Andrea Laurence author who has stories since she Coast girl trans constantly trying to develop a taste for smilgrits while caring for her boyfriend and her old bulldog. You can contact Andrea at her website: andrealaurence.com

USA TODAY bestselling author **Kat Cantrell** read her first Mills & Boon novel in third grade and has been scribbling in notebooks since she learned to spell. She's a former Harlequin So You Think You Can Write winner and former RWA Golden Heart finalist. Kat, her husband and their two boys live in north Texas.

Karen Booth is a Midwestern girl transplanted in the South, raised on '80s music and repeated readings of *Forever* by Judy Blume. When she's not writing about dreamy fictional men and the women who test them, she's in the garden, obsessing over college basketball, or spending time with her husband, college-age kids, and bratty cat.

Enemies to Lovers

Enemies to Lovers:
Business to Pleasure

ANDREA LAURENCE

KAT CANTRELL

KAREN BOOTH

MILLS & BOON

First Published in Great Britain 2022
By Mills & Boon, an imprint of HarperCollins*Publishers,* Ltd
1 London Bridge Street, London, SE1 9GF

www.harpercollins.co.uk

HarperCollins*Publishers*
1st Floor, Watermarque Building,
Ringsend Road, Dublin 4, Ireland

ENEMIES TO LOVERS: BUSINESS TO PLEASURE © 2022 Harlequin
Enterprises ULC.

Undeniable Demands © 2013 Andrea Laurence
Matched to Her Rival © 2014 Kat Cantrell
Pregnant by the Rival CEO © 2016 Karen Booth

ISBN 978-0-263-30558-6

MIX
Paper from
responsible sources
FSC™ C007454

This book is produced from independently certified FSC™ paper
to ensure responsible forest management.

For more information visit: www.harpercollins.co.uk/green

Printed and Bound in Spain using 100% Renewable electricity at
CPI Black Print, Barcelona

UNDENIABLE DEMANDS

ANDREA LAURENCE

To Vicki Lewis Thompson, Rhonda Nelson and
Kira Sinclair

You're the best plotting partners a girl could have.
You helped me take the smallest kernel of an idea
and develop it into a great multibook series.
I look forward to many more years of creativity,
laughter and good food with my ladies.

One

Wade hated the snow. Always had. You'd think a man born and raised in New England would feel differently or leave, but he'd done neither. Every November when the first few flakes started falling, a part of his soul would shrivel up until spring. That was why he'd booked himself a trip to Jamaica for the week before Christmas. He'd planned to return to the Edens', as always, for the holiday, but the frantic call he'd received from his foster sister, Julianne, had changed everything.

He had been loath to tell his assistant to cancel the trip, but perhaps if all went well, he could use the reservation after Christmas. He could ring in the New Year on a beach, drinking something frothy, with thoughts of his troubles buried deep.

Interesting choice of words.

The BMW SUV wound its way down the two-lane

road that led to the Garden of Eden Christmas Tree Farm. Wade preferred to drive his roadster, but rural Connecticut in winter was just not the place for it, so he'd left it in Manhattan. The SUV had snow tires, chains in the back and enough clearance not to scrape on chunks of ice in poorly cleared areas.

Spying the large red apple-shaped sign that marked the entrance to his foster parents' Christmas tree farm, Wade breathed a sigh of relief. He hadn't realized until that moment that he'd been holding his breath. Even under the less-than-ideal circumstances, returning home always made him feel better.

The farm was the only home he'd ever really had. None of the other foster homes had felt like one. He had no warm memories of living with his great-aunt before that, nor of his early years with his mother. But the Garden of Eden was just that: paradise. Especially for an abandoned young boy who could just as easily have become a career criminal as a millionaire in real estate.

The Edens changed everything. For him and every other child who had come to live there. He owed that couple his life. They were his parents, without question. Wade didn't know who his father was and had only seen his mother once since she dropped him at her aunt's doorstep as a toddler. When he thought of home and family, he thought of the farm and the family the Edens had pulled together.

They were able to have only one child of their own, their daughter, Julianne. For a time it seemed that their dreams of a house bustling with children who would help on the farm and one day take over the family business had been dashed. But then they decided to renovate an old barn into a bunkhouse perfect for rowdy boys and started taking in foster children.

Wade had been the first. Julianne had been in pigtails when he arrived, dragging her favorite doll behind her. Wade had been in his share of foster homes, and this time just felt different. He was not a burden. Not a way to get a check from the state. He was their son.

Which is why he wished he was visiting them for another reason. In his own mind, disappointing his parents would be the greatest sin he could commit. Even worse than the one he'd committed fifteen years ago that got him into this mess.

Wade turned the SUV into the driveway, then bypassed the parking lot and took the small road behind their large Federal-style house to where the family kept their cars. It was nearing the middle of the afternoon on a Friday, but even so, there were at least ten customer cars in the lot. It was December 21—only a few days until Christmas. His mother, Molly, would be in the gift shop, pushing sugar cookies, cider and hot chocolate on folks while they waited for Ken or one of the employees to haul and bag their new tree.

Wade felt the sudden, familiar urge to start trimming trees and hauling them out to people's cars. He'd done it for all of his teenage years and every Christmas break from Yale. It came naturally to want to jump back into the work. But first things first. He had to take care of the business that had brought him here instead of the warm beaches of Jamaica.

Julianne's call had been unexpected. None of the kids were very good about calling or visiting their parents or each other like they should. They were all busy, all successful, the way the Edens had wanted them to be. But their success also made it easy to forget to make time for the important people in their lives.

When Julianne had shown up at the farm for Thanksgiving with little warning, she'd been in for quite the surprise. Their father, Ken, was recovering from a heart attack. They hadn't called any of the kids because they didn't want them worrying about it or the crippling hospital bills.

Wade, Heath, Xander, Brody—any of the boys could've written a check and taken care of their problems, but Ken and Molly insisted they had it under control. Unfortunately, their solution was to sell a few plots of land they couldn't use for growing trees. They couldn't understand why the kids were so upset. And of course, the kids couldn't tell their parents the truth. That secret needed to remain buried in the past. And Wade was here to make sure it stayed that way.

If he was lucky, he could take one of the four-wheelers out to the property, buy the land back from the new owner and return before Molly could start wondering what he was up to. He wouldn't keep the purchase a secret from his parents, but he'd certainly rather they not fret over the whole situation until it was done.

Wade found the house empty, as expected. He left a note on the worn kitchen table, slipped into his heavy coat and boots and went out to grab one of the four-wheelers. He could've driven his SUV, but he didn't want to pull up in an expensive car and start waving money around at people.

Heath and Brody had both made visits to the farm since Julianne broke the news. Digging up as much information as they could, they found out that the person who had bought the smallest parcel of land was already living out there in some kind of camper. That sounded positive to him. They might need the money more than the land. But if they thought some rich guy was bullying them to sell it, they'd clamp down. Or jack up the price.

Wade took the four-wheeler down the well-worn path that went through the center of the farm. After selling eighty-five acres, the Edens still had two hundred acres left. Almost all of it was populated with balsam and Fraser fir trees. The northeastern portion of the property was sloped and rocky. They'd never had much success planting trees out there, so he'd understood why Ken had opted to sell it. He just wished his father hadn't.

By the time he rounded a corner on the trail and neared the border of the Edens' property, it was a little after two-thirty. The sky was clear and blue and the sun's rays pounded down on the snow, making it nearly blinding despite his sunglasses. He slowed and pulled out the new surveyor's map Brody had downloaded. The eighty-five acres that his parents had sold were split into two large tracts and one small one. Comparing the map to the GPS location on his phone, he could tell that just over the rise was the smallest, a ten-acre residential property. He was fairly certain this was the one he was after.

Wade refolded the map and looked around for any familiar landmarks. He'd deliberately chosen a spot he would remember. There had been a crooked maple tree and a rock that looked like a giant turtle. He scanned the landscape, but it appeared to him as though all the trees were crooked, and all the rocks were buried under a foot of snow. It was impossible to know for sure if this chunk of the property was the right one.

Damn. He'd thought for certain that he would know the spot when he saw it. That night fifteen years ago remained etched in his memory no matter how hard he tried to forget it. It was one of those moments that changes your whole life. Where you make a decision, right or wrong, and have to live with it forever.

Still, Wade was certain this was the right area. He didn't remember traveling far enough to reach the other plots. He'd been in too big a hurry to roam around the property all night trying to find the perfect spot. He eyed another maple tree, this one more crooked than the others. That had to be the one. He'd just have to buy the land back and hope that once spring came around, he would find the turtle rock at its base and know he'd bought the right plot.

Surging forward through the snow, he continued up to the rise and then started descending into the clearing toward what looked like some sort of shimmering silver mirage.

He pulled closer and realized it was the midafternoon sun reflecting off the superbly polished aluminum siding of an old Airstream trailer. You could have got a suntan from the rays coming off that thing. Parked beside it was an old Ford pickup truck with dually tires to haul the twenty-foot monster of a camper.

Wade stopped and killed the engine on the four-wheeler. There was no sign of life from inside the camper yet. Brody had searched online for the property sale records and found the new owner was V. A. Sullivan. Cornwall was a fairly small town, and he didn't remember any Sullivans when he went to school, so they must be new to the area. That was just as well. He didn't need to deal with anyone who remembered his troublesome days before the Edens and might give him grief.

His boots crunched through the snow until he reached the rounded doorway. It had a small window in it that he watched for movement when he knocked. Nothing. No sound of people inside, either.

Just great. He'd come all the way out here for nothing.

Wade was about to turn and head back home when he heard the telltale click of a shotgun safety. His head spun to the left, following the sound, and he found himself in the sights. The woman was standing about twenty feet away, bundled just as heavily as he was in a winter coat with a knit cap and sunglasses hiding most of her features. Long strands of fiery red hair peeked out from her hat and blew in the chilly wind. The distinctive color immediately caught his eye. He'd known a woman with hair that color a long time ago. It had been beautiful, like liquid flames. Appropriate, since he was playing with fire now.

On reflex, his hands went up. Getting shot by some overprotective, rural militia type was not on his agenda for the day. "Hey, there," he called out, trying to sound as friendly and nonthreatening as he could.

The woman hesitated, and then the shotgun dropped slightly. "Can I help you?"

"Are you Mrs. Sullivan?" Hopefully Mr. Sullivan wasn't out in the woods with a shotgun of his own.

"*Miss* Sullivan," she corrected. "What's it to you?"

A single female. Even better. Wade had a certain charm about him that served him well with the fairer sex. He smiled widely. "My name is Wade Mitchell. I wanted to talk to you about possibly—"

"Arrogant, pigheaded real-estate developer Wade Mitchell?" The woman took a few steps forward.

Wade frowned. She didn't seem to care for him at all. He wished to God the woman wasn't so bundled up so he could see who she was. Maybe then he could figure out why the mention of his name seemed to agitate her. Of course, he was wearing just as much winter gear as she was. "Yes, ma'am, although I wouldn't go so far as to use those adjectives. I wanted to see if you would be interested in…"

His words dropped off as the shotgun rose again. "Aw, hell," she lamented. "I thought it looked kinda like you under all those layers, but I thought, why would Wade Mitchell be in Cornwall making my life hell again after all this time?"

Wade's eyes widened behind his dark sunglasses. "I have no intention of making your life hell, Miss Sullivan."

"Get off my land."

"I'm sorry, have I done something to you?" He scanned his brain. Had he dated a Sullivan? Beaten up her brother? He had no memory of what he could've done to piss this woman off so badly.

The woman stomped across the snow, closing the gap between them with the gun still pointed directly at him. She pulled off her sunglasses to study him more closely, revealing a lovely heart-shaped face and pale eyes. Her skin was creamy, the perfect backdrop to the fiery strands of hair framing her face. When her blue eyes met his, he noticed a challenge there, as though she was daring him not to remember her.

Fortunately, Wade had an excellent memory. One good enough to know that he was in trouble. The fiery redhead glaring at him was a hard woman to forget. He'd certainly tried over the years, but from time to time, she'd slipped into his subconscious and haunted his dreams with her piercing, ice-blue gaze. A gaze that reflected the hurt of betrayal that he couldn't understand.

Property owner V. A. Sullivan was none other than Victoria Sullivan: green architect, eco-warrior and the employee he'd fired from his company seven years ago.

His stomach instantly sank. Of all the people who could've bought this property, it had to be her. Victoria Sullivan. The first person he'd ever fired from his company. It had pained him at the time, but he'd really had no choice. He had a strict policy on ethics violations. She hadn't taken the news well. And judging by her stiff posture and tightly gripped firearm, she was still upset about it.

"Victoria!" he said with a wide smile, trying to sound pleasantly surprised to see her after all this time. "I had no idea you were living out here now."

"Miss Sullivan," she corrected.

Wade nodded. "Of course. Could you please drop the gun? I'm unarmed."

"You won't be when the cops come." Her words were as icy cold as the snow, but eventually the gun disengaged and dropped to her side.

She pushed past him to the front door of the Airstream, pulling it open and climbing the stairs. "What do you want, Mr. Mitchell?"

As she hung at the top of the steps, looking back at him, Wade realized he needed to change his tactic, and fast. His original plan had been to tell the owner that he wanted the property for one of his development projects. If he told her that, she'd refuse him just to ruin his plans.

He'd have to appeal to a different side of her. That is, if he could explain himself before she started shooting.

"Miss Sullivan, I'd like to buy back this property from you."

* * *

Tori hung on the steps, the rage slowly uncoiling in her belly. This man was determined to ruin everything she held dear. He had taken away her reputation and very nearly her career. His turning on her suddenly had also damaged her ability to trust men. Out of the blue, he'd accused her of terrible things and tossed her out. She'd lost her first real apartment after he fired her.

And now that she was trying to settle down and establish herself again, he wanted to destroy her plans for her dream home. She just knew it. Her jaw set firmly, she made her decision before he even asked the question. If he were on fire, she wouldn't bother to spit on him.

"It's not for sale." She slipped inside and let the door slam behind her.

She was pulling off her coat, about to toss it onto the foldout bed, when she heard the door of the trailer open behind her. Tori spun on her heel and found the bastard standing in her tiny kitchen. He'd slipped out of his winter coat and tugged off his hat as he entered. He stood there now in a pair of dress pants and a plaid button-down shirt. The hunter-green of the top made his own green eyes seem even darker and more intriguing than she remembered. Because of the stocking cap he'd worn, his short, dark brown hair was messier than she'd ever seen it.

Without his slick suits and perfect hair, he looked nothing like the real-estate giant who had ruled over his company from the top floor. But he still had a commanding presence. She'd forgotten how tall he was: at least six foot two, with a powerful build. The large man seemed to take up all the space in her trailer, which had always had the perfect amount of room for her. It was as though he'd sucked up all the air, making her oddly warm and her camper uncomfortably small.

And she hated that about him.

Without hesitating, she picked up her shotgun again. Truthfully, it was loaded with shells full of recycled rubber pellets. She carried it with her to the compost bin in case she needed to scare off any foraging critters. She'd caught a black bear in the bin last week. The rubber pellets would send animals scurrying without seriously hurting them. Hopefully it would do the same with Wade Mitchell.

"Do you mind stepping back outside? I spent a lot of money to renovate this trailer and I'm not going to ruin it by shooting you in here."

Wade had only a momentary flash of alarm in his eyes before he smiled at her in a way that made her cheeks flush and her knees weaken. She remembered feeling that way whenever he would walk down the hallway past her cubicle and greet her with "good morning." She'd been fresh out of college and in awe of the two young mavericks with their up-and-coming real-estate development company. Alex Stanton was the golden playboy, but she was instantly drawn to the darker, more serious Wade. Then and now, his wide grin and strong, aristocratic features usually got him his way.

If she wasn't careful, she might fall prey to them again. She knew better than to trust a guy like him.

"Miss Sullivan, can we please talk about this without you constantly threatening to shoot me?"

"There's nothing to talk about." Tori kept the gun in one hand while she pulled off her hat and scarf with the other. She was burning up, and it had nothing to do with her new propane heating system. It was Wade and her overheated and long-ignored libido. She hated that the man who'd betrayed and fired her could still send her pulse racing after all this time. "And it's rude to come inside uninvited, so you deserve to be shot."

"I apologize," he said, laying his coat across the bench seat of her dining table. "But it is imperative that I discuss this with you today."

Oh, she was sure it was. No doubt he had bought the forty-acre property beside her and wanted her additional ten to add to whatever ridiculous project he was developing out here. There might be an army of backhoes and land movers over the horizon just waiting for her to sign off so they could start their work. But she wasn't giving up this land. This purchase had been years in the making. Her genealogy research had been what lured her up here, but from the first time she'd set foot in the area, she knew this was where she wanted to build her home.

Finding out the Edens were selling some property had been the chance of a lifetime. The lot was perfect. It sloped down, slightly, but would allow her to design a stilted, multistory home that had a living room with a wide vista of windows overlooking the valley below. Being surrounded by two hundred acres of tree farm on two sides guaranteed she wouldn't have a strip mall out her back door anytime soon.

She had a couple months in between projects to start designing and building her house. It was the perfect opportunity just when she had the time and money to jump on it. And he couldn't have it.

"I know that you're used to getting your way, Mr. Mitchell, but I'm afraid it isn't going to happen this time."

On cue, her electric teapot began to chirp on the

counter and spit out steam. She'd turned it on before she'd stepped out to put some trash in her compost bin, and now it was ready for her to extend some unintended hospitality. When she turned to look at Wade again, he had seated himself at her dining-table booth, a look of smug expectation in his eyes.

With a sigh, she set down the shotgun. It was hard to make tea when you were holding a heavy, loaded firearm.

"May I ask how much you paid for the land?"

"You may not, although I'm sure it's public record somewhere if you take the time to have one of the corporate minions you haven't fired look for it." She pulled out two teacups from her bamboo plywood cabinet above the sink. She shook her loose leaf tea into two infusers, put them in the cups and poured the hot water over them.

"My guess would be about a hundred and twenty-five thousand. There're no utilities run out here yet."

Tori refused to look at him. Of course the real estate guy could nail the price within a few thousand dollars. "What's your point?"

"My point is that I'll offer you double what you paid for it."

At that, Tori fumbled the jar of organic honey and sent it crashing to the Marmoleum floor. Fortunately, it didn't shatter. She quickly crouched down to grab it, but he had reached out for it as well and beat her to it. He held out the jar to her. Tori looked down at him, only inches away, and felt a familiar and unwelcome tingle deep in her belly. When she took the jar from his hand, her fingers brushed his and the tingle turned into a surge right to her core.

Jerking upright as though she'd been burned by his

touch, she quickly recovered and removed the infusers, then added a dollop of the honey to each cup. She plunked his tea down in front of him and took a seat on the opposite side of the table.

"That's ridiculous." She said the words knowing she meant both her reaction to him and his offer for her land. Tori knew better than to let herself fall for Wade's good looks or his seemingly good offer.

"Maybe. But that's what I'm offering."

"You're hiding something," she accused. "You're the guy who built your business buying cheap buildings and flipping them for a fortune. No way you'd pay one penny more than is necessary to turn a profit on whatever project you're wanting to build out here."

Wade turned to look her in the eye. A lock of brown hair had fallen into his face, giving him a boyish charm she had to steel her resolve against. "I'm not building anything out here. This isn't about money."

Tori scoffed. "You don't get to be a millionaire before you're thirty unless you're born into money or driven by it. Either way, everything is about money."

Wade watched her. He took a sip of his tea before he answered. "This is about family. That's more important to me than even money. This property belonged to my parents. They sold it without telling me or my other siblings. We never would've let them do that if we'd known. They worked too hard their whole lives for this land. We grew up here. Our childhood was here. If we'd known they were having financial problems, I would've taken care of things before they resorted to this."

Tori felt herself being sucked in by his story. The expression on his handsome face was one of sincere concern. The words sounded so convincing. But this was the same man who had praised her potential and work ethic, then fired her the next day. Ryan had also seemed sincere, and nearly every word out of his mouth over the past two years had been a lie.

She had been raised with a naive spirit by hippies who wanted only to experience life and culture. They didn't have a malicious bone in their bodies and never thought other people did, either.

Life had taught Tori differently. Wade had taught her differently. He had heard her pleas of innocence and turned his back on them. He hadn't believed her. So why should she believe him now?

The people who had sold her this land—Molly and Ken Eden—were a very sweet older couple. No way they'd spawned a son like Mitchell. They didn't even have the same last name. It wasn't even a well-planned lie. She wanted to be insulted by his lack of faith in her ability to see through his crap. Did he think she would just melt into a puddle at his feet the minute he knocked on the door and flashed those deep green eyes at her? Or started waving cash?

She didn't need Wade's money. She'd paid cash for this property. She was one of the most highly sought after green architects in America. She'd traveled thousands of miles in this Airstream to build environmentally friendly buildings, homes and businesses. Tori had several large and successful projects in Seattle, Santa Fe and San Francisco. She was wrapping up one in Philadelphia just after the first of the year. She did well enough that she could laugh at his offer. But it couldn't hurt to push him and see how far he was willing to take this.

"What if I said I would sell it back to you for half a million?" There was no way the land was worth that much unless there was oil, gold or diamonds hidden beneath her feet. She doubted it, though. She'd never heard of Wade Mitchell being interested in any of those things. The only thing about land he cared for was what he could build on top of it.

Wade didn't even flinch. "I would get out my checkbook and sign on the dotted line so you could find an even better piece of land and everyone would be happy. Let me assure you that nothing is more important than preserving my family and my history."

Wow. He was certainly desperate for this land. She almost felt bad for him. Any other person might have immediately given in and made his day. Four times the value was a great offer. A crazy offer. One that she was probably crazy to turn down. Even with her success, half a million was quite a lump of cash. Tori could certainly do a lot with it: buy new land, build her dream house without a mortgage attached to it, get a new hybrid pickup truck. She had to admit, if it were any other person sitting across the table from her, she'd probably take the money and tow her trailer off into the sunset.

But it wasn't any other person. It was Wade Mitchell. And she wasn't about to sell him this land. Not for any price. Just because it was worth it to watch him squirm. This would be as close to payback as she would ever get. It was his bad luck that he wanted *her* land.

"You're really quite good," she said, nodding and watching her tea instead of his handsome face. She wouldn't let herself get pulled in and swayed by his mesmerizing eyes and fabricated sob story. She'd already caught herself being a sucker once this year, and that was enough. Maybe if he came around in a few weeks, she'd let him be her dumb mistake of the New

Year. "Did you practice that speech long or was that off the cuff?"

Wade stiffened, pushing the half-empty cup of tea aside and shelving the charm. "Is all this animosity over your termination years ago?"

Now it was Tori's turn to stiffen in her chair. He made her seem petty for holding that over him all these years later. "Absolutely. I don't take affronts to my reputation lightly."

"You weren't worried about your reputation when you slept with one of our suppliers and put my company in jeopardy."

"I didn't sleep with anybody. I told you then that I didn't do any of the things you accused me of. Nothing has changed. Just because you didn't believe me doesn't mean I wasn't telling the truth."

"They were serious charges, and I needed to deal with them as such. I did what I had to do."

"And I'm doing what I have to do. I'm keeping this land. It's mine. Whether or not I like you or resent what you did is irrelevant."

"This isn't about me or you and your damaged pride. This is about Ken and Molly Eden and everything they worked for. I want to give them back what's rightfully theirs."

Tori straightened and shot him as lethal a gaze as she could manage. "You mean, *mine.* I signed those papers at the lawyer's office two months ago. I didn't hold a gun to their heads and make them sell me this land."

"Wouldn't have surprised me if you did," he said bitterly, glancing over at the shotgun sitting on the counter.

"They sold it all on their own. I paid them full asking price and covered all my own closing expenses, so it's not like I cheated them, either. I don't know whether you're their son or not, Mr. *Mitchell,* but let me just tell you that if you *are* their son, you're a crappy one. They told me about Ken's heart attack and all their medical expenses. Where have you been? In Manhattan? Worrying about making money?"

"You think I don't know that?" he challenged. Wade's eyes flashed with a touch of a temper she'd seen years before. "I'm not proud of it, but I can fix it."

Tori stood up from her seat. "You're just going to have to find another way to soothe your conscience. Send them on a cruise or something, because you aren't going to browbeat me into selling this land. And that's final. Please leave."

Wade stood, bringing his head a hairbreadth away from scraping the top of her camper. He took a step toward her, and his body loomed large and intimidating in such close proximity.

Tori couldn't help the surge of awareness that ran through her body as he came near. Apparently it was far easier to despise him from a distance. It had been a long time since she'd been in the same room as Wade, and she'd certainly never been this close to him, but her body remembered him. With him inches away, looking down at her with a focused, penetrating intensity, her spine wanted to turn to jelly. His warm scent, a familiar mix of spicy cologne and salty skin, swirled around her with every breath she drew into her lungs.

She finally took a step back, pressing herself against the kitchen counter. She didn't like being this close to Wade. It messed with her focus, and that just made her even more irritated. Tori couldn't let him use his size or sexuality to intimidate her.

"This isn't over," he said, pinning her with his dark green eyes before grabbing his coat and walking out into the cold.

Two

Wade remembered Victoria Sullivan as being smart and beautiful. Apparently she was also the most infuriating and stubborn woman he'd ever encountered.

Wade stomped back to his four-wheeler and stood there a moment, letting the cold sink in and douse the aggravating mix of anger and attraction surging through his veins. When he was back in control, he shrugged into his coat, jumped on the ATV and peeled out of her yard in a doughnut as he used to do as a teenager. The back tires sent a sheet of snow flying against the side of her trailer. It was juvenile, but she seemed to bring out the worst in him.

He was fuming as he plowed through the snow. It should be illegal for a woman that gorgeous to have a mouth that irritating. Honestly, once she'd peeled out of her jacket and revealed a snug pair of jeans and a fitted, long-sleeved T-shirt, he'd almost forgotten why he was there. It wasn't until she picked up her shotgun again that he realized he'd followed her inside without her permission.

Victoria had been one of his best and brightest architects. He'd hired her straight out of college when the company he and Alex had started was still small and spending more than it earned. She'd contributed quite a bit to making their first few big projects a success. He'd even considered asking her out to dinner. But then his assistant had come to him with concerns about seeing Victoria at a restaurant looking a little too cozy with one of their potential suppliers. She had been quite vocal about giving the man an upcoming contract, and the implication was clear. He fired her on the spot. Part of him regretted that. And not just because she had knockout curves, flawless skin and long, fiery red hair that made him warm under the collar.

He had wanted to believe her when she said she didn't do it. The thought of her with another man nearly made him crazy. But the logical part of his brain was infuriated by her audacious attempt to influence corporate contracts like that. Sleeping with a potential contractor was just as bad as taking bribes from one. Both compromised a person's objectivity and put the ethics of his company in question.

He would not have it, so he terminated her. He never dreamed the decision would come back to haunt him.

If she were any other woman, he would've asked her to dinner to talk over his offer and kissed her to keep the inflammatory words from flying out of her mouth. Her temper, as spicy as her hair, was a massive turn-on. He had a weakness for redheads.

But she wasn't another woman. She was holding on to seven years of bitterness along with the key to something more important to him than anything else. Protecting his family was his number one priority. Toying with Victoria like a cat with a mouse could cost him dearly. He needed her to sell him this land. He couldn't fail. As much as he'd like to resolve their differences between the sheets, it wasn't the answer in this situation. He doubted it would sway her, and she'd probably shoot him if he tried to kiss her.

"Arrogant and pigheaded," Wade grumbled, turning to steer the four-wheeler down the center aisle of trees toward the entrance. She thought she knew so much. Well, she forgot rich, powerful, ruthless and determined Wade Mitchell came in the same package. He would secure that land and protect his family one way or another.

Wade came to an abrupt stop as an old pickup truck, draped in Christmas lights and garland, pulled in front of him. Piled into the trailer it towed was a crowd of bundled-up people sitting on bales of hay and singing Christmas carols. The driver, Owen, threw a hand up at Wade, then continued back toward the house.

Hayrides, Santa visits, sugar cookies and hot chocolate. Picking out a tree at the Garden of Eden wasn't just a shopping trip. It was an experience. On the weekends in December, the farm was a madhouse. And it had to be. A good portion of their income came from just this one month. Sure, they did other things throughout the year, but Christmas tree farms depended on a good Christmas to stay afloat.

And lately, it hadn't been enough.

Wade blamed himself for that. When the boys grew up and moved away, the Edens had to hire in help. Owen had always worked on the farm, but as each year went by, more staff was added and their expenses went up. Throw in a mountain of hospital bills and competition from increasingly more realistic fake trees, and the Edens were lucky they'd survived this long.

Wade followed the truck to the house and then veered off to park the ATV back under the awning where they kept it. The farm would be closing soon, so he skipped the house and headed around to the tree-processing area. Heart attack be damned, he found his dad out there with a couple of teenage boys. They were leveling, drilling, shaking and net-bagging all the trees selected by the last round of customers.

As though he'd never left, Wade grabbed a tree and put it on the shaker to remove any loose needles. When it was done, Ken laid the tree out to drill. They carried special stands in the gift shop that ensured a perfectly straight tree.

Wade held it still while Ken drilled.

"You haven't lost your touch, kid. Need a job?"

Wade smiled. "I could work for about a week. Then I've got to get back to town."

"That's fine, fine. We'll be closed by then, anyway." Ken lifted the tree and gave it to one of the boys to run through the netter. When he turned back, he gave Wade a big welcome hug. "Good to see you, son."

"Good to see you, too, Dad. Is that the last of the trees for tonight?"

"Yep. With perfect timing, you've shown up just when all the hard work is finished. Come help me haul these trees out to the parking lot and we'll go see your mother."

Wade grasped a tree in each hand and followed his father through the snow to the parking lot where the last few cars waited for their trees. He watched his father carefully for signs of ill health as he hauled around the trees and helped families tie them into trunks and onto roofs. The man wasn't quite sixty yet and had always appeared to be at the peak of health. His brown hair was mostly gray now, but his blue eyes were still bright and alert, and he didn't hesitate in his physical work. Ken had always been a lean man, but a strong man. If nothing else, he looked a little leaner than usual.

"There's nothing wrong with me, so quit looking for it." Ken snatched the last tree from Wade and hauled it down to the pickup truck waiting for it.

Wade followed him, then stood quietly until the truck pulled away. "I wasn't looking for anything."

"Liar. Everyone has been doing it since your mother told Julianne about that damned attack I had. It was no big deal. I'm fine. They gave me a pill to take. End of story. Don't be sitting around waiting for me to drop dead so you can inherit this place."

Both men chuckled, knowing Wade could buy and sell the farm ten times over and had no interest in getting his claws on any inheritance. "You're looking good to me, Dad."

"Yeah." He slapped Wade on the back and started walking toward the gift shop. "Most days I feel okay. I'm slowing down a little. Feeling my age. But that's just reality. The attack threw me for a loop—just came out of the blue. But between the pills and your mother's dogged determination to feed me oatmeal and vegetables, I should be fine. What are you doing up here so early, Wade? You kids don't usually show up until Christmas Eve."

"I had some time in my schedule, so I thought I'd spend it with you guys. Help out. I know I don't visit enough."

"Well, that's a nice lie. Be sure to tell your mother

that. She'll eat it up. All of you boys are in a panic since you found out we sold that land."

"I wouldn't call it a panic."

"Wouldn't you, now? Four out of the five of you kids have been here in the past month, just randomly checking in. I'm sure Xander would've come, too, if congress wasn't in session fighting over the stupid budget."

Wade shrugged. "Well, what do you expect, Dad? You kept your heart attack a secret. You're having financial trouble and you don't tell any of us. You know we all make good money. There was no need to start selling off the farm."

"I didn't sell off the farm. I sold off some useless rocks and dirt that were costing more money than they earned. And yes, you make a good living. I haven't made a good living in quite a few years. One doesn't make up for the other."

"Dad—"

Ken stopped in front of the gift shop, his hand on the doorknob. "I don't want any of your money, Wade. I don't want a dime from any of you kids. The unexpected medical bills just sucked up our savings. The past few years had been lean and we'd cut back on things, including our insurance, to weather the rough patch. Selling off the extra land let us pay off all the bills, buy a new insurance plan and stick some money away. Less land means less taxes and less for me to worry about. Everything will be just fine."

He pushed open the door to the gift store, ending the conversation. Wade had no choice but to let the subject drop and follow him in. They were instantly bombarded with lights and sounds straight from Santa's workshop. Jingling bells chimed from the door; Christmas music played from overhead speakers. A television in the back was showing holiday cartoons on a constant loop near the area where children could write letters to Santa and play with toys while Mommy shopped and Daddy loaded the tree.

Multicolored lights draped from the ceiling. The scent of pine and mulling spices permeated the room. The fireplace crackled on one wall, inviting customers to sit in rocking chairs and drink the hot chocolate Molly provided free.

"Wade!" The tiny and pleasantly plump woman behind the counter came rushing out to wrap her arms around her oldest boy.

He leaned down to hug her as he'd always had to do, accepting the fussing as she straightened his hair and inspected him for signs of stress or fatigue. She always accused him of working too much. She was probably right, but he'd learned his work ethic from them. "Hey, Mama."

"What a surprise to have you here so soon. Is this just a visit or are you here for the holiday?"

"For the duration."

"That's wonderful," she said, her eyes twinkling with happiness and Christmas lights. "But wait." She paused. "I thought Heath told me you were in Jamaica this week."

"Plans changed. I'm here instead."

"He's checking up on us," Ken called from the counter where he was pouring himself a cup of cider.

"I don't care," she called back. "I'll take him however I can get him." Molly hugged him again, then frowned at her son. "I don't have anything prepared for dinner," she said, aghast at the idea. "I wish I'd known you were coming. I was just going to feed your father a sandwich."

"Whole wheat, fat-free turkey, no mayo, no flavor," Ken grumbled.

"Don't worry about feeding me, Mama. I was going to run into Cornwall to meet a couple of the guys at the Wet Hen and grab a few things from the store. I'll get something to eat at the diner when I'm done."

"All right. But I'm going to the store first thing in the morning, and I'll get stocked up on everything I need to feed a household of boys for the holiday!"

Wade smiled. His mother looked absolutely giddy at the idea of slaving over a stove for five hungry men. He recalled times from his youth when he and the other boys were hitting growth spurts all at once. They couldn't get enough food into their stomachs. Hopefully now they would be easier to take care of.

"Why don't you just give me a list and I'll pick it up while I'm out."

"We don't need your money," Ken called from the rocking chair by the fire, though he didn't turn to face them.

Molly frowned at her husband, and Wade could see she was torn. They did need the money, but Ken was being stubborn. "That would be very nice of you, Wade. I'll write up a few things." She returned to the counter and made out a short list. "This should get us through a few days. I'll go into town for a fresh turkey on Monday morning."

"Okay," he said, leaning down to kiss her cheek. "I'll be back soon. Maybe I'll bring home one of those coconut cream pies from Daisy's."

"That would be lovely. Drive safely in the snow."

Wade stepped through the jingling door and headed

out into the newly darkened night in search of pie, a dozen eggs, a sack of potatoes and some information on Victoria Sullivan.

When Tori got into her truck, she had every intention of going to Daisy's to get something to eat. Maybe swing by the store for some quick and easy-to-prepare food to get her through the holidays when the diner was closed. And yet before she could help herself, her truck pulled into the parking lot of the Wet Hen, the local bar.

"Let's face it," she lamented to her dashboard. "I need a drink."

Just one. Just enough to take the edge off the nerves Wade had agitated. And if it helped suppress the attraction that was buzzing through her veins, all the better.

Tori slid from the cab of her truck, slammed the heavy door behind her and slipped through the door of the Wet Hen. The sign outside claimed the bar had been in business since 1897. Truthfully, it looked as if it had. A renovation wouldn't hurt, but she supposed that was part of its charm. The bar was dark, with old, worn wood on the walls, the floors and the tables. The photos on the walls of various local heroes and the sports memorabilia from the high school seemed to be there more to camouflage cracks in the plaster than anything else. The amber lights did little to illuminate the place, but she supposed a bright light would not only ruin the atmosphere but force the local fire department to condemn it.

The place was pretty quiet for six on a Friday. She imagined business would pick up later unless people were tied up in last-minute holiday activities. She made her way to the empty bar and pulled up a stool. It was from her perch that she heard the laughter of a group of men in the back corner. When she turned, Tori quickly amended her plans. She needed two drinks. Especially with that cocky bastard watching her from the back of the bar.

What was Wade doing here? It was a small town, but wasn't there somewhere else he should be? At home with his all-important family, perhaps? But no, he was throwing back a couple with an odd assortment of old and young men from around town. She recognized her lawyer, Randy Miller, and the old bald sheriff from one of the local television advertisements about the dangers of holiday drinking and driving. There were a couple others there she didn't recognize.

And at the moment, every one of them was looking at her.

Had Wade been talking to them about her? The arrogant curl of his smile and the laughter in the eyes of the other men left no doubt. The irritation pressed up Tori's spine until she was sitting bolt upright in her seat.

She wanted to leave. Not just the bar, but the town. Maybe even the state. In an hour she could have the trailer hooked up and ready to go. Part of the beauty of being nomadic was that you could leave whenever things got uncomfortable. That's what her parents had always done. Hung around somewhere until it got boring or awkward and then moved on to someplace else. Tori had always had trouble imagining living in one community her entire life. There was no place to go when things blew up in your face.

But there were also advantages to being settled: longtime friends and neighbors. People you could count on. Stability. Roots. A place to call home and raise a family. After toying with the idea of having that kind of life with Ryan and then having it all collapse around her, Tori had decided she was tired of running. She might not have the life and family she'd dreamed about with Ryan, but she could have it with someone else if she sat still long enough to have a meaningful relationship.

Cornwall spoke to her. This was where her family had come from and this was where she wanted to stay. But if she was going to build her dream home here, she'd better learn how to tough it out. There was no towing off a house. Being the new girl in a small town was hard enough. Lacking in coping skills wasn't going to help the situation.

If Wade thought he could bully her into selling by turning the town against her, he was in for a surprise. She wasn't going to play along with his charade. If he could play dirty, so could she.

"What can I get you?" The bartender had finally made his way over to her end of the bar. He looked like the kind of guy you'd find at a 115-year-old bar named the Wet Hen. Thin, leathery and gray-haired with an ancient, blurry anchor tattooed on his forearm. The tag pinned to his apron said his name was Skippy. She'd never seen anyone less like a Skippy in her life.

"Gin and tonic with lime." Strong and to the point without stooping to shots. She was tempted to just chug a few big gulps of tequila so she'd no longer care about Wade and his cronies. But she couldn't lose control of her inhibitions, either. Lord knew what kind of trouble she'd get into.

Skippy placed a bowl of peanuts and a napkin on the counter for the drink he quickly poured. He looked as though he had a solid fifty years of experience mixing drinks. When the lowball glass plopped down in front of her, she took a large, quick sip. Damned if that wasn't the best gin and tonic she'd ever had.

Go Skippy.

The alcohol surged straight into her veins. She'd been too agitated to eat anything since Wade left, and her empty stomach gladly soaked up the wicked brew. Three sips into her drink, her worries from earlier had dulled into distant concerns that could be drowned out, along with the loud bursts of male laughter coming from the corner. Thank goodness.

It wasn't until she'd finished her drink and half a bowl of peanuts that she bothered to look in their direction again. Wade was still watching her, although this time the amusement on his face was gone. As the other men around the table chatted, he seemed to have narrowed his focus to her. The expression on his face was quite serious. And openly appreciative of whatever he was seeing.

When their gazes met, Tori felt a jolt of electricity that ran down her spine and prickled across her skin like delicate flames licking at her. It was almost as though his look caressed her physically and drew her into him. It was the same feeling she'd had when he touched her today, handing her the honey jar. Sudden. Unexpected. Powerful.

And totally and completely unwanted.

The clunk of a glass on the bar in front of her startled Tori out of Wade's tractor beam. When she turned, she saw a fresh glass, courtesy of Skippy.

"This one's on the oldest Eden boy."

It took Tori a minute to figure out that probably meant Wade. "You mean the dark-headed one in the green shirt with the smug expression on his face?"

Skippy leaned onto the bar and turned toward the men in the back. "Yep."

"I thought his last name was Mitchell."

"It is."

"Then why'd you call him an Eden boy?"

Skippy shrugged. "'Cause that's what he is."

Tori frowned. Wade's family tree seemed to be a touch more complicated than she'd anticipated. "Tell him I don't want it."

Skippy snorted and shook his head. "He's sitting with the mayor, the sheriff, the best lawyer in town and the city councilman who granted my liquor license. Sorry, kiddo, but I'm not getting involved. You'll have to tell him that yourself."

"Fine," Tori said. The drink was making her feel brave anyway. Scooping up the full glass, she slid off the stool a little too fluidly and made her way across the bar to the table of men in the back.

All five of them halted their conversation and turned to look at her when she approached.

"You're welcome, Miss Sullivan," Wade said with a smile that made her stomach flutter and pissed her off at the same time. He was too cocky for his own good.

"Actually, I wasn't coming to thank you. I'm returning it."

"Is something wrong with the drink?" Wade challenged.

"Nothing aside from it being purchased by you." She set it down on the edge of the table in front of him. "No thanks."

A couple of the men chuckled softly and another shifted uncomfortably in his seat. Wade ignored them all, his gaze laser-focused on her. "Oh, come on, now.

Don't be that way. It was a 'Welcome to Cornwall' drink. A taste of some local hospitality."

"I've lived here for two months and only four people have bothered to speak to me the entire time. It's a little late for a warm welcome. Especially coming from the man who's trying to run me out of town."

"That's harsh. You can stay in town. Just not on that particular spot. Maybe Randy here can help you buy a new place." Wade slapped the younger man beside him on the shoulder. "He tells me he handled the sale of my parents' property."

"*My* property," she emphasized. "What else did he tell you, Wade? Are there any loopholes you can use to nullify the sale? Or are you just snooping around town trying to find some dirt on me you can use for blackmail?"

Wade shrugged casually, and Tori could feel her blood nearly boil in her veins with anger. "Not everything is about you, Miss Sullivan. I'm visiting my friends while I'm in town. If they just so happen to have information about you, then great. I like to be well-informed. Especially when going up against a worthy adversary."

"Don't flatter me. You can dig all you want, but you're not going to find any dirt, because I haven't done anything wrong. I'm not selling you my property, Mr. Mitchell. And that's final." Tori spun on her heel and took two big steps away before she heard the sound of muffled snickers behind her and a poorly masked whisper that suggested Wade's skills in the bedroom might improve her attitude.

That was the last straw. Snapping her head around, she caught Wade smirking at her backside as though he agreed with his uncouth companion's assessment.

She returned to their table. "I'm sorry, what was that? I can assure you my attitude was just fine until you started bullying me around. You may live in a world where you always get your way, but it's not going to happen this time. And neither your money nor your penis is going to change that. I'm not interested in either of them."

With that, she picked up her drink, watching as Wade assessed her with curious eyes. He'd had the good sense to shelve the smirk. "On second thought," she said with a sickeningly sweet smile, "I think I will take this drink. You could use a little cooling off." With a flick of her wrist Tori emptied the glass into Wade's lap.

The icy cold drink shocked him upright out of the chair, sending ice cubes scattering across the floor. Tori turned and walked back to the bar, ignoring his stream of profanity muffled by his friends' howls of laughter. She paid her bill, leaving a nice tip for Skippy, and headed for the door.

Curiosity was nagging at her, but she wouldn't allow herself to turn around and see what Wade was doing. She would give anything to see that smug look wiped off his face, and she was pretty sure that would do it. But looking back meant that she cared. She didn't want to give Wade that satisfaction. Instead, she marched out the front door and headed to her truck. She was nearly to the corner of the building when she heard rapid, heavy footsteps coming up behind her.

"What is your problem?" Wade snarled over her shoulder.

As calmly as she could, Tori turned to look at him. Even with a tight jaw and an angry red flush tainting his perfect, aristocratic features, he was the most handsome man she'd ever seen in person. And she hated that that was her first thought when she looked at him. Those kinds of thoughts weren't helpful when dealing with the enemy. And that's what he was, despite the facade he put up to play nice and the way her body reacted when he was close by.

Judging by the snarl that had replaced his cajoling smile and the giant wet spot sprawled across his pants, she was pretty sure he was done playing nice. And that was fine by her. It would be much easier to deal with Wade when he wasn't trying to be charming. It just crossed the wires in her brain and made her think unproductive thoughts.

"My problem?" Tori said coolly. "I don't have a problem. You're the one who needs something, not me."

"And dumping a drink in my lap is the solution?"

Now it was Tori's turn to shrug dismissively, as he had. "It seemed like a good idea at the time. You all were having too much fun at my expense. Just because you have drinks with the mayor doesn't mean you can bully me."

Wade narrowed his green gaze at her, slowly stepping forward until she found herself backed up against the crumbling brick wall of the Hen. With one hand planted on the wall on each side of her, he'd made sure there was nowhere for her to go. Tori straightened her spine and looked defiantly at him as he closed in.

"I never had any intention of bullying you, Miss Sullivan."

Tori tried not to watch the soft curve of his lips as he spoke to her, but he was so close she had little choice. She remembered how she'd once fantasized about kissing those lips. Of course, that was before he turned on her and threw her out of his company on her rear end.

The surge of anger doused the old memories, and her gaze met his.

"What then?" she asked, her voice laced with sarcasm. "Were you going to take your friend's suggestion and seduce me? Certainly you're so masterful in the bedroom that one good romp would change my mind, right?"

Wade moved a fraction of an inch closer to her. For a moment Tori tensed, thinking he might be leaning in to kiss her. She wanted him to, and she didn't. She'd probably thoroughly enjoy it and then slap him when it was over. It was hard to think with him this close. He stopped short of touching his lips to hers. She could feel his warm breath on her skin.

"I've never had a woman offer me real estate after sex, but it wouldn't be the first time one of my lovers felt the need to repay me for a fantastically pleasurable night together."

Just the words *fantastically pleasurable* wrought a hard throb of need. She fought the urge to lean in to him. To discover what it would feel like to have his hard angles pressing into her soft curves. It had been a long time since she'd even let herself think of something like that. Not since things blew up with Ryan. She didn't trust herself to make the right choices, even with the right kind of man.

And this was the absolute wrong man to light up her libido. He was too smooth. Too charming and certain of himself. It didn't matter what he said or did, for every move he made was a strategic one. But that didn't mean her every move couldn't be a tactical one, as well. He already believed she could be manipulated through sex, or he never would've fired her. Let him think he was getting to her. Let him think he was winning.

Tori pressed a gentle hand to his chest. Her lips parted in invitation; a ragged breath of arousal escaped from her lungs. It wasn't hard to play along: she just gave in to her impulses. She could feel his heart racing just as quickly as her own. He was not immune to his own game. They were both playing with fire.

"What makes you think I want you?" she whispered.

Granting her silent wish, he leaned in and pressed himself against her. The warmth of his hard body radiated through his clothing. The salty scent of male skin mingled with pine. Wade let his lips graze, nestling touches light as feathers along her jaw to her earlobe. The sensitive hollow of her neck sizzled with a touch that tempted and teased without giving her what she really wanted: his mouth against her skin and his hands beneath her shirt.

"Oh, you want me," he whispered confidently into her ear. "Of that I'm certain." Pulling away and taking all the night's warmth with him, he met her gaze and smiled widely. "Good night, Miss Sullivan."

She watched him stroll confidently down the sidewalk and disappear around the corner. She waited until the night was silent and still before she let the air out of her lungs. That man had managed to build a fire in her she hadn't expected, especially considering how much she despised him. This was a dangerous game, but if he was trying to seduce her into selling, it would at least be more pleasurable than fighting. Especially when he lost.

A smile of amusement curled her lips. "Oh, you only think you won this round, Wade Mitchell. But the fun is just beginning."

Three

By the time Wade returned to the farm that night, the lights in the big house were all out except for the front porch and the kitchen. His parents had always been early to bed, early to rise, as most farmers were. Thank goodness for the bunkhouse.

The renovated barn referred to as "the bunkhouse" had been where all the boys slept and played as kids. The historic Federal-style house that came with the farm was large, but old in style and design, never renovated to have enough bedrooms and bathrooms to accommodate an ever-changing herd of boys and Julianne all at once. But none of the boys minded the separation.

The bunkhouse had been the perfect boys' retreat, and Julianne spent her fair share of time over there, as well. The entire downstairs was an open living area where they could do their homework, watch television, play video games and Ping-Pong, and roughhouse without breaking anything important. They even had their own mini-kitchen with a refrigerator, microwave and sink. As growing boys they were starving at all hours, and Molly didn't want them running across the yard to the house in the cold and dark.

Upstairs were two huge bedrooms and adjoining baths. The rooms had twin beds and a set of bunk beds to accommodate up to six foster boys at one time. In addition to Wade and his brothers, there had been other children who came but didn't stay long because they went back to their parents or were adopted by relatives. They rarely had an empty bed back then.

These days there were just the four of them, each having outgrown bunk beds. Molly had redecorated after they all moved out, and each room now had two queen-size beds. Typically the kids all arrived back at the farm at the same time: Christmas Eve. The big house hadn't gotten any larger in the past decade, so the boys found themselves back in the bunkhouse.

Since he was the only one there, Wade could stay in the upstairs guest room of the big house. At least until Christmas when the others arrived. But somehow that felt wrong. Instead, he carried Molly's requested groceries inside the big house, put them away and then locked the back door behind him. He grabbed the rest of his things from the hatch of his SUV and rolled his suitcase over to the bunkhouse.

Anticipating his move, Molly had left the porch light on, and on the mini-kitchen counter was a slice of lemon pound cake wrapped in cellophane and a note welcoming him home.

As he read the note he smiled and set the rest of his groceries beside it. He stashed a small case of water, cream cheese, Sumatran coffee beans and a six-pack of his favorite microbrewed dark ale in the fridge. He left the bagels and a bag of pretzels on the counter beside the cake.

God, it was nice to be home.

His loft apartment in Tribeca was nice—it should be, considering what he paid for it. But it didn't feel like home. With its big glass windows and concrete floors, it was a little too modern in design to feel welcoming. It was chic and functional, which is what he thought he liked when he bought it. But it wasn't until he set foot in this old barn with the battered table-tennis table and ancient two-hundred-pound television that he could truly relax.

Things hadn't changed much in the bunkhouse. The futon where he first made out with Anna Chissom was still in the corner. She'd been his first girlfriend, a shy, quiet redhead who kicked off a long string of auburn-haired women in his life. The latest, of course, was giving him the most grief. But he still wished he could pull Victoria down onto the futon and finish what they'd started outside that bar.

He'd done it intending to get under her skin and punish her for dumping that drink on him. Then he found he liked touching her. Teasing her. He enjoyed the flush upon her creamy fair skin. The soft parting of her lips inviting him to kiss her. She responded to him, whether she wanted to or not, exposing her weakness. Now he just had to take advantage of it. There were worse negotiating tactics. Yet she wasn't the only one suffering. He wanted to feel her mouth against his. And not just so she'd sell him her land.

Wade flopped back onto the couch and eyed his watch. It was only nine-thirty. He didn't normally go to bed until well after eleven, especially on the weekends. He was tempted to pull out his laptop and get some work done but was interrupted by the faint melody of his phone.

It was Brody's ringtone—the dramatic pipe-organ melody of the theme to *The Phantom of the Opera*. It was a long-running family joke, considering his computer-genius brother was pretty much living out the plotline as a scarred recluse. But when you had the kind of life that most of the Eden boys had lived, you developed a pretty thick skin and a dark sense of humor to make it through.

"Hey, Brody," Wade answered.

"Wade." His brother's tone was cautious and, as always, serious.

"No," Wade said, cutting off the next question. "I went out to the property to talk to the owner, but there's a...*complication*."

Brody sighed heavily. "I knew this wouldn't be as easy as you seemed to think."

"I said a complication, not a complete failure, Debbie Downer. It's just not going to be open-and-shut. The owner is reluctant to sell."

"Even at double the price?"

"I offered her half a million and she turned me down flat."

Brody groaned on the line. "Why on earth would she turn that down? Half a million dollars is a lot to just push aside."

"Well, it's partially my fault." And technically, it was. He had the feeling Victoria Sullivan might've sold the land if any of his brothers had shown up at her doorstep. But not Wade. Oh, no. She was bound and determined to get back at him for firing her, even though it was her own doing.

"What did you do?" Brody asked in the same sharp tone he'd always used as a child. Whenever one of the other boys lamented about being punished, those were always the first words out of his mouth. Brody was the one who never got into trouble, who never did anything wrong. He was too worried about being punished, thanks to his abusive father. Brody was always happiest sitting at his computer, whether he was playing games or helping Molly upgrade to the latest financial management software. He never got into trouble.

"I didn't *do* anything. She just doesn't like me. She used to work for me years ago."

"Did you sleep with her?"

Wade couldn't help snorting into the phone at his brother's assumption that this had to be a spurned lover. Compared to the lifestyle of his brother, he supposed he appeared to be a bit of a dog when it came to the ladies. "Then or now?" he teased.

"Either."

"No, I've never slept with her." Despite the fact that he would like to. Very much. He eyed the mostly dry spot on the crotch of his pants and smiled. She was a feisty one, for sure. He was certain they'd have a hell of a time in bed. But if she didn't like him enough to conduct a business deal, she probably didn't like him enough to take her clothes off for him.

Well, at least not yet. He'd seen the passion blazing in her pale blue eyes as he'd pinned her against that wall tonight. She wanted him, all right. But she was too stubborn to give in to it.

"I fired her. For cause, I might add. She still seems to be a little perturbed about that."

"I knew we should've sent Xander. No one can say no to him."

Their brother Xander was a Connecticut congressman. He was smooth, charming, likable and well-spoken. Everything a good politician needed to be. He would be perfect to handle the situation, if he were available. "Well, Xander is busy negotiating the country out of a huge deficit, so you're stuck with me. I can make this happen. I assure you. It just isn't going to get done in a day. She's going to take some convincing."

"What can I do to help it along? Run a background check? See if I can dig up any information on her?"

"That wouldn't hurt, although I doubt you'll come up with anything useful. At least, not anything blackmail worthy. I get the feeling her faux pas at my company was a fluke."

"Maybe there's something in her history you can use to soften her up. It will make me feel like I'm doing something."

Wade could hear the aggravation in his brother's voice. Brody wanted to help, but not much could be done from the supersecure corporate offices of his software empire in Boston. His brother was brilliant, had built a company that rivaled Google and Facebook, but Brody didn't go out in public. The only time anyone saw him was when he came home for Christmas or Easter. The rest of the time it was just he and his secretary, Agnes, on the top floor of his Boston high-rise.

It was a damn shame. If Brody's biological father ever got parole, Wade would make him wish he'd stayed in jail. The kind of bastard who would dump battery acid on his young son's face didn't deserve to see the light of day. Especially not when his son didn't get to see it, either.

"For now, some good intel may be all I need to convince her. She doesn't like me, but if I know what but-

tons to push, maybe I can change her mind. Look into
her company for me and some of her recent projects.
I'll send you the basic info to get started. I know she's
passionate about her work. That might be all it takes.
If I'm right, and this is the right property, once I secure it, there won't be any more trouble. If she holds
out, maybe you and I can go out in the dark over the
holiday and start digging holes."

"Digging holes in the dark?"

"You said you wanted to help," Wade pointed out,
only half joking. If the shovels came out, they had big,
big problems.

"Don't let it get to that point, Wade. This isn't a
missing time capsule we're looking for here. It's a dead
man's body. One that we all share some responsibility
for putting into the ground. It absolutely can't be found.
Do whatever it takes to fix this. It could ruin all our rep-
utations—maybe even our companies. Who wants to
do business with someone involved in the death of—"

"Just stop," Wade interrupted. He didn't even want
the words spoken aloud.

"This could kill Dad with his heart condition. I don't
want another death on my conscience."

Neither did Wade. It would probably do all that and
more. And if it didn't kill Ken, Wade was certain he
wouldn't be able to bear the look of disappointment on
his father's face. He'd spent his whole life trying to be
good enough. For his teenage birth mother, who had
dumped him on an old relative. For the foster families
that had passed him around like a hot potato. For the
Edens, who had treated him like their son. He couldn't,
wouldn't disappoint Ken and Molly.

He'd already failed fifteen years ago to protect his

brothers and sister as he should have. Wade wouldn't make that same mistake twice.

"I'll handle it," he promised. "One way or another."

"Welcome to the Garden of Eden Tree Farm. I hope we can help you have a very merry Christmas!"

The moment Tori crossed the threshold into the gift shop among the jingling of bells, Molly Eden greeted her from her post behind the counter. Tori had met the older woman once, at closing, but there had been paperwork to sign and not much time for chitchat.

Today she was determined to change that. Wade thought he could sneak around town and get information on her. Well, two could play at that game. And what better source than his mother? He claimed his family was more important than anything, even money. Spending some quality time with them under the guise of Christmas shopping was the perfect way to do a little digging of her own.

"Oh, Miss Sullivan!" Molly came out from behind the counter with a wide smile that was bookended by rosy cheeks. The woman was tiny and round, with gray-blond hair swept up into a neat bun at the back of her head. In about ten more years, once her hair had gone completely white, she'd make the perfect Mrs. Claus. And judging by her surroundings, Tori was pretty sure that was the plan all along.

"Please call me Tori."

"Only if you call me Molly, dear. We're neighbors, after all." Molly embraced her as though they were lifelong friends instead of acquaintances through real estate.

Tori smiled. She couldn't help it. The woman was

just so damn sweet. How was it that she could raise a sneaky corporate weasel like Wade? "That we are."

She noticed that nothing in the woman's tone or expression conveyed any hint of concern about the fact that Tori lived on her old land. The same was true when they'd met at closing. Neither she nor Ken had seemed bothered at all by it. In fact, Ken had appeared a little relieved. She remembered Ken had commented that they were getting to an age where nearly three hundred acres was a lot of land to deal with. Tori's piece was too rocky and sloped to grow trees. The other two larger plots were the same. No great loss there.

So why did it bother Wade so much that they'd sold it? It made Tori wonder if his parents even knew what he was up to. The burning, childish urge to tattle on him swirled in her gut. It would be so easy. Even a millionaire CEO could be brought down by the wrath of his mama.

But somehow that didn't seem like fighting fair. They hadn't taken the gloves off yet. She'd reserve that tactic until it was absolutely necessary. In the meantime, there wasn't any harm in being neighborly. She wasn't very good at it, since her neighbors typically changed out every few weeks, but she was willing to give it a try.

"So what brings you by today? Do you need a tree?"

"Oh, no," Tori said. "I don't have room for one in my little trailer. When the house is finished, I'll get one for sure. But for now I thought I might pick up one of the lovely fresh pine wreaths you put together. When I was down at Daisy's the other night, the waitress Rose was bragging on your artistic skills."

Molly was beaming with pride as she led Tori over to the display of wreaths. "Rose is such a sweetheart.

She used to date my Xander when they were in high school. I hate that it didn't work out."

They stopped in front of a stone wall covered in about ten different wreaths. There was a variety of sizes, all with decorations of different styles. Tori wasn't really in the market for a wreath, but she would buy one. If she didn't, she'd probably buy a package or two of the homemade fudge by the register, and she certainly didn't need that.

She picked the first one that really caught her eye. "That blue-and-silver wreath is gorgeous. I think I'll take that one."

"That's one of my favorites, too. Let me get the hook to get it down."

Molly headed off across the store, pausing only when the jingling of bells signaled someone else had come in. "Oh, Wade, perfect timing. Could you get that blue wreath down for me?"

Tori snapped her head around to see Wade shaking the snow off his boots on the entryway rug. Today he was wearing a deep red cashmere sweater with a white collared shirt beneath it. It made his shoulders look impossibly wide and strong. After being so close to him last night, she found it wasn't hard to imagine being wrapped in his arms. And being pressed against his chest… Tori shook her head to chase away the unproductive thoughts.

"Sure, Mama," he said without turning her way.

"And I want you to meet Tori Sullivan," Molly continued. "She's the one who bought that little piece of land near the ridge."

At that, Wade stiffened and turned in her direction. He frowned for only a moment, wiping the expression from his face before his mother could see it. He followed her over to the wreath display and, without speaking, lowered the blue-and-silver wreath into his mother's arms.

"Tori, this is my oldest son, Wade. He's in real estate in New York. Perhaps you two run in the same circles. Wade, Tori is an architect. She bought one of our lots, and she's designing a beautiful house to build up there."

"You flatter me," she said, avoiding Wade's gaze until she had to greet him. When she did, there was a polite blankness in his eyes. He was obviously going to pretend they had never met before. She was willing to play along with that for now. "It's nice to meet you, Wade." She held out her hand to him.

"And you, Tori," he said very formally, while managing to emphasize the pronunciation of her first name. It was the first time he'd called her that since he'd shown up at her trailer. Actually, it was the first time he'd ever called her "Tori." When she'd worked for his company, she'd gone by Victoria. She couldn't help but watch his lips as he said her name. There was something oddly seductive about the way his mouth moved that just wasn't there when he called her Miss Sullivan.

When he finally reached out and shook her hand, Tori realized a second too late that touching him was probably a bad idea. She was right. The minute his hand encompassed hers, it was as though she had dipped it into a warm bath. The heat of his soft touch engulfed her, sending a delicious surge of need up her arm that tightened her chest and made it hard to breathe. She found she couldn't pull away from him.

Her body was betraying her, and for what? A chaste, polite handshake?

But then she looked into his dark green eyes and realized it was more than that. He, too, felt the current of desire that traveled through their skin-on-skin contact. Unlike last night, when Wade was prepared and in control of the seduction, this seemed to catch him off guard. For just a brief moment the animosity and arrogance was stripped away, leaving him only with the expression of pure, unadulterated desire. He was fighting the urge to devour her, then and there.

His gaze was so penetrating, it felt like a caress. When his thumb gently stroked the back of her hand, her heart started racing, her breath quick in her throat the way it had been the night before when she thought he might kiss her. The feeling was intense. Too intense for a Christmas store with his mother only a few feet away.

Tori jerked away suddenly, hoping Molly didn't notice the invisible sparks as she rubbed her palm on her jeans to deaden the lingering sensation from his touch. Wade's eyes didn't stray from hers for a few moments, intently searching her as though he were looking into her soul. He turned away only when Molly spoke.

"Tori, I'm going to get this wreath boxed up for you. Do you have a hook to hang it?"

"No," she admitted, sounding oddly out of breath for someone standing still. "Pick whatever one you think will look the nicest with it, and I'll take that, too."

Molly grinned and dashed off to the other side of the store, leaving Wade and Tori alone.

"What are you doing here?" he asked, his tone unquestionably accusatory, yet low enough for his mother not to hear them.

Tori crossed her arms under her breasts, burying her still-burning hand. "Shopping, obviously."

This time, when his green gaze raked over her, there

was no heat behind it. Just irritation and suspicion. "Did you come here to get back at me for last night?"

"Get back at you for what? You claimed you were just hanging out with some friends. Do you think I came here to tattle on you to your mama?"

"No," he said, although the deep lines of the wary expression on his face gave away his lie.

Tori cracked a wicked grin, knowing she'd easily discovered an Achilles' heel. Of course, any son of a decent family had a soft spot where his mother was concerned. Even the pushy, arrogant sons. She opted to rub it in by parroting the line he'd used on her last night. "I'm here buying some Christmas decorations. If your mama just happens to supply me with some information about you, then great. I like to be well-informed. Especially when going up against a worthy adversary."

"Touché," he said drily before casting a quick glance over his shoulder to see where Molly was.

"I take it Ken and Molly don't know what you're trying to do to me?"

His head snapped back to look at her. *"Do to you?"* he whispered with a touch of incredulity in his voice. "Offering to pay you four times your property value is hardly twisting your arm. But no, they don't know about it, and I'd like to keep it that way. They don't need any more stress."

"If they don't care, why are you so determined to get it back? I don't understand."

A barrier went up inside Wade. Tori could almost feel the steel walls slamming into place. She'd obviously trodden into dangerous territory with him.

"I don't have to explain to you why this land is important to me. All you need to know is that I intend to get it back one way or another."

"So you seem to think."

Tori watched as Wade's hands curled into controlled fists at his side. She couldn't tell whether he wanted to kiss her senseless or bludgeon her with a nearby reindeer statue. But he couldn't do any of those things. Not with Molly nearby. Tori had no doubt he'd give her a piece of his mind the minute he could. She was kind of looking forward to it.

"Wade?" His mother's voice called over the cheerful carols playing in the store.

They both turned to look at his mother, and Tori noticed a curious expression on Molly's face. She seemed…intrigued by their quiet discussion. Tori hoped she hadn't mistaken their subdued animosity for real attraction. Tori wouldn't put it past her to try to fix them up. Yes, there was a current running beneath the surface, but it was pointless to consider what that meant. Fortunately, Wade's living in New York would easily put a damper on anything Molly tried to start up.

"Coming," Wade said before he shot Tori a heated warning glance and turned away. She watched him talk to Molly for a minute, then nod and walk out of the store without another word to her.

Tori let out a deep breath and realized she'd been holding it long enough for her lungs to start burning. Her whole body was tense from bickering with him and—if she was honest with herself—anxious with the need he built inside her with a simple touch. It was an extremely confusing combination.

"Your package is ready, dear."

Tori returned to the counter. "Thank you. I'm sure it will look great. The silver and blue against the shiny aluminum will be perfect."

"It will," she agreed. "What are you doing for Christmas? Do you have any family nearby?"

Tori shook her head. "No. My parents travel a lot. The last time they called, they were in Oregon. I'll probably call and check in with them Christmas Day, but I haven't spent an actual holiday with them in years."

"What about any brothers and sisters? Aunts? Cousins?"

"I'm an only child. And my family moved so much that we never really connected with our extended family."

"Hmph," Molly said thoughtfully, although Tori wasn't exactly sure what that meant. "Would you like to join me by the fireplace for some hot mulled cider?"

"I don't want to take up your time."

"Posh! The store is empty. Business won't pick up until later today, and then just with last-minute folk in a rush. Come on, I'll fix you a cup. I've also got some snickerdoodles I took out of the oven right before you came in."

Unable to turn down the Christmas pied piper, she followed Molly over to the refreshment stand, then to the rocking chairs in front of the fireplace.

"You guys really have a lovely place here. It's like a child's Christmas fantasy."

"Thank you. That's really what we were going for—a treasured holiday tradition as opposed to just a shopping trip. Ken and I have always loved children. We'd hoped to have at least five or six." Tori watched Molly gently finger the rim of her paper cup as she spoke. "When that didn't work out, of course, we started taking in foster kids. Wade was the first child we took in."

"Oh," Tori said, the pieces of her conversations with Wade and the bartender finally clicking into place. That was why he had a different last name from the people he considered his parents. He obviously adored Molly as though she were his biological mother. Perhaps not all of his story was meant to play on her emotions. It was possible he did want to preserve the land that had been a special home for him.

Did that change how she felt about selling her property? No. But it did change a little of how she felt about him.

"I didn't realize Wade was a foster child."

"Yes. Julianne is the only child nature blessed us with. The rest came to us through the Litchfield County Social Services office. We had so many over the years, but Wade, Brody, Xander and Heath were the ones who really became a part of our family. It gave us a lot of joy to give a home to children who really needed one. We'd hoped that one day we would be able to turn the farm over to one of them, but that probably won't happen. We raised them to dream big, and they did. Unfortunately, none of them dreamed of being a Christmas tree farmer."

Tori took a bite of one of the warm cookies and nearly moaned with pleasure. The cinnamon, sugar and butter were a divine combination. She'd honestly never had a cookie this good before. "Oh, Molly, this cookie is wonderful. I couldn't have expected anything less with everything you have here. I never had a Christmas tree growing up, but I always imagined buying one at a place like this."

"You've never had a Christmas tree?" Molly looked appalled.

"No. My family liked to travel. My mom homeschooled me so we could move from one town to the next every few weeks. The camper wasn't much bigger than the one I have now, so no real room for a tree. Sometimes, on Christmas morning, my parents would get up really early and decorate one of the nearby trees in the RV park where we were staying."

"Christmas in a camper." Tori could see the wheels turning in Molly's head. "Then I suppose a huge turkey with all the trimmings and homemade pies were out of the question."

Tori chuckled. "Not once in my life have I ever had that. My parents are hippies, really, so they were more into tofu and organic vegetables when I was young. And, yes, even if she'd wanted to cook a turkey, my mom didn't have the room or the equipment. Sometimes we'd eat at a Cracker Barrel when my dad got nostalgic for home-cooked food."

At that, Molly paled beside her. The rosy cheeks had vanished as though Tori had just told her there was no Santa Claus. "You're coming over to our place Monday night for Christmas Eve dinner."

Tori's eyes widened in surprise. "Oh, no," she insisted. Wade would think she'd deliberately done this. He'd make her miserable, glaring accusingly at her across the table all night. "I couldn't possibly intrude on your family dinner."

"Nonsense. Come up to the big house Monday night around five. We'll eat about six, but I want you to get there in time to meet everyone."

"Everyone?" What had Tori gotten herself into?

"It's just me and Ken and the kids. You'll get to meet my other boys. Brody will come up from Boston. He runs a software company. Xander is a congressman, so he's flying back from D.C. Heath, my youngest, will be up from Manhattan. He owns an advertising agency. And my daughter, Julianne, will be home from Long Island. She has a sculpting studio and art gallery in the Hamptons. I'm so excited. I only get them all together once a year. Christmas is a big deal for our family."

Holy crap. Molly made them sound wonderful, but Tori wondered if she wasn't wandering into a trap. How many of them knew about Wade's plans? Would she have his four siblings staring her down, as well? Tori didn't know if she could refuse three powerful CEOs and a congressman if they ganged up on her. She couldn't help imagining herself being slipped a roofie in her eggnog, waking up hog-tied in the basement and being forced to sign over her property.

"Really, thank you, but I already have plans." It wasn't technically a lie. She had planned to eat chicken soup and peanut butter and jelly sandwiches while watching old Christmas movies on DVD. Not good plans, but plans. Hopefully it was enough to appease the older woman.

Molly arched an elegant eyebrow at her. "I have seen your camper, dear. It's really lovely, but I can't imagine you putting together much more than a peanut butter sandwich and a can of soup in there."

Tori smiled. "How did you know what I was having?"

"Oh, Lordy," Molly wailed, dramatically getting up from her chair. "You're coming over for dinner, and that's final."

Tori trailed behind her, tossing her cup and napkin into the trash. She had to admit the idea of some real, home-cooked holiday food was tempting. But she would pay for it later. Wade would see to that. She could see that he got his stubbornness from his mother. The determined glint in Molly's light green eyes left no room for negotiation. Surely Wade would understand his mother was a force of nature.

"Can I bring anything?" Tori had no clue what she could possibly contribute, but her mother had raised her to at least be polite enough to offer.

Molly tried to hide her smile behind her hand and then shook her head. "Not at all. I'll have everything we need. Just bring your darling self, and we'll be waiting for you."

Tori nodded and walked to the cash register to pay for her wreath. She had no doubt Wade would be waiting for her Monday night. Armed and ready for battle.

Four

Tori couldn't make herself go inside the Edens' house. She felt stupid. It was the most unintimidating place she'd ever seen. The old white two-story home was lit with clear icicle lights, and each shutter-framed window had a wreath and candle gracing it. The two short columns that flanked the three stairs leading up to the front door were wrapped with garland and more lights. She could hear Christmas music and laughter from inside. Golden light shone through the downstairs windows and onto the snow.

It was beautiful. Welcoming. The kind of house you wanted to go caroling to because you knew the owners would give you hot cocoa and cookies.

But there was no walking up the steps. Instead, she stood there freezing, clutching the potted poinsettia she'd brought as a hostess gift.

This was a mistake. She just knew it. Tori had spent

the past few hours pacing in her Airstream, trying to think of a way to get out of coming tonight. And when she wasn't pacing, she was looking around at her empty trailer, considering whether she really preferred to watch sentimental old black-and-white Christmas movies and feast alone on peanut butter and chicken soup.

It was Christmas Eve, a day of family and celebration and community. Unfortunately, she wasn't quick to make friends, and small towns were notoriously hard to crack. The only people she knew in Cornwall were her real-estate lawyer, who was apparently best buddies with her enemy; Rose, the waitress at Daisy's diner; and Wade and Molly. That made for a fairly unmerry Christmas this year if she turned down this invitation.

She just couldn't have two miserable Christmases in a row. Last year she'd hoped to spend it with her boyfriend, Ryan. They both traveled so much with their work, but it had seemed that meeting for the holidays in Colorado would be possible. Instead, he'd canceled at the last second, leaving her with a whopping bill for a winter bungalow for one.

Later she discovered he'd never had any intention of coming. He was married with three kids. Ryan was going to be home with his family no matter what he told her. Dating Tori had been perfect for him because she was always moving around and never pressuring him for more. Their relationship was sustained by phone calls, emails and long weekends together. When she'd mentioned moving permanently to Connecticut, only a few hours from his home near Boston, he panicked and broke it off. Finding out about his whole other life had been just the icing on that miserable cake.

He hadn't been the first womanizer to steal her heart and probably wouldn't be the last. She just had a soft spot for smooth, seductive liars. She confused their calculated moves for cultivated charm, but whatever the label, the relationships didn't end well. Slick and likable, they seduced you with words to get what they wanted, then they walked away, uncaring of the shambles they left behind.

Unfortunately, Wade was one of those men, and despite her better judgment, she could feel the attraction building inside her. She wanted him, even as she plotted and planned to make him suffer for the way he'd treated her. She simply couldn't get her brain and her body on the same page. Would having dinner with his family at Christmas make the situation better or worse?

She supposed that all depended on how he reacted to her being there. Perhaps the best way to make him suffer would be to have a good time tonight. Not let him get to her, by rousing either her anger or her desire for him. Having an excellent meal with the enemy was far better than a subpar meal feeling virtuous and lonely.

"I will have a good time," she said out loud, her breath creating a soft cloud of fog in the cold.

"Of course you will. But if you keep standing out here, you're going to get frostbite."

Tori whipped her head around and saw a man standing in the snow a few feet away from her with an armful of firewood. He looked as if he was in his late twenties, tall and strongly built, with short, light brown hair and a wide disarming smile. Her heart was still racing with surprise when she shook her head and laughed. "You scared the daylights out of me."

"Sorry," he said, although his mischievous expression did not lead her to believe it. "You must be Miss Sullivan."

"Tori, yes," she said, shifting the plant in her arms

so she could reach out to shake his hand. "Which one are you?"

"Heath. I'm the baby, if that helps."

The tall muscular man in front of her hardly qualified as a baby. He held the heavy logs in one arm to shake her hand as though they were made of Styrofoam.

Then a thought struck her. Heath knew who she was and was expecting her. Did Wade know she was coming? "Did your mother tell you I was coming to dinner?"

"She told me when I was peeling potatoes on KP."

"Does Wade know?"

"Nope," Heath said with a wicked gleam of pleasure in his eyes. "What's the fun in that?"

Tori's lips twisted in concern. She wanted to see the expression of surprise and irritation on Wade's face when she walked in, unannounced, to his family Christmas party. Apparently so did Heath. But it still felt like a bit of a trap. "Am I walking into the lion's den here?"

Heath shrugged. "Eh, they're fun lions. They'll play with you before they eat you. Come on, let's go in. I'm freezing out here, and the sooner we get in there, the sooner I get pie."

There was no avoiding it now, despite Heath's assurance that she would be eaten. Hopefully she could get some of this famous pie first. Tori let the youngest Eden boy usher her up the stairs, and he held the door open.

"Look what I found outside!" he announced.

Tori had barely recovered from the sudden rush of warmth and light when she was struck with five sets of eyes. She clutched the plant tightly in her hands and tried to gather some holiday cheer in her expression. It probably ended up coming out a little pained.

ANDREA LAURENCE
67

Molly and a younger woman who looked very much like her looked up from their napkin folding at the large dining room table. Standing in the living room talking were Ken and another of the boys. This one looked vaguely familiar and a bit like Heath, actually. Another, younger man watched her from his crouch in front of the fireplace. Their expressions varied. Curiosity, cheer, surprise and even a touch of anxiety from the one tending to the fire.

But Wade was nowhere in sight.

"Oh, Tori, you came," Molly said, rounding the dining room table to greet her.

"She was just standing in the snow. What did you tell her about us, Ma?" Heath broke away from Tori's side to carry the wood over to the brother by the fireplace.

"You hush," Molly chided and accepted the poinsettia Tori offered. "This is beautiful. Thank you. I told you that you didn't need to bring anything, dear."

"You told me I didn't need to bring any food," Tori corrected with a smile for her warm welcome.

"You're very sweet. Merry Christmas to you." Molly leaned in to give her a big hug. "Ken," she said as she pulled away, "could you introduce her to everyone while I find a place for this and check on the turkey?"

"Sure thing." The tall, lean frame of Ken Eden ambled toward her, a friendly smile on his face. "Hey there, Miss Sullivan. Merry Christmas."

"Merry Christmas to you, too. And call me Tori, please."

Ken nodded. "Now, you met Heath. He's the youngest and most troublesome of the group."

"I heard that!" a voice shouted from the general direction of the fireplace.

"He also has excellent hearing. This is Xander."

"Xander Langston," Tori said, reaching out to shake the man's hand. Molly had mentioned one of her sons was a politician, but Tori didn't connect the pieces until she saw the man she recognized from television news and advertisements. She'd had no idea Xander Langston was also one of the "Eden boys" until she saw him standing by the couch.

Xander smiled, greeting her with a polished finesse that practicing politics must have perfected. "Welcome, Tori. Sounds like you've heard my name before. Are you a registered voter?" he asked with a touch of humor in his light hazel eyes that let her know he was trying to be funny.

"Not here. My previous residence was a PO box in Philadelphia, but I'll be changing that."

"Excellent. I hope spending time with my family doesn't negatively influence your vote."

"Stop campaigning, Xander." The young woman from the dining room came over, shoving the congressman aside with her shoulder. "Sorry, he has trouble turning it off. I'm Julianne."

"This is my baby girl," Ken said, his blue eyes brightening at the sight of his daughter. "She's the most talented artist you'll ever meet."

"Daddy," she chided in a tone very much like her mother's. "I'm glad you could join us tonight, Tori. We need some more estrogen in this house."

Tori shook her hand. The Edens' only daughter was quite beautiful and looked very much like she imagined Molly had appeared when she was younger. She had long golden-blond hair, light green eyes and a smile that lit up the room. A person's eyes just naturally went to her.

"Brody, quit playing with the fireplace and come meet our guest."

The last of the brothers put down the fireplace poker and made his way over. There was a reluctance in his movements that made Tori wonder if this brother was a part of Wade's plot. He'd made a point of mentioning that all of the children wanted the land back. The others didn't seem to look at her or treat her differently than any other dinner guest.

Then she saw it. As he stepped into the shimmering light of the Christmas tree, the previously darkened side of his face was illuminated. Tori sucked in a surprised breath and stiffened her whole body to keep from reacting inappropriately. Almost the entire left side of Brody's face was horribly scarred; the skin puckered and twisted into a horrible mask. She couldn't even imagine what kind of injury would leave a mark like that.

She noticed that Brody had deliberately hesitated at the edge of the group, almost giving her time to react and process everything before he greeted her. He'd apparently lived with this, and people's reactions, for quite some time. She felt the sudden urge to put him at ease. As quickly as she could, Tori made eye contact and smiled. "It's nice to meet you, Brody."

He reached out and shook her hand, nodding gently to himself. "Nice of you to come," he said, the corners of his mouth curving up in subdued welcome. The unmarred side of his face was quite handsome. She could tell that if he really, truly smiled, it would be very charming. He had beautiful dark blue eyes with thick coal-black lashes that his injury hadn't touched. His gaze was initially wary, perhaps anxious at meeting someone new, but the smile eventually made its way into his sapphire depths.

Julianne frowned, looking around the living room. "Where's Wade?"

"Bringing in the last of the Christmas presents from Brody's car. How exactly did I get saddled with this job on my own? What are all of you doin—"

Wade stopped in front of the Christmas tree, his arms overflowing with brightly wrapped packages. His gaze zeroed in on Tori in the crowd of his family members. Her hair must have made her stand out. For a moment, a confused mix of emotions played across his eyes. There was a flash of anger, irritation, concern, surprise... Then his gaze flicked over to his father, and Wade's jaw tightened to hold in whatever words Tori's sudden appearance brought to his mind.

"Wade, have you met our new neighbor?" Ken seemed oblivious to his son's consternation.

"Yes, I have." Wade lowered the presents to the floor, leaving them beside the small mountain of gifts that was already arranged there. He dusted his hands off on his jeans and pushed the sleeves of his hunter-green sweater up the strong bulge of his muscled fore-arms. He took a deep breath, cast a few meaningful glances to his siblings and walked over to the group. "Mama introduced us in the shop a couple days ago. I didn't realize you were coming to dinner tonight." Wade speared her with a sharp, accusing gaze.

Tori straightened and put on a polite smile. He was unhappy about her being here. Good. He shouldn't be the only one who got to run around town with a smug grin on his face. "Yes, Molly insisted I come tonight so I wouldn't spend Christmas alone. She's very sweet."

"And stubborn," Heath added with a grin.

"Glad you could join us tonight," Ken said, with a reassuring hand to her shoulder. "Dinner should be ready soon."

From there, the group seemed to disperse. Julianne and Ken disappeared into the kitchen to help Molly. Brody and Heath went back to building the world's greatest fire. Xander made noises about presents in his car and slipped out the back door where Wade had just come in. It left Tori and Wade alone in the entry-way, surrounded by twinkling lights and Bing Crosby crooning in the background.

Wade watched her intensely for a moment, letting the pressure of his anger out while no one was watching. His face had grown a bit red from the strain of holding it in for so long. He quickly threw a glance over his shoulder for witnesses before he spoke. "May I take your coat?" The words were stilted. Formal. As they'd been Saturday in the gift shop.

Nodding, Tori stuffed her gloves into her pockets and slipped out of her jacket. Wade took it from her and walked a few feet to the closet. She watched him slip the coat onto a hanger, meticulously straightening it as he spoke. "What the hell do you think you're doing?" His voice was extremely low, almost a hiss.

"Having Christmas dinner," Tori retorted. "Your mother invited me, and there was no telling the woman no."

Wade turned toward her, his brow furrowed. He was still irritated, but some of the red blotches were fading from his neck. He had to know there was no arguing with Molly Eden. She was a force of nature. "You could've had the decency to fake the swine flu and cancel."

Tori crossed her arms over her chest. "It's Christmas

Eve. So sue me if I'd rather spend it with other people than sit alone in my trailer. It was a nice invitation, and I accepted it. You can stand there and believe it's part of my supersecret plan to undermine your dastardly plot. And maybe it is. But there's nothing you can do about it except smile and eat some turkey, unless you want to make a scene and ruin your mother's holiday."

Wade thrust her coat into the closet and shut the door as forcefully as he could without audibly slamming it. He turned to her with venom in his dark eyes. "I told you my family is the most important thing in the world to me. It's the reason I'm willing to pay you more than anyone in their right mind would pay for that land. To preserve my family. You can come here and have dinner. But you'd damn well better know that I won't sit back and let you toy with any of them."

"I'm not out to manipulate people like you are, Wade. I have no intention of doing anything to your family."

"You'd better hope you're right."

"Or what?" Tori challenged.

Wade opened his mouth to answer, but his gaze moved over her shoulder to someone behind her. His defensive posture melted away, his expression softening.

Then Tori heard Heath's amusement-laced voice behind her. "Hey, you guys are standing under the mistletoe."

"Mistletoe?" Molly came running from the kitchen, a gleam of excitement in her eyes.

Wade and Tori both looked above their heads and back at each other with a touch of dismay. Dangling from the ceiling was a small sprig of green leaves tied with a festive red ribbon. What the hell was mistletoe doing in the house? Everyone here was related. If not by blood, by circumstance. His mother never hung mistletoe....

Then it hit him. She'd invited Tori to dinner. She'd hung mistletoe. Molly was plotting. The woman had five children in their late twenties or early thirties and not the slightest forecast of weddings and grandbabies in her future. She must have gotten it in her head that Tori would be perfect for one of her boys. Maybe even him. What was she thinking?

By now, the entire family had piled back into the living room to watch.

"Mama," Wade complained. "Why did you hang this stuff? It's silly."

"It's tradition," Molly countered. "This is the first year I've been able to hang it, so you bet your sweet bippy you're going to play along and make me happy."

Wade swallowed the lump in his throat and turned from his family to look at Tori. She looked even more anxious than he felt. She was stiff, her light blue eyes wide with shock from the unexpected declaration. Her cheeks were slightly flushed. He didn't know if it was from their argument or the embarrassment of kissing him like this.

Two seconds earlier they'd been fighting, and now he had to kiss her in front of his entire family. Several times over the past few days he'd fantasized about doing just that. Running his hands through the silken fire of her hair. Halting the flow of poisonous words from her mouth by kissing her into silence.

But not now. Not like this. Not in front of everyone.

"If you don't do it, I will," Heath offered from the

back. Julianne threw an irritated elbow into his ribs, doubling him over. "Ow, Jules!"

That made Wade frown. He sure as hell wouldn't let Heath anywhere near Tori or the mistletoe. He'd punch his brother in the jaw for even thinking about kissing Tori.

He'd worry about what that meant later.

"Just hurry up and get it over with."

Tori's voice distracted him from his brother's taunt. He frowned at the redhead. Even though the sensible thing to do would be to give her a quick peck and move on, he didn't like her attitude. Never in his life had a woman asked him to "hurry up and get it over with." It made him want to pull her into his arms and kiss her breathless. He wanted her to eat her words.

But doing that in front of his family was dangerous. Brody would worry that he'd let sex distract him from their goal. Molly would start knitting booties. He needed to just kiss her so they could have dinner and send Tori on her way.

"Kiss her!" someone shouted. He wasn't sure who.

Wade took a step forward, Tori's whole body tensing as he did. Leaning in to her, he didn't hesitate to bring his lips to hers. He had every intention of giving her the kind of kiss appropriate for a stranger caught in this awkward ritual. But the moment his skin touched hers, it was just like before. The handshake in the gift shop had nearly thrown him for a loop. Touching her so innocently had sent his blood boiling, and he hadn't been able to make himself pull away.

Just like now.

Tori's mouth was soft and more welcoming than he'd expected. There was no tight-lipped resignation. Instead, she leaned in to him just slightly, tasting like the honey she'd put in his tea a few days earlier. The gesture was enough to coax him into closing his eyes and deepening the kiss. His right hand slipped up to caress her cheek.

The surge of desire that ran through his body urged him forward, keeping him from pulling back the way his brain knew he needed to. In the back of his mind he registered that Tori wasn't pulling away, either. There was something stronger than both of them holding them in place. A tingle of electricity danced across the palm of his hand where he touched her. He wanted to wrap his arms around her. He wanted to forget about their circumstances and press his body against hers.

A loud wolf whistle from one of his brothers startled both of them out of it. As if receiving an unexpected slap, Wade jerked back. Tori did the same. He looked at her, a little startled by his reaction to her. The intensity had completely caught him off guard. Judging by the wide-eyed expression on Tori's face, she was equally confused by what had just happened.

Glancing behind her, he saw that his whole family stood with mixed expressions on their faces. A few were surprised, Brody was irritated, Heath was amused. Only his mother was grinning, a smug satisfaction in her eyes. Wade could tell she was picking out the perfect color of pastel yarn at that very moment.

"Well," Ken said, breaking the awkward silence. "I think it's time to carve this bird. Everyone finish up and make your drinks."

The family scattered again, Molly reluctantly returning to her duties and leaving Wade and Tori alone. He looked back to her, and his chest suddenly felt tight and uncomfortable. The white collared shirt under his sweater was choking him. He was unpleasantly warm, despite being on the opposite side of the room from the fireplace.

Maybe it had nothing to do with his clothes. It was her. She looked more beautiful than she ever had. Her pale skin was flushed a rosy pink. Her lips were moist and slightly parted. The light blue of her eyes seemed darker around the edges than before. Maybe it was the dark blue of her scoop-neck sweater that drew out the color. It highlighted the long column of her neck and the delicate line of her collarbones. Between them, a small cameo hung on a gold chain. It was the ivory silhouette of a woman set against a blue background that reminded him of his mother's Wedgwood.

Wade wanted to sweep the necklace aside and plant kisses in the hollow of her throat. He wanted to know how her skin would taste and smell. He sucked in a deep breath to draw in her scent. It was a smoky mix of sweet flowers, like honeysuckle, and the herbal undertone of burning incense. It was surprisingly seductive.

"What was that?" Tori's voice was small and without the biting tone she normally hurled at him.

"Just a kiss," he answered, dismissing the powerful feeling that had set fire running through his veins when they touched. He wasn't ready to let her know how it had affected him. How she affected him. That would put him at a distinct disadvantage in their negotiations.

Her blue eyes searched his face for a moment before she sighed and looked away. There was a touch of disappointment in her expression as though she'd expected him to acknowledge it was more than that. She nodded softly and took a step away from him. "I'm going to wash my hands before dinner."

Wade pointed out the small half bath beneath the stairs and watched her walk away. The sweater was enticing, but more so were the charcoal-gray skirt and knee-high leather boots she wore with it. There was a sway to her hips when she walked that was deliciously outlined by the fit of the skirt, and the slit in the back offered him a momentary flash of thigh with each step. It made him wish the bathroom were farther away so he could continue to watch her walk.

Brody stepped into the path of his view just as she pulled the door closed behind her. A frown lined his brother's face as he thrust a mug of mulled cider into Wade's hand. "Here. There's no whiskey in it. I figured you were being dumb enough without alcohol."

Wade scowled at his brother but accepted the drink. "You worry too much. It's all part of my plan," he lied, hoping it sounded like forethought on his part. "I'm softening her up. Then, when you dig up some good information on her I can use, she'll be putty in my hands."

Heath came past them to put his own coat into the closet. "Hey, Wade, I thought you were supposed to be buying Tori's land, not checking her for tonsillitis."

"Both of you just cool it. I know what I'm doing."

Brody's dark blue gaze narrowed at him. Wade often wondered if his brother's personality would be different if he had been born into better circumstances. Would he be less serious? More open to life?

"Try not to scowl at her, Brody. Make her feel welcome, more at ease. It will help. You said you wanted to do something. Here's your chance."

Brody sighed. "I know. I just wasn't prepared to see her walk in. I wish Mama had told me she was coming. She knows I don't like those kinds of surprises."

Wade nodded. "Neither do I." He knew his brother didn't like to meet new people. It was a painful ritual he had to repeat every time someone came face-to-face with him for the first time. "How did she do?"

"Better than most. She didn't run screaming or anything. Although, I need to tell Julianne not to sit her across from me at the table. I'm sure it wouldn't help her appetite to look at me the whole time."

Wade sighed and took a sip of his cider. "Stop it. No self-flagellation during the holidays. Would you rather she sits across from me?"

"Hmm," Brody said thoughtfully. "You two might end up playing footsie at this rate. Maybe across from Xander or Heath."

"Dinner is ready," Molly announced from the entryway to the kitchen. "Is everyone ready?"

The bathroom door opened and Tori came out much more composed than when she went in. Wade watched her paint a smile on her face and curl her hands into fists before she took a few steps toward the dining room. The kiss seemed to have thrown her for a loop. He was glad. Perhaps keeping her off balance was the best thing to do. Kill her with kindness. Use any information Brody came up with to charm her. Being nice might confuse her, make her like him and his family. Maybe then she could understand how important buying the land back was to him.

"Wade, I've put you here," Julianne said, indicating a chair on the far side of the table.

He nodded and made his way over. His sister smiled wickedly at him as she seated Tori next to him and Brody to her left, his good side facing the guest. The rest of the family took their places.

The table was laid with a red-and-gold tablecloth that was barely visible beneath the edge-to-edge casserole dishes, platters and bowls. In the center were thick red pillar candles, poinsettias and golden ribbons that sparkled in the light. As always, Molly had outdone herself.

As tradition dictated, they stood at the table and held hands. Wade reached out and took Tori's hand, trying hard to focus on his father's words instead of how her touch affected him.

"I'm thankful that all of us are back together again. It's been a tough year for everyone," Ken began. "But certainly not the worst we've ever had. We're fighters. We have each been blessed with perseverance and drive and have been brought together for a reason. May we each have a glorious and prosperous New Year and may we each find ourselves back here again next year, blessed in life, love and happiness."

Wade felt Tori gently squeeze his hand. A lump formed in his throat. She understood. At least, she understood his family. She could never truly understand what he was dealing with. He doubted she had such dark secrets buried in her past. Few people did.

Ken smiled. "Merry Christmas, everyone. Let's eat."

Five

Tori was glad she hadn't chickened out after that kiss. She had stood in the bathroom for longer than necessary and toyed with the idea of trying to climb out the tiny window. Reason and hunger trumped her flight reflex, and for that she was grateful. She was stuffed almost as full as the turkey had been before the feasting started. She'd had no idea what a real Christmas dinner was like—one cooked without chafing fuel or charcoal briquettes—until now. There had been mashed potatoes and chestnut-oyster bread stuffing covered in gravy. Maple-glazed carrots. Hot yeast rolls. Then dessert. Good Lord. She'd never known pumpkin pie could melt on your tongue like that.

Everyone had been very friendly, engaging her in their conversations, including Wade. There was a lot of family banter, laughter and tall tales. Tori supposed this was what it was like to have a large family. Growing up as an only child, she'd always longed for a home with a family like this. She'd imagined holidays with merriment and shared stories from childhood.

Tori had sometimes thought that when she married and built her home she'd want to have a lot of children. Four. Maybe five, like the Edens. When things fell apart with Ryan after two years, she'd decided to go ahead and build her dream house anyway. Hopefully love and children would follow. But at the rate she was going, the dreams of that large family were dwindling away. She might end up living in that big house alone.

Perhaps that was why every attempt to start drawing up an architectural design had failed. Even her pen knew there was no point in a home without lively discussion or shared memories to be made there.

Tori turned to listen to Heath as he very animatedly talked about one of his obnoxious advertising clients. They were all such great storytellers. After hearing Ken talk, she knew where the children had learned their skills.

It was a welcome distraction from the night's wildly swirling undercurrents. Having Wade only a few inches away all night had been its own form of torture. She couldn't help but be hyperaware of him. For one thing, he was like a radiator. She could feel the heat of his body penetrating her sweater. Tori tended to run cold, and it took everything she had not to curl against his side and lean into his warmth.

They also kept touching one another. First, holding hands during the blessing before dinner. Then passing food around the table. Without fail their fingers would brush or their shoulders would bump. Innocent, meaningless touches that sent a jolt through her body each time. And the kiss certainly hadn't helped. Whenever her mind drifted away from dinner, it would go back to the moment under the mistletoe.

She hadn't expected anything like that. Wade had had a look on his face as though he were being marched to the guillotine. Clenched jaw, blank eyes. He hadn't wanted to kiss her. And yet, once he did…everything changed. And it really did feel as if everything was different. In less than a minute the way she thought about Wade, the way she looked at him, the way she perceived him shifted on its axis.

Tori dragged her fork through the streaks of whipped cream left on her dessert plate and pondered the kiss. There was a tenderness in his touch that surprised her. A need thrummed through the glide of his fingertips across her skin. It made her want to wrap her arms around his neck and pull him close. Wade! Of all the people to make her react like that… A part of her wished she had found herself under the mistletoe with any of the other brothers. They were all handsome and successful. She could do worse, even considering scowling Brody.

But it had to be Wade, the one she was determined to keep her defenses up against. He was out to push her aside and get what he wanted at any price. She had to remember that.

But somehow that kiss had put a dent in her armor. Sitting so close to him during dinner, Tori couldn't help but wonder if he knew it. He'd made it clear that first night that he would do whatever it took to change her mind, including seducing her. But the mistletoe kiss wasn't planned. And she got the feeling from his reaction that it wasn't just a scheme.

So what was that kiss all about? He'd blown off her question when she asked. She didn't know why. It was more than just a kiss. More than his ruthless drive. At least, it felt that way to her. Maybe it was just her old attraction to him coloring her impressions.

Tori glanced at Wade beside her. He was watching her. He was facing Heath as his brother talked, but his gaze had strayed to her. There was no anger or animosity in his green eyes. Only desire swirling with the flicker of candlelight. His eyes invited her closer. Dared her to stand under the mistletoe with him again.

No, she had been right. It had been more than just a simple kiss.

Taking a deep breath, Tori turned away and found herself facing Brody. He stiffened when he noticed her move toward him. She could tell he was extremely uncomfortable with her there. While almost everyone else at the table was relaxed and chatting, Brody was board straight in his seat and quiet. He wouldn't look at her, but every now and again his gaze would stray to her, then nervously back to the others at the table.

She hoped she wasn't the cause of his discomfort. Tori would hate it if his holiday was ruined because of her surprise arrival. Why had they seated him beside her if he would be miserable? She didn't know what she could do to make it better. Speaking to him made it worse. So she shifted back toward Wade and felt Brody subtly relax into his chair.

"Can we open a present tonight?" Julianne asked as she got up from the table with a stack of dessert plates she had collected.

"You know the rules," Molly chided. "Only Tori gets her present tonight."

Tori was in the process of standing with her own dish when she paused, hearing her name. "What?"

"Why does Tori get to open her gift?" Heath asked.

"Not once in eighteen years have you ever let one of us open a gift early."

"Stop whining, Heath," Ken said. "Tori is getting her present tonight because she won't be here in the morning when we do gifts."

Tori frowned and pushed in her chair. "No more, please. Having me over for dinner was kind enough, really."

Molly shook her head. "It's too late. If you don't take it, it will be a waste." She turned on her heel and headed into the kitchen, ending the argument.

The next few minutes were a blur of activity. Tori was shooed from the kitchen but watched the activity with interest for a while. Everyone took on a task. Not just the women as she had expected. Wade and Brody pushed up their sleeves and started washing and drying pans. Ken brought in dishes from the dining room. Julianne loaded the dishwasher. Xander loaded plastic containers with extra food. Heath bagged the trash and carried it outside. Molly watched over the process like a tiny drill sergeant.

Feeling useless, Tori went to sit in front of the fireplace. Brody and Heath's fire was quite excellent, and it warmed her back. The old house was beautiful, but a touch drafty, and being near the blaze was a prime spot.

Looking around, she found the same decorating enthusiasm from the gift shop carried over into the house. The fireplace and railing up the stairs were draped in garland. There were candles and poinsettias and other sparkly things everywhere. The tree was the grand centerpiece of the living room. She had expected a tree decorated with coordinating ribbons and glass globes, but this was a family tree. There was a mishmash of ornaments and pieces made with felt, clothespins and glitter glue. Crafts from the children's younger days. Multicolored lights. A shiny gold star on the top. It was perfect.

The rest of the room was equally interesting. There were built-in bookcases filled with leather-bound books, knickknacks and a million picture frames. It was a fascinating thing to Tori. Her family was minimalist out of necessity. They had a strict policy that if they didn't use something for six months, it was gone. And if it didn't serve more than one function, there was no sense in getting it at all.

Tori was distracted by footsteps on the dark hardwood floor. What should've taken at least an hour in the kitchen was done in less than ten minutes. The family poured back into the living room far earlier than Tori had expected.

They all held mugs of cider. Wade had two, one of which he handed to her as he sat down on the stone hearth beside her. She took it with a touch of hesitation. "Did you put something in this?" she asked quietly enough for only him to hear.

He smiled widely, his dangerous charm making it obvious that he could have if he wanted to. "No. Just cider."

With no real choice but to believe him, she sipped the drink. It was warm with cinnamon and caramel undertones. It tasted just the way Christmas should. Not the slightest hint of any chemicals.

"Ken," Molly urged, "go get Tori's gift from the shop, would you, please?"

"I'll get it, Dad." Wade leaped up and beat his father out the door.

Tori sat anxiously awaiting what he was bringing her. He returned a few minutes later with a tiny potted Christmas tree. It was about two feet tall, and it was decorated with tiny balls of birdseed that looked like ornaments, and strands of cranberries and popcorn threaded around it like garland. It was adorably festive and just the right size for her Airstream.

"Is that really for me?" she asked, wishing she had brought something else with the poinsettia. It didn't seem like enough for all their kindness.

"Absolutely," Molly said, beaming with the excitement of gift-giving. "Anyone else would've gotten a larger tree."

Wade approached her with the tree in his arms. "When Mama mentioned you'd never had a Christmas tree, the entire family was rightfully appalled. Everyone needs a Christmas tree, as far as the Edens are concerned." Wade set the tree on the small end table beside her. "This balsam fir is alive and well-potted, so when it's warmer you can plant it somewhere. The decorations are for the birds, quite literally. You can set the tree outside after Christmas, and they'll happily eat up all the decorations so you don't have to find a place to store them."

Tori couldn't help the look of surprise on her face. The gift itself was thoughtful enough, but there was also an attention to detail that she appreciated. These people knew nothing about her, and yet they'd chosen the most perfect present. She didn't know what to say, so she just reached out to touch the ornaments and admire her tree instead of the man who brought it to her.

"It's beautiful," she finally got out. "Thank you for the tree. And for having me to dinner. You may have single-handedly salvaged my holiday."

Wade smiled, and Tori's breath caught in her throat. He'd never smiled at her that way. There was always a challenge, a hard edge of negotiation in his expression, even when he was trying to charm her. Tonight, for the holiday, he seemed to have put that aside. Now his smile was just pure joy. It lit up his face, making him more breathtakingly handsome than he'd ever been.

She swallowed hard and took a sip of her cider to distract herself. Wade sat down beside her again and took up his own mug. Tori held her breath, just knowing that the rapid pound of her heartbeat was loud enough for him to hear sitting so close.

Fortunately, someone suggested Julianne play some carols on the ancient-looking upright piano in the corner. That would be loud enough to muffle the sound. Heath goaded his sister until she took her place at the bench and started playing. She began with "The First Noel," and everyone sat quietly listening to her play.

Tori was relieved to have some time without having to maintain a conversation with someone. She wasn't an introvert, per se, but she did spend a lot of time alone. She'd gotten a little rusty at basic small talk. Eating dinner had taken up a lot of that time until now. Lifting her mug, she happily sipped her mulled cider and listened to the music.

"You may want to leave before too long," Wade suggested.

Tori turned to him with a frown curling her mouth down. Just when she thought they'd called a truce. "Are you ready to be rid of me already?"

"No," he said, turning to the piano and leaning toward her. "But you should know we're hard-core on tradition around here. Once Julianne plays a couple songs, a group of grown men is going to watch *How the Grinch Stole Christmas* on an old VHS tape. Then

Dad will read 'A Visit from Saint Nicholas' to all of us before bed."

Tori smiled. She could hardly imagine a room of powerful CEOs watching cartoons. "It sounds sweet. Are there footie pajamas involved?"

"No, thankfully they don't make them in my size. When we were kids, yeah, it was cute. Now it's just getting old and sad, but we haven't provided the requisite grandchildren to pass on the tradition."

"Mmm…" she murmured, taking the last sip of her cider as the final notes of Julianne's song rang out. "I'd better go, then."

"I'll walk you out. My mom is loading you down with leftovers, so I'll carry your tree."

Tori arched an eyebrow at Wade but didn't argue. As she rose, Molly got up as well, and the two women headed into the kitchen where Tori disposed of her mug in the sink. Wade was right: Molly had packed a bag full of containers to feed her for a few days. Molly gave Tori a big hug, thanked her for coming and walked her to the door.

Tori was careful to avoid the mistletoe this time as she grabbed her coat and flung it over her arm. She waved good-night to everyone, then headed out the door with Wade behind her.

They crunched through the snow to where she'd parked her truck without saying a word. She unlocked the passenger door and set the leftovers on the floorboard. Wade put the tree on the bench, and Tori fastened it into place with the seat belt. "That should hold it steady," she said, tossing her bulky jacket inside and slamming the heavy door closed.

Wade was standing beside her, leaning casually against the truck. She expected him to go back into the house—he didn't even have his coat on—but he stayed firmly in place. His green eyes were black in the dark night, fixed on her face. The intensity of his gaze made her skin flush and a tingle run down the length of her spine.

"That wasn't so bad, was it?" she teased, unsure what else to say with him watching her so closely.

"No, it wasn't. I rather enjoyed it. I hope you had a good time. My family seems to like you."

"I did have a good time. They seem like really great people."

"They are. I would do anything to protect them."

Tori felt the mood shift. He wasn't just talking about Christmas dinner anymore. She'd hoped they could shelve this argument for at least one night.

"I know there's a part of you that thinks I'm the big bad wolf out to steal your property. The fact of the matter is that without getting lawyers involved and doing some fairly ugly things that would hurt my parents and their reputation, I can't take this land from you. And I can't force you to sell it. But I hope that meeting my family tonight helps you understand where I'm coming from and how important this is to me. So you know that I've been telling you the truth the whole time."

Wade took a step forward, invading her space. If he was deliberately trying to use his size to intimidate her, his plan was backfiring. She was anything but intimidated. When he was that close, she was thoroughly turned on and extremely distracted from the conversation.

"I need you…" he began, wrapping a gentle hand around her upper arm. Tori couldn't help leaning in to him, her brain short-circuiting with his touch and his words. "…to believe me, Tori."

Tori sighed, an expression of disappointment wrinkling her delicate nose. "Wade, what difference does it make if I believe you or not? You want my land. I don't want to sell it to you. It's a fairly cut-and-dried scenario."

Wade shrugged. "Nothing is that simple. Years of experience have taught me that there is always room to negotiate. Everyone has a pressure point. For some people, it's a dollar amount. That's obviously not the case with you or we would've resolved this the first day. I didn't plan for you to be here tonight, but maybe some good can come of it. Perhaps you have a soft spot for family that would help you understand. I don't want to be the bad guy. I like you, Tori. You're spunky. And beautiful when you aren't pointing a gun at me."

He watched Tori's eyes widen and her mouth softly part at his compliment. "You're just flattering me to get your way," she accused, shrugging off his hand.

"I won't lie to you. I do want the land. But I also want to get to know you better. And for you to like me. I'd like to ask you out to dinner sometime. A nice romantic dinner without my family's prying eyes watching our every move. The perfect scenario ends with both of us achieving everything we want."

"How do you know anything about what I want?"

Wade looked into Tori's eyes. They reflected a confusion he could sense in every inch of her tense body language. She wanted him. She despised him. He was walking a fine line between the two sides. He decided to push her until her desire won the battle. He leaned in and gently brushed a strand of red hair out of her face, barely grazing her forehead and cheek with his fingertips. Tori sucked in a ragged breath when he touched her. He spoke low, almost like a lover's whisper. "Maybe I don't. So tell me, what do you want, Tori?"

She swallowed hard but didn't pull away from him. "I want…" Her voice trailed away as though she couldn't find the right words. "I didn't think you'd stoop so low as to try to romance the land out from under me," she replied, choosing to ignore his question. "As if you even could."

So she was onto him. That might make the seduction harder, but not impossible. "You doubt my abilities?" He grinned a wide, mischievous smile at her and pulled back to give her some room to breathe. He'd rattled her enough.

"No, but perhaps you underestimate my ability to resist you. Tell me, what was that kiss about?"

That was a damn good question. What *was* that kiss about? Tori was the last woman he needed to be attracted to, but his reaction to her was undeniable. Stupid, but undeniable. At best, he could try to use their attraction to tip the scales in his favor. "I told you already. I'm after the win-win scenario."

"I'm not going to sell you my land, Wade. If that's all tonight was about, all that kiss was about, then you can take your Christmas tree and go back inside."

Tori shifted her boots in the snow and crossed her arms under her breasts. The act of defiance did little to discourage the thoughts about her running through his mind. It had only focused his brain on the perky orbs of her breasts that pressed against her chenille sweater and threatened to erupt over the top of her scoop neckline.

It made his mouth water to think about gliding his hands over the soft fabric and kneading her supple flesh. He had the fierce urge to run his tongue along her collarbone and the crest of her breasts.

When he tore his gaze away and looked her in the eye again, he knew he'd been caught in the act. Her eyes widened, and he was struck by what a gorgeous shade of blue they were. Her eyes were a lovely shade of light blue that reminded him of the ice-blue eyes of his friend's Siberian husky. Cool, wary and penetrating. They were also sparkling with the hint of a desire she didn't want to acknowledge. She dropped her hands back to her sides to ruin the display she created.

"Actually, no. That isn't all that it's about." He didn't elaborate, but the pointed way he watched her lips as she tentatively licked them should have spelled it out for her.

Whether it was due to the cold or to his blatant admiration, her creamy cheeks turned a rosy pink and her breath came out rapidly in foglike bursts. He wondered if that was how she would look when she was flushed and breathless from his passionate caresses.

He hadn't been lying when he said he wanted her to like him. That he wanted to ask her out to dinner sometime. When they argued, his blood boiled with irritation and arousal all at once. Wade liked a challenge. Tori was certainly that.

Sure, he intended to get that land back one way or another, but that was a separate issue. Business versus pleasure. He wished she could see the difference, but the women he'd known had a tendency to tangle issues together into an impossible knot. Tori was no different where this was concerned.

Initially he'd thought that indulging in their undeniable connection would complicate the issue. But kissing her in the foyer had changed everything. Denying the electricity between them might actually make their problems worse. He was certainly getting cranky returning to his bunkhouse room every night, alone, with Tori on his mind. Tonight he would have to share the room with Brody and listen to his opinion on the matter.

That wouldn't help the tension building up, either. Perhaps if he and Tori blew off a little steam together, the situation wouldn't seem quite so dire. On her end, at least. On his end, it was most certainly dire, no matter how much pent-up sexual frustration taunted him.

His perfect solution would be to get the land back, offer her enough money that she could buy land that was even better for her needs, and have her in his bed for a while. There didn't have to be a bad guy in this story if she would be open-minded to the options. He wasn't above abusing their sexual chemistry to get his way—if they happened to end up in bed together, so be it.

And at the moment, he wished it would happen sooner rather than later.

"This is also about the chemistry between us." Wade took another step toward her and she didn't back away. His hand went to her face, tipping her chin up to look at him. Even in heeled boots, she had to strain to look him in the eye this close. "I'm not the only one to feel it, am I?"

Tori gave just a subtle shake of her head. He could detect it only by his hand against her smooth skin. "I feel it," she whispered.

She stepped closer until their bodies were nearly touching. He was suddenly aware of the scent of her perfume again, an alluring earthy and floral mix. It made his whole body tighten with anticipation of touching her the way he'd wanted to earlier but couldn't. Now he was free to act without the eyes of his family and their obnoxious critiques.

Wade didn't need any more of an invitation. He dived into her, capturing her lips and cupping her upturned face in his hands. She was soft and open to him.

He felt her hands press against his chest, not to push him away, but to feel him through the thick wool of his sweater. Wade moaned against her mouth as her silky tongue glided along his own. It sent a sharp barb of pleasure through his body, urging him to take more than he should tonight. His hands fell from her face to slip around her waist. He tugged her to him, relishing the feel of her soft body against his hard angles.

Without pulling away, he inched them backward through the snow until her back was pressed against the cold metal of her truck door. She gasped but didn't resist it. In fact, it seemed to light a fire in her. When his mouth left hers to finally taste the hollow of her throat, Tori wrapped her arms around his neck, her silky stocking-clad leg sliding up the outside of his thigh to hook around his hip and draw him in.

The throbbing of his groin pressing into her was almost as uncomfortable as the needling cold on his exposed skin. His hot lips scorched across her frosty throat in a delicious contrast. It wasn't until her pebble-hard nipples pressed into his chest that reality intruded. He was practically devouring her in twenty-degree weather, and neither of them had on a coat.

Forcing himself to pull away, he took one last gentle kiss and backed off. Wade sucked in a large breath of painfully icy air to kill his arousal. He couldn't walk back into the house like this. He grabbed her upper arms and pulled her away from the frigid metal siding of her truck. "I'm sorry," he said. "You've got to be freezing. I didn't think about that at the time."

"To the contrary," she said, her lips swollen and her

cheeks still red. "I'm feeling quite warm for some reason." She smiled sheepishly and brushed a long strand of red hair behind her ear.

Damn. He'd forgotten to touch her hair. He'd ached to do that from the first moment he saw it.

"You don't have a coat on, either," she said. "You'd better get back inside or you'll spend your Christmas Day sick instead of with your family. You don't want to miss the Grinch."

Wade smiled and shook his head. "I'm certain they'll wait for me, whether I want them to or not." There were unnecessary words swirling in his gut that he had the urge to say before he left. They probably wouldn't help the situation, but he couldn't keep them inside. "I want you to know that all this doesn't have anything to do with the land."

Tori stood on her toes to press a soft goodbye kiss to his lips. "I know," she whispered faintly against his mouth.

He had to force his hands into fists buried deep in his pant pockets to keep from reaching for her again.

"I'm glad this one wasn't in front of your whole family," she said with a grin. Before he could respond, Tori turned and ran around to the other side of the truck. "Merry Christmas, Wade." She climbed inside and the engine roared to life.

Tori gave a quick wave as she turned her truck and pulled away from the Garden of Eden. Wade watched her disappear into the darkness, and then ran his hand through his hair.

"Merry Christmas, Tori."

Six

Thursday night, Tori sat in her favorite seat at the counter of Daisy's Diner. Now that the holiday had passed and the leftovers Molly forced on her were all eaten, it was back to her usual haunt.

Over the past few weeks she'd made her first friend in the waitress who handled the counter there. Her name tag said "Rosalyn," but she told Tori to just call her Rose. Rose was off on Wednesday nights, but any other day of the week Tori would be at Daisy's for dinner.

"Hey there, Tori. What will it be tonight?" Rose asked, leaning casually against the countertop.

Her eyes barely glanced at the menu before she made her decision. "How about the chicken pot pie and some hot tea?"

Rose smiled. "You got it." She spun from the counter and disappeared into the back, returning a few minutes later with a teacup and a small kettle of hot water. "I'm surprised you didn't starve over the holiday with us closed," Rose said with a smile.

"I was able to depend on the kindness of strangers," Tori admitted. "The Edens invited me over for dinner."

Rose perked up in quite a peculiar way. "The Edens, huh? Are they *all* in town for Christmas?"

"Yes. At least they were. I met all of them on Christmas Eve. Some of them may have left by now."

The waitress nodded, a hint of disappointment in her dark brown eyes. She turned and Tori followed Rose's line of sight to where her son was sitting alone in a corner booth. The little boy was eight or nine, and whenever Tori came in, he was doing homework or playing his handheld video games while Rose worked.

"I always had a soft spot for Xander. We dated on and off in high school before he left for college. He had a smile that would make my heart just melt. Very charming. It's no wonder he's a politician. He has a way with people."

Tori nodded in agreement. "He was very nice. I was more worried about Wade, though. He's been giving me some trouble."

"Worried? Why? My sister went to high school with him." A sly grin spread across Rose's face. "A lot of women in this town wouldn't mind Wade Mitchell giving them trouble. Some say he's the pick of the litter."

Tori chuckled, a hint of bitterness beneath it. "Well, those people would say differently if they had something he wanted. He's very persistent and downright irritating when he doesn't get his way."

"What could you possibly have that he wants? You just got here."

"He wants my land."

Rose frowned. "The land you just bought?"

She nodded and sipped her tea. "It belonged to his family and he wants to buy it back."

"I don't know why he'd want it. None of the kids have ever shown much interest in the farm. But I'll tell you, if I had to have someone causing me trouble, I'd take an Eden boy in a heartbeat. At least you'd have something nice to look at while you suffered."

That was certainly true. All the Eden boys were attractive. Even Brody, if you could look past the scars and the attitude. If given her choice of the lot, the decision wouldn't be difficult. Wade was certainly her type: dark hair, soulful eyes, a wicked smile... Unfortunately, the magnificent view was a distraction she couldn't afford. "As nice as that all sounds, he's becoming a major pain in my—"

"Well, speak of the devil." Rose straightened immediately and started fidgeting with her dark brown ponytail. Tori turned in her seat and found Wade there, hanging up his coat on a rack by the door. She turned back before he could see her, hoping he wouldn't notice her. Unfortunately, Rose was strutting around so conspicuously in front of her that he was certain to look her way eventually.

"Hey, Rosie," Wade said, sitting down at the counter a few seats away. "How've you been?"

Rose slid down the counter as if she'd been pulled in by his tractor beam. "Good. How about you?"

"Busy. How's your dad doing these days?"

Tori watched the smile fade from Rose's face. "He's okay. I'm sure he's bored out of his skull, but twenty-three hours a day in a cell will do that to you."

Wade straightened in surprise. Apparently he hadn't kept up with the latest Cornwall gossip. Even Tori knew that Rose's dad had gone to jail last year. She didn't know what for, exactly, but it didn't sound as though he would be getting out anytime soon.

"Oh, I hadn't heard he was, uh… I'm sorry. *Um*…do you guys have the pot roast special tonight?"

Rose smiled again and let the uncomfortable subject drop. "That's only on Mondays. But we've got the sliced roast beef with mushroom gravy and mashed potatoes. It's almost as good."

"That'll do. And a lemon-lime soda, please."

"You bet." Rose shot Tori a wink and disappeared into the kitchen.

Alone at the counter with him, Tori couldn't decide if she should shrink into herself and hope she became invisible or sit up tall and dare him to say something to her. She hadn't seen him since Christmas Eve. Since they kissed. And now she didn't quite know how to act. Was he still the enemy? Her body didn't think so, but her brain disagreed. He could be exploiting their natural attraction to get his way. She would have to err on the side of caution and continue under the assumption he was the enemy, kisses or no, until he stopped asking to buy her land. She couldn't trust his motives.

And yet she didn't want to fight with him anymore. It was all too confusing.

She opted for a happy medium, quietly sipping her tea and waiting for her dinner to arrive. Tori focused so intently on it that she noticed only a familiar heat, and when she looked up, Wade was on the stool beside her. She hadn't even realized he'd moved.

"Hello, Tori."

She turned in her seat to look at him. He was wearing dark tailored jeans and a black cashmere sweater that fit his broad shoulders beautifully. She itched to reach out and brush the soft fabric as an excuse to touch him again.

"Wade," she responded simply. She was afraid she'd give away too much if she said anything more.

Wade smiled broadly, undeterred by her cool reception. He took the drink Rose offered him before she disappeared into the kitchen again, leaving Tori high and dry. He took a sip before he spoke. "Do you eat here a lot?"

"Most nights. You've seen my kitchen." She was certain her confusion was etched on her face, but there was nothing she could do about it. "You're awfully friendly tonight."

"Why wouldn't I be? The last time I saw you, we made out against the side of your truck."

Tori's cheeks lit up as bright as her hair. "Don't say it like that," she said, wishing her pot pie would come and give her something to focus on instead of her memories of making out with Wade. She couldn't think of anything else with his scent so close, tempting her to do it again.

Wade grinned and she was glad she was sitting down and didn't have to worry about her knees giving out from under her. She wished she didn't amuse him so much. If he smiled less and sat farther away, she might not be fighting this pointless attraction to the man she was trying very hard not to like. A man she *shouldn't* like, considering he fired her, made her lose her apartment and was hell-bent on taking away her second chance at settling down.

It was that stupid smile that did it.

"Okay," he agreed, leaning in to whisper the words softly in her ear. "The last time I saw you, I drank in your lips like a sweet wine I couldn't get enough of."

Rose approached at that moment, heard Wade's low words, then immediately spun on her heel and vanished. Tori knew she'd hear more about that later, but she could hardly care with Wade's deep voice vibrating through her. A shiver ran down Tori's spine when he spoke, and gooseflesh drew up all over her skin. His warm breath on her neck took her back to the snow, to the truck, to the kisses she couldn't forget. Why did he have this power over her? "I s-suppose that's a better way to put it," she stuttered. "And yet you haven't darkened my doorstep since then."

"I wanted to, believe me. But I had to put in the family time. We only get together once a year. The last of them left today, so I'm free to begin harassing you again."

Honestly, she'd felt his presence even with him gone. The past few days he'd plagued her thoughts, overrun her dreams and disrupted her focus. Memories of his kisses lingered. She was on edge thinking he might show up any minute to continue his petition to buy the land. Or better yet, to pick up where they'd left off. He might as well have been sitting in her camper since Monday night.

"Why did you stay behind when the others left?" she said, pushing the thoughts of his touch out of her mind.

"A few things needed my attention," he said.

She swallowed hard. "Like what?"

"Like you." His lips curled in a smug grin. He knew he was pushing all the right buttons. "So how long have you been here in Cornwall?"

The change in discussion nearly gave her whiplash, but the topic was thankfully a safe one. "Two months. I had been looking at this area for a while before that but hadn't found any land that suited the house I want to build."

"Shouldn't an architect build a house to suit the land, not the other way around?"

"Perhaps." She shrugged. "But this is going to be my one and only home. The place where I live for the rest of my life. I've been thinking about what I want for years, and I finally have the money and time to make it happen. That plot of land is perfect for what I envision. I refuse to settle."

"Understandable. How are the plans coming for the house?"

Tori's lips twisted with concern before she spoke. "Not as quickly as I'd like. But you can't rush perfection. I hope to have the blueprints finalized this week and break ground before the end of January."

Wade's eyes widened almost imperceptibly and his brow furrowed with thoughts he didn't choose to share. "Why Cornwall? You're not from around here, are you?"

"No and yes. I'm not from anywhere. My parents and I traveled my whole life. But I came to visit this area on a long weekend while I was working in Philadelphia, and I fell in love with it."

Wade was listening intently, and it bothered her. The conversation seemed innocent enough. What was his angle? He couldn't really care. Was he just making small talk or was he trying to get information he could use against her later? Maybe he'd try to stall her building permits and frustrate her into selling.

"I've lived around here my whole life."

"Cornwall?"

"Not exactly. Here and there in Litchfield County. I bounced around through a lot of different foster homes at first. I came to Cornwall when I was ten and stayed here until I went off to Yale."

"Is that where you met Stanton?" Alex Stanton had been Wade's business partner when she first went to work for him.

"Yes. We started our own company together after college, and then after you left, we decided to split up and focus on different types of projects. He wanted to branch out, go nationwide and, eventually, international. I wanted to focus on Manhattan, so I've been on my own a few years now."

"Now the two of you can make money twice as fast."

"Precisely the idea behind our dastardly plan."

Damned if she didn't smile at him. He had a way of making her like him no matter how badly she didn't want to. He was only a few days into his petition and he had already managed to charm her. He'd kissed her. How long could she hold out against this? How long until he tired and gave up?

"So, tell me about some of your green innovations. I've been hoping to add more into my projects."

At that, Tori outright frowned. He really was taking every available angle to butter her up. "Really?"

"Yes, really. I've been investing heavily in a couple of green companies over the past few years. They're really making some great strides in products that are earth friendly and, I hope soon, affordable for consumers. I think more people will use them when the price isn't so intimidating."

That surprised her. When you're in the business of renovating and reselling buildings, every penny spent cuts into the profit. She never expected him to be the kind who would invest in green products. But she was glad he did. She wished more people would. "I agree.

That's why I try to get as much exposure for my work as possible. I want to increase interest and demand, which will hopefully make some of these innovations mainstream and drive down the price."

"It's hard to do. My folks have managed to run an organic farm without the crippling prices breaking their profit margin, but it's taken decades to perfect it."

Tori's brows shot up over her teacup. "The tree farm is organic?"

"For the past twenty years."

Wade was full of good surprises tonight. She wouldn't admit it to anyone, but she was actually enjoying her conversation with him. It felt almost like a fun, casual first date.

Did she just use the word date?

"I've been looking at some of your recent projects online. You really do great work. The building in Philadelphia is stunning."

Tori blushed again. If he was playing her, he was good at it. She couldn't help but believe him. Her latest project really was incredible. Her best apart from her own house, which was going to be her greatest work. "Thank you. It's almost done. The ribbon cutting is scheduled for just after the New Year."

"I wish we hadn't lost you at our company. Your talents would've been put to good use."

It sounded like a compliment, but this time it rubbed her the wrong way. Tori was about to say something rude about how he shouldn't have fired her, but Rose returned then, placing a piping-hot dish of chicken pot pie on the counter in front of her. It was the perfect opportunity for her to focus on something else.

The pie had a golden flaky crust that Tori yearned to bust open with her fork. Typically, she'd leaned toward club sandwiches and grilled chicken plates, but dinner with the Edens had been a gateway meal. Now she was on a personal mission to make up for twenty-eight years of home-cooking deprivation.

"That smells great," he said, leaning closer to her and inhaling the enticing aroma. "Don't let me stop you from enjoying your meal."

Tori opened her mouth to argue with him about etiquette, but Rose came by with his plate, too. Now she couldn't even refuse out of politeness.

"Perfect," he said, eyeing his roast beef. "Now we can eat together. Not exactly what I envisioned for our first date, but it will do."

"Date?" Tori's head snapped up from her plate. The man must be reading her mind. It was the only answer.

"I told you I wanted to take you out to dinner," he said before popping a bite of beef into his mouth and swallowing. "I was thinking more of wine and candlelight, but we can save that for our second date."

"We're dating now?" It was news to her. News that made her heart flutter momentarily in her chest as though she were a teenager.

Wade shrugged. "Why label it? We're just enjoying each other's company and getting to know one another. What are you doing tomorrow night?"

Tori paused with a bite of chicken and vegetables in midair. "Why?"

Dropping his fork to his plate, Wade spun on his stool to face her. His brow was furrowed with irritation, but the light in his green eyes indicated it was more exasperation than anything else. "Why must you make everything so difficult? It's a simple question. Do you have plans Friday night or not?"

"No." It was the truth. She worked during the day

on the blueprints for the house, fielding calls and holding virtual meetings on other projects, but most of her
evenings were spent reading or messing around on her
computer until she got sleepy.

"Well, you do now. I'm going to take you out on a
proper dinner date."

Wade had to admit this was the first time he'd ever
dressed in an Armani suit, gotten into his BMW and
driven to a trailer to pick up a woman for dinner. As he
climbed out of the SUV, he was pleased that the sunny
day, while cold, had managed to melt most of the snow
and reveal the well-packed gravel of her temporary
driveway. A couple more warm days and he might be
able to find the turtle-shaped rock on her property that
served as a makeshift headstone.

He had tried to talk himself into canceling this date
several times today. He was attracted to Tori, but he
could suppress that urge if he needed to. Asking her out
had very little to do with his desire for her. As much
as he didn't like the idea, getting close to Tori was the
best way to soften her up. She'd gone from a hellcat to
a kitten after spending time with his family. The information Brody had supplied him with about her business
had made her putty in his hands. He was confident that
a date or two would wear her down.

It had to. If Tori intended to break ground on the
house in a few weeks' time, he had to hurry. There
wasn't time to finesse this situation. He had to win
Tori over one way or another, and this seemed to be
the quickest way. She was attracted to him. If the past
was any indication, that might be enough to influence
her decision.

It was sleazy. Underhanded. And absolutely necessary. He couldn't fail his family.

As he made his way to her front door, he enjoyed feeling the crunch of gravel against the soles of his dress shoes. He'd opted not to wear his snow boots and was hoping Tori had done the same. The knee-high boots she'd worn at Christmas were nice, but he was a self-proclaimed ankle guy. Just another reason for him to despise the cold and ice of New England winters. His favorite part of the female body was tucked away until spring.

He had his fingers crossed that she would step out of that Airstream in one of her sexy pairs of heels. Back when she'd worked for him, he could always count on finding her near the copier or in the break room wearing an attractive yet professional outfit and a pair of luscious heels. It had been the highlight of his day.

He gave a quick rap on the aluminum door and waited for her to answer. A moment later it swung open, and he stepped back to hold it for her. Cling to it was more like it.

The elevated camper gave him a prime view of a pair of black patent leather pumps with a strap around each delicate ankle. His heart almost skipped a beat as his gaze traveled up the length of her calves to the dark red bandage dress that clung to her round, full hips. The neckline was off the shoulder, and dipped low to give a tantalizing yet tasteful view of her breasts.

Tori smiled and slipped into a black full-length wool coat before stepping down to join him. Her thick auburn hair was swept up into a twist, exposing the long, pale line of her neck and sparkling ruby earrings. Her pale eyes looked mysterious and exotic lined in black with a smoky shadow.

She was, in a word, breathtaking.

He reached out a hand to help her down the stairs and then pushed the door shut behind her. "You look beautiful," he said.

"Thank you," Tori replied. The blush of her cheeks was made even more evident by the powerful red of her dress peeking out from under her coat. "You look very nice, too. I don't think I've seen you in a suit since we worked together."

Wade smiled and held out his arm to lead her to the passenger side of his car. "I wear them all the time in real life. On the farm, I'd just get pine sap on it. More rugged attire is required out here, as you know."

Tori eased into the heated leather seat and pulled her legs in. "Yes, these heels aren't very practical in the country."

"That's a damn shame," Wade said as he slammed her door closed. He then got in on his side.

Tori waited until they were on the highway before she spoke again. "So where are we going?"

"A little French place I know on the west side. It's a far cry from Daisy's Diner, I have to tell you."

"Wait, I think I've heard of that place. Incredible food, but almost impossible to get in?"

"That's the place."

"How did you get reservations? You just asked me out last night. It's Friday, one of the busiest nights. I've heard people can wait months for a table."

Wade turned to her with his cockiest smile. "I know people."

"Oh, that's very impressive," she mocked.

"I went to high school with the executive chef. We've stayed good friends over the years. Whenever I'm in town, all I have to do is call and I've got a table held for me."

"That must go over well with all the women you take there."

Wade tried not to make a face, but he couldn't help it. She made him sound like a tomcat running around west Connecticut. "I'm usually alone or with one of my brothers," he said. "I think this is the first date I've ever taken there. I'm usually not in Cornwall long enough to romance anyone."

Tori nodded and turned to glance out the window at the rapidly darkening sky. "So when do you head back to the big bad city?"

"I don't know," Wade admitted.

And he didn't know. His plan had been to secure the land, spend Christmas with his family and hop the next plane to Jamaica. He should be gone by now, but that hadn't panned out. All his brothers and Julianne had returned to their respective homes. And he was still there. Without the land. And without a ticket to a warm tropical locale.

When all this was over, he was going to demand a vacation on Brody's private Caribbean island. He owed Wade after all the grief he'd served him the past few days.

"Don't you have a business to get back to?"

"Not until after the New Year. My company shuts down for two weeks so my employees can enjoy the holidays."

"Was it your intention to spend those two weeks here, badgering me?"

"No. By now I'd intended to be on a beach, soaking in the sun and badgering a waitress for another drink."

Tori turned to him. "So you'll stay in Cornwall until you wear me down, right?"

Wade met her gaze momentarily before turning back to the road. "Yes."

"And what if I deliberately stalled just to keep you around?"

Wade slowed the SUV to turn into the parking lot of the restaurant. For a packed night, there weren't many cars, but the dining room was small and didn't have many tables. Or a menu, for that matter. They served a series of tasting courses, chef's choice. Wade pulled into a spot and turned off the car.

Unbuckling his seat belt, he pivoted to face her. "If you're really interested in keeping me around, there are better ways to go about it."

"Like what?" she asked. The challenge lighted her eyes like sparkling hunks of aquamarine.

"Like making wild, passionate love to me until I can't bear to leave your side."

Tori's mouth dropped open. Her lips moved in vain for a moment, but there were no words. He seemed to have that effect on her, and he had to admit he liked it. Wade grinned wickedly and climbed from the car. He came around and opened the door for her, taking her hand as she slid from the seat.

They walked to the restaurant with his arm around her waist. He liked the feel of her body against his side. She fit perfectly there, and he needed only to turn his head toward her to breathe in the floral scent of her shampoo. It made him want to spread the strands across a silky pillowcase and bury his face in them. Soon. Hopefully.

Just as they opened the door, he leaned in and whispered, "And I hope you'll put that new plan into place tonight after dessert."

The sounds of the restaurant eclipsed any response she might have cobbled together. He focused instead on greeting the hostess, the executive chef's wife, and following her to an intimate table for two by the fireplace. Wade helped Tori out of her coat, then handed both their jackets over to the hostess to be checked.

Moments later their server, Richard, arrived with two glasses of white wine. After welcoming them and introducing himself, he placed the glasses on the table, adding, "We're starting tonight with an '83 sauvignon blanc and a tasting of caviar and white asparagus."

A second server swooped in behind Richard with their first plates, and then both of them disappeared into the kitchen.

"I hope you're hungry," Wade said, admiring the artistry of their first dish. "There's nine more courses."

They'd need every bit of spare room to eat all the food and wine presented to them. There was a *fois gras* terrine, butter-poached lobster, potatoes with black truffles, lamb, sorbet and the most delicate white chocolate mousse with cherries he'd ever put into his mouth. The food and wine flowed as easily as their conversation.

Wade had been concerned at first that their usual antagonistic banter might ruin the evening. As much as fighting with Tori aroused him, he wanted tonight to be about something else. The more she got to know him, the more she seemed to open up to him. The information Brody had been able to uncover about Tori had proved fairly useful so far. Talking about her work and her passion for environmental causes had opened a door to him.

Tonight the romantic atmosphere and the multiple courses of wine seemed to help her relax and enjoy herself. After about the third course, he could see the tension ease from her shoulders and a lazy pleasure settle into her eyes. She laughed and flirted, smiled and watched him over her glass with warmth in her gaze. He liked this side of Tori just as much as, if not more than, her fiery red side.

They talked about their work and their college experiences. Tori shared details about her travels as a child and all the things she'd seen. Wade had to admit he was a touch jealous that she had seen so many things at such a young age. When he was young, he was poor. And now that he was no longer poor, he was too busy to travel.

In turn she asked him a lot about his high school years and growing up with brothers and sisters. They had lived quite different lives.

Before he knew it, he looked up and found they were the only customers left in the restaurant. There was only the sultry music playing in the background and the crackling of the fireplace beside them. Even the servers seemed to blend into the background, well-trained not to interfere with their customers' romantic evenings.

"Did you say you never went to prom?"

Tori looked up from her last half-eaten plate. "No prom. No high school graduation. None of the normal stuff."

"Do you like to dance?"

She hesitated a moment before she answered. "I don't know. I've never actually danced with a man before. I mean, I went to a few nightclubs in college, but not real dancing. There's never really been the opportunity. No school dances, no family weddings…"

Wade frowned and eyed the area just beside their table. "That is a travesty." He stood, placing his napkin in his seat, and reached out for Tori's hand. "Come here."

Despite a flash of wariness in her eyes, Tori didn't argue with his demand, and he was glad. Instead, she rose gracefully from her chair and took the few steps over to the open area that was the perfect dance floor for two.

Wade pulled her into his arms, giving her time to adjust to the proper stance before pressing her body against his own and rocking in gentle time with the music. At first she was stiff in his arms. He worried that it was him, but her glance kept nervously shifting down to her feet. She was uncomfortable not knowing how to dance.

"I don't think I'm very good at this," she said, worrying her lip with her teeth.

"Just relax," he cooed into her ear. "No one is watching. It's only you and me." Wade splayed his hand across her lower back, pressing her into him and guiding her movements. "Close your eyes and feel the music. Feel the movement."

Tori closed her eyes, her body relaxing after a few moments. Then she leaned in and placed her head on his shoulder. Wade reveled in the feel of her in his arms, closing his own eyes to block out everything but the experience of holding her.

Her skin was like satin against his. The soft curves of her body fit into each hard ridge of his own. He could feel the crush of her breasts against the wall of his chest and the rapidly beating heart behind it. The rhythm of it matched the pounding in his own rib cage. The blood had started rushing in his veins the moment he touched her. Every nerve in his body was tingling with arousal and anxiety.

Despite all the complications and reasons he shouldn't want Tori, he did. He wanted her very badly. And he was fairly certain she felt the same way.

Tori shifted in his arms, and he opened his eyes to see her pull away just enough to look him in the eye.

"I'm ready," she said.

"For what?"

The corners of her red lips curled up in a seductive smile. "To make you never want to leave my side again."

Seven

Tori had never seen a man pay a check so quickly. A wad of large bills was tossed onto the table, and he grasped her hand to lead her out of the restaurant. They paused only long enough to collect their coats, and then they were back on the road.

Whereas on the way to the restaurant his engine had purred, now the German motor roared and devoured the highway ahead of them. The speed only fueled the desire burning inside her. Its flames licked at her skin, flushing her pink and melting her core into a pool of liquid need. She wasn't exactly sure where they were going, but she didn't care. She just wanted to get there fast.

Her left hand crept across the gap between them and planted itself firmly on his thigh. Her fingers rubbed over the soft material of his suit, his muscles tensing beneath her grip. The speedometer surged in response, and the reaction urged her on. She stroked his leg, inching ever higher.

When she glanced up at Wade, his face was rock hard, his jaw locked and his eyes burrowing into the road. His knuckles were white as they gripped the leather steering wheel. He was fighting hard for control. So far, he seemed to have it managed.

That made Tori want to push him. The road was deserted and dark. With a wicked smile, she moved her hand higher, dipping between his thighs. She found the firm heat of him struggling against the confines of his pants. Wade jerked and groaned at her touch, but the SUV remained steady and in control as they traveled.

With curious fingertips she explored him. She gently stroked his length and swallowed hard when he extended beyond her expectations. She wet her lips in anticipation and clamped her thighs tightly together to quell the ache building inside her. She wanted him so badly. Even back when she was his employee, she'd fantasized about this. At least before...

No. She wasn't going to ruin tonight with thoughts about the past. She'd always wanted a taste of Wade Mitchell, and tonight she was going to have it. When she spied the apple-shaped sign of the tree farm, a rush of relief washed over her. They were almost there.

As the SUV's tires met the gravel of the driveway, Tori palmed his fly with one last firm stroke. Wade growled low, whipping the car to a stop. They'd parked in front of a building that looked like a barn, but without the hayloft, large swinging doors and livestock. Thank goodness they weren't heading to the big house. As much as she wanted him, she just couldn't... Not there with Ken and Molly so close by.

The engine went quiet. Wade stretched his hands to

relax the tense muscles and turned in his seat. His gaze dropped to her hand, which was still touching him, and shifted back up to meet hers. "I've got to get you in the house before I'm forced to make love to you in the backseat like a teenage boy."

Instead of responding, Tori gave him another firm squeeze. Wade's hand grabbed her wrist and tugged her away before she could move again. "No, seriously," he said, his eyes closed. "It's not very comfortable back there."

"Okay," Tori agreed with a grin. "But only because having sex in a bedroom without wheels is a rare treat for me." With a laugh, she climbed out of the SUV, too anxious to wait for him to open her door. He met her around the other side and took her hand, leading her to the front door.

Once inside the building, Wade locked the dead bolt behind them and swept her into his arms. His mouth crushed hers, devouring her with an enthusiasm her body had been craving since their fourth course. Tori let her purse fall to the ground and wrapped her arms around his neck. She was glad she'd chosen to wear these heels, because they brought his mouth closer to hers and aligned their bodies perfectly. His erection pressed into her lower belly, and she tilted her hips to grind against it. A growl vibrated across her lips, followed by the glide of his tongue along hers.

Wade's hands moved up her back until they reached her zipper. A hum ran along her spine to the base as it glided down and exposed her back to the cool air. His fingers delved beneath the fabric to caress her skin and undo the snaps of her strapless bra.

As much as she hated to break away from him, she knew she needed to if she wanted to feel her bare skin on his. Tori pressed against his chest until his lips left hers. His warm hands cupped her shoulders, pushing her dress down until it pooled around her ankles with her bra. Now she was wearing only her lace panties, sheer thigh-high stockings and heels. She could feel his eyes on her, drinking in every inch of her body. Tori thought she would feel self-conscious, but the fire in his eyes was undeniable. He wanted her. There might be other layers of conflict between them, but his desire was genuine.

To tempt him, she reached behind her head to pull out the few pins that held her hair in the twist. Her breasts reached out to him as she moved, the tight nipples aching for his touch. His gaze went to them, his tongue darting across his lower lip as he watched. Instead of reaching for her, he tugged down his tie and threw it to the ground.

Once the pins were removed, the thick red curls fell down over her bare shoulders. She gently shook her head and stepped out of her dress.

"God, you're beautiful," he said, his voice a hoarse whisper. "Come here."

Tori closed the gap between them. Her palms ran over his chest and up to his shoulders to slip his jacket off. It fell to the floor beside his tie, and Tori made quick work of the dress shirt buttons.

When Wade shrugged out of his shirt, Tori's breath caught in her throat. His chest was broad and chiseled, with each muscle well-defined. A dark sprinkle of chest hair trailed down to his stomach. Her gaze followed the line of it down, but before she could reach for his belt, he reached for her wrist and tugged her to him. She slammed into his chest, her nipples pressing against the firm, tan skin she'd just been admiring.

His mouth found hers again and then traveled down her throat. He nipped at her skin with his teeth, soothing it with his lips and tongue. Wade buried his hands in her hair, rubbing the strands between his fingertips. She closed her eyes and just focused on the sensations he coaxed.

Wade's hand slid down her back, caressed a round cheek through the lace of her panties, then continued along the back of her thigh. He tugged her leg up around his hip, then wrapped his arm around her waist. With his mouth still on her throat, he lifted her off the ground, hooking her other leg around him.

Clinging to his shoulders, Tori squealed at the sudden movement. Then with a laugh she threw her head back, arching her spine and offering her breasts to him. He accepted, taking one nipple into his mouth as he walked them slowly through the large open room. The tug of pleasure shot straight to her center, and Tori groaned loudly. She thought she remembered him saying his brothers had left, but she didn't know that for sure. She hoped no one else was here, but frankly she didn't care. She needed him now.

"Bed?" she whispered.

His lips parted with her flesh only long enough to say, "Upstairs."

Tori glanced at the staircase behind them. They'd been moving toward it since he picked her up. He began to carry her up the stairs, but she shook her head. "Too far," she gasped between ragged breaths. "Right here."

"On the stairs?"

"Yes, now."

Wade didn't argue. He eased her onto one of the steps, the plush carpeting meeting her bare skin. She leaned back onto her elbows, sprawled across the steps as he pulled away to look at her. His breath was rapid, his chest rising and falling as if he'd been running a marathon. His gaze slowly traveled up her body until it met her eyes. The green depths were almost penetrating.

He didn't look away as he unfastened his belt and eased down his own pants and briefs. Tori caught only a quick glance of his magnificent body and the flash of foil in his palm before he was crouched down, kneeling on a step between her leather-wrapped ankles. He lifted one leg and planted a kiss on her ankle, then on her inner calf and knee. He placed a searing kiss on her inner thigh just above the lace band of her stocking. Tori's leg quivered in his hands, his hot breath near torture on her exposed center. His fingertips glided across her panties, hooking around the edge before tugging them down her legs and tossing them to the bottom step.

Tori let out a heavy sigh as his body moved back up to cover her own. His blazing-hot skin glided deliciously across hers. The man was as hot-blooded as they came, like a furnace. He picked up where he'd left off, placing a kiss on her hip bone, then on her belly. The evening stubble on his chin scratched and tickled her delicate skin. His mouth moved over her stomach to the valley between her breasts. Braced on his elbows, he took his time teasing each nipple into fierce, throbbing peaks with his tongue.

She could feel the brush of his arousal along her inner thigh. Her whole body ached to have him inside her, but Wade didn't appear to be in the same hurry she was. "Wade, please," she said, her hands tugging impatiently on his upper arms.

He pulled away for just a moment, quickly sheathing

himself in latex and moving back between her thighs. This time he covered her completely, and she was glad. She'd quickly become accustomed to his warmth, and losing it, even for a few moments, had left her shivering. Now that he was back where he belonged, Tori tilted her head to look him in the eyes. Wade dipped down to kiss her again. As his tongue slowly penetrated her, so did the rest of him. He surged forward. Inch by inch he filled her. Tori held her breath and eased her legs open farther to accept all of him.

When at last he was buried deep inside her, Wade stilled. His lips parted from hers so he could suck in a ragged breath. "Victoria," he murmured against her lips, "you feel so incredible."

His words were nearly as sexy as the almost pained expression on his face as he said them. Tori drew her stocking-clad legs up and wrapped them around his waist. That movement alone was enough to draw a hiss from his lips. She placed a hand on each side of his face. Feeling the rough stubble in her palms, she drew him down for another soft, brief kiss. "Love me," she said.

A flash of challenge lit in his eyes. Pulling back, he thrust into her again without breaking their visual connection. This time it was Tori who cried out. Before she could recover, he moved again and again. The desire that had been building inside her for the past few hours was now a constant throb of pleasure. The ache of it increased with their every movement.

Everything else faded away but that feeling. There was no land to be bought. No lost job. No animosity between them. Not even the burn of the rug on their elbows or the bite of the stair across her back registered. There was only their frenzied drive to fulfill the need.

Tori clung to him, panting and whispering words of

encouragement in his ear. "Yes," she repeated, the pressure building inside reaching the critical point. "Yes, Wade, yes!" Tori cried out as the wave of her climax crashed over her. Her body trembled against his as he quickened his pace and found his own release. The roar was almost deafening as he poured everything he had into her, then collapsed.

Tori held him to her, the sweat of their bare skin mingling together, until their rapid breaths finally slowed. It was only then, when the passionate fog had lifted, that she could find the strength to speak again.

"Let's go find a real bed," she said.

Wade woke up to the delicious smell of coffee and bacon. He smiled, shifted and rolled over, expecting to see the other side of the bed empty. Instead he found himself looking at Tori's bare back.

Molly.

Wade flopped back against his pillows in disgust. The movement was enough to wake Tori. She tugged the sheets modestly over her breasts and sat up, a touch disoriented. When she turned to look at Wade, he was struck by how beautiful she looked, tousled. Her red hair was wild, her lips swollen from a night of kisses. She looked like a woman who had been thoroughly and completely loved the night before.

And he'd be inclined to pick up where they left off if he didn't think his mother was downstairs.

"Good morning," he said.

"Morning," she said with a yawn and a long, feline stretch that accentuated the bare curve of her back. Then her delicate nose wrinkled and her brow furrowed. "Are you cooking something?" she asked.

"No."

"But I—" Tori brought her hand up to her mouth. "Molly isn't downstairs, is she? My panties are…" She lifted the sheet, then quickly brought it back down. "Oh, no. They're still on the stairs."

Wade sat up and shook his head. "Don't worry about all that. I'm not a teenager anymore. And if I know my mother, she's probably pleased as punch to find our clothes strewn across the living room. She knew I was taking you out to dinner last night."

"Are you sure she won't be upset?"

"Extremely. The woman hung mistletoe. She knows exactly what she's doing."

"And what's that?"

Wade swallowed hard and swung his legs out over the edge of the bed. "Working on grandchildren."

He pulled on a pair of his pajama pants from his luggage, turning his back to Tori to hide the laugh her wide, panicked eyes brought on.

"I, uh, I—I mean…"

"Relax. I'm sure the next generation of Edens has yet to be spawned. I'll go run her off."

Wade opened the bedroom door and slipped down the stairs to the ground floor. His mother was nowhere to be found, but she'd certainly been in the bunkhouse. Their clothes from the living room floor—not the panties, thankfully—had been picked up and neatly laid over the arm of the couch. The coffeepot was on and dripping the last of a fresh pot. There was a pitcher of orange juice and a foil-wrapped casserole dish on the counter. In the center of the breakfast table was a vase filled with some of the greenhouse-grown roses left over from the pine centerpieces she sold in the shop.

"Is it safe?"

Wade turned to find Tori standing a few steps from

the bottom of the staircase, a blanket wrapped around her like a toga.

"Yes, she's gone. She brought us breakfast."

Tori stooped down at the bottom of the stairs, snatching up her panties. She found her purse by the front door and stuffed the panties inside to hide the evidence in case someone came back. "Breakfast?"

"Yes, are you hungry?"

She smiled sheepishly. "After the meal last night I thought I might never eat again. But I did manage to work up quite an appetite."

That was for sure. After they made it upstairs, they'd taken a shower together, starting another round of love-making they finished in the bed.

"Would you like coffee or orange juice?"

"Juice," she said, reaching for her red dress. "This seems like a little much for breakfast, but I didn't plan for an overnight trip."

"Upstairs in the bedroom drawer are some shirts you're welcome to try on. They'll be big, but it's better than a cocktail dress. And under the sink are some extra toiletries that Molly keeps here in case one of us forgets something. There should be a new toothbrush and anything else you might need."

Tori nodded and slunk back toward the stairs. "That's great. I'll be right back."

By the time she came back downstairs in an oversize Yale alumni sweatshirt, Wade had made them both a plate with breakfast casserole and diced fruit that Molly had left in the fridge. He handed her a glass of orange juice as she sat down at the table.

"This looks wonderful. Molly really didn't have to go to all this trouble."

Wade sat down with a mug of coffee and shook his head. "She lives for this. Don't let her fool you."

Tori took a few bites, quietly eating and avoiding making eye contact with Wade. He wasn't sure if the typical morning after had been made more awkward, or less, by his mother's culinary interference.

"How are you this morning?" he asked.

Tori brushed her loose hair behind her ear and took a sip of juice before she answered. "Honestly, I'm a little weirded out that your mother knows we slept together, and I'm still trying to process that fact myself."

"Do you regret last night?"

"No," she said. "But sex always changes things. I'm not quite sure what's going to happen from here."

"I believe we go out on another date."

Tori frowned. "I don't know if I'm ready for that. Three dates in a week. With a man who wants my land and fired me from my first real job."

"That still bothers you, doesn't it?"

"Yes," she admitted. "Despite what you believe, I didn't do anything wrong. I didn't so much as shake that guy's hand, much less handle anything else. I was so naive. And when you fired me, it felt like I'd lost everything. My apartment, my confidence in my abilities. Even a little of my trust in men."

Now it was Wade's turn to frown. "I damaged your ability to trust men?"

Tori shrugged. "In a way. More me not being able to trust that I know what I'm doing in a relationship. I had been attracted to you. You were the boss, and I knew it was a bad idea, but I couldn't help it. Sometimes I wondered if the feeling was mutual. Those couple of nights that we worked late together, I thought I'd felt a spark of something."

"You did. I wanted very badly to ask you out, but I wasn't sure if it would be appropriate, since you worked for me."

Tori sighed and sat back in her chair. "I'm glad I didn't imagine that. One afternoon I remember asking your assistant, Lauren, what she thought, since I figured she knew you best. She said I was way off. That I wasn't your type at all. Then you fired me, and I figured I must've been imagining things."

Hearing the name of his former admin was like finding a missing piece to an old mental puzzle. "Lauren," he said.

"Yes. What about her?"

"What else did she tell you about me and my tastes?"

Tori paused for a second and turned to look at him. "You don't think…?"

"She made it all up," he said with certainty. Something about Tori's ethics violation had always troubled him, but he could never put his finger on what, aside from him not wanting to believe she could do it. There had been a real connection between them. That was probably why the idea of her with another man was more painful than it should've been. "Lauren is the one who told me she saw you having an intimate dinner with one of our suppliers. The next day you started making recommendations… The timing was too suspicious."

"He had a superior product. He didn't have to seduce me for an endorsement. But why would she say that about me when it wasn't true?"

With that piece in place, the entire picture became painfully clear. "I am so sorry," he said, shaking his head. "This was all my fault."

"How? If Lauren did it, why are you to blame?"

Wade had ended up firing Lauren only a few months after Tori. She'd seemed sweet at first. After Tori left, she developed some extremely suggestive behaviors. She made it no secret she wanted Wade, although he wasn't interested at all. After catching her being rude on the phone to Julianne, thinking she was a girlfriend and not his sister, he had to let her go. She was an efficient employee, but she was letting a misplaced territoriality compromise her performance.

"She must've been jealous of you. I don't know why I didn't connect this before. I asked her one afternoon if she could help me find out what kind of flowers you liked. I was going to send some to your home and ask if you'd like to have dinner."

"I never got any flowers," Tori replied.

"I never got to send them. Lauren showed up with her story about you the next day. It never occurred to me that she was jealous enough of you to sabotage your whole career like that, but that has to be it. Not long after you left, Lauren made it quite obvious that she was interested in me. I'm sorry I didn't believe you."

Tori nodded and glanced down at the remains of her breakfast. "There was no way to prove it either way. You did what you had to do."

"I feel horrible. I want to make it up to you somehow."

"That's not necessary," she said. "I know I've given you a lot of grief over it, but look at where I am now. It might have been a rocky transition, but things turned out the way they were meant to. If I had continued to work for you, I'd probably still be there, making you money, but I never would've gone for my dream. When I lost my job, I took the chance to start my own company, and it was the best thing I could've done. When

I think of it that way, I don't know…maybe I should be thanking you."

"Yet you've been angry with me all this time?"

"I was hurt because you didn't believe me. It was easy to blame you for the upheaval in my life that came after it. The truth is probably that I wasn't ready to settle down in one place yet. I was just rebelling from my parents. Who knows, if you hadn't fired me, I might've quit a few weeks later and started wandering again."

"What made you ready to settle down now? Here?"

"I started doing genealogy a few years back as a way to connect with my roots. My parents were so nomadic I never really met any extended family or knew where we came from. A little digging uncovered that my father's family was from this area, a few generations back. Cornwall was where they settled after migrating to America from Ireland."

She took a sip of juice before continuing. "I came up here on a whim once, when I had a free weekend away from the project in Philadelphia. I just drove around, mostly. But then I spied this beautiful wooded area and I pulled over and started walking around. For the first time in my life, I felt like I was home. Like I'd spiritually dropped anchor. I wanted to stay here. So I started looking for land to buy. I couldn't have found a more perfect piece of property than the one your parents were offering. I snatched it up and started hatching plans to build my dream house."

Seeing the excitement light up Tori's face, Wade felt smacked in the gut with guilt. She longed for a connection to her family and a chance to build a real home. And he wanted her to. He felt crappy for keeping her from that dream. But he couldn't risk the body being found, even for her dreams. "And once again, I've charged into your life and tried to ruin it all."

She chuckled softly but didn't contradict him. "Life should never be boring."

Wade watched a touch of sadness creep into her eyes. Sadness that he knew he was partially responsible for. It made him want to sweep her into his arms and kiss her until she was too wrapped up in them to be distressed. He wanted to distract her with something so fantastic she wouldn't think about the past for at least a few days.

"I want to take you to New York."

She looked up, startled by the sudden change in topic. "New York? Why?"

"I want to make amends for the past and take you someplace as exciting and beautiful as you are. I want to spend New Year's Eve with you in Times Square."

"Are you kidding me?" She laughed. "I'd pretty much prefer to be anywhere over freezing to death in a mad crush of people in Times Square. I'll be happy to watch the ball drop via my television, though thank you for asking me."

Wade smiled and reached across the table to take her hand. "We're going to New York. Pack your bags because I'm picking you up Monday morning. We're going to see a show. We're going to eat some great food. And when that ball drops, you and I are going to be right there to watch it."

Tori squirmed but didn't pull away. "I don't know, Wade. As nice as that sounds, I don't want to spend my night outside in the cold with a million other people. I'd rather spend it alone with you."

Wade smiled; a plan was forming in his head that would satisfy both their desires. "Who said anything about being outside?"

Eight

"Oh. My. Dear. Lord."

Wade tipped the bellhop and followed Tori's voice into the penthouse suite's master bedroom. He found her standing in front of the wall of windows that lined the room from floor to ceiling. The view overlooked Times Square and the hustle and bustle of the theater district. He'd had this exact view in mind when he renovated this building. His architect had designed this suite, and these windows, for the precise experience Wade had planned for tonight.

"This is amazing. You can see everything from here. How did you get us a room like this on such short notice?"

"Easy," he said, sneaking up behind her to wrap his arms around her waist and tug her against him. "I just called and asked for it. Although it helps when you know the owner and renovated the hotel."

"Ah…" she said, curling into his warmth. "I should've known better than to think you'd be down there with the crowds tonight. Look how many people are already standing around and there's hours to go."

"I've done that before," he said, biting at her earlobe. "When I was younger and poorer. It was fun. But I'd much rather watch the ball drop tonight with your naked body pressed against this glass."

Tori responded by arching her back and pressing her hips into his throbbing desire. He growled against her neck. "And the best part is that these windows are one-way glass."

"Nobody can see in, even at night with the lights on?"

"Correct." Wade's hand snaked across her stomach and up to caress one firm breast through the silky fabric of her blouse. Tori gasped softly when his thumb brushed over the hard peak of her nipple. "No one can see me do this, even if they were right on the other side of the window."

"That should prove interesting," she whispered, near purring.

"Indeed," Wade said, undoing the top button of her shirt. "We have all night to test our theory." He moved down for the second button. Then the doorbell rang.

Blast. He'd ordered room service, hadn't he? It seemed like a good idea at the time. He just hadn't realized how much driving in the car with her would turn him on. Maybe it was the memories of their drive home from the restaurant that had made it hard to focus on the road.…

Tori pulled away, smiling when she saw the pained expression on his face. "Sorry. Are we expecting someone?"

"Dinner."

She arched an eyebrow and breezed past him to the front door of the suite. "You mean you aren't taking me out somewhere?"

"On New Year's Eve? In the theater district? No, sorry. You said you didn't like the crowds, and there's no way to avoid them tonight unless we dine in."

Tori opened the door, and a man rolled in a cart covered in silver domes. He pushed the cart over to the dining room table and transferred the platters, unveiling them one by one. There was lobster, prime rib, herb-roasted potatoes, haricots verts and a platter of plump red strawberries with a bowl of chocolate fondue in the center. Last of all he placed on the table an ice bucket containing a bottle of champagne, and two glasses.

Wade tipped the server. The man thanked him before disappearing just as quickly as he'd arrived.

"This is quite a spread you've ordered. You've done nothing but feed me indulgent food since we met."

"Nothing?" he asked with a mischievous grin.

"Okay, well, it's not all you've done, but we certainly haven't worked off all these calories, either. I'm going to grow out of my clothes."

"Well…" Wade approached her and continued undoing the buttons of her blouse where he'd left off. "We'd better remedy that, right away."

By the time they got around to dinner, it was nearly cold, but salvageable. The only warm food remaining was the ramekin of chocolate fondue, which was heated by a candle to keep it fluid for dipping. It didn't matter. Tori had worked up a huge appetite and wasn't feeling very particular.

"The festivities will be starting soon, and the view

in the dining room isn't as grand. How do you feel about a picnic here in the bedroom?" Wade asked as Tori slipped into the bathroom.

"Sounds great. Is it safe to say we're staying in for the night?"

"That was the plan."

"Okay," she called, eyeing her wardrobe bag hanging beside her in the bathroom. Wade hadn't really told her what they were going to be doing, so she'd packed a variety of clothing. Unzipping the bag a few inches, she spied the beaded neckline of the dress she'd been dying to wear.

It was a fully beaded midnight-blue gown with a halter neckline and a slit up the side that went almost to her hip. It had been an impulse purchase. Tori rarely bought things like that because her storage space was at a premium in the Airstream. She'd simply had to own the dress and figured she'd worry later about what she would wear it to. She'd packed it for their trip thinking they might go someplace fancy. But why not wear it tonight?

She was spending New Year's Eve in a glamorous penthouse overlooking Times Square. She was about to dine on lobster and champagne with a handsome date. The dress would be perfectly suited for a night like this if they were in a chic restaurant or at a party in a grand ballroom. It should be just as suitable for a private dinner for two.

With a giggle of girlish excitement, she fully unzipped the bag and slipped into the gown. The indulgent purchase had been sealed the moment she'd first tried it on. It fitted as though it were made just for her, hugging each curve. Tori reapplied her lipstick, ran her fingers through her hair and went back into the bedroom.

Wade had carried the food into the master bedroom and spread out a blanket for a picnic on the floor by the window. He had slipped back into his trousers but left off the dress shirt. It was thrown across a chair in the living room the last time she saw it, but Tori was glad he'd left it off. Wade had a magnificent chest, and she couldn't spend enough time admiring the hard lines and the dark curls of his chest hair. Unfortunately she hadn't found a reason for him to just stay shirtless all the time.

He was kneeling on the blanket, pouring flutes of champagne, when he looked up at her—and froze. His jaw fell open, and his gaze took in every inch of her body. He licked his lips before he spoke. "You did hear me say we were staying in, right?"

"Yes," she said with a smile. "But I felt like dressing up a little bit for the occasion." Tori held out her arms and spun around for effect. "Do you like it?"

He swallowed hard. "Very much."

"Is it too much for a picnic on the floor?"

"Not at all." He reached out his hand and helped her down onto the blanket. "Looking that beautiful, you can do whatever the hell you like."

Tori blushed. She felt beautiful in this dress, but hearing him say it made her all the happier that she'd decided to put it on, impractical as it was. She settled down beside him, curling her legs to the side and spreading the gown out around her.

Wade handed her a glass of champagne and held up his own for a toast. "To…letting go of the past and embracing a new year and new beginnings."

It was the perfect toast for them in so many ways. Over the past week it did seem as though they had come so far. There was a time in her life when the mention of his name would've sent her into a rampage. Now, sitting across from him, she felt that everything had changed. Thoughts of Wade brought on tingly, warm sensations and a nervous, excited feeling in her stomach.

Tori clinked her glass flute to his. "To new beginnings," she echoed. And that was really what she wanted. A fresh start. Knowing the truth about the circumstances around her firing made the past, the past. She could finally set down the grudge she'd held all these years, and she was glad. She didn't want that dark cloud hanging over their relationship.

Relationship.

Is that what this had become? Things had moved so quickly, but it certainly felt like something more than a fling. But a relationship required more than just attraction and compatibility. It also required trust. She wasn't sure that she had much left. Wade had damaged it pretty badly. Whatever ability she'd regained after several years had been shattered by Ryan. Was trusting a man even possible? And trusting a man like Wade Mitchell? That seemed out of the question. Even with their past resolved, he still wanted her property. That hadn't changed.

Taking a sip of her champagne, she realized how badly she wanted to trust him. This had started out as a game between them. A battle of wills to see who would crack under pleasure, so to speak. But now…she feared it was her. Wade seemed as though he'd put the game behind them, as she had, but she couldn't know for sure. She wanted something more between them. Tori wanted to build her dream house. And if she was honest with herself, she wanted Wade living in it with her.

The thought made her champagne hard to swallow. How had she made that kind of leap in just a few short days? Maybe it wasn't much of a leap. She'd wanted him years ago. Fantasized about more. Perhaps that was why his supposed betrayal hurt her so badly. The feelings had remained, buried under her anger and rushing to the surface the moment the barricades were brushed away.

"I'm starving," Wade said, oblivious to the thoughts running through her mind.

She forced the champagne down her throat to respond. "Me, too." Better for her to focus on food than on her dangerous thoughts.

Wade made them both plates, and they sat eating quietly. They'd spent so much time together in the car on the drive down that they were clearly out of small talk. That left only serious discussions. She wasn't sure either of them was ready for that.

Tori was biting into a chocolate-coated strawberry when Wade set aside his plate and looked down at his watch. "It's getting close to midnight," he said. "We don't want to miss it. I'll pour more champagne."

Tori nodded and accepted his hand to stand up. She went to the window. The dim lights in the bedroom suite allowed her to see everything outside. The lights and activity in the square were stunning. It was amazing that so many people could be in one place at one time. Crowds were gathered around stages where musicians performed for broadcast specials. The sound was probably deafening, yet not a peep made it through to their room. She had seen this scene on television every year, but somehow looking down on it was a completely new experience.

As was the warmth at her bare back as Wade came up behind her. He brought an arm around her to hold out her refilled glass of champagne. On a nearby table, he'd set down the platter of strawberries and chocolate.

His hands gently swept her hair over one shoulder. His lips seared a trail across her bare skin, sending a shiver of anticipation down her spine. It didn't matter how many times she'd had him, she wanted more. Her need almost seemed to get worse, like an escalating addiction. Her body reacted in an instant to his touch. Her breasts tightened within the confines of her gown. Her belly clenched with need.

Wade's fingertips sought out the clasp of her dress at her neck. With a snap it came undone. The fabric slipped over her skin, gliding to the ground with the heavy thump of beads. Tori kicked the dress aside and placed her drink on the table with the fruit. He followed suit, obviously needing both of his hands for what he had planned.

Grasping her by the waist, he turned her to face him. "We've still got a few minutes," he said. "Plenty of time for some dessert."

Without his powerful green gaze leaving hers, he plucked a strawberry from the platter and dipped it in chocolate. He held the fruit in front of her lips, but before she could bite into it, he dropped it to her collarbone. He dragged the berry down her throat to the hollow between her breasts. It left a warm trail of chocolate in its wake. The plump, red fruit circled one breast, teasing at her aching nipple, then traveled to the other. Nearly devoid of chocolate now, the strawberry made its way back to her lips.

She took a bite, the sweet juice instantly filling her mouth. Tori chewed and swallowed as Wade patiently held the rest of the berry for her to finish it. "Don't you want any?" she asked.

"No," he said with a wicked grin. "I prefer the chocolate." Wade set the rest of the berry aside and leaned in to kiss her. His lips tasted of champagne. He buried his fingers in her hair and moaned against her mouth. Tori drank him in, feeling a touch light-headed from his kisses and the alcohol.

When he did pull away, it was to clean up the mess he'd made. He bent Tori back over his arm, and she offered up her throat and breasts to him. He started with her neck, tasting and teasing her with his tongue as he licked every drop of chocolate from her skin. The scalding heat of his lips moved down her chest, following the berry's path to curl around each breast. He bathed each nipple, coaxing it into painfully hard peaks, then biting gently until she cried out.

By now, Tori was certain the chocolate was long gone, but Wade was nothing if not thorough. He traveled back up to her lips and murmured against them, "It's almost time. I don't want you to miss seeing it."

He spun Tori in his arms until she was facing the window and the chaotic scene below. She felt oddly exposed, standing completely naked in front of the glass. It was an exhilarating feeling. Dangerous, yet safe, since no one could see her. Firm hands pressed at her back until she bent forward and braced her hands against the glass. Wade's palm glided leisurely down her spine. He gripped her hips, tugging her bottom back against his hard desire.

"One minute to go. Let's see if you can last that long." Wade sought out her moist center with his fingers. They glided expertly over her, coaxing the building tension of release deep inside.

Tori's fingers clutched uselessly at the glass, but it was all she could do. In front of her there was nothing but the lights of the cityscape, as though they were making love on the roof. She gasped as a finger pene-

trated her, her muscles tightening around him. A wave
of pleasure rocked her, but it wasn't enough. "Wade,"
she said, an edge of desperation creeping into her voice.

"Fifteen seconds." He leaned over her and placed a
burning kiss between her shoulder blades.

Tori glanced over her shoulder and saw him kick
aside his trousers. Soon. Thank goodness. She needed
him now. All of him. "Ten, nine, eight," she whispered as the numbers began counting down, the building pressure of her orgasm certain to beat the clock.
"Seven, six, five."

His fingers glided over her moist flesh, taking her
closer to the edge. "Four, three, two, one," Wade said,
thrusting inside her at the stroke of midnight.

The infamous ball dropped to the base, the number
of the New Year lighting up, but Tori hardly gave it a
glance before closing her eyes and absorbing the pleasurable impact on her body. He barely moved in her
before she came undone. As the cheers and shouts rang
out in the city below, Tori heard only her own cries.

Wade filled her, pushed her, thrilled her and touched
her as no man ever had before. He took her to a place
she hadn't known existed, and she wanted to stay there
with him in this moment forever.

"Oh, Wade," she gasped as the last throbs of pleasure dissipated.

Wade's arms snaked around her waist, tugging her
up until her bare back pressed against his chest. "I could
make love to you all night and never have enough."

"There's quite a few hours left," she teased, breathless.

"Is that a challenge?" he asked, thrusting hard into her.

Tori laughed and tightened her muscles around him.
"Absolutely."

In one quick move Wade pulled away and swept Tori up into his arms. She squealed in surprise, but before she could recover, he dropped her, bouncing, to the bed.

He was back over her in an instant, driving into her body with renewed fervor. The laughter died in her throat as the pleasure began coursing through her veins once again. This time when her release came, so did his. He groaned low against her neck and lost himself inside her body.

Tori cradled him against her as his trembling arms and legs threatened to give way beneath him. After he caught his breath, she tipped his chin up so he could look at her. There was a green fire blazing in his eyes, and she was pleased she was responsible for it. She brought her lips to his, this kiss tender and meaningful.

"Happy New Year, Wade."

The rest of the champagne was forgotten, the strawberries abandoned. Wade didn't care. He had his red-haired beauty in his arms, and that was all he wanted. For the first time in months—hell, years—Wade felt at peace. It was possible that he'd never felt like this. The world was stable on its axis. Tori had done that. The woman whose spirit he had been determined to crush so he could get what he wanted.

Now, with her head resting on his chest and the flaming silk of her hair sprawled over her shoulders and his stomach, he knew he couldn't go through with it. His plan to seduce her had backfired.

The implications were dire. It made him almost sick to his stomach to think of what it might mean for his family. If the body was ever uncovered, it would ruin everything. But that was his mistake. His price to pay. Not Tori's.

There had to be another way. He'd figure something out. He always did.

"Wade, are you still awake?"

"Yes."

Tori rolled off his chest and looked at him. "What was this trip about, really?"

Wade frowned. "What do you mean?"

"The hotel, the food, the champagne—that's a lot of effort just to make up for the whole job thing."

He supposed it might seem that way, but he didn't mind. Having money and powerful connections allowed him the luxury of doing things for people when he wanted to. "You're worth the effort."

"You are, too, you know."

Wade had the sudden urge to climb out of bed and go get a drink, but Tori had her arms clasped around him like steel manacles. He swallowed hard. "You're just supposed to say thank you."

"Thank you." Tori held him in place with her icy blue eyes. "What happened to you, Wade?"

He knew what she meant without her elaborating. He was surprised. Few people ever bothered to ask him about his life before the Edens, so he didn't tell the story very often. Those who mattered in his life already knew. Except Tori. She mattered. More than he ever wanted or expected her to.

"A person doesn't become such an overachiever, so driven to prove himself, without a reason," she pressed. "You don't have to do things to impress me. I don't need ten-course French dinners and penthouses in Manhattan to want to spend time with you. What are you trying to prove? And to whom?"

With a sigh Wade let his head drop back against the

pillows. If he had to talk about it, at least it was dark and he didn't have to look at her. "For a long time I thought I was trying to be a good son for the Edens. To repay them for taking me in and helping me turn my life around. All the good it did me, since they wouldn't accept my money when I tried to give it to them. Then I wondered if maybe I wasn't trying to prove to…those who left…that I was worth keeping."

"Like your mother?"

"Yes. And others. My mother was still in high school when she got pregnant. I wasn't exactly part of her plans. So, after she had me, she played at being a mom for a while. When that didn't work out, she took me over to her aunt's house. What was supposed to be a couple hours of babysitting turned into seven years. She just never came back."

Wade could hear Tori's breath catch in her throat. He didn't want her pity. That was why he never told anyone about this. He'd rather people saw him as the strong, powerful businessman. That was the point, wasn't it? To keep this part hidden? And yet he wanted to tell her everything now that he'd started talking. He wanted to let Tori in.

"My aunt never married and wasn't particularly interested in having children, but it wasn't bad with her. I didn't know any different. When she died of breast cancer and my mother was still off the grid, I ended up in the foster system. She had never terminated her parental rights, so I couldn't be adopted even if someone had wanted to. I doubt anyone but the Edens would have. I bounced around a lot. I was an angry child. Rebellious. A trouble starter. I had a lot of crap to work through for a ten-year-old, but it was how I coped. I guess it was easier to push people away than to get close to someone who would eventually cast me aside. But the Edens didn't fall for that game. They wouldn't let me push them away. They believed in me. So I changed my tactic to be the best man I could possibly be."

"And now you're successful, powerful and have a family that loves you."

"And you know what that got me?" he said, a bitter edge creeping into his voice.

"What?"

"A mother showing up on my doorstep with her hand out."

"What did you do?"

"Well, as you said, I'm always out to prove myself, so I did what I felt I should. I gave her a lump sum of cash and bought her a house as far from New York as I could get—in San Diego. And I made her sign a contract agreeing to never contact me or anyone in my family again, or she'd have to repay me for everything."

Tori's grip on him tightened ever so slightly. "And she agreed to that?"

Wade had not been there for the contract negotiation, but his lawyer told him she couldn't sign fast enough. There was a part of him that had hoped she wouldn't. That she had changed and wanted to get to know the son she'd abandoned. He'd been a fool for even entertaining that fantasy. "Without hesitating. So in the end, my money and my success didn't prove anything to anyone."

"What about to yourself?"

Especially not to himself. No one else on earth was able to see inside him and know what he was truly like the way he could. Strip away the money and the suits and what was he left with? When things were important, truly important, he failed.

He couldn't protect his family the way he should have. If he had done his job, Heath never would've had to do what no thirteen-year-old boy should have to do. Julianne wouldn't have to carry those dark memories with her. His parents wouldn't be secretly selling off pieces of the farm to stay afloat. No success in business could make up for that kind of personal failure.

"Is that even possible?" he asked. "Can someone like me ever reach the point where they've achieved enough? How would I know when I've expunged my sins? There's always the opportunity to disappoint myself. Or someone else."

"You haven't disappointed me."

Wade chuckled. "I haven't, now? Well, considering I fired you erroneously, harassed you mercilessly and want to take your land away from you, I imagine you have very low standards."

Tori sat up on one elbow and looked down at him. "I don't have low standards. I think I'm just better at seeing past the bull."

"And where did you learn that skill? Traipsing across America studying the human condition?"

"Something like that," she admitted. "Attending the school of life has its perks and its pitfalls. I think never building real relationships handicapped me when I grew older. I was too trusting because I'd never had the opportunity to be hurt. I didn't build relationships, like you, but because I couldn't. We were gone too quickly. I was naive."

"You?"

"Yes." She smiled. "I wasn't always so cynical. The

real world brought that. What life didn't teach me, my ex-boyfriend did."

She hadn't mentioned much about her past relationships, but Wade picked up on the pained tone in her voice. The darkness couldn't veil that. "What did he do?"

Tori sighed and shrugged. "Like I said, I was too trusting. He took advantage of the fact that I was always moving. I wasn't going to pressure him for marriage or a commitment, even after years together, because I wasn't in that place."

Wade could tell where this was going. "He was married."

"With three kids. Living happily outside Boston. When I told him I was thinking of buying land in Connecticut, he came unglued."

"And that was the last man you dated?"

Tori nodded.

Wade already felt like crap for the way things had gone down between him and Tori. Knowing she was trying to recover her trust in men when he showed up, scheming to manipulate her, made it that much worse. She deserved more than just a luxurious weekend in Manhattan. She deserved a week in Paris. Or better yet, for him to go away and leave her life and her plans alone.

"Tori," he started, not quite sure at first what he was going to say. "I'm sorry."

"For what?"

Wade swallowed the lump in his throat. He had so many feelings swirling in his gut. So many things he wanted to say to her. But he couldn't put them into words. Wouldn't. At least not until after he'd dealt with the situation that had brought him here in the first place. Whether he intended it or not, Tori could get hurt. And he didn't want to say or do anything now that might make the pain that much sharper.

"For everything," he whispered.

Nine

Tori strolled into Daisy's Diner a few days later with a bounce in her step and a smile on her face that wouldn't fade away. Her trip to New York with Wade had been wonderful. Magical. Romantic. Everything she'd hoped for and more than she'd dreamed it could be. They'd strolled through the city, window-shopping and sightseeing. They went to a show. They talked and spent hours in each other's arms. And then it was time to come home.

Back to Connecticut—and reality. She hadn't seen Wade since they'd returned to Cornwall. They both had things to do. She was certain he would have to return to his life in Manhattan soon, although he hadn't mentioned it and she hadn't asked. He had a business to run. And she had a house to build. But they'd opted to meet here tonight for dinner.

"Hey, there," Rose said as Tori walked past her usual seat. "No counter service today?"

"No." She smiled. "I have a date tonight, so I thought a booth might be better."

"Oh, really." Rose poured a mug of hot water for Tori's tea and came out from behind the counter with two menus tucked under her arm. She sat across from Tori in the corner booth she'd selected. "Spill it," she demanded, pushing the hot water over to her customer.

Tori began fidgeting with the mug, knowing her cheeks were probably as red as her hair now. "Wade is meeting me here."

"Wade Mitchell? The man who was making you crazy a week ago?"

"The same."

Rose flung her dark ponytail back over her shoulder and leaned in closer. "So, you wanna tell me what happened between then and now?"

Tori could barely explain it. Everything had changed. Even the past, if that were possible. "It feels like the world has shifted."

Rose sat back against the padded pleather of the booth, her brown eyes wide. "You're in love with him."

"What?" Tori perked up at her friend's bold assessment. "No, no. That's silly. It's only been a few days."

Rose crossed her arms over her chest and refused to budge on the subject. "I can assure you, with the Eden boys, a few days is all it takes."

The words were like a fist to her gut. The truth barreling into her at fifty miles an hour. She was in love with him.

"I...I like him a lot," she countered, even as her mind raced with a different version of the facts. "We have a good time together. But it's nothing more than that. He's leaving to go home shortly, so it would be stupid of me to go and fall in love with him."

Rose nodded mechanically, clearly disbelieving every word of Tori's argument. Tori understood. She didn't believe her own words, either. And they were sensible. She shouldn't be in love with Wade. He *was* leaving. They *weren't* serious. She couldn't trust him because he still wanted her land. None of that added up to a fairy-tale romance. Just another disaster waiting to happen like before.

She wished someone would tell her heart that.

The heart in question started pounding madly in her chest when she looked up and spied Wade coming in the entrance. "He's here," she whispered.

Rose dutifully got up and flashed a smile to Wade on her way back to the counter. "What can I get you to drink tonight?"

"Coffee, thanks," Wade said. "It's freezing out there." He slipped out of his jacket and tossed it into the booth before sliding in where Rose had been sitting.

Wade looked so handsome tonight. He was wearing a dark blue collared shirt with thin gray pinstripes. His skin was freshly shaved and slightly pink from the sting of the icy wind outside. Tori wanted to reach out and touch his face. She wanted to breathe in his cologne. Some of her clothing had come home smelling like him after their trip. She hadn't been able to make herself go to the Laundromat to wash them yet.

Tori suddenly felt like a shy, smitten teenager sitting with him. Her realization of love only a minute before left her feeling vulnerable even though there was no way he could know how she felt. She certainly wasn't about to tell him. She had barely come to terms with it herself, although sitting on the edge of her bed sniffing a sweater should've been her first clue.

"How are you?" he asked.

Tori smiled, although it felt nervous and forced to her. She hoped it didn't look that way. "Good. You?"

"Good," he said. Wade looked down at the menu and began thoroughly studying it without elaborating.

Tori winced and hid her face with her own menu. Did he notice? Things felt weird when they'd never felt weird before. It was all her doing. She needed to act normal. This was the same man she'd spent a good part of the past week with. Naked. After that, dinner in the local restaurant should be no big deal. She just had to relax.

Rose came back with the coffee; she took their orders and the menus. Now neither of them had anything to hide behind. Once Rose disappeared into the kitchen, Tori took a deep breath. "I had a nice time in New York. Thank you for taking me. You know you didn't have to go to that much trouble."

"No trouble at all. I had a great time, too. I'm glad we were able to go. It was certainly more exciting than spending New Year's Eve here with my folks. They never even make it up to midnight. As kids, we used to stay up in the bunkhouse and watch Dick Clark on television after they went to bed."

"It must be strange to stay up here this long without the others. Are you heading back to New York soon?" Tori almost didn't want to know how much time she had left, but she had to ask.

Wade nodded. "In a couple days. I still have a few things to take care of before I go back."

"That's right. You still haven't bought my land," she said with a weak smile. She'd enjoyed the past few days without the topic coming up. "Time is a-ticking on that."

He glanced down at his mug and took a sip. "I guess I'm not going to worry too much about that anymore."

Tori's brow shot up in surprise. She didn't hide it well at all. "What?"

"You don't want to sell it to me. I can't make you. I don't know what I could offer to change your mind, so there's no point in fighting over it anymore."

What should've been a victorious moment didn't feel quite how she'd expected. Going up against Wade, she'd always secretly thought she would lose. One way or another he would wear her down. And now, although he'd named her the victor, it didn't seem as if she'd won. After the past few days, a part of her didn't want to beat him. The thought had crossed Tori's mind that if he'd stay, she'd consider selling it to him. She wanted to build a home, not just a house. Somehow having Wade there with her was an integral piece of her design.

Selling him the land would make him happy. She wanted him to be happy. She could find another piece of land, but replacing Wade's place in her heart felt nearly impossible.

And yet, she felt a tug of hope deep inside. If he no longer wanted her property, maybe she could have both him and the land. She'd known trusting Wade would be an issue as long as he had this ulterior motive. If that was gone, what could that mean? Had he really given up wanting the land or did he care too much about her to hurt her like that? He hadn't said anything about how he felt for her. If he was going back to New York and life as usual, he probably felt nothing at all but had just run out of time.

She'd be left with no reason to hate him when it was all over.

"I'd like to spend the last few days with you before I go."

She hadn't expected that at all. If he wasn't just romancing the property away from her, maybe there was more here than she'd thought. With a sigh of dismay, Tori shook her head. Wade always seemed to want the things she couldn't give. "I have to leave tomorrow. I'm going to Philadelphia for a few days. They're having the ribbon-cutting ceremony on my building down there on Saturday afternoon. I've got to wrap up all the loose ends. I probably won't be back until the seventh or eighth."

"Oh." Wade's expression was curious. A hint of disappointment mixed in with something else she couldn't put her finger on. She could almost see his mind spinning. She remembered that expression from watching him at his desk when she worked with him.

"You could come with me," she suggested.

He looked at her and shook his head. "I can't. I'll need to be back in Manhattan before that."

"I guess I'll have to catch up with you in the city sometime. Or the next time you're up this way."

Wade nodded, his expression guarded. He must've realized, as she had, that this would be their last date. Their last night together. "Do you have another project coming up that you'll be traveling to soon?"

"Not for a few months. I'm going to Vermont for a while this summer to design a ski lodge. Until then, I'll be here, working on building my house."

"Do you have the final plans drawn up yet?"

Yes and no. She had twenty plans completed, but for some reason her clarity about what she wanted had become muddled over the holidays. "I have to make a few final decisions. That's all. I should be able to get the contractors in place to break ground in the next few weeks."

Wade's green eyes widened just a touch at her words, but Rose brought their plates and the expression vanished. "I should give you Troy Caldwell's number. He's got a great building team that does excellent work."

Tori nodded and tried to focus on her food. She'd heard Caldwell was the guy to work with around here. She just hadn't gotten around to speaking with him before the holidays. It seemed that once she got back from Philadelphia, she'd have plenty of time. Wade would be long gone.

The rest of the meal was spent discussing the neutral topics of local electricians and concrete companies. Every now and again Tori would look up to find Wade watching her. There was a hesitation in his voice, a touch of worry lining his eyes. She wasn't certain she was the cause of it, though. He seemed a million miles away tonight. Maybe the stresses of being away from work were distracting him.

Tori was absentmindedly drawing the design for the front of her home across her plate with her fork and leftover ketchup when Wade's voice startled her. It seemed he wasn't the only one distracted this evening.

"Would you like to come back to the bunkhouse for some dessert? Molly baked a really nice chocolate cream cheese Bundt cake this morning."

His words were asking her if she'd like to join him for dessert, but the intensity of his gaze promised more than that. He wanted to have her in his arms one last time before they parted ways.

Tori knew she should say no. It would be so much easier if she just walked away now. She could take her land, her dignity and what was left of her heart back to her Airstream.

Instead, she found herself meeting his gaze and nodding yes. She wasn't quite ready to say goodbye to Wade.

Yet.

They'd spent another incredible night together. He hated to wake her up that morning but knew she had a schedule to keep. He would rather have lain in bed all day with her ear pressed to his heart and her hair strewed across his chest. He had to admit he'd gotten used to having her there when he woke up—grumpy face, wild hair and all.

But he had to.

After they'd reluctantly gotten out of bed, Wade made his way downstairs. Molly hadn't sneaked in with breakfast today, so Wade made coffee and toasted bagels while Tori showered.

They ate quietly together. There was an awkwardness in the air. For all intents and purposes, their relationship was over. They'd had their last date, their last chance to make love and this was their final breakfast.

Unlike other relationships that ended in angry fireworks or bitter barbs, their relationship would die quietly, because it was the practical thing to do. Neither of them really wanted to say goodbye, but neither was willing to say or do anything to change it. This needed to be the end.

When they were finished, he walked her out to her truck. They loitered at the door, so many unspoken things lingering between them. But Wade wouldn't say what he wanted to. Not until he'd finished what he came here for. And to do that, Tori needed to go to

Philadelphia. If he was successful, maybe he'd call her. Or maybe he'd be smart and just let this whole thing go. If she ever found out the truth about his past, it would be over anyway.

But that didn't mean he didn't want one last embrace. He wrapped his arms around Tori, hugging her tight to his chest. She clung just as fiercely to him, letting go only when he pulled away for their last kiss. He pressed his lips to hers, losing himself in the soft feel of her. There was no heat in the kiss. Just…goodbye.

When he stepped back, Tori quickly slipped on her sunglasses and climbed into the truck. He thought he saw the glint of tears in her eyes for a moment, but it could've been the morning sun blinding her.

"Goodbye, Wade," she said, slamming the truck door closed before he could respond. The engine roared to life, and he watched the truck disappear down the road to the highway.

It was over. And he didn't like it at all. But now it was time to put his plan into action.

If there was one thing Wade knew for certain, it was that he could call Heath at any hour, with any number of crazy requests, and his younger brother would be up for it. Brody second-guessed everything. Xander worried about how things might look. But Heath… He was the impulsive brother, and that was exactly what Wade needed. He headed back inside the bunkhouse to get his phone.

"Hey there, big brother," Heath answered. "What's happening?"

"You busy tomorrow?" Wade cut to the chase. His brother knew him well enough not to take offense. Neither of them usually had the time to waste on pleasantries.

"I don't have to be. What do you need?"

"You, a high-quality metal detector and a large plastic tarp."

"What, no shovels?" Heath joked.

"Dad has those. And the backhoe if we need it."

He'd been using the backhoe that day fifteen years ago as part of his chores on the farm. When he needed to bury the body, it seemed like the quickest and easiest thing to use, since he was working alone. No one would think twice about him driving it around the property. But the grave wasn't really that deep. He hadn't taken the time to bury the body seven or eight feet as he should have.

With Heath's help they could probably skip it this time. "We'll definitely need the metal detector. The snow has mostly melted, so it should be easier, but I still have fifteen years working against me on this. You up for an unorthodox treasure hunt?"

"Sure, yeah," Heath said without hesitation. "Whatever we have to do. I mean, hell, it's my ass if this all goes down wrong. You bet I'll help however I can to keep this a secret. I take it the plan to buy the land didn't work out."

"Nope. This is plan B."

Brody would've lectured him about the failure of plan A, but Heath always rolled with the punches. "What's plan B, exactly?"

"Find the body and move it back onto the family land while she's out of town. Can you come up tomorrow?"

"I can. I'll make some calls and dig up a good metal detector tonight, then leave in the morning."

Tori should have felt excited. There were hundreds of people gathered around the new arts-and-sciences center she'd designed. The press was there, snapping pictures and filming pieces for the nightly news. The mayor had personally shaken her hand and told her she'd done a beautiful job. This was huge exposure for her business.

But she wasn't excited. She was…lonely. This was a big moment for her, and she had no one to share it with. She pasted the smile back on her face for the photos and fought the tears that threatened to ruin the moment.

She wanted to share all of this with Wade. She wanted him standing next to her, beaming with pride. And yet he wasn't there. Why? Because of a stupid piece of land.

That's what it had become to her. She had imagined that it would be a magical thing to own a piece of the earth and make her mark on it by building her dream house. But the reality was much different. Even before Wade had shown up and started throwing money around, she'd begun to have her doubts. She'd dug in her heels only because he wanted something she had.

But he'd changed his mind. Wade wasn't going to fight her for it anymore. Why? Maybe for the same reason she no longer wanted to keep it. If this land was the only thing standing between them, he could have it.

The mayor cut the ribbon, and the crowd cheered amid the blinding flash of cameras. The dignitaries stepped back and the front doors were held open for everyone to go inside. There would be folks wandering around all afternoon sipping champagne, eating appetizers and talking about the virtues of green architecture as though they understood it.

As she watched the crowd file in, she knew she should go in with them. Answer questions. Do interviews. But she hadn't felt so desperate to get out of a place in her whole life.

If she left now, she could be home in a few hours. Wade should still be at the farm. And then she could tell him.

Tell him what? That she loved him? That he could have the land because it was nothing but dirt and rock without him in her life? Maybe. If she could work up the nerve.

Turning away from the building, Tori headed for the parking lot and her truck. She had a few hours' drive to figure out what she wanted to say. But she knew she had to go to Wade. Now.

It was probably thirty degrees outside, but Wade was sweating as though it were summertime. They hadn't even started seriously digging yet. That was probably why. They hadn't found what he was looking for so they could start digging. The afternoon had not gone as well as he'd hoped. The snow had melted, revealing a landscape just as confusing as before. No turtle-shaped rocks. No crooked trees like he remembered. Maybe his memory was faulty. Maybe he'd just been a freaked-out kid that night and the whole incident had gotten scrambled in his mind. He wished someone had gone out there with him.

They'd taken to just running the metal detector over every inch of the property. Periodically, they'd get a hit and they'd dig furiously into the frozen ground, only to find an old quarter or a screw. Heath would move on with the metal detector and Wade would stomp the ground back into place. There was another snowstorm in the forecast for tomorrow. By the time Tori returned, the evidence of their search would be buried for a few weeks and hopefully undetectable.

The sun had set not too long ago, and the darkness was making their job even harder than the rock-hard dirt. Heath had turned on the headlight on one of the four-wheelers, and they both carried flashlights, but they were getting discouraged.

"Wade, I don't see any rocks that look like a turtle. Not even if I scrunch my eyes up and look sideways."

"I know." Wade sighed. Maybe this whole plan was a bad idea. Even if they could find the right place, moving a fifteen-year-old corpse couldn't be easy. It's not as if he would be in one piece anymore.

"I'm not getting much with the metal detector. You're sure he still had that ring on when you buried him?"

"Yes." Wade remembered the large gold ring with the black stone in the center. How could he forget it? He'd had an imprint of it punched into his face once. "I remember because I thought about taking it off so no one could identify him. But I didn't know what to do with it. I decided it was better to just leave it on, since he would've taken it with him when he left."

"I guess that was a good idea. We'd never find him without it."

"I'm beginning to think we won't find him even with it." Wade looked across the dark landscape of Tori's property. The rocky ridge where she planned to build the house was off to the back. There was no way he could've buried anything there, even with the back-hoe. Maybe the construction crew that would build her house wouldn't find anything. Maybe, despite his failures, this secret would stay buried.

"Are you sure it's on her plot and not one of the others?" Heath asked.

At this point, Wade couldn't afford to consider that possibility. To know he'd wasted all this time on the wrong property? And if there was one thing he knew, it was that the owner of the largest plot, a large commercial development company, wasn't going to sell for any amount of money. Brody had done some research, and they were building a small resort retreat. They'd already started working out there.

"No, I'm not sure," Wade admitted through gritted teeth. "But I swear I didn't go that far. This area looks right. It's got to be right."

Heath nodded and started swinging the metal detector over a different segment of land.

"Let's load up and call it a night. We can try again in the morning before it starts to snow."

They each grabbed their shovels and equipment and had started walking back to their four-wheelers when they were suddenly bathed in bright white lights. Headlights.

Wade froze in place like a deer. He clutched his incriminating tools tighter in his fists. Who was it? He couldn't tell. They were blinded, unable to see anything but the bright white orbs aimed in their direction.

Was it the sheriff? No. He wasn't that lucky. He knew the sheriff and could talk his way out of this. The lights were way too high for a patrol car. It was a truck. An older truck, judging by the loud rumble of the engine.

An old truck.

Wade swallowed hard. She couldn't be back already. Not this soon. The ribbon-cutting ceremony was today. Tori would've had to drive straight back after it ended to be here already. She said Monday or Tuesday at the earliest. Why would she have rushed home again?

The answer was on the tip of his tongue, but he didn't even want to think it, much less say it. The way she'd looked at him last night had been different. Something had changed. He'd tried to deny it at dinner, and when he made love to her. He told himself it was just because they both knew it was the end for them.

Wade was a fool to ignore the truth. Tori had fallen in love with him. He couldn't be certain, but maybe she'd decided to come home early before he returned to New York so she could see him again. Or maybe she'd gotten brave enough to tell him how she felt.

And instead she'd caught him red-handed on her property with a shovel and a metal detector. Damn.

Heath leaned in to him, finally daring to move. "Are they just going to watch us or get out of the truck? You think they're calling the cops?"

Wade shook his head. "I doubt it. I think it's Tori."

"Oh, man," Heath said. "I thought she wasn't coming back for a couple of days. What are you going to tell her? You can't tell her the truth."

That was a great question. He'd have to think of something, because the truth was completely off the table. "I have no idea. But you just get on your four-wheeler and go, okay? She and I need to talk alone."

"I'm not going to leave you out here. Doesn't she have a shotgun?"

Wade had forgotten about the shotgun. Hopefully it was locked in the Airstream and not with her in the truck. "Yes, you are. Seriously. I'll be okay. Go, now. It's better that way."

Heath shrugged and turned away from the light to go to his ATV. He loaded his things, cranked the engine and disappeared into the trees. It wasn't until he was gone that Wade heard the truck's engine die. The lights stayed on when the heavy door clicked open.

Wade still couldn't see, but he could hear boots crunching on the gravel. Then a woman's silhouette appeared between him and the truck's headlights. He'd know those curves anywhere.

Tori stopped a few feet away. He was about to say something to explain himself when she suddenly charged forward. Her hand reared back to slap him, and he was going to let her. His hands were full. What was he going to do? Swing a shovel at her? He deserved it, anyway.

Instead, she hesitated for a moment and her hand finally fell back to her side. Tori took a step back, her breath ragged in the darkness. He could finally make out her features in the light. Her eyes were wide, her jaw clenched tight. "You bastard!" she said. "All this time. All those nights we spent together were a lie. You were just using me. Lulling me into complacency so you could slip in and get what you wanted."

"Tori, it wasn't like that." Wade tossed the shovel onto the ground and reached for her, but she took another step back.

"Don't you dare. Don't you try to smooth everything over with your charming lies. I've fallen for enough of those already. I can't believe this." Tori buried her fingers in her hair and clutched her skull. She turned from him and started pacing through the yard like a caged lioness. "I can't believe I let myself trust you when I knew you were the last person I could trust."

"I'm sorry, I—"

"That night in the diner was especially well done," she continued, her sharp tone leaning toward the sarcastic and bitter. "Letting me believe that I'd won. That you had given up trying to take the land from me. And I just ate it up. Watched you with love-stricken doe eyes and sucked up all the crap you threw my way."

"That wasn't a lie. I don't want to take your land. I knew I would hate myself for doing that to you. I couldn't."

"So, what? You decided you'd just wait until I left and steal what you really wanted? Save yourself the trouble and the half-million-dollar expense?"

Wade looked down at the ground, the expression on his face too guilty to be washed out by the bright lamps shining on him. "You don't understand."

"No, I don't understand. And maybe I would, but you've wrapped everything up in a web of lies so thick I couldn't see the truth even if it was right in front of me. What is it that you're after, Wade? It's obviously not the land and your family legacy, as you said before. What do I have on this property that is so valuable to you? What could be so damn important that you would ruin everything…" Her voice trailed off.

Tori's voice trembled at the end, and it made his chest ache to hear her like that. He'd never wanted to hurt her. He'd spent his whole life trying to care for and protect the important people in his life. Why would he want to hurt her? He wanted so badly to tell Tori the truth. But that secret wasn't just his to protect. He couldn't betray his family, even for her. He'd failed his brothers and sister once. Wade absolutely could not do that to them again. No matter how he might feel about Tori. "I can't tell you that. I want to. Believe me, I do. But I can't."

Tori chuckled bitterly and crossed her arms defensively over her chest. "Of course you can't tell me. I can't believe I trusted you. That I let myself fall… *No.*" She corrected herself with a firm shake of her head. "The only thing I fell for was your sob story about family. I'm not about to do that twice."

"Tori, please." Wade reached for her, but she moved out of the way.

She held out her hand for him to keep his distance. "You don't get to touch me anymore." Turning on her heel, she marched back toward her truck. She killed the lights, slammed the door and headed for her trailer.

Wade took a few steps to follow her. He wanted to talk to her. To help her understand.

"You know," she said, "when I was in Philadelphia today, I had started to think that maybe this land wasn't so important after all. I can build a house here, but if the things that make it a home are…somewhere else… what is the point? It seemed so vital for you to preserve your family legacy. So I decided you should. I got in my truck as soon as the ceremony was over, and I came home to tell you that I wanted to sell you the land. And some other things that aren't relevant anymore."

Wade closed his eyes, her words hitting him hard in the gut. She'd trusted him. She cared enough about him to give him the one thing he wanted. And he had ruined it by sneaking behind her back and trying to steal the gift before she could give it. He was an impatient ass, and there were no words in his defense.

"Can I ask one thing? Maybe this is a question you can actually answer."

Wade looked up at her. She was standing on the metal stairs and gripping the door handle with white-knuckled intensity. The patio light illuminated the shimmer in her blue eyes as she watched him. Just the slightest thing could send those tears spilling down her cheeks, but she fought to hold on.

"I'll answer if I can."

"Was all of this just about the land to you? The dinners, the trip to New York, the chocolate-covered strawberries... I know at first it was a game of wits for both of us, but along the way it changed for me. I'd hoped it changed for you, too. Was it all just an attempt to charm me into giving you what you wanted, or did any of that mean something to you?"

Yes, it meant something. He wanted to yell it. He wanted to scoop her up into his arms and kiss her until she couldn't be angry with him anymore. But her furrowed brow and glassy eyes made him wonder if the truth would make things better or worse. Would it hurt her more to know that what they had had was special and he'd ruined it? Or to believe that it all had been a game?

"Tori, I—"

"Wait," she interrupted. "Forget I asked. I think I'd rather not know the truth. Goodbye, Wade."

Wade saw one of the tears escape down her cheek as she opened the door and disappeared inside.

Ten

"You look like hell."

Wade looked up from his desk to see Heath standing in the doorway of his office. He had to admit he wasn't surprised by the impromptu arrival of his youngest brother. He'd been dodging calls, texts and emails from his siblings for over a week. He'd canceled dinner plans at Brody's place. Before too long, he'd figured, they'd send someone to track him down. Since Heath lived and worked in Manhattan, too, he was the obvious stuckee.

Wade looked down at his watch. "Eight days, thirteen hours and forty-two minutes. That means Linda in accounting wins the office pool."

"Very funny," Heath said, coming into the office and shutting the door behind him. "What's going on with you lately? You've been too quiet."

Wade shrugged. "I've been busy. Work always picks

up after the holidays, and it takes a while for everyone to get back into the swing of things."

"Uh-huh." Heath wandered over to the minibar and pulled out a soda from the stash. "Do the other people you say that to actually believe you?"

With a heavy sigh, Wade sank back into his leather executive chair. "No one else ever bothers to ask how I am, so I haven't gotten much practice in yet."

"Tell the truth. How are you?"

"I'm fine."

Heath sat in one of Wade's guest chairs and propped his feet up on the edge of the large mahogany desk. He scrutinized Wade with his hazel gaze as he casually sipped his drink. "Brody was right," he said after a few silent moments.

Wade frowned at his brother. "Brody was right about what? I haven't even spoken to him since I had to cancel our dinner plans."

"Doesn't matter. He was still right. You're in love."

The declaration sent Wade bolt upright in his chair. What did Brody know about being in love? The man was a hermit. "That's ridiculous."

Heath shook his head. "She loves you, too, you know."

"Since when did my entire family become psychic?"

"Mama saw her at the grocery store. Said she was an absolute mess. She's not sure what went on between you two, but she's very unhappy about it."

"I don't date to please Mama. She needs to focus her matchmaking skills on you for a change."

"She shouldn't waste her time," he said with a wide grin. "I'm already married."

"You're hilarious. Keep telling that story and she'll move on to demanding those grandchildren she wants."

Heath shuddered in his seat and took a large swig of soda to wash away the bitter aftertaste of Wade's suggestion. "The point is that she's miserable. You're miserable."

"I'm not miserable."

"You're not Jolly Old Saint Nick, either. You've been avoiding everyone. You've got bags under your eyes large enough to store loose change. Your tie doesn't even match your shirt, man. You're obviously not sleeping."

Wade looked down at the blue shirt and green plaid tie he was wearing. He could've sworn he'd reached for the blue striped one. Must've grabbed the wrong tie and not noticed. Not sleeping for a few days would do that to a guy, he supposed. "I've got new neighbors. They've been louder than usual, and after a few weeks at the farm, I got used to the quiet."

"And it has absolutely nothing to do with the red-head whose heart you broke last week?"

Heath just wasn't about to let this go. Wade knew that if he didn't say something soon, Heath was liable to put him in a headlock and knuckle his scalp until he confessed.

Wade opted to answer the question without really answering it. "She's better off without me."

"Isn't that for her to decide?"

Wade shrugged. "It doesn't matter. She hates me."

"I doubt that. She was just hurt. Your betrayal was that much worse because she let herself fall in love with you."

"She didn't say that."

"Why on earth would she? Anyway, she didn't need to say it. We both know why she rushed home from

Philadelphia. And even if she does hate you now, that doesn't change anything. *You're* still in love with *her*."

Wade's chest started to ache at the mere thought. The pain had plagued him since the door of Tori's Airstream slammed shut in his face. It had woken him up the few times he had managed to fall asleep. He'd started popping antacids. He'd even done a Google search for "heart attack symptoms" to make sure he wasn't dying. As best he could tell, he wasn't on death's door. He was just in love with a woman who hated him.

"She's never going to forgive me for lying to her. And I can't tell her the truth about what we were looking for. I can't just go to her and tell her I love her and that she's just got to trust me."

"You know, fifteen years ago our lives took an unexpected turn. For the most part we've been able to carry on with our lives. Sure, we remember. Our consciences are burdened with it. We worry we handled it wrong and made a bigger mess of the situation. We pray that no one ever finds out what happened. But for more than twenty-three hours out of every day, I can live my life like it never happened. Can you?"

"Usually. Until I found out Dad sold the land."

"But before that…were you happy?"

Happy was a funny word. Wade didn't like using it. "I was content. 'Happy' sounds like puppies and rainbows. I was pleased with how my life was going."

"And now?"

"And now…I guess, to use your words, I'm miserable."

"We've decided you should tell her the truth."

Wade's brow shot up at his brother's words. "We? Did you all hold some secret council meeting without me?"

"Yes," he said, very matter-of-factly. "Via Skype. We talked it over and decided that you shouldn't give up your chance at real happiness just to protect us."

Wade almost laughed for a moment before he realized Heath wasn't kidding. They had no idea what they were asking him to do. He'd spent his whole life trying to protect them. Trying to make up for that night. He couldn't just flip-flop because they said it was okay. It wasn't okay. "I'm not going to expose everyone, including myself, just for a woman."

"She's not just any woman, Wade. She's the woman you love. Do you want to marry her?"

The image of Tori in an ivory lace gown instantly sprang into his mind. Her red-gold hair was pulled back into an elegant twist. Her peaches-and-cream skin rosy from excitement and champagne. He'd never even thought about it before, and yet the vision of her in his mind was so real that he couldn't push it aside. "If she'd have me."

"Then you can tell her. After the wedding."

Wade opened his mouth, then realized what they had in mind. If he married Tori, he could tell her everything and she couldn't be compelled to testify against them.

"She's not going to marry me unless I tell her the truth. And I can't tell her the truth unless she marries me. So, really, I get nowhere with this."

Heath shrugged. "I disagree. When I came in the door, you were 'fine.' Now you're a man in love who wants to get married. I think you're way ahead. Now you just have to go tell her."

"Yeah, sure. Tori, I love you and I want to marry you. And once you marry me, I can tell you all about how I buried some guy on your property and I'm afraid you'll dig him up while building your dream house."

"Those aren't the words I'd recommend. But if you show up there, tell her you love her, offer her a ring to prove you're serious and explain where you're coming from with all this, I think she'll understand."

Wade frowned at his brother, then turned back to stare at his desk blotter. He'd lain in bed night after night replaying those last moments with Tori. If he'd said or done something else, might it have ended differently? Sometimes the door slammed in his face just the way it had happened. But once, Tori had listened to his words. She'd forgiven him. And that was the time he'd imagined telling her the truth.

He wanted so badly to go back and have another try. Heath insisted he still had a chance to turn things around. He had permission to tell her what she wanted to know, but he wasn't sure if it would make a difference. Could Tori really trust him enough? What if it was too little, too late? Was it possible she was still in love with him after everything that had happened between them?

Wade closed his eyes and pictured Tori as she'd been Friday morning before she left for Philadelphia. Her pale blue eyes were wary, but the love he saw there was undeniable. Maybe he hadn't lost his chance yet. God, he hoped so. He couldn't function like this for much longer. He'd have a real heart attack before too long from the stress and the copious amounts of caffeine he was drinking to compensate for lost sleep.

He had to give it a shot. The gaping hole in his chest begged him to at least try. If she turned him down, he would not have lost anything he hadn't already given away.

Heath looked at his brother. His expression was about as serious as it ever got. "This will work out."

He sure as hell hoped so.

"You always were the optimist in the family." Wade rolled his chair up to the desk with a new fire to put his plan into action. "Okay, Mr. Advertising Executive, direct me to the most environmentally conscious jeweler on the market."

"I should've known—" Heath grinned "—that you would pick the only woman on earth able to resist the little blue box. Let me call one of my guys who handles most of our jewelry accounts. But be warned—odds are it won't be local. You might have to wait a couple days."

Absolutely not. He would be in Connecticut tomorrow, come hell or high water. "That's unacceptable," he said.

"Well, then, get ready to get on a plane."

Wade nodded and rang his admin to clear his calendar for the rest of today and tomorrow. He'd fly to the ends of the earth to get Tori back.

"It's crap. All crap." Tori ripped the sheet of paper off the pad, then crumpled her latest blueprint into a ball and tossed it into the overflowing wastepaper basket. It had to be the hundredth design she'd sketched in the past week, but she hated them all. Even the ones she'd been really happy with before Wade came into her life.

Now everything felt wrong.

Maybe this whole settling-down thing was just a bad idea. Maybe her mother was right when she said that they had a wandering spirit that shied away from the tethers of the typical American dream. A month ago it had seemed like a great plan. She had been bursting with ideas. Fantasizing about her new closet with room for more than five pairs of shoes. Just the thought of a full-size kitchen and an actual living room with a couch and big-screen television was enough to get her blood pumping with excitement.

Now the only thing that set her heart to racing was Wade. And he was long gone, along with the piece of her he'd taken with him.

Tori cussed and flung her pencil across the Airstream. It bounced off her cabinet door and rolled toward the bathroom. She watched it move across the floor, stopping at the butt of her shotgun, which was leaning against the door frame.

It brought to mind the first day he'd shown up on her property. His charming smile. His infuriating arrogance. The way she'd threatened to shoot him. How was she supposed to carry on with her plans when even the sight of her shotgun brought memories of him to mind? Living on his parents' old property would guarantee that she could never get away from Wade Mitchell.

But Tori didn't want to get away from him. She wanted the charming liar back in her arms. She sat staring blankly at her notepad, thinking about what had happened. Since he left, replaying the scene in her mind had given her some clarity. It had allowed her to focus on the words she'd refused to listen to in her anger.

Whatever it was he wanted was important. The land itself had no real value to him, just whatever was on it. Given she didn't even know what it was, it wasn't something she would ever miss. A part of her understood his reasoning. If he could take or move what he needed, Tori could keep her land and they could both be happy. Maybe even happy together.

If only she hadn't decided to come home early.

Tori looked back down at her fresh sheet of paper. The blank squares were taunting her. Picking up a new pencil, she took a deep breath and tried something different. How would she design a house for both her and Wade to live in?

She started with his office. It had an entire wall of windows that opened up on a view of the valley below like the ones overlooking Times Square in their hotel suite. On the opposite wall were floor-to-ceiling bookshelves. A see-through fireplace connected his office to the great room. Both spaces would have twelve-foot ceilings and huge panes of glass. One panel would slide out to let them onto the deck. She sketched in a hot tub where they could sit together in the evenings, talk and drink wine.

Wine... Tori started sketching a dream kitchen with a staircase that led down into a wine cellar. Her pencil moved feverishly now, the rooms flowing together perfectly. Nearly an hour passed before she sat back and looked at the design.

This was the house she wanted. The one with Wade in it. Her gaze moved over the second-story guest bedroom that was right off the master suite. It would be perfect for a nursery. She could just see the ivory-and-green wallpaper, the mobile over the crib. The sunlight that streamed in would provide the perfect amount of natural light. Wade could sit in the rocking chair and read bedtime stories....

That was the thought that brought the tears to her eyes that she'd fought for days.

Tori grasped the corner of the sketch, ready to rip it off and trash it with the others, but she just couldn't. This was the house she wanted.

The rumbling sound of a car pulling onto her property pulled her attention away from the design. Unable to see from her seat, she got up and walked over to the window.

The corner of a red hood with a BMW logo nearly sent her heart into her throat. She stumbled back against the sink, gripping the counter to keep her knees from giving out under her. Wade had returned to New York a week ago. Why was he here now? To apologize? To offer her more money? Her mind raced with different options, but she shook each one aside. The only way to know for sure was to go out there and find out.

Glancing to her right, she picked up the shotgun and went to the door. She was in love with him, but she was still angry and hurt by what he'd done. He needed to know that.

Tori swung open the door and stepped down into the snow. A snowstorm had blown through the day after she came home, blanketing the property in white and making it impossible for her to look around and search for clues about what he was after.

When she turned, Wade was standing near the hood of his SUV, his arms raised in surrender. In one hand was a bundle of tulips wrapped in florist paper. "Don't shoot," he said with the smile she'd missed.

She raised the gun and studied his face. He looked older, more tired than she remembered. Hopefully he'd had as bad a week as she had. Knowing he might have suffered without her helped soothe her pride a bit. "What do you want?"

"I came here to make you an offer."

It took everything Tori had not to pull the trigger and cover his body in painful welts. An offer? Here she was, designing their home, decorating their damn nursery, and he came here focused on the same old agenda.

"You're too late," she said. "I wouldn't sell you this

land for every dime you have. Flowers won't help, either."

Wade nodded. A flicker of amusement in his eyes sent a flame of irritation through her veins. "That's fine. I'm not here to buy the land."

Tori frowned. "If you don't want my land, what do you want, Wade?"

"I want you."

The intensity in his expression was undeniable. His green eyes were burrowing into her. It made it hard to breathe. He wanted her. *Her.* Not the land. Not what was hidden on it. Her. Her heart leaped in her chest for a moment, but she refused to so much as blink on the exterior. She wasn't going to let him off that easily. "I'm not interested in any more dinner dates. All I got out of that was indigestion and rug burn."

A smile curled Wade's lips. Instinctively she wanted to smile back, but she wouldn't.

"That's okay," he said. "I'm not here to ask you on a date. I'm here to tell you that I'm in love with you."

Tori's hands started trembling, the shotgun unsteady in her grasp. She stood there with her mouth open but without words as Wade came closer.

"Let's just set this down, shall we?" He eased the gun from her hands and laid it in the snow a few feet away. "I'd rather not have our love story turn into one of those tragic tales." Wade handed her the bouquet of tulips. They were her favorite flower. She hadn't ever told him that.

"How did you know?" she asked.

"Brody is a genius. You can find out almost anything with a computer. I've waited seven years to give you those flowers." He put his hands on her upper arms, gently rubbing her skin to warm her. "I've been miserable since we fought. I can't get that night out of my head. I can't sleep. All I can see is the look on your face when you walked away, and it breaks my heart. I'd give anything to see you smile again. Today, and every day of the rest of my life."

If the mention of love wasn't enough, he was making sounds like he wanted to…to…

"I want to tell you the truth. Every bit of it. But it's not just my secret to keep. There are others who could get hurt if the story were to be made public. But I can tell you this much… I was once very young and very stupid. When faced with something no child should have to handle, I made the wrong decision. I believe the evidence of that night is somewhere on your property. I've been doing everything I can think of to make sure no one ever finds it. I've done some things in the past few weeks that I'm not proud of. But I did what I felt I had to do to protect my family. You know how important they are to me. I would protect them with my life, just as I would protect yours. And for now I have to continue to protect their secret, just as I would protect a secret of yours."

Tori could see the pain in Wade's expression. His past was eating at him, gnawing at his gut on a daily basis. She was amazed that she hadn't noticed it before now, but maybe he just kept it too well hidden. He was letting down walls for her. Because she wanted him to. Even if he couldn't tell her everything, he was making the effort. And she could appreciate that. If she could be certain of nothing else, she knew that Wade would do anything for the people he loved. And if he loved her as he said he did, she would be just as fiercely protected.

The sense of security and stability that washed over her in that moment was unprecedented. A lifetime of moving from place to place had never provided it. Even buying this land hadn't provided it. But she'd found it in allowing herself to trust Wade and be protected by him.

"One day, I hope to be able to tell you the rest of the story. And that you'll hear everything I've done and trust me when I say that, right or wrong, I only ever had the best of intentions. I pray for your understanding because you are a beautiful, intelligent woman and I adore you. You make me happy just lying in bed listening to you breathe. I want to wake up every morning to your messy hair and pouty face. And I want to do it here, in Connecticut, in the house you designed."

Tori gasped. "You'd move here?"

He nodded. "I would. There isn't much I can do in the office that I can't do from here with teleconferences and virtual meetings. I might have to go to the city from time to time, but when I do, I want to take you with me. I don't think I like the idea of traveling without my wife."

"But I—" Tori started, then stopped. She watched as Wade eased down onto one knee in the snow. Reaching into his coat pocket, he pulled out a small wooden box wrapped in a gold ribbon. "Wade…" she said, disbelieving. The flowers slipped from her fingers to the snow.

"Victoria Sullivan," he began, unwrapping the bow. He eased open the hinge and held the box up to her. "Would you do me the honor of being my wife?"

Tori glanced down at the engagement ring in his hands. The nearly two carat round diamond was set in a multirow pave diamond band of platinum. It sparkled so brightly with the sunlight reflecting off the snow that she was almost blinded. She had stood in the snow very nearly dumbstruck for the past few minutes, but now she knew she had to find the right thing to say. And it should be easy, since she'd been screaming it in her head since he knelt in the snow.

"Yes," she said, tears pooling in her eyes from the light and the emotions ready to spill out of her.

Wade stood back up, slipping the ring onto her finger. It fit perfectly.

She tore her eyes away from the ring to look up at the man who would soon be her husband. "I love you," she said.

"And I love you." He leaned down to kiss her, almost the official sealing of the deal he'd come here to offer her.

Tori melted into his arms, losing herself in the feeling of being with the man she thought she'd lost forever. Her blood instantly began to heat with the desire he easily stirred in her. Just when she was ready to tug him into the Airstream and make love to her fiancé for the first time, he pulled away and looked down at her with a smug grin.

"Do you have any idea how hard it was to find the perfect diamond for you?"

Tori frowned. "Am I that picky?"

"I don't know if you are, but I certainly am. It had to be perfect. So perfect, I was willing to fly to San Francisco and back to buy it from a jeweler there. This ring is from an environmentally conscious and well-regulated Canadian diamond mine. Certified conflict-free. The band is made of recycled platinum. Hell, the ring box is even made from Rimu wood, whatever that is."

Tori grinned. Wade could have marched right into Tiffany's, bought any ring he wanted, and she would've said yes. But he didn't. He traveled all the way to the West Coast and back to get the ring he knew she would want. That was more precious than the large, flawless stone in the center.

"Rimu is a sustainable wood from New Zealand. And I love it. There isn't a more beautiful and perfect ring in all the world. Absolutely perfect."

"Like you," he said.

Rising on tiptoe, she kissed him again. "Now, let's go inside and get you out of those wet pants."

Wade's brow shot up at her suggestion. He glanced down at the wet knees of his trousers, then back at the Airstream behind him. "Okay, but after that, you need to get back to work designing that house."

"Why?"

"Because," he said, "I'm afraid if I make love to you the way I want to, we're going to roll this sucker down the hill and into a ditch. I need a house. Without wheels. ASAP."

"I'll do my best," Tori said. Taking his hand in hers, she led him over to the Airstream. "Until then," she said, laughing, "if this trailer's a rockin'..."

Epilogue

Two months later

"Remind me again why we're hiding eggs? In the dark?" Tori looked across the silver, moon-illuminated yard at Wade and Brody. They were both chucking the plastic Easter eggs under bushes and behind tree trunks.

Brody straightened and shrugged. "It's tradition. Like watching the Grinch at Christmas. Don't question our methods."

"But there aren't any children to find them."

"It doesn't matter," he explained. "For as long as I have lived on this farm, Wade and I have hidden Easter eggs for the younger kids. I swear to you, if Julianne and Heath wake up and there are no eggs to find, bunny heads will roll."

"You know, when Wade first told me about this, I

thought he meant the Edens hosted a community egg hunt here on the farm. I didn't realize I'd be out in the middle of the night hiding candy for your twenty-seven-year-old brother."

"It's good practice," Wade replied with a wink. "If Mama has her way, there will be grandkids hunting here in no time."

"Yeah, well," she muttered, "I don't know why all the pressure is on me when there are four other kids in this family. We need to get Brody a girl."

"Ha, ha," Brody said flatly. "You're funny. Why don't you get me a unicorn and a time machine while you're at it? Then I can go back to the nineties and gouge my father with the unicorn horn before he could ruin my chances of ever dating."

Tori shook her head and put an egg under the steps of the front porch. Over the past few months she'd gotten to know Wade's family better, including the grumpy and serious Brody. She found that he wasn't really that grumpy or that serious. He had a marshmallow center under that hard-candy shell. It made her want to help other people see though his defenses, as well.

"How do you expect to meet women if you never go out in public?" Wade teased. "Have one ordered on the internet and delivered to your office?"

Brody chucked an egg at Wade. The plastic shell separated on impact with his chest, sending candy scattering across the grass. "I imagine the shipping would be outrageous on that, so no. I have a woman in my life, thank you very much."

Wade retaliated with his own egg. Brody ducked and his egg missed, hitting the tree behind him and flying open. "Agnes doesn't count. She's your fiftysomething secretary. And she's married with grandchildren."

"Don't I know it," Brody complained. "She started making noises a few weeks ago about her anniversary coming up in the fall. She says she wants to take some time off for it."

"That's nice. Are they going on a trip to celebrate?" Tori asked.

"Yes," Brody responded with a heavy sigh. "It's a milestone year. Apparently they've booked a three-week Mediterranean cruise."

"That sounds wonderfully romantic," she said.

Brody shook his head, unconvinced. "Not for me."

"Agnes is Brody's connection to the outside world," Wade explained. "Without her, he's helpless as a babe."

"I am not helpless. There are just some things that I can't do from my office. Or that are easier to have her handle. Like picking up my dry cleaning."

Tori couldn't imagine living in Brody's world without contact with other people. From what Wade had told her, he had a housekeeper who worked at his home during the day while he was gone, but she always left before he got back. And he had his secretary. Aside from family visits, that was it. He lived in seclusion. "What are you going to do when she goes?"

"I don't know," Brody said. He put the last of his eggs in the curled-up nest of the garden hose. "I've been trying not to think about it. I've got months before I have to make a decision."

"I'm sure you can hire a temp from a local agency to come in while she's gone."

Brody frowned at her. "I don't like new people."

"I'm new, and you like me."

"That's because I realized Wade was hopelessly in love and there was no getting rid of you."

Wade came up behind Tori and wrapped his arms

around her waist. She curled against him, seeking out his warmth in the chilly night air.

"You have to keep yourself open to the opportunities around you," he said to his brother. "You never know what you might find. Great things can show up where you least expect them."

Brody looked at the two of them and shook his head. "People in love are disgusting."

"Disgustingly happy," Wade countered, placing a warm kiss just under Tori's earlobe. The touch sent a shiver down her spine that made her want to dump her basket of eggs and drag him back to the Airstream.

"Happily ever after," she agreed.

* * * * *

MATCHED TO HER RIVAL

KAT CANTRELL

To Jill Marsal, agent extraordinaire, because you stuck with me through all the revisions of this book and together, we made it great. And because this one was your favourite of the three.

One

In the media business—and in life—presentation trumped everything else, and Dax Wakefield never underestimated the value of putting on a good show.

Careful attention to every detail was the reason his far-flung media empire had succeeded beyond his wildest dreams. So why was KDLS, the former jewel of his crown, turning in such dismal ratings?

Dax stopped at the receptionist's desk in the lobby of the news station he'd come to fix. "Hey, Rebecca. How's Brian's math grade this semester?"

The receptionist's smile widened as she fluffed her hair and threw her shoulders back to make sure he noticed her impressive figure.

He noticed. A man who enjoyed the female form as much as Dax always noticed.

"Good morning, Mr. Wakefield," Rebecca chirped. "He made a C on his last report card. Such an improvement. It's been like six months since I mentioned his grades. How on earth did you remember?"

Because Dax made it a point to keep at least one personal detail about all his employees front and center when speaking to them. The mark of success wasn't simply who had the most money, but who had the best-run business, and no one could do it all by themselves. If people liked working for you, they stuck around, and turned themselves inside out to perform.

Usually. Dax had a few questions for Robert Smith, the station manager, about the latest ratings. Someone was tripping up somewhere.

Dax tapped his temple and grinned. "My mama encourages me to use this bad boy for good instead of evil. Is Robert around?"

The receptionist nodded and buzzed the lock on the security door. "They're taping a segment. I'm sure he's hovering near the set."

"Say hi to Brian for me," Dax called as he sailed through the frosted glass door and into the greatest show on earth—the morning news.

Cameramen and gaffers mixed it up, harried producers with electronic tablets stepped over thick cables on their way to the sound booth, and in the middle of it all sat KDLS's star anchor, Monica McCreary. She was conversing on camera with a petite dark-haired woman who had great legs, despite being on the shorter side. She'd done a lot with what she had and he appreciated the effort.

Dax paused at the edge of the organized chaos and crossed his arms, locking gazes with the station manager. With a nod, Robert scurried across the ocean of people and equipment to join him.

"Saw the ratings, huh?" Robert murmured.

That was a quality Dax fully appreciated in his employees—the ability to read his mind.

Low ratings irritated him because there was no excuse. Sensationalism was key, and if nothing newsworthy happened, it was their job to create something worth watching, and ensure that something had Wakefield Media stamped on it.

"Yep." Dax left it at that, for now. He had all day and the crew was in the middle of taping. "What's this segment?"

"Dallas business owners. We feature one a week. Local interest stuff."

Great Legs owned her own business? Interesting. Smart women equaled a huge turn-on.

"What's she do? Cupcakes?"

Even from this distance, the woman exuded energy—a perky little cheerleader type who never met a curlicue or excess of decoration she didn't like. He could see her dolloping frosting on a cupcake and charging an exorbitant price for it.

Dax could go for a cupcake. Literally and figuratively. Maybe even at the same time.

"Nah. She runs a dating service." Robert nodded at the pair of women under the spotlight. "EA International. Caters to exclusive clients."

The back of Dax's neck heated instantly and all thoughts of cupcakes went out the window.

"I'm familiar with the company."

Through narrowed eyes, Dax zeroed in on the Dallas business owner who had cost him his oldest friend. Someone who called herself a matchmaker should be withered and stooped, with gray hair. It was such an antiquated notion. And it should be against the law.

The anchor laughed at something the matchmaker said and leaned forward. "So you're Dallas's answer to a fairy godmother?"

"I like to think of myself as one. Who doesn't need a bit of magic in their lives?" Her sleek dark hair swung freely as she talked with her hands, expression animated.

"You recently matched the Delamerian prince with his fiancée, right?" Monica winked. "Women everywhere are cursing that, I'm sure."

"I can't take credit." The matchmaker smiled and it transformed her entire demeanor. "Prince Alain—Finn—

and Juliet had a previous relationship. I just helped them realize it wasn't over."

Dax couldn't stop watching her.

As much as he hated to admit it, the matchmaker lit up the set. KDLS's star news anchor was more of a minor celestial body compared to the matchmaker's sun.

And Dax was never one to underestimate star power.

Or the element of surprise.

He strode onto the set and dismissed the anchor with a jerk of his head. "I'll take over from here, Monica. Thanks."

Despite the unusual request, Monica smiled and vacated her chair without comment. No one else so much as blinked. No one who worked for him, anyway.

As he parked in Monica's still-warm chair, the petite dynamo opposite him nearly bowled him over when she blurted out, "What's going on? Who are you?"

A man who recognized a golden opportunity for improved ratings.

"Dax Wakefield. I own the station," he said smoothly. "And this interview has officially started over. It's Elise, right?"

Her confusion leveled out and she crossed her spectacular legs, easing back in the chair carefully. "Yes, but you can call me Ms. Arundel."

Ah, so she recognized his name. Let the fun begin.

He chuckled darkly. "How about if I call you Ms. Hocus-Pocus instead? Isn't that your gig, pulling fast ones on unsuspecting clients? You bibbidi-bobbidi-boo women into relationships with wealthy men."

This interview had also officially become the best way to dish up a side of revenge—served cold. If this ratings gold mine led to discrediting EA International, so much the better. Someone had to save the world from this matchmaker's mercenary female clients.

"That's not what I do." Elise's gaze cut from his face

to his torso and her expression did not melt into the typical sensuous smile that said she'd be happy to further discuss whatever he wanted to talk about over drinks. Unlike most women.

It whetted his appetite to get sparks on the screen another way.

"Enlighten us then," he allowed magnanimously with a wave of his hand.

"I match soul mates." Elise, pardon-me-Ms.-Arundel, cleared her throat and recrossed her legs as if she couldn't find a comfortable pose. "Some people need more help than others. Successful men seldom have time or the patience to sort through potential love interests. I do it for them. At the same time, a man with means needs a certain kind of mate, one not easily found. I widen the potential pool by polishing a few of my female clients into diamonds worthy of the highest social circles."

"Oh, come now. You're training these women to be gold diggers."

That was certainly what she'd done with Daniella White, whose last name was now Reynolds because she'd managed to snare Dax's college friend Leo. Who then promptly screwed Dax over in favor of his wife. A fifteen-year friendship down the drain. Over a woman.

Elise's smile hardened. "You're suggesting women need a class on how to marry a man for his money? I doubt anyone with that goal needs help honing her strategy. I'm in the business of making women's lives better by introducing them to their soul mates."

"Why not pay for them to go to college and let them find their own dates?" Dax countered swiftly.

The onlookers shifted and murmured but neither Dax nor Elise so much as glanced away from their staring contest. An indefinable crackle sliced through the air between them. It was going to be beautiful on camera.

"There are scholarship opportunities out there already. I'm filling another niche, helping people connect. I'm good at what I do. You of all people should know that."

Oh, she had not just gone there. Nearly nose to nose now, he smiled, the best method to keep 'em guessing. "Why would I know that? Because you single-handedly ruined both a business venture and a long-standing friendship when you introduced Leo to his gold digger?"

So, apparently that wound was still raw.

College roommates who'd seen the world through the same lens, he and Leo believed wholeheartedly in the power of success and brotherhood. Females were to be appreciated until they outlived their usefulness. Until Daniella, who somehow got Leo to fall in love with her and then she'd brainwashed his oldest friend into losing his ruthless business edge.

Not that he believed Daniella was 100 percent at fault. She'd been the instigator but Leo had pulled the plug on the deal with Dax. Both he and Leo had suffered a seven-figure loss. Then Leo ended their friendship for no reason.

The pain of his friend's betrayal still had the power to punch quite a hole through his stomach. That was why it never paid to trust people. Anyone you let in eventually stomped all over you.

"No!" She huffed a sigh of frustration and shut her eyes for a beat, clearly trying to come up with a snappy response. Good luck with that. There wasn't one.

But she tried anyway. "Because I single-handedly helped two people find each other and fall in love. Something real and lasting happened before your eyes and you had a front-row seat. Leo and Dannie are remarkably compatible and share values. That's what my computer does. Matches people according to who they are."

"The magic you alluded to earlier," Dax commented with raised eyebrows. "Right? It's all smoke and mirrors, though. You tell these people they're compatible and they fall for it. The power of suggestion. Quite brilliant, actually."

And he meant it. If anyone knew the benefit of smoke and mirrors, he did. It kept everyone distracted from what was really going on behind the curtain, where the mess was.

A red stain spilled across Elise's cheeks, but she didn't back down. "You're a cynical man, Dax Wakefield. Just because you don't believe in happily ever after doesn't mean it can't happen."

"True." He conceded the point with a nod. "And false. I readily admit to being cynical but happily ever after is a myth. Long-term relationships consist of two people who've agreed to put up with each other. No ridiculous lies about loving each other forever required."

"That's…" Apparently she couldn't come up with a word to describe it. So he helped her out.

"Reality?"

His mother had proven it by walking out on his father when Dax was seven. His father had never recovered from the hope she'd eventually come back. Poor sap.

"Sad," she corrected with a brittle smile. "You must be so lonely."

He blinked. "That's one I've never been called before. I could have five different dates lined up for tonight in about thirty seconds."

"Oh, you're in worse shape than I thought." With another slide of her legs that Dax couldn't quite ignore, she leaned toward him. "You need to meet the love of your life. Immediately. I can help you."

His own bark of laughter startled him. Because it wasn't funny. "Which part wasn't clear? The part where I said you were a phony or the part where I don't believe in love?"

"It was all very clear," she said quietly. "You're trying to prove my business, my life's work, is a sham. You can't, because I can find the darkest of hearts a match. Even yours. You want to prove something? Put your name in my computer."

Double ouch. He'd been bamboozled. And he'd never seen it coming.

Against all odds, he dredged up a healthy amount of respect for Elise Arundel.

Hell. He actually kind of liked her style.

Elise wiped her clammy hands on her skirt and prayed the pompous Mr. Wakefield didn't notice. This was not the scripted, safe interview she'd been promised or she never would have agreed to sit on this stage under all these burning hot lights, with what felt like a million pairs of eyes boring a hole through her.

Thinking on her feet was not her strong suit.

Neither was dealing with wealthy, spoiled, too-handsome, arrogant playboys who despised everything she believed in.

And she'd just invited him to test her skills. Had she accidentally inhaled paint thinner?

It hardly mattered. He'd never take her up on it. Guys like Dax didn't darken the door of a matchmaker. Shallow, unemotional relationships were a snap to find, especially for someone who clearly had a lot of practice enticing women into bed. And was likely an ace at keeping them there.

Dax stroked his jaw absently and contemplated her. "Are you offering to find me a match?"

"Not just a match," she corrected immediately and tore her gaze from the thumb running under his chiseled cheekbone. "True love. My gig is happily ever after."

Yes. It was, and she hadn't failed one single couple yet. She wasn't about to start today.

Matching hearts fulfilled her in so many ways. It almost made up for not finding her own match. But hope sprang eternal. If her mother's five marriages and dozens of affairs hadn't squeezed optimism and a belief in the power of love out of her, Dax Wakefield couldn't kill them either.

"So tell me about your own happily ever after. Is Mr. Arundel your one true love?"

"I'm single," she admitted readily. It was a common question from clients who wanted her credentials and the standard answer came easily now. "But it's not a commentary on my services. You don't decide against using a travel agent just because she hasn't been to the resort you're booking, right?"

"Right. But I would wonder why she became a travel agent if she doesn't ever get on a plane."

The crowd snickered and the muscles in her legs tensed. *Oh, spotlight how do I hate thee? Let me count the ways...*

She'd be happy to get on a plane if the right man came along. But clients were always right for someone else, not her, and well...she wasn't the best at walking up to interesting men in public and introducing herself. Friday nights with a chick flick always seemed safer than battling the doubts that she wasn't quite good enough, successful enough, or thin enough for dating.

She'd only agreed to this interview to promote her business. It was a necessary evil, and nothing other than EA International's success could entice her into making such a public spectacle.

"I always fly first class myself, Mr. Wakefield," she responded and if only her voice hadn't squeaked, the delivery would have been perfect. "As soon as you're ready to board, see me and I'll put you on the right plane in the right seat to the right destination.

"What do I have to do?" he asked. "Fill out a profile online?"

Was he actually considering it? She swallowed and the

really bad feeling she'd tamped down earlier roared back into her chest.

Talk him out of it.

It was a stupid idea in the first place. But how else could she have responded? He was disparaging not only her profession but a company with her name on it.

"Online profiles don't work," she said. "In order to find your soul mate, I have to know *you*. Personally."

Dax's eyelids drifted lower and he flashed a slumberous smile that absolutely should not have sent a zing through her stomach. "That sounds intriguing. Just how personal does this get, Ms. Arundel?"

Was he *flirting?* Well, she wasn't. This was cold, hard business. "Very. I ask a series of intensive questions. By the time I'm finished, I'll know you better than your own mother."

Something dark skittered through Dax's eyes but he covered it swiftly. "Tall order. But I don't kiss and tell, especially not to my mama. If I do this, what happens if I don't find true love? You'll be exposed as a fraud. Are you sure you're up for that?"

"I'm not worried," she lied. "The only thing I ask is that you take this seriously. No cheating. If you commit to the process and don't find true love, do your best to spread word far and wide that I'm not as good as I say I am."

But she *was* that good. She'd written the matching algorithm herself, pouring countless hours into the code until it was bulletproof. People often perplexed her, but a program either worked or it didn't, and she never gave up until she fixed the bug. Numbers were her refuge, her place of peace.

A well-written line of code didn't care how many chocolate bars she ate. Or how easily chocolate settled on her hips.

"That's quite a deal." His gaze narrowed. "But it's too easy. There's no way I can lose."

Because he believed she was pulling a fast one on her clients and that he'd never fall for it. "You're right. You don't lose either way. If you don't find love, you get to tear my business apart in whatever way makes sense to you. If you do find love, well…" She shrugged. "You'll be happy. And you'll owe me."

One brow quirked up and she refused to find it charming.

"Love isn't its own reward?"

He was toying with her. And he wasn't going to get away with it. "I run a business, Mr. Wakefield. Surely you can appreciate that I have expenses. Smoke and mirrors aren't free."

His rich laugh hit her crossways. Yeah, he had a nice laugh. It was the only nice anything he had that she'd admit to noticing. Dannie had certainly hit the mark when she described Dax Wakefield to Elise as "yummy with an extra helping of cocky and a side of reptile."

"Careful, Ms. Arundel. You don't want to give away all your secrets on the morning news."

He shook his head, and his carefully coiffed hair bounced back into place. A guy as well put-together as Dax Wakefield hadn't even needed an hour with a makeup artist to be camera-ready. It was so unfair.

"I'm not giving anything away. Especially not my matchmaking abilities." Elise sat back in her chair. The farther away she was from Pretty Boy, the better. "So if you find true love, you'll agree to advertise my business. As a satisfied client."

His eyebrows shot up and the evidence of surprise gave her a little thrill that she wasn't at all ashamed to wallow in.

If this had been about anything other than EA International, the company she'd breathed life into for seven years, she'd have been at a loss for words, stumbling around looking for the exit.

But attacking her business made it personal. And for what? Because his friend had broken the guy code? Dax needed someone to blame for Leo's falling in love with Dannie, obviously, not that he'd admit it. Elise made a convenient scapegoat.

"You want me to advertise your services?" Incredulity laced his deep voice.

"If you find love, sure. I should get something out of this experiment, too. A satisfied client is the best reference." A satisfied client who'd previously denounced her skill set in public was worth more than a million dollars in advertising. "I'll even waive my fee if you do."

"Now you've got me curious. What's the going rate for true love these days?"

"Five hundred thousand dollars," she said flatly.

"That's outrageous." But he looked impressed nonetheless. About time she got his attention.

"I have dozens of clients who disagree. I guarantee my fees, too. If you don't find your soul mate, I refund your money. Well, not yours," she conceded with a nod. "You get to put me out of business."

That's when she realized her mistake. You could only find a soul mate for someone who had a soul. Dax Wakefield had obviously sold his a long time ago. This was never going to work. Her code would probably chew him up and spit him out.

She had to get off this stage before all these eyes and lights and camera lenses baked her like a pie.

Rubbing his hands together with something resembling glee, he winked. "A proposition I can't lose. I'm so on board with that, I'll even do you one better than a simple reference. Five hundred K buys a fifteen-second spot during the Super Bowl. If you pull a rabbit out of your hat and match me with my true love, I'll sing your praises right before halftime in a commercial starring *moi*."

"You will not." She let her gaze travel over his smooth, too-handsome face, searching for a clue to his real intentions.

Nothing but sincerity radiated back. "I will. Except I won't have to. You'll need a lot more than smoke and mirrors to win."

Win. As though this was a race.

"Why, because even if you fall in love, you'll pretend you haven't?"

A lethal edge sharpened his expression. "I gave you my word, Ms. Arundel. I might be a cynic, but I'm not a liar."

She'd offended him. His edges smoothed out so quickly, she would have thought she'd imagined it. But she knew what she'd seen. Dax Wakefield would not allow himself to win any other way than fair and square. And that decided it.

This...contest between them was about *her* as much as it was about EA International. As much about Dax's views on love and relationships versus hers. If she matched him with his soul mate—not if, *when*—she'd prove once and for all that it didn't matter what she looked like on the outside. Matching people who wanted to fall in love was easy. Finding a match for a self-professed cynic would be a stellar achievement worthy of everyone's praise.

Her brain was her best asset and she'd demonstrate it publicly. The short fat girl inside who wanted her mother to love her regardless of Elise's weight and height would finally be vanquished.

"Then it's a deal." Without hesitation, she slid her hand into his and shook on it.

Something bold and electric passed between them, but she refused to even glance at their joined fingers. Unfortunately, whatever it was that felt dangerous and the slightest bit thrilling came from deep inside her and needed only Dax's dark gaze to intensify it.

Oh, goodness. What had she just agreed to?

Two

The uncut footage was exceptional. Elise Arundel glowed on camera, just as Dax thought she would. The woman was stunning, animated. A real live wire. He peered at the monitor over the producer's shoulder and earned a withering glare from the man trying to do his job.

"Fine," Dax conceded with a nod to the producer. "Finish editing it and air the interview. It's solid."

Dallas's answer to a fairy godmother was going to wave her magic wand and give KDLS the highest ratings the news show had seen in two weeks. Maybe even in this whole fiscal year.

It was totally worth having to go through the motions of whatever ridiculous process Ms. Arundel cooked up. The failure to find him a soul mate would be so humiliating, Dax might not even go through with denouncing her company afterward.

But that all depended on how miserable Elise deliberately tried to make him. He had no doubt she'd give it her best shot.

Within fifteen minutes, the producer had the interview clip queued and ready. The station crew watched it unfold on the monitors. As Dax hammered the matchmaker, she held her own. The camera even captured the one instance she'd caught him off balance.

Okay, so it had happened twice, but no one other than

Dax would notice—he was nothing if not a master at ensuring that everyone saw him precisely as he meant for them to.

Elise Arundel was something else, he'd give her that.

Shame those great legs were attached to such a misguided romantic, whom he should hate a lot more than he actually did. She'd refused to take any crap and the one-up she'd laid on him with the satisfied client bit…well, she'd done exactly what he'd have done in her shoes.

It had been kind of awesome. Or it would have been if he'd escaped without agreeing to put his name in her computer.

Dax spent the rest of the day immersed in meetings with the station crew, hammering each department as easily as he had Elise. They had some preliminary numbers by lunch on the fairy godmother interview—and they were very good indeed—but one stellar day of ratings would not begin to make up for the last quarter.

As Dax slid into the driver's seat of his Audi, his phone beeped and he thumbed up the text message.

Jenna: You could have dates lined up with five different women? Since you're about to meet the love of your life…which is apparently not me…let's make it four. I never want to see you again.

Dax cursed. How bad was it that he'd forgotten Jenna would most assuredly watch the program? Maybe the worse crime was the fact that he'd forgotten entirely about the redhead he'd been dating for four—no, five—weeks. Or was it closer to six?

He cursed again. That relationship had stretched past its expiration date, but he'd been reluctant to give it up. Obviously Jenna had read more into it than she should have. They'd been having fun and he'd told her that was the extent of it. Regardless, she deserved better than to find out she had more of an investment than Dax from a TV program.

He was officially the worst sort of dog and should be shot.

Next time, he'd be clearer up front—Dax Wakefield subscribed to the Pleasure Principle. He liked his women fun, sexy and above all, unattached. Anything deeper than that was work, which he had enough of. Women should be about decadent indulgence. If it didn't feel good, why do it?

He drove home to the loft he'd bought in Deep Ellum before it was trendy and mentally scrolled through his contacts for just such a woman. Not one name jumped out. Probably every woman he'd ever spoken to had seen the clip. Didn't seem as if there were much point in getting shot down a few more times tonight.

But jeez, spending the night alone sucked.

Stomach growling, Dax dumped his messenger bag at the door and strode to the stainless-steel-and-black-granite kitchen to survey the contents of his cupboard.

While pasta boiled, he amused himself by recalling Elise's diabolical smile as she suggested Dax put his name in her computer. Sweet dreams were made of dark-haired, petite women.

He wasn't looking forward to being grilled about his favorite color and where he went to college so Ms. Arundel could pull a random woman's name out of her computer. But he was, oddly enough, looking forward to sparring with her some more.

The next morning, Dax opted to drive to his office downtown. He usually walked, both to get in the exercise and to avoid dealing with Dallas traffic, but Elise had scheduled their first session at the mutually agreed-upon time of 10:00 a.m.

By nine forty-seven, he'd participated in three conference calls, signed a contract for the purchase of a regional newspaper, read and replied to an in-box full of emails, and drunk two cups of coffee. Dax lived for Wakefield Media.

And now he'd have to sacrifice some of his day to the Fairy Godmother. Because he said he would.

Dax's mother was a coldhearted, untrustworthy woman, but in leaving, had taught him the importance of living up to your word. That was why he rarely promised anything.

EA International resided in a tasteful two-story office building in Uptown. The clean, low-key logo on the door spoke of elegance and sophistication, exactly the right tone to strike when your clients were high-powered executives and entrepreneurs.

The receptionist took his name. Dax proceeded to wait until finally she showed him to a room with two leather chairs and a low table strewn with picture books, one sporting a blue-and-gold fish on the cover and another, a waterfall.

Boring. Did Ms. Arundel hope to lull her clients into a semi-stupor while she let them cool their heels? Looked as though he was about to find out.

Elise clacked into the room, high heels against the hardwood floor announcing her presence. He glanced up slowly, taking in her heels, those well-built legs, her form-fitting scarlet skirt and jacket. Normally he liked taller women, but couldn't remember why just then. He kept going, thoroughly enjoying the trip to her face, which he'd forgotten was so arresting.

Her energy swept across him and prickled his skin, unnerving him for a moment. "You're late."

Her composed expression didn't waver. "You were late first."

Not that late. Ten minutes. Maybe. Regardless, she'd made him wait in this pseudo dentist's office on purpose. Score one for the matchmaker. "Trying to teach me a lesson?"

"I assumed you weren't going to show and took a call.

I am running a business here." She settled into the second chair and her knee grazed his.

She didn't even seem to notice. His knee tingled but she simply crossed her legs and bounced one siren-red pump casually.

Just as casually, Dax tossed the fish book back on the table. "Busy day. The show does not go on without a lot of hands-on from yours truly."

But that didn't really excuse his tardiness. They were both business owners and he'd disrespected her. Unintentionally, but point taken.

"You committed to this. The profile session takes several hours. Put up or shut up."

Hours? He nearly groaned. How could it possibly take that long to find out he liked football, hated the Dallas Cowboys, drank beer but only dark and imported, and preferred the beach to the mountains?

Dax drew out his phone. "Give me your cell phone number." One of her eyebrows lowered and it was so cute, he laughed. "I'm not going to prank call you. If this is going to take hours, we'll have to split up the sessions. Then I can text you if I'm going to be late to the next one."

"Really?"

He shrugged, not certain why the derision in her tone raised his hackles. "Most women think it's considerate to let them know if they're held up. My apologies for assuming you fell into the category of females who appreciate a considerate man."

"Apology accepted. Now you know I'm in the category of woman who thinks texting is a cop-out. Try an actual phone call sometime." She smiled, baring her teeth, which softened the message not at all. "Better yet, just be punctual. Period."

She'd *accepted* his quasi-apology, as if he'd meant to really convey regret instead of sarcasm.

"Personal questions and punctuality?" He *tsk*ed to cover what he suspected might be another laugh trying to get out. When was the last time he'd been taken to task so expertly? Like never. "You drive a hard bargain, Ms. Arundel."

And she'd managed to evade giving out her digits. Slick. Not that he really wanted to call her. But still. It was kind of an amusing turnabout to be refused an attractive woman's phone number.

"You can call me Elise."

"Really?" It was petty repetition of her earlier succinct response. But in his shock, he'd let it slip.

"We're going to be working together. I'd like it if you were more comfortable with me. Hopefully it'll help you be more honest when answering the profile questions."

What was it about her and the truth? Did he look that much like a guy who skated the edge between black and white? "I told you I'm not a liar, whether I call you Elise, Ms. Arundel or sweetheart."

The hardness in her gaze melted, turning her irises a gooey shade of chocolate, and she sighed. "My turn to apologize. I can tell you don't want to be here and I'm a little touchy about it."

It was a rare woman who saw something other than what he meant for her to, and he did not want Elise to know anything about him, let alone against his will. Time for a little damage control.

"My turn to be confused. I do want to be here or I wouldn't have agreed to our deal. Why would you think otherwise?"

She evaluated his expression for a moment and tucked the straight fall of dark hair behind her ear, revealing a pale column of neck he had an unexplainable urge to explore. See if he could melt those hard eyes a little more. Unadulterated need coiled in his belly.

Down, boy.

Elise hated him. He didn't like her or anything she stood for. He was here to be matched with a woman who would be the next in a long line of ex-girlfriends and then declare EA International fraudulent. Because there was no way he'd lose this wager.

"Usually when someone is late, it's psychological," she said with a small tilt of her head, as if she'd found a puzzle to solve but couldn't quite get the right angle to view it.

"Are you trying to analyze me?"

She scowled. "It's not bargain-basement analysis. I have a degree in psychology."

"Yeah? Me, too."

They stared at each other for a moment, long enough for the intense spike in his abdomen to kick-start his perverse gene.

What was it about a smart woman that never failed to intrigue the hell out of him?

She broke eye contact and scribbled furiously in her notebook, color in her cheeks heightened.

She'd been affected by the heat, too.

He wanted to know more about Elise Arundel without divulging anything about himself that wasn't surface-level inanity.

"The information about my major was a freebie," he said. "Anything else personal you want to know is going to cost you."

If they were talking about Elise—and didn't every woman on the planet prefer to talk about herself?—Dax wouldn't inadvertently reveal privileged information. That curtain was closed, and no one got to see backstage.

Elise was almost afraid to ask. "Cost me what?"

When Dax's smoke-colored eyes zeroed in on her, she was positive she should be both afraid *and* sorry. His irises weren't the black smoke of an angry forest fire, but the wispy gray of a late November hearth fire that had just begun to blaze. The kind of fire that promised many delicious, warm things to come. And could easily burn down the entire block if left unchecked.

"It'll cost you a response in kind. Whatever you ask me, you have to answer, too."

"That's not how this works. I'm not trying to match myself."

Though she'd been in the system for seven years.

She'd entered her profile first, building the code around the questions and answers. On the off chance a match came through, well, there was nothing wrong with finding her soul mate with her own process, was there?

"Come on. Be a sport. It'll help me be more comfortable with baring my soul to you."

She shook her head hard enough to flip the ends of her hair into her mouth. "The questions are not all that soul-baring."

Scrambling wasn't her forte any more than thinking on her feet, because that was a total misrepresentation. The questions were designed to strip away surface-level BS and find the real person underneath. If that wasn't soul-baring, she didn't know what was. How else could the algorithm find a perfect match? The devil was in the details, and she had a feeling Dax's details could upstage Satan himself.

"Let's find out," he said easily. "What's the first one?"

"Name," she croaked.

"Daxton Ryan Wakefield. Daxton is my grandmother's maiden name. Ryan is my father's name." He shuddered in mock terror. "I feel exposed sharing my history with a virtual stranger. Help a guy out. Your turn."

This was so not a good idea. But he'd threatened her business, her livelihood. To prove her skills, his profile had to be right. Otherwise, he might be matched with an almost–soul mate or worse, someone completely incompatible. Dax wasn't a typical paying client, and she couldn't treat him like one. What was the harm in throwing him one bone? It wasn't as if she had to answer all of the questions, just enough to get him talking.

"Shannon Elise Arundel."

How in the world had that slipped out? She hadn't told anyone that her real first name was Shannon in years. Her shudder of terror wasn't faked.

Shannon, put down that cake. Shannon, have you weighed yourself today? Shannon, you might be vertically challenged but you don't have to be horizontally challenged too.

The words were always delivered with the disapproving frown her mother saved for occasions of great disappointment. Frowning caused wrinkles and Brenna Burke hated wrinkles more than photographers.

Dax circled his finger in a get-on-with-the-rest motion. "No comment about how your father was Irish and wanted to make sure you had a bit of the old country in your name?"

"Nope. My name is very boring."

Her mother was the Irish one, with milky skin and glowing red hair that graced magazine covers and runways for twenty years. Brenna Burke, one of the world's original supermodels, had given birth to a short Black Irish daughter prone to gaining weight by simply looking at cookies. It was a sin of the highest order in Brenna's mind that Elise had a brain instead of beauty.

Dax quirked his mouth in feigned disappointment. "That's okay. We can't all have interesting stories attached to our names. Where did you grow up?"

"This is not a date." The eye roll happened involuntarily, but the exasperation in her voice was deliberate. "I'm asking the questions."

"It's kind of like a date," he mused brightly as if the

thought fascinated him. "Getting to know each other. Awkward silences. Both of us dressed just a little bit more carefully than normal."

She glanced down at her BCBG suit, which she'd snipped the tags from that morning. Because red made her feel strong and fierce, and a session with Dax called for both. So what? "This is how I dress every day."

Now she felt self-conscious. Did the suit and five-inch stilettos seem as though she was trying too hard?

"Then I'm really looking forward to seeing what you look like tomorrow." He waggled his brows.

"Let's move on," she said before Dax drove her insane. "This is not a date, nor is it kind of like a date, and I'm getting to know you, not the other way around. So I can find you a match."

"Too bad. A date is the best place to see me in action." When she snorted, he inclined his head with a mischievous smile. "That's not what I meant, but since you started it, my favorite part of dates is anticipating the first kiss. What's yours?"

She lifted her gaze from his parted lips and blinked at the rising heat in his expression. The man had no shame. Flirting with his matchmaker, whose business he was also trying to destroy.

"Jedi mind tricks only work on the weak-minded. Tell me more about what you like about dating. It's a great place to start."

He grinned and winked. "Deflection only works on those who graduated at the bottom of their class. But I'll let it pass this time. I like long walks on the beach, hot tubs and dinner for two on the terrace."

Clearly this was slated to be the battle of who had the better psychology degree. Fine. *You want to play, let's play.*

"Why don't you try again, but this time without the *Love*

Connection sound bite? I didn't ask what you liked to *do* on dates. I asked what you like about *dating*."

"I like sex," he said flatly. "In order to get that, dating is a tiresome requirement. Is that what you're looking for?"

"Not really. Plus it's not true." His irises flashed from hearth-fire smoke to forest-fire smoke instantly and she backpedaled. "I don't mean you're lying. Get a grip. I mean, you don't have to date someone to have sex. Lots of women would gladly line up for a roll in the sheets with a successful, sophisticated man."

Who had a face too beautiful to be real, the physique of an elite athlete and eyelashes her mother would kill for. Not that she'd noticed.

"Would you?"

"I don't do one-night stands."

She frowned. When was the last time she'd even been on a date? Oh, yeah, six months ago—Kory, with a *K*. She should have known that one wouldn't work out the instant he'd introduced himself as such.

"There you go. A woman who would isn't worth my time."

Her head snapped back. Was that a compliment? More flirting? The truth?

"So you aren't just looking for sex. You want to put some effort into a relationship. Have drinks, spend some time together. And you want to know things about the women you date, their history, their likes and dislikes. Why?"

He contemplated her as he sat back in his chair, thumb to his jaw, a habit she'd noticed he fell into when she made the wheels in his convoluted head turn. Good.

"You're much more talented than I imagined," he allowed with a jerk of his chin. "I'm so impressed, I'm going to tell you why. It's so I can buy her something she'd genuinely appreciate and give it to her on our next date."

So the woman in question would sleep with him, no

doubt. And it probably never failed. "Another example of a considerate man?"

"Sure. Women like to be treated well. I like women. Ergo, it's no chore to do my best to make them happy."

There had to be something wrong with that, but she couldn't find the fault to save her life. Plus, the glow from his compliment still burned brightly. "If only all men subscribed to that theory. What do you find attractive in a woman?"

"Brains," he said instantly and she didn't even bother to write that down.

"You can't tell if a woman has brains from across the room," she responded drily. "If you walk into a bar, who catches your eye?"

"I don't meet women in bars, and last time I walked into one, I got four stitches right here." He tapped his left eyebrow, which was bisected by a faint line, and his chagrined smile was so infectious, she couldn't help but laugh.

"Okay, you win that round. But I have to note something. Redhead, blonde? Voluptuous, athletic?"

"Would you believe it if I said I have no preference? Or at least that used to be true." He swept her with a sizzling once-over that curled her toes involuntarily. "I might be reconsidering."

"The more you try to unsettle me, the less it works," she advised him and cursed the catch in her throat that told him her actual state far better than her words. This was ridiculous and getting them nowhere. "You promised to take this seriously and all I know about you so far is that distraction and verbal sleight of hand are your standard operating procedure. What are you hiding?"

The flicker of astonishment darting through his expression vanished when a knock sounded on the door. Dang it. She'd hardly begun to dig into the good stuff.

Elise's assistant, Angie, stuck her head in and said, "Your next appointment is here."

Both she and Dax shot startled glances at their watches. When he hadn't shown, she'd scheduled another appointment. How had the minutes vanished so quickly?

He stood immediately. "I'm late for a meeting."

What did it say that they'd both lost track of the hour? She nodded. "Tomorrow, then. Same time, same bat channel?"

He grinned. "You've got yourself a date, Ms. Arundel."

Three

Dax whistled a nameless tune as he pulled open the door to EA International. Deliberately late, and not at all sorry.

Today, he was in charge, and Elise would not get the drop on him again. He'd give her enough information to make it seem that he was going along willingly, simultaneously dragging out their interaction a little longer. Long enough to figure out what about Elise got under his skin, anyway. Then he was done here.

"Morning, Angie." Dax smiled at the receptionist and handed her the vase of stargazer lilies he'd brought. "For you. Is Ms. Arundel's calendar free?"

Angie moistened her lips and smiled in return. "Cleared, just as you requested yesterday. Thanks for the flowers. They're beautiful."

"I'll show myself to Ms. Arundel's office." He winked. "Don't tell her I'm coming. It's a surprise."

When Dax blew through the door of Elise's office, the location of which he'd noted yesterday on his way out, the look on her face was more wary disbelief than surprise.

"Look what the cat dragged in," was all she said and ignored him in favor of typing on her laptop. The clacking was too rhythmic to produce actual comprehensible sentences.

Faking it. For him. Warmed his heart.

"I'm taking you to lunch," he informed her. "Get your handbag and shut that thing down."

That earned her attention. She pierced him with that laser-sharp gaze he suspected had the power to drill right through his skull and read his mind like a book. "Are you this egotistical with all women? I'm shocked you ever get a second date."

"Yet I do. Have lunch with me and you'll find out why." He quirked a brow at her and pulled out the big guns. "Unless you're afraid."

She didn't scowl, didn't immediately negate the statement. Instead, she smiled and clicked the laptop closed. "Can't stand being under the spotlight, can you? If you don't like the setting I use to walk through the profile questions, just tell me."

A spontaneous and unexpected laugh shot from his mouth. Why was it such a surprise that she was on to him?

He held up both hands. "I surrender. You're right. That little room with the fish book is like being in therapy. Restaurants are more relaxed."

Elise opened a desk drawer and withdrew a brown leather bag. "Since my schedule is mysteriously clear, lunch it is. On one condition." She cocked her head, sending her dark hair swinging against her chin. "Don't evade, change the subject or try to outsmart me. Answer the questions so we can be done."

"Aww. You're not enjoying this?" He was. It was the most fun he'd had with a woman he wasn't dating in his life.

"You're quite honestly the most difficult, disturbing, contrary client I've ever dealt with." She swept passed him in a cloud of unidentifiable perfume that hit him in the solar plexus, and then she shot back over her shoulder, "Which means you're paying. But I'm driving."

He grinned and followed her to the parking lot, then slid

into the passenger seat of the sleek Corvette she motioned to. He would have opened her door, but she beat him to it.

New car smell wrapped around him. "Nice ride. I pegged you for more of a Toyota girl."

She shrugged. "Even fairy godmothers like to arrive at the ball in style."

"I'm not threatened by a woman driving, by the way." He crossed his arms so he didn't accidentally brush shoulders with Elise. The seats were really close together. Perfect for lovers. Not so good for business associates. "Just in case you were worried."

Elise selected an out-of-the-way bistro-type place without asking him and told the hostess they'd prefer to sit outside, also without his input. The wrought iron chairs and tables on the terrace added French charm and the wine list was passable, so he didn't mind. But two could play that game, so he ordered a bottle of Chianti and nodded to the waiter to pour Elise a glass whether she wanted one or not.

"To loosen you up?" she asked pertly and picked up her glass to sniff the bloodred wine with appreciation.

"Nah. To loosen you up." He dinged their rims together and watched her drink. Elise liked red wine. He filed that tidbit away. "I didn't actually agree to your condition, you know."

"I noticed. I'm banking on the fact that you're a busy man and can't continually take time away from work to finish something you don't want to be doing in the first place. So don't disappoint me. What's the difference between love, romance and sex?"

Dax choked on the wine he'd just swallowed and spent his time recovering. "Give a guy a warning before you lay that kind of question on him."

"Warning. Question imminent. Warning. Question imminent," she intoned in such a perfect robot voice, he sputtered over a second sip, laughing this time.

For an uptight matchmaker, she had an offbeat sense of humor. He liked it. More than he should. It was starting to affect his focus and the more Elise charmed him, the less he remembered why it was important to punish her for Leo's defection.

"Let's see," he said brusquely. "Fiction, Sade and yes, please."

"Excuse me?"

"The answer to your question. Love equals fiction, Sade is romantic music and critical to set the mood, and I would assume 'yes, please' is self-explanatory in relation to sex."

"That's not precisely what I was looking for."

"Then tell me what you would say. So I have an example to go by."

"You never give up, do you?"

"Took you long enough to figure that out. So?" he prompted with raised eyebrows.

She sighed. "They're intertwined so closely you can't remove one without destroying the value of the other two."

"That's a loaded statement. Tell me more before I proceed to tear it apart." He propped his chin on his hand and ignored the halibut a waiter placed in front of him, which he scarcely recalled ordering.

Her lips mushed together in apparent indecision. Or frustration. Hard to tell with her.

"You can have sex without being in love or putting on romantic music. But it's so much better with both. Without love and romance, sex is meaningless and empty."

As she warmed to the topic, her expression softened and that, plus the provocative subject matter, plus the warm breeze playing with her hair, plus...whatever it was about her that drew him all swirled together and spread like a sip of very old, very rare cognac in his chest. "Go on."

"On the flip side, you can certainly make a romantic gesture toward someone you're in love with and not end up in bed. But the fact that you've been intimate magnifies it. Makes it more romantic. See what I mean?"

"Philosophy." He nodded sagely and wondered if the thing going on inside might be a heart attack. "I see. You want to understand how I feel about the three, not give you examples. Rookie mistake. Won't happen again."

"Ha. You did it on purpose so you could probe me."

That was so close to the truth, the back of his neck heated. Next his ears would turn red and no woman got to have that strong of an effect on him. "Yeah, well, guess what? I like the spotlight. When you accused me of that earlier, it was nothing but a classic case of projection. You don't like the spotlight so you assumed that was the reason I didn't want to sit under yours."

She didn't so much as flinch. "Then what is the reason you went to such great lengths to get me out of the office?"

The shrewd glint in the depths of those chocolaty irises tipped him off that he hadn't been as slick with the schedule-clearing as he believed. Odds were, she'd also figured out that she'd hit a couple of nerves yesterday and lunch was designed to prevent that from happening again.

"That's your turf." He waved at the crowd of tables, people and ambiance. "This is mine."

"And I'm on it, with nary a peep. Cut me some slack. Tell me what your ideal mate brings to the relationship."

"A lack of interest in what's behind the curtain," he said instantly as if the answer had been there all along. Though he'd never so much as thought about the question, not once, and certainly wouldn't have told her if she hadn't made the excellent point about the turf change.

But lack of interest wasn't quite right. It was more the ability to turn a blind eye. Someone who saw through the curtain and didn't care that backstage resembled post-tornado wreckage.

Was that why he broke up with women after the standard four weeks—none thus far had that X-ray-vision-slash-blind-eye quality?

"Good." Elise scribbled in her ever-present notebook. "Now tell me what you bring to her."

When she'd called the questions intensive, she wasn't kidding. "What, presents aren't enough?"

"Don't be flip. Unless you want me to assume you bring nothing to a relationship and that's why you shy away from them." A light dawned in her eyes. "Oh. That's it, isn't it? You don't think you have anything to offer."

"Wait a minute. That's not what I said." This conversation had veered way too far off the rails for comfort.

He'd agreed to this ridiculous idea of being matched only because he never thought it would work. Instead, Elise challenged his deep-seated beliefs at every turn with a series of below-the-belt hits. That was not supposed to happen.

"Then say what you mean," she suggested quietly. "For once. If you found that woman, the one who didn't care what was behind your curtain, what do you have to offer her in return?"

"I don't know." It was the most honest answer he could give. And the most unsettling.

He shoveled food in his mouth in case she asked a follow-up question.

What *did* he have to offer in a relationship? He'd never considered it important to examine, largely because he never intended to have a relationship. But he felt deficient all at once.

"Fair enough. I get that these questions are designed to help people who are looking for love. You're not. So we'll move on to the lightning round." Her sunny tone said she knew she was letting him off the hook and it was okay.

Oddly grateful, he nodded and relaxed. "I rule at lightning rounds."

"We'll see, Mr. Wakefield. Glass half-full, or half-empty?"

"Technically, it's always full of both air and water." Her

laugh rumbled through him and he breathed a little easier. Things were clicking along at a much safer level now, and eating held more appeal.

"That's a good one. Apple or banana?"

"What is that, a Freudian question? Apple, of course."

"Actually, apples have biblical connotations. I might interpret it as you can't stay away from the tree of knowledge," she said with a smirk. "What relieves stress?"

"Sex."

She rolled her eyes. "I probably didn't need to ask that one. Do you believe in karma?"

These were easy, surface-level questions. She should have started with them. "No way. Lots of people never get what's coming to them."

"That is *so* true." She chuckled with appreciation and shook her head.

"Don't freak out but I do believe you're enjoying this after all."

Her smile slipped but she didn't look away. This might not be a date, but he couldn't deny that lunch with Elise was the most interesting experience he'd had with a woman, period. Even ones he was dating.

The longer this went on, the harder it was going to be to denounce her publicly. She was good—much better than he'd prepared for—and to criticize her abilities would likely reflect just as poorly on him as it did her.

Worse, he was afraid he'd started to like her. He should probably do something about that before she got too far under his skin.

By one o'clock, Elise's side hurt from laughing. Wine at lunch should be banned. Or required. She couldn't decide which.

"I have to get back to the office," she said reluctantly.

Reluctantly? She had a ton of things to do. And this

was lunch with Dax. Whom she hated…or rather didn't like very much. Actually, he was pretty funny and maybe a little charming. Of course he was—he had lots of practice wooing women.

Dax made a face. "Yeah. Duty calls."

He stood and gallantly took her hand, while simultaneously pulling her chair away. It was amazingly well-coordinated. Probably because he'd done it a million times.

They strolled to the car and she pretended that she didn't notice how slowly, and she didn't immediately fish her keys from her bag. Dax put his palm on the driver's-side door, leaning against it casually, so she couldn't have opened it anyway. Deliberately on his part, she was sure.

She should call him on it.

"Tomorrow, then?" he asked.

Elise shook her head. "I'm out of the office tomorrow. I have a thing with my mother."

Brenna had an appointment with a plastic surgeon in Dallas because the ones in L.A. stopped living up to her expectations. Apparently she couldn't find one who could make her look thirty again.

"All day?" Dax seemed disappointed. "You can't squeeze in an hour for me?"

No way was he disappointed. She shook her head. The wine was affecting her more than she'd thought.

"I have to pick her up from the airport and then take her to the doctor." Oh, that might have been too much information. "I need to ask for your discretion. She wouldn't like it if she knew I was talking to others about her private affairs."

"Because your mother is famous or something?"

Elise heaved a sigh. "I assumed you checked up on me and therefore already knew I was Brenna Burke's daughter. I should have kept my mouth shut."

Stupid wine.

"Brenna Burke is your mother?" Dax whistled. "I had a poster of her above my bed when I was a teenager. The one where she wore the bikini made of leaves. Good times."

"Thanks, I needed the image in my head of you fantasizing about my mother." That's precisely why she never mentioned Brenna. Not only because of the ick factor, but also because no one ever whistled over Elise. It was demoralizing. "You know she was thirty-five in that photo, right?"

Elise called it her mother's I'm-not-old stage, when the hot runway models were closer to her nine-year-old daughter's age than Brenna's, and the offers of work had all but dried up.

I should have waited to have kids, Brenna had told her. *Mistake Number One talked me into it. Being pregnant and off the circuit ruined me.*

Bitter, aging supermodels took out their frustration on those around them, including Elise's father, dubbed Mistake Number One when he grew tired of Brenna's attitude and left. Adult Elise knew all this from her psychology classes. Still hurt, even years later.

"So?" Dax sighed lustily. "I didn't care. She was smoking hot."

"Yeah. So I've been told." She feigned sudden interest in her manicure, unable to take the appreciation for her mother in Dax's expression.

"Elise." His voice held a note of…warmth. Compassion.

Somehow, he'd steered her around, spine against the car, and then he was right there, sandwiching her between his masculine presence and the Vette.

He tipped her head up with a fist and locked those smoky irises on hers and she couldn't breathe. "Tastes change. I like to think I've evolved since I was fourteen. Older women aren't so appealing anymore."

She shrugged. "Whatever. It hardly matters."

"It does." The screeches and hums of the parking lot

and chatter of other diners faded away as he cocked his head and focused on her. "I hurt your feelings. I'm sorry."

How in the world had he figured that out? Somehow, that fact alone made it easy to admit the truth. She probably couldn't have hidden it anyway. "It's hard to have a mother known for her looks when you're so average, you know?"

He shifted closer, though she would have sworn there wasn't much space between them in the first place.

"You're the least average woman I've ever met, and you know what else? Beauty fades. That's why it's important to use what's up here." He circled an index finger around her temple, oh so slowly, and the electrified feel of his touch on her skin spread through her entire body.

"That's my line," she murmured. "I went to college and started my own business because I never wanted a life where my looks mattered."

After watching her mother crash and burn with Mistake Number Two and then Three without finding the happiness she seemed to want so desperately, Elise learned early on that a relationship built on physical attraction didn't work. It also taught her that outward appearance hardly factored in matters of the heart.

Compatibility and striving to find someone who made you better were the keys to a relationship. She'd built EA International on those principles, and it hadn't failed yet.

Dax was so close; she inhaled his exotic scent on her next breath. It screamed *male—and how.*

"Me, too. Unlike your mother, I never wanted to make a career out of modeling." When her eyebrows shot up, he chuckled. "Figured you checked up on me and knew that Calvin Klein put me through college. Guess you'll be looking me up when you get home."

A lit stick of dynamite between her and the laptop couldn't stop that from happening. "My mother put me through college. Reluctantly, but I insisted."

Funny how they'd both paid for college with modeling dollars and then took similar paths to chart their own destinies. She never would have guessed they had anything in common, let alone such important guiding experiences.

Dax's gaze drifted lower and focused on her mouth. Because he was thinking about kissing her. She could read it all over his expression.

Emergency. This wasn't a date. She'd led him on somehow. They didn't like each other, and worse, he shied away from everything she desired—love, marriage, a soul mate. She was supposed to be matching him with one of her clients.

First and foremost, she'd given him permission to *ruin her business* if he didn't find the love of his life. And she was compromising the entire thing.

All of it swirled into a big black burst of panic. Had she lost her mind?

Ducking clumsily out of his semi-embrace, she smiled brightly. "So I'll call you to schedule the next session. Ready to go?"

His expression shuttered and he nodded. "Sure. I'll leave you my card with my number."

In awkward silence, they rode back to EA International where Dax's car was parked.

Despite knowing he thought happily ever after was a myth, despite knowing he faked interest in her as a method of distraction, despite knowing he stood to lose $500,000 and pretended to misunderstand her questions or refused to answer them strictly to prevent it—despite all that, she'd wanted him to kiss her.

Dax Wakefield was better at seducing a woman than she'd credited.

When Elise got to her office, she locked the door and sank into the chair. Her head fell forward into her cupped palms, too wined-and-Daxed to stay upright any longer. If he flipped her out this much without laying those gorgeously defined lips on hers, how much worse would it be if he'd actually done it?

She couldn't take another session with him.

Match him now.

She had enough information. Dax might have thought he was being sneaky by probing her for answers to the questions in kind but he'd revealed more about himself in the getting there than he likely realized.

While the match program booted up, Elise stuck a stick of gum in her mouth in hopes it would stave off the intense desire for chocolate. She always craved chocolate, but it was worse when she was under stress.

Maybe she should take a page from Dax and relieve her stress with sex.

But not with him. No sir.

Almost of their own accord, her fingers keyed his name into the browser. Provocative photos spilled onto the screen of a younger Dax with washboard abs and formfitting briefs scarcely covering the good parts. Her mouth went dry. The man was a former underwear model with a psychology degree, a wicked sense of humor and a multibillion-dollar media empire.

Who in the world did she have in her system to match *that*?

Usually she had a pretty good idea who the match would be ahead of time. One of the benefits of administering the profile sessions herself—she knew her clients very well.

A slice of fear ripped through her. What if the program couldn't find a match? It happened occasionally. The algorithms were so precise that sometimes clients had to wait a few months, until she entered new clients.

Dax would never accept that excuse. He'd call foul and claim victory right then and there. Either he'd crow about proving Elise a sham or worse, claim she'd withheld the name on purpose to avoid the fallout when the match wasn't the love of his life.

Newly determined, she shut down the almost-naked pictures of Dax and flipped to the profile screen. She flew through the personal information section and consulted her notes before starting on the personality questions.

That went easily, too. In fact, she didn't even have to glance at the scribbled words in her notebook.

Do you want to be in love? She typed yes. He did, he just hadn't found the right person yet, or he wouldn't have agreed to be matched. Plus, she'd watched his face when he described a woman who didn't care about whatever he hid behind his curtain. That man wanted to connect really, really badly with someone who got him.

How do you sabotage relationships? She snorted and typed "by only dating women he has no chance of falling in love with."

When she reached the last question, she breathed a sigh of relief. Not so bad. Thank goodness she wouldn't have to see him again. A quick phone call to set up his first meet with the match and she'd be done with Dax Wakefield.

She hit Save and ran the match algorithm. Results came back instantly. Fantastic. She might even treat herself to half a carton of Chunky Monkey as a reward. She clicked on the pop-up link and Dax's match was…*Elise Arundel*.

No! She blinked, but the letters didn't change.

That was so wrong, she couldn't even put words together to say how wrong.

She ran the compiler again. *Elise Arundel.*

Stomach cramping with dread, she vised her temples. That's what she got for not asking him all the questions. For letting her professional ethics slide away in the wake of the whirlwind named Dax.

He'd think she did it on purpose—because she'd started

to fall for his slick charm. If she actually told him she was his match, he'd smirk with that knowing glint in his eyes and…

She'd skewed the results. That had to be it. Talk about your Freudian slipups—she'd been thinking about the almost-kiss and the almost-naked pictures and his laugh and thus answered the questions incorrectly.

Besides, the short, fat girl inside could never be enough to change Dax Wakefield's mind about love. She had to match him with someone else.

Her fingers shook and she could hardly type, but those answers had to change. He didn't want to be in love. Total projection on her part to say that he did, exactly as he'd accused her of earlier. She fixed that one, then the next one and eventually worked her way back through the profile

There. She clicked Run and shut her eyes.

This time, the pop-up opened to reveal…Candace Waters.

Perfect. Candy was a gorgeous blonde with a high-school education. Dax would love running intellectual circles around her and Candy liked football. They'd get along famously.

No one ever had to know Elise had nearly screwed up.

Four

When an unrecognized number flashed on Dax's phone, he almost didn't answer it.

Instead of working, as he should be, he'd been watching his phone, hoping Elise might call today.

He couldn't get that moment against the car out of his head, that brief flicker in her gaze that said she didn't hate him anymore and better yet, didn't see him as a match to be pawned off on some other female. Before he'd had time to explore what she did feel, she'd bolted, leaving him to wonder if he'd imagined it.

He should call her already. It was only a conversation to schedule the next session, which would likely be the last. What was the big deal about calling? It wasn't as if she'd answer the main line at EA International anyway. He could schedule the appointment through Angie and go on with his day.

The quicker they finished the sessions, the closer Elise would be to be finding him a match, at which point he'd prove beyond a shadow of a doubt that Elise's matchmaking service fronted as a school for gold diggers. Then, the cold place inside that had developed during the rift with Leo could be warmed nicely by the flames of EA International roasting on the morning news.

A prospect that held less and less appeal the more time he spent with Elise.

The dilemma ate at him, and if he didn't see her again, he didn't have to think about it. That's why he didn't call.

But Dax answered his phone, mentally preparing to spiel off a contract's status or sales figures—pending the caller's identification. "Wakefield."

"It's Elise Arundel." The smooth syllables hit him in all the right places. "Do you have a few minutes?"

He should have called her. Elise had a sexy phone voice.

Grinning like a loon for who knew what reason, Dax settled back in his chair and put his feet out. "Depends on what for. If it's lightning round two, yes."

Elise's chuckle was a little on the nervous side. "I'm afraid that's not the reason for my call. Actually, I have good news on that front. More sessions aren't required after all. I've got your match."

Oh, wow. This thing had just become nauseatingly real.

"Already? That is good news," Dax said heartily. It *was* good news. The best. He didn't have to see Elise again, exactly as he wanted.

And a little voice inside was singing, *Liar, liar, pants on fire.*

"So," Elise chimed in quickly, "I'm calling to set up your first meet with your match, Candace. She prefers to be called Candy, though."

"Candy." That was something you ate, not someone you dated, and sounded suspiciously like a name for a coed. "She's legal, right?"

"You mean is she over the age of eighteen?" Elise's withering tone put the grin back on his face. "What kind of matchmaker do you take me for? She's twenty-eight and works as a paralegal for Browne and Morgan."

"Just checking. What's the drill? I'm supposed to call her and set up a date or something?"

"That's up to you. I've emailed her picture to you, and

I've sent yours to her. If you're both agreeable to meeting, I'd be happy to coordinate or you can go it alone from here."

Curiosity got the best of him and he shouldered the phone to his ear so he could click through his email. There it was—"Sender: Elise Arundel, Subject: Candace Waters." He opened it and a picture of Candy popped onto the screen.

Holy hell. She was *gorgeous*. Like men-falling-over-themselves-to-get-her-a-drink gorgeous. Not at all what he was expecting. "Is she one of your makeover success stories?"

If so, Elise might have a bit more magic in her wand than he'd credited.

"Not everyone is in need of a makeover. Candy came to me as is."

Nice. Not a gold digger then. He took a closer look. She was blonde-with-a-capital-B, wearing a wicked smile that promised she had the moves to back it up. He would have noticed her across the room in a heartbeat.

For the first time, he got an inkling that this whole deal might be legitimate. "She'll do."

Then he returned to planet earth. There was a much greater chance that Candy had something really wrong with her if she'd resorted to a matchmaker to find a date.

"I had a feeling you'd like her," Elise said wryly. "She's perfect for you."

Because something was really wrong with him too?

Elise was obviously running around wielding her psychology degree like a blunt instrument. She'd probably come up with all kinds of bogus analyses about his inability to commit and his mama issues—bogus because he didn't have a problem committing as long as the thing had Wakefield Media stamped on it. Females were a different story. He'd die before letting a woman down the way his mother had let down his father, and he'd never met someone worth making that kind of promise to.

No doubt Elise had warned Candy about what she'd gotten herself into. Maybe she'd given Candy hints about how to get under his skin. Elise certainly had figured out how to do that well enough. And of course Elise had a vested interest in making sure Candy made him happy. This woman he'd been matched with might even be a plant. Some actress Elise had paid to get him to fall in love with her.

That…*schemer*.

Thank God he never had to see Elise again. A paralegal sounded like a blessed reprieve from razor-sharp matchmakers with great legs.

"I'll call her. Then I expect you'll want a full report afterward, right?"

The line went dead silent.

"Still there, Elise?"

"Not a *full* report."

"About whether she's my soul mate. Get your mind out of the gutter."

For some reason, that made Elise laugh and muscles he hadn't realized were tense relaxed.

"Yeah, I do want that report. I guess we never really laid down the ground rules of how this deal was going to go. Do we need an unbiased third party to verify the results?"

A judge? Suddenly, he felt like a bug pinned to cork. "The fewer people involved in this, the better. I'll call you afterward and we'll go from there. How's that?"

"Uncomplicated. I can get on board with that. Have a good time with Candy. Talk to you later."

The line went dead for the second time and Dax immediately saved Elise's number to his contacts. It gave him a dark little kick to have the matchmaker's phone number when she'd been so adamantly against giving it to him.

Then he dialed Candy's number, which Elise had included with the picture. His perverse gene wanted to find out if Candy was on the up-and-up. If Elise had hired someone to date him, he'd cry foul so fast it would make her head spin. And he'd never admit it was exactly what he'd have done.

Dax handed the valet his Audi's key fob and strolled into the wine bar Candy had selected for their first meet. She wasn't difficult to find—every eye in the room was on the sultry blonde perched on a bar stool.

Then every eye in the room turned to fixate on him as he moved forward to buss Candy on the cheek. "Hi. Nice place."

They'd conversed on the phone a couple of times. She had a pleasant voice and seemed sane, so here they were.

She peered up at him out of china doll–blue eyes that were a little less electric in person than they'd been on his laptop screen. No big deal. Her sensual vibe definitely worked for his Pleasure Principle—she'd feel good, all right, and better the second time.

"You look exactly like your picture," she said, her voice a touch breathier than it had been on the phone. "I thought you'd swiped it from a magazine and you'd turn out to be average-looking. I'm glad I was wrong."

Dax knew what reflected back at him in the mirror; he wasn't blind, and time had been kind to his features. It was stupid to be disappointed that she'd commented on his looks first. But why did his cheekbones have to be the first thing women noticed about him?

Most women. He could have been wearing a paper bag over his head for all the notice Elise had taken of his outward appearance. One of the first things she'd said to him was that he was lonely.

And as Candy blinked at him with a hint of coquettishness, he experienced an odd sense of what Elise meant. Until a woman ripped that curtain back and saw the man underneath the skin, it was all just going through the motions. And Dax dated women incapable of penetrating his cynical hide.

How had he just realized that?

And how *dare* Elise make him question his dating philosophy? If she was so smart, why hadn't she figured out he was dating the wrong women?

Besides, he wasn't. The women he dated were fine. Ms. Arundel was *not* ruining this date with her psychobabble.

He slid into the vacant bar stool next to Candy, swiveled it toward her and gave her his best, most practiced smile. It always knocked 'em dead. "You look like your picture, too. Have you ever modeled?"

Dax signaled to the bartender to bring a wine menu and tapped the Chilean red without glancing at it for more than a moment. Ordering wine was a necessary skill and he'd had plenty of opportunity to develop it. Regardless of whether this woman was his soul mate or Elise's accomplice, she'd appreciate his taste.

She nodded. "Since I was fourteen. Regional print mostly, department stores, catalogs, that kind of thing. Celebrities took over cosmetics so I never had a chance there, but eventually all the offers stopped. My mom made me get a job with benefits when I turned twenty-five."

It had been a throwaway question, one you asked a woman as a compliment, but she'd taken it seriously, reeking of sincerity as she'd talked. "So you're a paralegal now?"

She wrinkled her nose and laughed. The combination was cute. Not perky cheerleader let-me-make-you-a-cupcake cute. Actually, it wasn't so cute at all, in retrospect.

"Yes, I research legal briefs all day," she said. "It's not what I imagined myself doing, but it was so hard to find a job. If a woman interviewed me, I got shown the door immediately. Men were worse. You can bet they made it clear the job was mine if I agreed to 'after hours' work."

Candy shuddered delicately and Dax had no problem interpreting what "after hours" meant. "Discrimination at its finest."

"Most people think it's a nice problem to have. It's not. I get so beat down by people who judge me by my looks." Crossing her legs casually, Candy leaned forward and rested an elbow on the bar to casually dangle her hand an inch above Dax's knee. "That's why I signed up with EA International. I can't meet men the traditional way."

Her body language screamed *I'm into you*. The benefit of understanding human psychology—people rarely surprised him. And Candy was legit. He'd stake his life on it.

"I get that. Who wants to meet someone in a crowded bar, knowing they only came up and talked to you because of your face?" Dax sipped his wine and realized somewhere along the way, he'd actually relaxed. He was on a date with a nice, attractive woman and they had several things in common. It was comfortable ground. "You like football?"

"Sure. It's mindless, you know? Easy to follow."

He did know. That was why he liked it, too. Wakefield Media took 99 percent of his gray matter on a regular basis; it was fantastic to veg out on Sundays, the one day a week he didn't focus on work. "We should catch a game sometime."

Elise might very well be legit, too. Candy was exactly his type, almost to the letter. Dax's neck went a little hot. Wasn't that an interesting turnabout? People in general might not surprise him, but Elise almost never failed to.

"I'd like that." Candy smiled widely enough to display a mouthful of expensively capped teeth. "Tailgating is my favorite part. It's like a six-hour party every Saturday and Sunday."

Dax liked a good party. But *six-hour* parties…every Saturday *and* Sunday? "You watch college ball too?"

"I guess. Is that who plays on Sundays? I forget which one is which. I, um, actually don't watch the game most of the time." Laughing, she shook her head carefully so that strands of hair brushed her bare shoulders and drew attention to her cleavage simultaneously. It was impressive. And it was his turn to give her some signals in kind. He knew this dance well.

Candy's phone beeped. His was on silent, which he considered an unbreakable date rule. Obviously she didn't subscribe to it.

"Oh, pardon me," she tittered in that fake way designed to make it seem like an accident her phone wasn't off, when it was anything but. "I have to check in with my friend so she knows you didn't slip something in my drink and drag me ino a dark alley."

"No problem."

Okay, she got a pass on that one. It did make sense to be safe.

As she thumbed back a reply and then another one, Dax glanced at his own phone while his date texted with her girlfriend.

He had a couple of texts himself. As Candy was still facedown in her phone—likely sending messages to her female posse about Dax with the words "delish" and "rich" in all caps—he glanced at his own messages. They were both from Elise and, for some reason, that made him grin.

How's it going?

Must be going well since you're not answering.

His smile widened as he responded: She's great.

And left it at that. Elise could wait for her full report. While Candy finished texting what must be half the female population of Dallas, Dax sipped his wine and amused himself by imagining a certain matchmaker cooling her jets as she waited for additional details. Which he wasn't going to give her until he was good and ready.

* * *

Elise sat on her hands so she couldn't tap out a reply. Dax was on a date with Candy and she had no business bothering him with inane text messages.

But there was so much riding on this. Of all the women in her database, Candace Waters had the best shot at keeping Dax from vilifying Elise's company. Well, and obviously she wanted Candy to find the love of her life too. Dax was charming, sinfully hot even with his clothes on, and quick on the draw with that intelligent sense of humor. What wasn't to like? If you were into that kind of man, which Candy totally should be.

But what if Dax didn't like Candy? "She's great" didn't really say a whole lot, but then they'd only just met. Elise had to give them both a chance to find out more about each other and trust the process that she herself had created.

To keep her hands busy, she tried typing up copy for an ad campaign that needed to go out immediately. January was just around the corner, which was traditionally a demanding time for EA International. The one-two punch of Christmas and then Valentine's Day got people motivated to find someone special.

Once Dax grilled Candy for all her personal history and figured out what she'd like, what kind of Christmas gift would he buy her?

Yeah, the ad copy wasn't working as a distraction either.

She grabbed her phone and texted Dax back: That's it? Great? Do you like her?

In agony, she stared at the phone waiting for the reply. Nothing.

Dax was ignoring her. On purpose. Not sending a message was as pointed a message as actually sending one.

Butt out, her blank screen said.

Now she really had to stop obsessing. She pushed the

button to power off the phone and tossed it on the couch where she couldn't see it.

Maybe she should comb through some applications for her makeover program. Juliet had been such a challenge and then such a triumph, Elise hadn't taken on a new project yet. There were so many deserving applicants, from the one who'd been caring for her three younger brothers after the death of their parents, to another who'd been in the foster care system her whole life and just wanted to find someone who would love her forever.

Decision made, Elise sat down in her home office to contact them both. These two women had stayed on her mind for a reason, and she could handle two houseguests at the same time. Dannie would help out with the hair and makeup sessions, and after the infusion of cash from Prince Alain's match fee, Elise could afford to feed and clothe two women for a couple of months.

She never charged for her makeover services, instead choosing to gift these destitute women with new lives. Elise's magic wand might be the only opportunity they would have to succeed.

Done. She glanced at the time as she saved the women's information to EA International's database using a remote connection. Eight whole minutes had passed.

Why was she so *antsy?*

Because she'd butchered Dax's profile questions the first time. What if she'd messed it up the second time and Candy wasn't really his soul mate?

Armed with a bowl of grapes and a tall glass of ice water, she opened the algorithm code, grimly determined to sort through how it had arrived at the original match so she could reasonably conclude if it had completed the second match correctly.

After fifteen minutes of wishing the grapes were chocolate and staring at code until her eyes crossed, she couldn't stand it. Retrieving her phone from its place of banishment, she powered it on. And powered it off before it fully booted up.

What was she doing? She might as well drive to the restaurant and peer through the window like a stalker. And worse, she had a feeling she might have done exactly that if she had a clue where Dax and Candy had met.

Ridiculous. She'd check for text messages once and then find a movie or something to watch.

She powered on the phone. Nothing.

That…*man*. She couldn't think of a bad enough word to encapsulate how infuriating Dax Wakefield was. He knew how much this meant to her. Knew she was on pins and needles. How hard would it have been to type, "She's beautiful and fun. I like her a lot"?

Not hard. He wasn't doing it because ignoring Elise was part of the game, to make her think the date was going from bad to worse, so she'd sit here and stew about losing.

In reality, he was laughing it up with Candy, having an awesome time drinking red wine and talking about their similar interests. Right now, he was probably watching her over his wineglass with those smoky bedroom eyes and somehow getting Candy to admit things she'd never told anyone before.

Maybe they'd moved to the parking lot and Dax had Candy cornered against her car, breathless and…that was going too far for a first date. They should be taking things slowly, not jumping right into something physical, the way Dax most assuredly did with all his previous women.

Immediately, Elise pulled up the text app: Candy doesn't go all the way on a first date.

She groaned. Dax had officially fried her brain. She hit the delete button.

Oh, God, had she just hit Send? *Please, please, please*, she prayed, hoping against hope she'd deleted the message as she'd meant to, and scoured her phone's folders for the answer.

Which she instead got in the form of a message from Dax: Speaking from personal experience?

Her stomach flopped at the same time she laughed, quite against her will. He'd made the faux pas okay and comical in one shot. How did he *do* that?

At least she'd gotten him to respond. She replied: You specified no one-night stands. She's in it for the long haul.

Dax: I wouldn't have called her otherwise.

That flopped her stomach in a different way. If this worked, Dax and Candy might very well get married. Most of the couples she matched did. She was in the business of introducing soul mates, after all.

Why did the thought of Dax and Candy falling blissfully in love make Elise want to cry?

The prospect of another round of holidays alone coupled with the stress of dealing with Dax—that was it. They were both killing her. Slowly.

And…if someone as cynical about relationships as Dax found his happily ever after, what did it say that she couldn't find hers?

Five

Candy laughed again and launched into another convoluted story about her dog. Dax was more than a little sorry he'd asked if she had any hobbies. Who knew a dog could be a hobby? Or that a grown woman would actually shop for outfits for said dog?

He signaled the bartender for another round and not for the first time, his attention wandered.

She finally wrapped up her monologue and leaned forward to give him an eyeful of her strategically exposed cleavage, which meant he wasn't paying enough attention to her. It was the fourth time she'd done it in thirty minutes, not that he was counting. Her signals were just so uncomplicated and easy to read.

Despite Elise's warning to the contrary, Candy was most definitely open to ending the night skin-on-skin. She would be energetic and creative in bed and yeah, it would be pleasurable.

But in the morning, she'd wake up intending to pursue a long-term, very serious relationship. Big difference from his usual dates. Regardless, he should embrace the spirit of what Elise had set up here, so when it failed, his conscience was clear.

Time to pay attention to his date. After all, she was supposed to be his soul mate. She certainly had a distinct lack of interest in what was going on behind his curtain. Likely she hadn't noticed he had one.

Giving Candy another practiced smile, he nodded to the door and stood, palm extended. "Shall we find a place to have a bite to eat?"

It was how these things worked—if drinks went well, you asked the woman to dinner. If not, you said you'd call her and escaped. Not that he'd claim drinks had gone particularly well, but maybe over dinner Candy would reveal some hidden depths he couldn't resist.

Without bothering to play coy, she took his hand and slid off the bar stool, rising to her full height. "I'd love to."

Jeez, her legs were long. Too long. She was almost as tall as Dax.

"Pardon me while I powder my nose," she said, and turned to sway across the room with a one-two gait.

Dax was meant to think it was sexy. He *should* think it was sexy. But, all at once, nothing about Candy seemed sexy. The lady had moves and a clear interest in demonstrating them. She was exactly the type of woman he went for in a big way. Something was broken here.

His phone vibrated in his pocket, distracting him totally from Candy's departure. His lips curled up involuntarily. He pulled it out, expecting to see another text from Elise. Which it was.

I hope you're not checking your messages in front of Candy. Because that would be rude.

He laughed, painfully aware it was the first genuine amusement he'd felt all evening. He hit Reply: Then stop texting me.

Elise: .

He groaned through another laugh. A blank message. Her sense of humor slayed him.

Candy materialized in front of him far sooner than expected. "Ready?" she said.

"Sure." He pocketed his phone and followed his date out into the chilly night. She didn't have a coat, deliberately of course, so Dax could offer her his. Then she'd accidentally-on-purpose leave something in the pocket—lipstick, an earring; it varied from woman to woman—so she'd have an excuse to call him.

He shrugged out of his jacket anyway and handed it to her, earning a grateful smile as she slung it around her shoulders.

That's what he had to offer in a relationship—a coat. Nothing more. And it wasn't fair to Candy, who came into this date thinking there might be a possibility of something magical. The back of his neck heated. If Candy was his soul mate, she deserved better.

This was jacked up. He never should have called her. But how else could he have handled this? To prove Elise ran a sham business, he had to go on the date. Who knew said date would be exactly like every other date he'd ever been on, which had worked quite well for a long time, and yet not feel right?

As they walked to the valet stand, Candy stumbled, just a little and with practiced grace. Dax rolled his eyes even as he slung a steadying arm around her waist. She peered up at him in invitation. *Kiss me and let's get this party started,* she said without saying a word.

He could have scripted this date ahead of time and not missed a trick. Wearily, he eyed Candy's plumped lips, knew how good it would feel when she melted into him. On paper, they made sense together, for the short term anyway.

And he had no interest in her whatsoever. The perfect woman wasn't so perfect. What was *wrong* with him?

Elise was wrong with him. She'd set him up on a date with a woman who had all these long-term, soul-mate, mumbo-jumbo expectations and it was seriously cramping his style.

And okay, it pricked at his conscience too. Which had picked a fine time to surface.

Elise had ruined his ability to have fun on a date. She'd pay for that.

"I'm sorry, Candy, but this isn't going to work out."

"Oh." Candy straightened, her face hardening. "But we were matched. By Elise. I was really happy with her choice. But you're not?"

Obviously she'd not been clued in that this date was also part of an experiment. And a wager. Yet another mark against Elise.

"She did a great job matching us. You're exactly the kind of woman I like."

"Then what's the problem?"

"I'm not interested in a relationship, and it would be unfair to you for us to continue." The standard excuse rolled from his tongue.

"You forgot to say it's not you, it's me." Candy had obviously heard the excuse before too. She flung his jacket at him with surprising force. "Thanks for the drinks. Have a nice life."

She flounced to the valet and tapped her foot while the uniformed kid raced to get her car. Then she roared out of the parking lot with a screech.

Not only had Elise ruined him, she'd set him up in a catch-22. There was no way he could have fallen for Candy, not when it meant he'd lose the wager. Plus, all of Elise's profile questions kept getting in the way, making him think about his intentions. *That* was the problem, not the sound bite he'd spieled off to Candy.

The valet pulled Dax's car into the lane and hopped out. Dax slipped him a folded bill and got behind the wheel. The closer he drove to his loft, the deeper his blood boiled. Thanks to a certain matchmaker, he'd be spending yet another night alone, his least favorite thing to do.

He pulled onto a side street and hit the call button on his phone before checking the time. Almost nine.

Elise answered on the first ring, so he didn't worry about interrupting her plans too much.

"Expecting my call?" he said with as much irony as he could. She must have been sitting there watching her phone like a hawk. On a Friday night. Looked like Elise could use a bit of her own magic to find a date.

"Um, yeah," she said, her voice husky as though she'd been running laps, and it sent heat to his blood in a whole different way. "You said you'd give me the full report. Isn't this it?"

He'd totally forgotten about that, but it was absolutely the reason for his call now. "Text me your address. It's an in-person kind of report."

He ended the call and an instant later, the message appeared.

Who said I was at home?

She was *not* allowed to make him laugh when he was still so furious with her.

The address came through a moment later and the grin popped out before he'd realized it. *Let's rock and roll, Ms. Arundel.*

Looked like he wouldn't be returning to his empty loft just yet after all.

Elise answered the door of her uptown condo wearing jeans and a soft yellow sweater, all perky and cupcake-y though she'd only had a few minutes' warning before Dax appeared on her front porch. He tried really hard to not notice how the sweater brought out gold highlights in her eyes. He was mad at her for…something.

"That was fast," she said and raised her eyebrows in that cool, infuriating way that said she had his number. "Did you observe the speed limit at any point on your way here?"

"Gonna give me a ticket?" He crossed his arms and leaned a shoulder on the door frame, because she'd very pointedly not invited him in. That was okay. The view was pretty good from here.

"No, a guess. The date must not have gone well if you were in that much of a hurry to get here."

"You think I wanted to see you instead?"

How had she arrived at that conclusion?

But then hadn't he compared Candy to Elise all night and never found a thing in Candy's favor? Hadn't he anticipated this showdown with Elise during the drive over and looked forward to it far more than he'd anticipated having a naked Candy in his arms?

Well, it was stupid to pretend otherwise, regardless of how ridiculous it sounded. The facts spoke for themselves. He'd wanted to see Elise. He liked baiting her.

She stared at him as if he'd grown an extra nose. "No, ding-dong. Because you wanted to lord it over me that I didn't match you with your soul mate."

"Yeah." He nodded by rote and mentally kicked himself. *Ding-dong.* It might be funny if it wasn't so true. "That's why I sped over here. To tell you Candy was perfect, but it didn't work out."

Perfect for the man he'd shown Elise, anyway. She'd failed to dig beneath the surface and find the perfect woman for the man behind the curtain. *Not as good as you think you are, huh, Ms. Hocus-Pocus?*

Elise cocked her head, contemplating him. "I know she's perfect. I matched you with her. But you never really gave it a chance, did you?"

No point in pretending on that front. "What do you want me to say, Elise? I never made any bones about the fact that I'm not interested in a relationship."

No, that wasn't entirely true. He wasn't interested in a relationship with anyone he'd ever met and part of him was disappointed Elise hadn't pulled someone out of her hat who could change his mind.

But that would have been impossible because she didn't exist.

Dax sighed, weary all of a sudden. "Look, the idea of true love is as bogus as the idea of feeding a bunch of data into a program and expecting something magical to come out."

The porch light highlighted a strange shadow in her expression. "It's not magic. The algorithm is incredibly complex."

"I'm sure the software company told you that when they sold it to you but there's no way a developer can be that precise with intangibles. Admit it, you're—"

"I wrote the program," she interrupted, so softly he had strain to hear her.

Then the words sank in and he forgot all about getting her to admit the matches were actually just random pairings. "*You* wrote the program? You have a psychology degree."

The shadows deepened in her expression and he felt like crap for opening his mouth without censor. He'd hurt her feelings, not once but twice. At what point had she started to care what he thought of her?

"I do have a psychology degree. A master's. My bachelor's degree is in computer science."

"A *master's?*"

"That's right." Her jaw tightened. "I almost went on for the PhD in psychology but decided to take the plunge with EA International instead. I can always go back to school later."

"But…you wrote the program?"

She might very well be the sharpest woman he'd ever met. And not just because she'd earned an advanced degree. Because she defied his expectations in ways he'd only begun to appreciate.

Her slight form held a wealth of secrets, things he'd never imagined might lie beneath the surface. Things he'd never dreamed would be so stimulating—intellectually *and* physically. After an incredibly frustrating night in the company of an inane woman who dressed dogs for fun, he wanted to uncover every fascinating bit of Elise Arundel.

"Is it *really* so hard to believe?" She crossed her arms, closing herself off from him. It was way past time for a heartfelt apology.

"It's not that I don't believe it, it's just so incredibly sexy." That was not even close to an apology and he needed to shut up, like yesterday. "I mean, I wasn't kidding. Brains turn me on."

Her eyebrows drew together. "Really? Because I have one in a jar on my kitchen counter. I've never found it particularly attractive but to each his own."

In a spectacularly unappealing combo, he snorted and laughed at the same time. "Wait. You're kidding, right?"

She rolled her eyes, but a suspicious tug at her lips told him she was having a hard time not laughing. "I do not now, nor have I ever, had a pickled brain in my possession."

"It was worth the clarification." A host of things unsaid passed between them, most of them indecipherable. He wanted to unscramble her in the worst way. "How bad is to admit that a conversation about pickled brains is the most scintillating one I've had this evening?"

With a sigh, Elise butted the door all the way open with the flat of her hand. "You better come in. I have a feeling I need to be sitting down for the full report."

Inside—exactly where he wanted to be, but not to discuss Candy. Dax trailed the matchmaker through a classically decorated condo with rich, jewel-toned accents. "So this is where all the magic happens?"

"The women who go through my makeover program stay here, yes." Elise flopped on the sofa, clearly unconcerned about appearing graceful.

She had no pretense. It was almost as if she didn't care whether he found her attractive. She wasn't even wearing lipstick. The only time he'd ever seen a woman without lipstick was after he'd kissed it off. Women of his acquaintance always put their best face forward.

But Elise hadn't invited him in for any sort of behind-closed-doors activities. She wanted the lowdown on his date with another woman. This was like sailing through uncharted waters during a hurricane.

Slightly off stride, he sank into the plush armchair near the couch.

"Tell me what happened with Candy," she instructed without preamble. "Every last detail. I have to know precisely what didn't work, if anything did work, more abou—"

"Whoa. Why do you have to know all that?" That bug-on-cork feeling was back and on a Friday night in the company of an interesting woman, no variation of this conversation sounded like it would lead to the kind of fun he'd rather be having.

Her stare was nothing short of withering. "So I can get it right the second time."

"What second time?"

"I promised to match you with the love of your life. Admittedly, I like to get it right the first time, but I'm okay with one mistake. Two is unacceptable. So I need details."

Another date? He almost groaned. Somehow he'd thought they could let that lie, at least for a blessed hour or two. The wager was over. She'd lost. Didn't she realize that?

"Elise…"

She gazed across the coffee table separating them, and he couldn't do it. Couldn't denounce her as a fraud, couldn't tell her flat out that she wasn't the fairy godmother she seemed to think she was, couldn't stand the thought of hurting her feelings again.

Then there was the whole problem of this strange draw he felt every time he thought about Elise. Without this mission of hers to match him with his mythical soul mate, he'd have no excuse to see her again, and the thought made him twitchy.

She held up her hand in protest. "I know what you're going to say. You don't kiss and tell. I'm not asking you to."

"I didn't kiss Candy. And that wasn't what I was going to say."

"You didn't kiss her?" Elise looked a little shocked. "Why not?"

"Because I didn't like her. I only kiss women I like."

"But the other day at the bistro, you almost kissed *me*. I know you were about to. Don't bother to deny it."

As Dax did actually know the value of silence on occasion, he crossed his arms and waited until all the columns in her head added up. A blush rose on her cheeks. Really, he shouldn't enjoy that so much.

And he probably shouldn't have admitted he liked her. Not even to himself, but definitely not to her. Too late now.

"Stop being ridiculous," she said. "All this talk about how I'm sexy because I wrote a computer program and trying to throw me off balance with cryptic comments designed to make me believe you like me—it's not going to work."

She thought he was lying. Better yet, she thought he'd told her those things for nefarious purposes, as a way to manipulate her, and she wanted to be clear there was no chance of her falling for it. If he hadn't liked her already, that alone would have clinched it, and hell if he knew why.

Thoroughly intrigued, he leaned forward, elbows on his knees. "What exactly am I working here?"

"The same thing you've been working since moment

one. Distraction. If I'm all flustered and thinking about you kissing me, I'll mess up and match you with the wrong woman. Then I lose. It's brilliant, actually."

And instantly, he hit his stride. The wager, the full report he'd come to deliver, soul mates and matches—all of it got shoved to the back burner in favor of the gem buried in Elise's statement.

He zeroed right in on the kicker. "You're thinking about kissing me?"

Kissing Dax was, in fact, *all* Elise had been thinking about.

Did they make human muzzles? Because she needed one. "I said you were *trying* to get me to think about it. So I'd be distracted. It doesn't work."

Because she didn't need to think about kissing him to be distracted. That had happened the moment she'd opened the door to all that solid masculinity encased in a well-cut body. She didn't know for sure that he still had the washboard abs. But it was a safe bet. And it was easy to fantasize about when she already had a handy image emblazoned across her mind's eye of him half-naked.

Casually, Dax pulled at the sleeve of his date-night suit, which shouldn't have looked so different on him than what he'd worn all the other times she'd seen him. But it was clearly custom-made from gorgeous silk, and in it, he somehow he managed to look delicious and dangerous at the same time.

"Really," he said. It was a statement, not a question, as though he didn't believe her.

Probably because he knew she was skirting the truth. Why had she invited him in? Or given him her address in the first place? This was her sanctuary, and she rarely allowed anyone to intrude.

Dax got a pass because she *had* messed up. "You can't

distract me. I've got a one-track mind and it's set on finding the perfect woman for you. Candy wasn't it. I get that.
But her name came up due to the unorthodox profile sessions. We have to do the last one and do it the right way."

For all the good it would do. Who else did she have
in her database to match with Dax? Mentally, she sorted
through the candidates and tried to do some of the percent-
ages in her head.

And forgot how to add as a slow smile spread across his
face, heavy with promise and a side of wicked. "Shall we
put that to the test?"

"Um…" Her brain went a little fuzzy as he pierced her
with those smoky eyes and raked heat through her abdomen
without moving an inch. "Put what to the test?"

Then he stirred and she wished he'd stayed still.

He flowed to his feet and resettled next to her on the
couch. "Whether I can distract you or not."

Barely a finger width separated them and she held her
breath because oh my God, he smelled like sin and salva-
tion and she had the worst urge to nuzzle behind his ear.

This was not part of the deal. She was *not* attracted
to Dax Wakefield. It was unthinkable, unacceptable. She
had no experience with a predatory man who had a new
woman in his bed more often than he replaced his tube of
toothpaste.

How could this have happened? Did her previously co-
matose libido not understand what a player this man was?
How greatly he disdained long-term commitment and true
love?

The man was her lonely heart's worst nightmare
wrapped in a delectable package. She might as well hand
him a mallet and lie down at his feet so he could get to
smashing her insides flat right away.

He was meant for his true soul mate, who would be the
right woman to change his mind about love. Elise was not it.

Pulse hammering, she stared him down, praying he couldn't actually see her panic swirling. Now would be a great time for some pithy comeback to materialize in her fuzzy brain, but then he slipped his hand under hers and raised it to his lips.

Her fingertips grazed his mouth and his eyelids drifted lower, as if he found it pleasurable. Fascinating. Little old Elise Arundel could make a walking deity like Dax feel pleasure. Who would have thought?

Watching her intently, he pursed his lips and sucked, ever so slightly, on her index finger, and the answering tug between her legs wasn't so slight. Honeyed warmth radiated outward, flushing over her skin, and a hitch in her lungs made it hard to catch a breath.

"What are you doing?" she asked hoarsely.

"Seeing what you taste like," he murmured and slid her hand across his stubbly jaw, holding it against his skin. "And it was good enough to want more."

Before she could blink, his head inclined and his lips trailed across hers, nibbling lightly, exploring, teasing, until he found what must have been the angle he sought. Instantly, their mouths fused into a ragingly hot kiss.

Elise's long-dormant body thundered to life and broke into a rousing rendition of the Hallelujah Chorus.

His hands cupped her neck, tilting her head back so he could take it deeper. Hot and rough, his tongue slicked across hers, and she felt strong responding licks deep in her core. A cry rose up in her throat and came out as a moan.

Those strong and deft hands drifted lower on her back, dipping under the hem of her sweater, spreading across her bare skin at the arch of her waist.

Stop right there.

He did.

She really wished he'd kept going.

They both shifted closer, twining like vines. Then he

pushed with his palm against the small of her back and shoved her torso into his. Oh, my, it was hard against the roused tips of her breasts, which were sensitive enough to feel him through layers of cloth.

This wasn't the PG-rated kiss she'd been thinking about since the almost-kiss of the parking lot. This one had *rated R* slapped all over it. Fisting great wads of his shirt in her hands, she clung to him as he kissed her, shamelessly reveling in it, soaking up every second.

Until she remembered this was all designed as a distraction.

Pulling away was harder than it should have been. Chest rising and falling rapidly, she put a foot of couch between them. Not enough. She hit the floor and kept going, whirling only when the coffee table was between her and the hot-tongued man on the couch.

"Good kisser," she said breathlessly and cursed her fragmented voice. "I'll note it on your profile."

His heavy-lidded gaze tracked her closely. "I wasn't finished. Come back and see what else I'm good at. You want to be thorough on the profile, don't you?"

"I can't do that." If he triggered such a severe reaction with merely a kiss, what would her body do with more?

"Scared?"

"Of you? Not hardly." The scoff was delivered so convincingly, she almost believed it herself.

A light dawned in his expression and she had the distinct impression he'd just figured out exactly how much he scared her. That sent another round of panic into the abyss of her stomach.

"There's just no need," she clarified, desperately trying to counter the effects of being kissed senseless. "We put it to the test, and while the kiss was pleasant, it certainly didn't distract me from the next steps. When do you want to schedule the last session?"

Dax groaned the way someone does when you tell them they have to get a root canal followed by a tax audit. "I'd rather kiss you some more. Why are you all the way over there?"

"We're not doing this, Dax. Hear me now, because I can't stress this enough. You and I are not happening." She held up a finger as he started to speak. "No. Not any variation of you and I. We have a deal, a wager, and nothing more. I have to do my job. It's my life, my business. Let me do it."

He contemplated her for a long moment. "This is important to you."

"Of course it is! You threatened to destroy my reputation, which will effectively ruin the company I've built over the last seven years. How would you like it if I had the power to do that to you and then spent all my time trying to seduce you into losing?"

"Elise." He waited until she glanced at him to continue. "I'm sorry. That was not my intent. I like kissing you. That's all. If you want to do another session, I'll be there. Name the time."

Oh, how *dare* he be all understanding and apologetic and smoky-eyed? "How about if I call you?"

She needed Dax gone before she did anything else stupid, like set off on an exploratory mission to see if he still had underwear-model abs under that suit.

"Sure. I can give you some space. Call me when you're ready to pick up where we left off."

Of course he'd seen right through her and then dumped a heck of a double entendre in her lap. Pick up where they left off with the sessions—or with the kiss? And which way would he interpret it?

Which way would she mean it?

She'd just realized something painful and ridiculous. The text messages during his date, letting him kiss her, the supreme sadness of imagining him blissfully in love with his soul mate; it all rolled up into an undeniable truth—she didn't want Dax to be with anyone else.

And she couldn't let herself be with him, even for what would undoubtedly be the best night of her life. It was the morning after when she woke up alone, knowing she hadn't been enough to keep him, and all the mornings alone from then on, that she couldn't do.

That was the best reason of all to get him matched with someone else in a big hurry.

Six

At precisely seven-thirty the next evening, Elise's door-bell rang. And yes, Dax was exactly who she expected to see grinning at her on the other side of the door, both hands behind his back.

"I said I'd call you."

Not that she'd really thought he'd wait around for the phone to ring, but he could have given her at least twenty-four hours to figure out how to call him without creating the impression she wanted him to pick up *exactly* where that kiss had left off.

Which would be really difficult to convey, when truth-fully, she did. And now her house was spotless because every time she considered picking up the phone, she cleaned something instead.

"I know. But I'm taking this seriously. For real. Your office isn't the best place to get answers to your questions. So we're going to do it here."

"Here? At my house?" *Bad, bad idea.* "You want to do the profile session on a Saturday night?"

Didn't he have a new woman lined up already? Candy hadn't worked out, but a man like Dax surely wouldn't wait around for Elise to find him some action. Saturday night equaled hot date, didn't it?

"I don't think you fully appreciated the point I made about getting to know me best while on a date." With a flourish, he pulled something from behind his back. A DVD she didn't recognize. "So we're going to watch a movie."

"The profile session is going to be a date?" *She* was his hot date. How in the world had she not seen this coming?

It was straight out of Psych 101—to get the cheese, she had to complete the maze. But why? What was his motivation for forcing her to navigate a date in the first place?

"More of a compromise," he allowed with a nod. "This is not anything close to what I've ever done on a date. But the setting is innocuous and we can both relax. I don't feel like you're grilling me, you don't feel like it's work."

That sounded remarkably like the excuse he'd used to get her to go to lunch, which had proved to be rather effective, in retrospect. "What if I'm busy?"

"Cancel your plans. You want to know what makes me tick?" His eyebrows lifted in invitation. "I'm offering you a shot. Watch the movie. Drink some wine. If you do that for me, I'll answer any question you ask honestly."

Dax gestured with his other hand, which clutched a bottle of cabernet sporting a label she'd only ever seen behind glass at a pricey restaurant.

She shook her head. "This is a thinly veiled attempt to seduce me again."

The sizzling once-over he treated her to should not have curled her toes. Of course, if he'd given her a warning before he showed up, she could have put on shoes.

"I'm not trying to tilt the scales by coming on to you," he insisted. "Trust me, if I wanted you naked, this is not how I would go about it."

As she well knew his seduction routine, she opted to keep her mouth shut. For once.

"I, Daxton Wakefield, will not touch you one single time this whole evening." He marked the statement by crossing his heart solemnly with the DVD case. "Unless you ask me to."

"You're safe on that front. Not that I'm agreeing to this, but what did you bring?" She nodded at the movie against her better judgment.

He shrugged. "An advanced screening copy of *Stardate 2215*. It's that big-budget sci-fi flick coming out Christmas day."

She eyed him. "That's not in theaters yet. How did you get a copy?"

"I have friends in low places." He grinned mischievously. "One of the benefits of being in the media business. I called in a few favors. You like sci-fi and I wanted to pick something I knew you hadn't seen."

Speechless, she held on to the door so she didn't end up in a heap at his feet. She'd never told him what kind of movies she liked, but somehow he'd figured it out, and then went to great lengths to get one. Her heart knocked up against her principles and it was not cool.

Not a seduction, my foot.

But she really wanted to see that movie. And she really wanted to get Dax Wakefield matched to someone else so she could stop thinking about kissing him.

"Truce?" He held out the DVD and the wine with a conciliatory smile and he looked so freaking gorgeous in his $400 jeans and long-sleeved V-neck, she wanted to lap him up like whipped cream.

If that bit of absurdity didn't decide against this idea for her, nothing would.

"I haven't eaten dinner yet."

"Jeez, Elise." He huffed out a noise of disgust. "You're the most difficult woman to not have a date with in the entire United States. Order a pizza. Order twelve. You may have free rein with my credit card if that's what it takes to get me over your threshold."

"Why are you so dead-set on this? Honestly."

He dropped his arms, wine and DVD falling to his sides.

"Believe it or not, this is me leveling the field. You deserve a genuine chance at doing your thing with the questions and the algorithm. This is an atmosphere conducive to giving you that."

Sincerity laced his words, but to clarify, she said, "Because you don't like my office."

Something flitted through his expression and whatever it was scared her a great deal more than the kiss. "Because I have an extremely full week ahead and daylight hours are scarce. I want to give you my undivided attention, without watching the clock."

Her heart knocked again.

"You've just won an evening with a matchmaker." She stepped out of the door frame and allowed Dax passage into the foyer for the second time in two days.

She should have her head examined.

True to his word, he strolled past her without touching, went to the living room and set the wine on the coffee table.

She fetched wineglasses and he ordered the pizza. They settled onto the couch and three sips in, she finally relaxed. "This cabernet is amazing. Where did you find it?"

"In my wine rack." He handed her the remote without grazing her fingers. It was carefully done. "I was saving it for a special occasion."

"Right. Pizza and a movie is special."

He didn't move, didn't touch her at all, but she felt the look he gave her in all the places his kiss had warmed the night before. "The company is the occasion, Elise."

Prickles swept across her cheeks. The curse of the fair-skinned Irish. She might as well take out a billboard proclaiming her innermost thoughts. "We'll get through the profile session much faster if you quit detouring to flatter me with platitudes."

His head tilted as if he'd stopped to contemplate a particularly intriguing Picasso. "Why do you find it so hard to believe that I like you?"

Because he made a habit of working emotions to his advantage. Because he was a swan and she was not. Because to believe would be akin to trusting him.

But she ignored all that in favor of the most important reason. "You don't ruin the reputation of someone you hold in fond regard. If you really like me, prove it. Let's end this now."

"To be fair, I didn't know I was going to like you when I made that deal. But if you do your job, you've got nothing to worry about, do you?" He lifted his glass in a mock toast.

A part of her had hoped he'd take the opportunity to call it off, and she shouldn't be so disappointed he hadn't. Why—because she'd internalized his pretty words? Thought maybe he'd realized she was actually a very nice person and hadn't deliberately set out to ruin his friendship with Leo?

"Hey."

"Hey, what?" she said a touch defensively, pretty sure she had no call to be snippy.

"It's a compliment that I'm holding fast to our deal. You're a smart, savvy woman and if I didn't respect the hell out of you, I'd have let you bow out long before now."

"Bow out? You mean give up and quit? No way."

When he grinned, she deflated a little. He'd phrased it like that on purpose to get her dander up and allow him to slide the nice stuff by her. How did he know how to handle her so well?

"That's why I like you," he said decisively. "We're both fighters. Why else would I be here to put myself through your profile wringer? I can't claim the matchmaking process is bogus unless I submit to it wholly. Then we both know the victor deserves to win."

Now he'd dragged ethics into this mess. She shook her head in disbelief. Against all odds, she liked him too. Somehow he'd stripped everything away and laid out some very profound truths. Of all the ways he could have convinced her he really liked her, how had he done it by *not* calling off their deal?

He respected her skills, respected her as a business woman, and she'd been on the defensive since moment one. It was okay to let her guard down. Dax had more than earned it.

"It's hard for me to trust people," she said slowly, watching him to see if he had a clue how difficult a confession this was. "That's why I give you so much grief."

He nodded once without taking his eyes off her. "I wasn't confused. And for the record, same goes."

He stretched his hand out in invitation and she didn't hesitate to take it. Palm to palm, silent mutual agreement passed between them. Warmth filled her as the intensity of the moment unfolded into something that felt like kinship.

Neither of them trusted easily, but each of them had found a safe place here in this circle of two. At least for tonight.

Dax stopped paying the slightest bit of attention to the movie about fifteen minutes in. Watching Elise was much more fun.

She got into the movie the same way she did everything else—with passion. And it was beautiful. He particularly liked the part where she forgot they were holding hands.

There was nothing sexual about it. He didn't use it as an excuse to slide a suggestive fingertip across her knuckle. He didn't yank on her hand and let her spill into his lap, even though nothing short of amnesia was going to get that hot kiss out of his head.

Far be it from him to disrupt the status quo. The status quo was surprisingly pleasant. He'd agreed not to come on to her, and he'd stick to it, no matter how many more times she gave him a hard-on just by looking at him.

Promises meant something to him and he wanted Elise to understand that.

And oddly enough, when he knew there wasn't a snowball's chance for anything above pizza and a movie, it was liberating in a way he'd never expected.

It was new. And interesting. Instead of practicing his exit strategy, he relaxed and enjoyed the company of a beautiful woman who made him laugh. He couldn't wait to find out what happened next.

The pizza arrived, and he let her hand slip from his without protest, but his palm cooled far too quickly.

Elise set the box on the coffee table and handed Dax a bright red ceramic plate. The savory, meaty smell of pepperoni and cheese melded with the fresh-baked crust and his stomach rumbled. Neither of them hesitated to dig in.

Dax couldn't remember ever eating with a woman in front of the TV. It was something couples did. And he'd never been part of one. Never wanted to be, and furthermore, never wanted to give someone the impression there'd be more couple-like things to come.

But this wasn't a date and Elise wasn't going to get the wrong idea. It was nice.

"Thanks for the pizza," she said around a mouthful, which she couldn't seem to get down her throat fast enough. "I never eat it and I forgot how good it is. You do amazing things with a credit card."

She'd meant it as a joke but it hit him strangely and he had a hard time swallowing the suddenly tasteless bite in his own mouth.

Yes, his bank account could finance a small country, and he made sure the women he dated benefited from his hard work, usually in the form of jewelry or the occasional surprise overnight trip to New York or San Francisco. He'd never given it much thought.

Until now. What *did* he have to offer a woman in a relationship? A coat and a credit card. Thanks to his friendly neighborhood matchmaker, it seemed shallow and not... enough. What if Elise did the impossible and introduced him to his soul mate? She was smart and had a good track record. She could actually pull it off.

By definition, his soul mate would be that woman worth making lifelong promises to.

Did he really want to meet her and be so inadequately prepared?

"You're supposed to be asking me questions." Dax gave up on the pizza and opted to drown his sudden bout of relationship scruples with more wine.

Eyebrows raised, Elise chewed faster.

"I suppose I am," she said and washed down the last of her pizza with a healthy swallow of cabernet, then shot him a sideways glance. "Say, you're pretty good. I did forget about work, just like you predicted."

He crossed his arms so he didn't reach for her hand again. It bothered him that he wanted to in the same breath as bringing up the profile questions designed to match him with another woman. "Yeah, yeah, I'm a genius. Ask me a question."

After pausing the movie, Elise sat back against the sofa cushion, peering at him over the rim of her glass. "What does contentment look like?"

This. His brain spit out the answer unchecked. Thankfully, he kept it from spilling out of his mouth. "I spend my day chasing success. I've never strived for contentment."

Which didn't necessarily mean he hadn't found it.

"What if Wakefield Media collapsed tomorrow but you had that woman next to you, the one who doesn't care about what's behind your curtain? Would you still be able to find a way to be content as long as you had her?"

No surprise that Elise remembered what he'd said at

lunch the other day. How long would it take her to figure out he actually *wanted* someone to care?

Nothing was going to happen to Wakefield Media. It was hypothetical, just like the soul mate. So if this was all theoretical, why not have both?

"What if having the woman *and* success makes me content? Is that allowed?"

Somehow, the idea buried itself in his chest and he imagined that woman snuggled into his bed at the end of a long day, not because he'd brought her home, but because she lived there. And they were together but it wasn't strictly for sex—it was about emotional support and understanding—and making love heightened all of that.

Dax could trust she'd stick around. Forever.

"If that's what contentment looks like to you, then of course."

Her catlike smile drove the point home. She'd gotten a response out of him even though he'd have sworn he'd never so much as thought about how to define contentment.

He had to chuckle. "Well played."

Now that he'd defined it, the image of that woman wouldn't dissolve. She didn't have a face or a body type, but the blurred shape was there in his mind and he couldn't shake it.

What was he supposed to do with that?

With a nod at his concession, Elise sipped her wine and contemplated him. "What do you do with your free time?"

Dax grinned and opted to bite back the inappropriate comment about his after-hours activities. "Should I pick something that makes it sound like I have an interesting hobby?"

"No, you should say what you like."

"I like to people-watch," he said.

"Tell me more about that. What's great about people-watching?"

"Spoken in true therapist fashion." He meant it as a joke and she took it as one. He liked amusing her, and it was easy to do so. "People-watching is the best way to figure out what motivates the masses. And it never gets old."

She was really, really good at this, especially when he wasn't trying to weasel his way out of having his psyche split open. Actually, she had a knack for yanking things out of his brain even when he *was* looking for a way to avoid answering her questions.

So there was no point in being anything less than honest. Plus, this environment, this bubble with only the two of them, created a sort of haven, where it didn't seem so terrible to say whatever he felt.

"Go on," she encouraged with a small wave. "Why do you have to figure out what motivates people?"

"Wakefield Media isn't just a top-grossing media company. It's a top-grossing company, period. That's not an accident. I got a degree in psychology instead of business because it's crucial to have a keen understanding of what brings people back for more, especially in the entertainment space."

Wine and pizza totally forgotten, she listened with rapt attention as if he'd been outlining the secrets of the universe, which she couldn't get enough of. "And people-watching helps?"

For a woman who'd moaned so appreciatively over the pizza, she had amazing willpower. She'd only eaten one piece. She was so interested in what he said, food took a backseat. It was a little heady to be worthy of so much focus.

"People can be notoriously loyal to certain shows, and conversely, very fickle. You'd be shocked at how much you can pick up about why when you just sit and observe how people interact."

Her soft smile punched him in the gut. "Your insights must be something else."

"I bet yours would be as good. Do it with me some time."

Now why had he gone and said that? Hadn't he gotten a big enough clue that she didn't want to hang out with him? Look how hard it had been to get her to agree to pizza and a movie.

The wine must be messing with his head.

"I'd like that. It's a date," she said without a trace of sarcasm and he did a double take.

The wine was messing with her head too, obviously.

"A date that's not a date because we're not dating?" She'd been undeniably clear about that last night. Otherwise, he'd never have agreed to keep his hands off of her.

And look what that promise had netted him—this was bar none the most enjoyable evening he'd had in ages, including the ones that did involve sex.

"Right. We're not dating. We're…friends?" she offered hesitantly.

A denial sprang to his lips and then died. *Friends*. Is that what was happening here? Did that explain why he felt as though he could tell Elise anything?

"I don't know. I've never been friends with a woman. Aren't there rules?"

She made a face. "Like we're not supposed to cancel our plans with each other when someone we *are* dating calls?"

"Like I'm not supposed to fantasize about kissing you again." The answering heat in her expression told him volumes about her own fantasies. "Because if that's against the rules, I can't be friends with you."

She looked down, that gorgeous blush staining her cheeks. "You're not supposed to be doing that anyway. Regardless."

He tipped up her chin and forced her to meet his eyes

again because that heat in hers liquefied him. And he craved that feeling only she could produce. "I can't stop."

As he'd just broken his promise not to touch her, he tore his hand away from her creamy skin with reluctance and shoved it under his thigh.

Elise messed with his head. No wine required.

She blinked, banking all the sexy behind a blank wall. "You'll find it surprisingly easy to stop as soon as I match you with someone else. She'll help you forget all about that kiss, which never should have happened in the first place."

There it was again, slapping him in the face. Elise wasn't interested in him. Her main goal was to get him paired off with someone else as soon as possible.

And that was the problem. He didn't want to be matched with another Candy. The thought of another date with another woman who was perfect for him on paper but not quite right in reality…he couldn't do it.

He wanted that blurred woman snuggled into his bed, ready to offer companionship, understanding. Contentment. Instantly, she snapped into focus, dark hair swinging and wearing nothing but a gorgeous smile.

Elise.

Yes. He wanted Elise, and when Dax Wakefield wanted something, he got it.

But if he pursued her, would this easiness between them fall apart? After all, she wasn't his soul mate and that in and of itself meant she couldn't be that woman in his imagination, with whom he could envision a future.

What a paradox. He'd finally arrived at a place in his life where he could admit he'd grown weary of the endless revolving door of his bedroom. And the woman he pictured taking a longer-term spot in his bed wanted to be *friends,* right after she hooked him up with someone else. Whom he did not want to meet.

Where did that leave the wager between them?

Seven

Bright and early Monday morning, Elise sat in her office and plugged the last of the data into the system. Dax had answered every single question and she firmly believed he'd been honest, or at least as honest as he knew how to be when the content involved elements a perpetual player hardly contemplated. But they'd stayed on track Saturday night—mostly—and finished the profile. Finally.

This would be her hour of victory. She'd built a thriving business using nothing but her belief in true love and her brain. Not one thin dime had come from Brenna, and Elise had fought hard to keep herself afloat during the lean years. She would not let all her work crumble.

She was good at helping people find happiness. Matching Dax with someone who could give him that would be her crowning achievement.

She hit Run on the compiler.

Elise Arundel.

Her forehead dropped to the keyboard with a spectacular crash. She couldn't decide whether to laugh or cry.

Of course her name had come up again. The almost-kiss had been enough to skew the results the first time. Now she had a much bigger mess on her hands because she couldn't get the *oh-my-God* real kiss off her mind. Or the not-a-date with Dax, which should have only been about completing the profile, but instead had eclipsed every evening Elise had ever spent with a man. Which were admittedly few.

They'd bonded over pizza and mutual distrust. And—major points—he'd never made a single move on her. When he confessed he still thought about kissing her, it had been delivered with such heartbreaking honesty, she couldn't chastise him for it.

But his admission served as a healthy reminder. Dax liked women and was practiced at getting them. That's why it felt so genuine—because it was. And once he got her, she'd start dreaming of white dresses while he steadily lost interest. They were *not* a good match.

It didn't stop her from thinking about kissing him in return.

Her mixed feelings about Dax had so thoroughly compromised her matchmaking abilities she might as well give up here and now. It wasn't as though she could fiddle around with the results this time, not when it was so clear she couldn't be impartial. Not after Dax had made such a big deal about ethics.

She groaned and banged her head a couple more times on the keyboard. He was going to have a field day with this. Even if she explained that matchmaking was as much an art as a science, which was why she administered the profile sessions herself, he'd cross his arms and wait for her to confess this matchmaking business was bogus.

But it wasn't, not for all her other clients. Just this one.

The truth was, she abhorred the idea of Dax being matched with another woman so much, she'd subconsciously made sure he wouldn't be. It was unfair to his soul mate—who was still out there somewhere—and unfair to Dax. He was surprisingly sweet and funny and he deserved to be with a woman he could fall in love with. He deserved to be happy.

And she was screwing with his future. Not to mention

the future of EA International, which would be short-lived after Dax crucified her matchmaking skills. That would be exactly what *she* deserved.

How in the world could she get out of this?

A brisk knock on her open door startled her into sitting up. Angie poked her head in, and the smirk on her assistant's face did not help matters.

"Mr. Wakefield is here," she said, her gaze cutting to the lobby suggestively.

"Here?" Automatically, Elise smoothed hair off her forehead and cursed. Little square indentations in the shape of keys lined her skin. "As in, here in the office?"

Maybe she could pretend to be out. At least until the imprint of the keyboard vanished and she figured out what she was going to tell him about his match. Because of course that was why he'd jetted over here without calling. He wanted a name.

"I've yet to develop hologram technology," Dax said smoothly as he strolled right past Angie, filling the room instantly. "But I'm working on it. In the meantime, I still come in person."

Hiding a smile but not very well, Angie made herself scarce.

Elise took a small private moment to gorge herself on the visual panorama of male perfection before her. She'd been so wrong. His everyday suit was anything but ordinary and he was as lickable in it as he was in everything else. And then her traitorous brain reminded her he was most lickable *out* of everything else.

Her mouth incredibly dry, she croaked, "I thought you were busy this week. That's what pizza was all about, right?"

He didn't bother with the chair intended for guests. Instead, he rounded the desk and stopped not a foot from her, casually leaning against the wood as if he owned it.

"I am. Busy," he clarified, his gaze avidly raking over her, as if he'd stumbled over a Van Gogh mural amid street graffiti and couldn't quite believe his luck. "I left several people in a conference room, who are this very minute hashing out an important deal without me. I got up and walked out."

For a man who claimed his company was more important than anything, even contentment, it seemed an odd thing to do. "Why?"

His smoky irises captured hers and she fell into a long, sizzling miasma of delicious tension and awareness.

"I wanted to see you," he said simply.

Her heart thumped once and settled back into a new rhythm where small things like finding his real soul mate didn't matter. The wager didn't matter. The rest of her life alone didn't matter. Only the man mattered.

And he wanted to be with her.

"Oh. Well, here I am. Now what?"

He extended his hand in invitation. "I haven't been able to think about anything other than sitting on a park bench with you and watching the world go by. Come with me."

Her chair crashed against the back wall as she leaped up. She didn't glance at the clock or shut her computer down, just took his hand and followed him.

Most men took her hints and left her alone, more than happy to let her stew in her trust issues. Not this one. Thank goodness. She could worry about how wrong they were for each other and how she had to find someone right for him later.

Fall nipped the air and Elise shivered as she and Dax exited the building. Her brain damage apparently extended to braving the elements in a lightweight wool dress and boots.

"Hang on a sec. I need to go back and get my coat."

She turned when Dax spun her back. "Wait. Wear mine." Shrugging out of his suit jacket, he draped it around her shoulders and took great care in guiding her arms through the sleeves. Then he stood there with the lapels gripped in his fists, staring down at her as if the act of sharing his warmth had great significance.

"You didn't have to do that," she said as she rolled up the sleeves self-consciously. But she had to do something with her hands besides put them square on his pectorals as she wanted to. "My coat is right in—"

"Humor me. It's the first time I've given a woman my coat because she needed it. I like it on you."

"I like it on me, too." She hunched down in it, stirring up that delicious blend of scent that was Dax, danger and decadence all rolled into one. She could live in this jacket, sleep in it, walk around naked with the silk liner brushing her skin...

Too bad she'd have to give it back.

They strolled down the block to the small urban park across the street from EA International's office building. Dax told her a funny story about a loose dog wreaking havoc at one of his news station studios and she laughed through the whole thing. Their hands brushed occasionally and she pretended she didn't notice, which was difficult considering her pulse shot into the stratosphere with every accidental touch.

She kept expecting him to casually take her hand, as he'd done Saturday night. Just two people holding hands, no big deal. But he didn't.

No wonder her feelings were so mixed. She could never figure out what to expect. For a long time, she'd convinced herself he only came on to her so she'd lose the wager. Now she wasn't so sure.

Dax indicated an unoccupied bench in the central area of the park, dappled by sunlight and perfectly situated to view a square block of office buildings. People streamed to and from the revolving doors, talking to each other, checking their phones, eyeing the traffic to dart across the street.

She'd opted to sit close, but not too close, to Dax. At least until she understood what this was all about. They might have bonded over the fact that neither of them trusted easily, but that didn't mean she'd developed any better ability to do so.

"How does this people-watching deal go?" She nodded at the beehive of activity around them.

He shrugged. "Mostly I let my mind wander and impressions come to me. Like that couple."

She followed his pointed finger to the youngish boy and girl engaged in a passionate kiss against the brick wall of a freestanding Starbucks.

"Eighteen to twenty-five," he mused. "Likely attending the art school around the corner. They both own smartphones but not tablets, have cable TV but not the premium channels, read Yahoo news but not the financial pages, and can tell me the titles of at least five songs on Billboard's Top 100, but not the names of any politicians currently in office except the president."

Mouth slightly agape, she laughed. "You made all that up."

Dax focused his smoky eyes on her instead of the couple and the temperature inside his jacket neared thermonuclear. "He has a bag with the art school logo and they both have phones in their back pockets. The rest is solid market research for that age group. The details might be slightly off, but not the entertainment habits."

"Impressive. Do you ever try to find out if you're right?"

He gave her a look and stretched his arm across the back of the bench, behind Elise's shoulders. "I'm not wrong. But feel free to go ask them yourself."

Carefully, she avoided accidentally leaning back against his arm. Because she wanted to. And didn't have any clue how to navigate this unexpected interval with Dax, or what to think, what to feel.

"Uh…" The couple didn't appear too interested in being interrupted and all at once, she longed to be that into someone, where the passing world faded from existence. "That's okay."

His answering smile relaxed her. Marginally.

Unfortunately, she had a strong suspicion she could get that into Dax.

"Your turn," he said. "What do you see in those two?"

Without censor, she spit out thoughts as they came to her.

"They're at an age where love is still exciting but has the potential to be that much more painful because they're throwing themselves into it without reservation. They're not living together yet, but headed in that direction. He's met her parents but she hasn't met his, because he's from out of state, so it's too expensive to go home with a girl unless it's serious. Next Christmas he'll invite her," she allowed. "And he'll propose on New Year's because it's less predictable than Christmas Eve."

Dax's lips pursed. "That's entirely conjecture."

He was going to make her work for it, just as she'd done to him.

"Is not. He has on a Choctaw Casino T-shirt, which is in Oklahoma, and if they lived together, they'd be at home, kissing each other in private. The rest is years of studying couples and what drives them to fall in love." She recoiled at the smirk on his face. "So, you can cite research but I can't?"

"Cite research all you want. *Validated* research." As he talked, he grew more animated and angled toward her. "You can't study how people fall in love. Emotions are not quantifiable."

"Says the guy with a psychology degree. How did Skinner determine that mice responded more favorably to partial reinforcement? Not by asking them whether they prefer Yahoo or Google news."

A grin flashed on his face and hit her with the force of a floodlight.

She fought a smile of her own and lost. "You study, you make a hypothesis, you test it and *voilà*. You have a certified conclusion."

Only with Dax could she enjoy a heated argument about her first and only love, the science of the heart.

"So tell me, Dr. Arundel." His gaze swept her with some of that heat in a pointed way she couldn't pretend to miss. "What's your hypothesis about me? Break me down the way you did that couple."

The honks and chattering people filled the sudden silence as she searched his face for some clue to what he was after. Besides the obvious. Clearly he was still thinking about kissing her.

And she was pretty sure she wouldn't utter one single peep in protest.

Great. If she couldn't trust him and she couldn't trust herself to remember why they wouldn't work, why was she still sitting here in the presence of a master at seduction?

"Honestly?" He nodded but she still chose her words carefully. "You don't like to be alone, and women fill that gap. You want her to challenge you, to make it worth your while to stick around, which never happens, so you break it off before she gets too attached. It's a kindness, because you don't really want to hurt her. It's not her fault she's not the one."

His expression didn't change but something unsettled flowed through the depths of his eyes.

"What makes you think I'm looking for the one?" he said lightly. But she wasn't fooled. His frame vibrated with tension.

She'd hit a nerve. So she pressed it, hard.

"You never would have agreed to be matched if you weren't. And you certainly wouldn't keep coming back, especially after it didn't work out with Candy."

He shifted and their knees nested together suggestively. Slowly, he reached out and traced the line of her jaw, tucking an errant lock of hair behind her ear, watching her the entire time.

"I came for the match and stayed for the matchmaker."

"Dax, about that—"

"Relax."

His fingers slid through her hair, threading it until he'd reached the back of her neck. She was supposed to *relax* when he touched her like that?

"You're off the hook," he murmured. "I'm officially calling off our wager. Don't be disappointed."

He'd read her mind. Again.

Relief coursed through her body, flooding her so swiftly, she almost cried. She didn't have to confess that she'd skewed the results. He'd never have to know she'd abandoned her ethics.

But without the wager in place, she had no shield against the onslaught of Dax. No excuse to hold him at arm's length. Much, *much* worse, she had no excuse to continue their association.

"You don't think I can match you?"

"I think you can sell ice to Eskimos. But the fact of the matter is I don't want to meet any more women."

"But you have to," she blurted out. If he didn't, how would he ever meet the love of his life? She might have abandoned her ethics, but not the belief that everyone deserved to be deliriously happy.

Calmly, Dax shook his head. "I *don't* have to. I've already met the one I want. You."

A thousand nonverbal sentiments pinged between them, immobilizing her.

She wasn't right for him. He wasn't right for her. They didn't make sense together and she couldn't let herself think otherwise. Not even for a moment.

The best way to stop wishing for things that couldn't be was to match him with someone else, wager or no wager. Then he could be happy.

Elise froze and forcibly removed his hand from her silky hair.

Now that was a shame. He liked the feel of her.

"Me?" she squeaked.

"Come on. Where did you think I was headed?" Apparently, telling a woman you wanted to see her wasn't enough of a clue that you were into her. "It would be a travesty to continue this matchmaking deal when it's not going to happen."

"What's not going to happen? Finding you a match?" Indignation laced her question.

But then he'd known she wouldn't go down without a fight. He'd have been disappointed otherwise. It had taken him most of Sunday to figure out how to maneuver past all her roadblocks. He still wasn't sure if he'd hit on the right plan. Chances were, she'd drop a few more unanticipated blockades.

That's what made it great.

"The concept was flawed from the beginning. And we both know it. Why not call a spade a spade and move on? We've got something between us." He held up a finger to stem the flow of protests from her mouth. "We do. You can't deny it. Let's see what happens if we focus on that instead of this ridiculous wager."

"I already know what's going to happen." A couple of suits walked by and she lowered her voice. "You'll take me to bed, it'll be glorious and you'll be insufferably smug about it. Hit repeat the next night and the next, for what… about three weeks?"

He bit back a grin. "Or four. So what's the problem?"

His grin slipped as she sighed painfully. "That's not what I want."

"You'd rather I fumble around with no clue how to find your G-spot and then act like it's okay when I come before you? Because I grew out of that before I hit my twenties. The smug part might be a little insufferable, but…" He winked. "I think you'll forgive me."

"You know what I'm saying, Dax. Don't be difficult."

He was being difficult?

"You want promises right out of the gate?" His temper flared and he reined it in. "I don't operate like that. No one does."

"Not promises. Just an understanding that we have the same basic goals for a relationship."

He groaned. "This is not a computer program where you get to see the code before executing it. Why can't we take it day by day? Why can't it be like it was Saturday night?" His thumb found the hollow of her ear again. He spread his fingers against her warm neck and she didn't slap his hand away. "Today is pretty good, too. Isn't it?"

Her eyes shut for a brief moment. "Yeah. It's nice. But we want different things and it's not smart to start something when that hasn't changed. Am I supposed to give up the hope for a committed, loving relationship in exchange for a few weeks of great sex?"

"Who said you have to give up anything? Maybe you're going to gain something." A lot of something if he had his way. He waggled his brows. "What have you got against great sex?"

"I'm a fan of great sex, actually." She crossed her legs, pulling herself in tighter. "It's especially great when I can count on it to be great for a long time instead of wondering when the end is coming."

"Let's break down precisely what it is that you want, shall we?" His head tilted as he contemplated the slight woman who'd had him on the edge of his seat since day one. "You want desperately to find your soul mate but when a guy isn't exactly what you envisioned, you run screaming in the other direction. There's no middle ground."

Her fair skin flushed red. "That's not true."

It was, and she needed someone real to get her over her hang-ups and visions of fantasy lovers dancing in her head. "You have check boxes in your mind, profile questions that you want answered a certain way before you'll go for it. No guy could ever perfectly fit the mold. So you stay home on Saturday nights and bury yourself in futuristic worlds to avoid finding out your soul mate doesn't exist."

"Soul mates do exist! I've seen it."

"For some people." It was a huge reversal for him to admit that much, and she didn't miss it. "But maybe not for me, or for you. Did you ever think of that?"

"Never. Every male I've ever met, that's the first thing I wonder. Is he my soul mate?"

Every male? Even him? "But you don't take that first step toward finding out."

"Just as you evaluate every woman to see if she's the one, decide she can't be, and then don't stick around long enough to let her disappoint you."

Deflection. They were both pretty well versed in it when the subject material grew too hot, and digging into the fact that no one ever measured up—for either of them—was smoking. Escaping unsinged seemed more and more unlikely. But neither of them had jumped out of the fire yet.

She was scared. He got that. It squeezed his chest, and what was he supposed to do with that? After all, *he* was the one who scared her.

"Yeah," he allowed. "But I'm willing to admit it. Are you?"

She slumped down in his jacket, which almost swallowed her. Her wry smile warmed him tremendously. She looked so sweet and delectable sitting there wearing a jacket she hadn't tried to manipulate her way into, and an urgent desire to strip her out of it built with alarming speed.

"It's not fair, you know," she complained. "Why can't you be just a little stupid?"

He laughed long and hard at that and didn't mind that she'd evaded his challenge. He already knew the answer anyway.

"I should ask you the same thing. If you'd relax your brain for a minute, we could avoid all this."

"Avoid what? Psychoanalyzing each other under the table?"

"Hell no. That's the part about us that turns me on the most."

"There's no us," she said and looked away. Her cheeks flushed again, planting the strangest desire to put his lips on that pink spot. "What happened to being friends?"

"Would it make things easier for you to stick a label on this thing between us? I'm okay with calling us friends if you are. But be prepared for an extra dose of friendliness."

She snorted. "Let's skip the labels."

"Agreed. With all the labels off the table, let's just see what happens if I do this."

He tipped her chin up and drew her lips close, a hairbreadth from his, letting her get used to the idea before committing.

Her whole body stilled.

He wanted Elise-on-Fire, as she'd been on the couch the first time he'd kissed her, before she freaked out. And he felt not one iota of remorse in pushing her buttons in order to get her there.

"Scared?" he murmured against her lips. "Wanna go home and watch *Blade Runner* for the four-thousandth time?"

"Not with you," she shot back, grazing his mouth as she enunciated, and it was such a deliberate tease, it shouldn't have sent a long, dark spike of lust through his gut.

He pulled back a fraction, gratified when she swayed after him. "Rather do something else with me? All you have to do is ask."

Her irises flared, and he fell into the chocolaty depths. The expanse between them was an ocean, an eternity, the length of the universe, and he wanted to close the gap in the worst way. Holding back hurt. Badly. But he wanted to see if she'd take the plunge.

"Dax," she murmured and her breath fanned his face as she slid both hands on either side of his jaw. "There is something I want to do with you. Something I've been thinking about for a long time."

Whatever it was, he'd do it. This not-quite-a-kiss had him so thoroughly hot it was a wonder he didn't spontaneously combust. "What's that, sweetheart?"

"I want to beat you at your own game," she whispered and the gap vanished.

Hungrily, she devoured him, tongue slick against his, claiming it masterfully. Her hands guided his head to angle against her mouth more deeply, and fire shot through his groin, nearly triggering a premature release the likes of which he'd not had to fight back in almost two decades.

Groaning, he tried to gain some control, but she eased him backward, hands gliding along his chest like poetry, fingers working beneath the hem to feel him up, and he couldn't stand it.

"Elise," he growled as she nipped at his ear. At the same moment, her fingernails scraped down his abs. White-hot lust zigzagged through the southern hemisphere.

They were in public. On purpose—to prevent anything too out-of-control from happening. Of course Elise had smashed that idea to smithereens.

He firmed his mouth and slowed it down. Way down. Languorously, he tasted her as he would fine wine and she softened under his kiss.

Emboldened now that he had the upper hand, he palmed the small of her back and hefted her torso against his. She moaned and angled her head to suck him in deeper, and he nearly lost his balance. Shifting to the back of the bench, he gripped her tighter, losing himself in the wave of sensations until he hardly knew which way was up.

They either needed to stop right now or take this behind closed doors. He pulled back reluctantly with a butterfly caress of his mouth against her temple.

It had to be the former. It was the middle of the day; he had to get back to work and see about the mess he'd left behind. She probably needed time to assess. Analyze. Work through her checklists and talk herself off the ledge.

Breathing hard, she pursed kiss-stung lips and peered at him under seductively lowered lashes. "Did I win?"

Eight

They held hands as they strolled back to Elise's office and she reveled in every moment of it. Dax didn't pause by his car, clearly intending to walk her all the way back inside. Maybe he was caught up in the rush and reluctant to part ways, too.

Wouldn't that be something? Dax Wakefield affected by Elise Arundel.

What was she *doing* with him?

For once, she had no idea and furthermore, didn't care. Or at least she didn't right now. Dax had a magic mouth, capable of altering her brain activity.

"Don't make plans for tonight," Dax said as they mounted the steps to her office. "I'll bring dinner to your house and we'll stay in."

That worked, and she refused to worry about lingering questions such as whether he intended to seduce her after dinner or if it would be a hands-off night. Maybe she'd seduce him before dinner instead.

She grinned, unable to keep the bubble of sheer bliss inside. This was her turn, her opportunity to get the guy.

"A date that's really a date because we're dating now?" she asked.

Insisting she still had to find him a different match had been an excuse, one contrived to avoid wanting him for herself—and to deny that the whole idea scared her. It still did. But it was her turn to be happy and hopefully make Dax happy at the same time. What could it hurt to try?

He scowled without any real heat. "Dating sounds like a label."

"I'm biting my tongue as we speak."

Unfortunately, she suspected she'd be doing a lot of that in the coming weeks. Somehow Dax had made it seem possible to forgo not only labels, but also guarantees about the future. But that didn't mean her personality had changed. She still wanted a happily ever after. She still wanted Dax to find true love.

The park-bench confessional had revealed more than either of them intended, of that she was sure. It was the only thing she was sure of. But she desperately wanted to believe that the raw revelations had opened them both up to trying something new in a relationship. Sticking around for Dax and day-by-day for her.

It required an extreme level of trust she wasn't sure she had in her. Day-by-day might be a blessing in disguise—it gave her time to figure out if she could trust Dax without wholly committing her fragile heart.

Dax opened the door to EA International and uttered an extremely profane word. She followed his gaze to see four women crowded around Angie's reception desk, all of whom turned in unison at the sound of the door. He dropped her hand without comment.

The park-bench kiss euphoria drained when she recognized Candy. The other three women, a brunette, a blonde and a redhead, weren't familiar but they all had a similar look about them as if they shared a hair stylist. And, like Candy, they all could have stepped from the pages of a magazine.

New clients referred by Candy? That seemed unlikely considering things hadn't worked out with Dax. And Elise had yet to find Candy's soul mate. Guiltily, she made a mental note to go through Candy's profile again to see if she could fix that.

"Is this an ambush?" Dax asked and she did a double take at his granite expression.

"An ambush?" Elise repeated with a half laugh.

That was no way to speak to potential customers. She skirted him and approached the women with a smile. "I'm Elise Arundel. Can I help you?"

"We're here to protest." The redhead stepped to the front and gestured to the other ladies to show she spoke for the group. Not only did these women have similar styles, they also wore identical glowers.

Elise took a tiny step backward in her boots and wished she'd bought the Gucci ones with the higher heel.

"Protest?" Automatically, she shook her head because the word had no context. "I don't understand."

Angie shot to her feet, straightening her wool skirt several times with nervous fingers. "I'm sorry, Elise. I was about to ask them to leave."

Dax took Elise's elbow, his fingers firm against the sleeve of his jacket, and nodded to the redhead. "Elise, this is Jenna Crisp, a former girlfriend. You know Candy. Angelica Moreau is the one on the left and Sherilyn Mc-Carthy is on the right. Also former girlfriends."

These were some of Dax's ex-girlfriends. She couldn't help but study the women with a more critical eye. It seemed Dax had been totally honest when he claimed to have no preference when it came to a woman's physical attributes. The women, though all beautiful and poised and polished, were as different as night and day.

Hard evidence of how truthfully Dax had answered at least one of the profile questions led her to wonder if he'd been forthright on all of them from the very beginning.

Which meant he really did think love was pure fiction.

A funny little flutter beat through Elise's stomach. Dax's hand on her arm was meant to comfort her—or hold her back—and she honestly didn't know which one she needed. "What exactly are you here to protest?"

Had Dax texted them with the news that he was inter-

ested in Elise or posted it to his Facebook timeline? He'd
have to be very slick to have done so without Elise noticing and besides, why would he? None of this made any
sense. It might be upsetting for a former girlfriend to find
out Dax had moved on, but surely not surprising—the man
was still underwear-model worthy, even fifteen years later,
and could give Casanova *and* Don Juan kissing lessons.

Jenna crossed her arms and addressed Elise without
glancing at Dax. "We're here in the best interest of your
female clients. We're protesting you taking him on as a
potential match. Don't foist him off on another unsuspecting woman."

Unable to stop blinking, Elise gaped at Jenna, extremely
aware of the other women's hardened gazes. Those lined
and mascaraed eyes might as well be spotlights.

"I'm sorry, what?"

A hot flush swept up from her neck to spread across her
cheekbones. All those eyes on her, including Dax's and Angie's, had done their job to make her uncomfortable. After
all, she was wearing Dax's huge jacket, which told its own
story, but also turned her figure blocky, like a stout oak
tree in a forest of willows.

"He's not interested in a relationship." Candy cleared her
throat. "He told me. Flat out. I thought it was so strange.
Why would he go to a matchmaker? Then Jenna and I met
by accident at Turtle Creek Salon and I found out he's only
in your system as part of some wager the two of you made."

The other ladies nodded and the brunette said, "That's
where we met Jenna and Candy too, at the salon."

They *did* share a hairdresser. Elise would congratulate
herself on the good eye if it made one bit of difference. Her
knees shook and she locked them.

Jenna waved at Dax. "He's a cold, heartless SOB who'll
screw you over without a scrap of remorse. No woman deserves that in a match. You have to drop him as a client."

Dax's jacket gained about fifty pounds, weighing heavily on her shoulders. These women had no idea Elise had been kissing Dax not ten minutes ago and making plans to have dinner. But Jenna wasn't talking to her directly. Dax wasn't going to screw Elise over.

"This has gone on long enough." Dax stepped in front of Elise to position himself between her and the ex-girlfriends. "Say anything you like about me, but don't involve Elise in your grievances. She has a right to take on whomever she pleases as a client and you have no call to be here."

Dax's staunch defense hit her in the heart and spread. He was a gentleman underneath his gorgeous exterior, and she appreciated the inside *and* the outside equally.

This was a really bad time to discover she might care about him more than she'd realized.

Jenna glared at Dax, fairly vibrating with animosity. "We were still together when you agreed to be a client. Did you tell her that? One would assume your matchmaker might like to know you weren't actually single."

The bottom dropped out of Elise's stomach. Surely that wasn't true. Jenna was spewing half truths in retaliation for Dax's imagined transgressions. That's what all of this was about—scorned women spewing their fury.

The blonde—Sherilyn, if Elise's beleaguered brain recalled correctly—flipped her curls behind her back and put a well-manicured comforting hand on Jenna's shoulder.

"We were dating, yes." Dax's eyes glittered. "But I was very much single. I did not promise you anything beyond our last date. If you chose to read a commitment into it, that's unfortunate, but it has nothing to do with my business at EA International. Nothing to do with Elise. You're using her to exact revenge on me and it won't work."

Let's take things day by day.

It was almost the same as saying no promises past the last date. Elise suspected Dax gave that speech often.

No, Dax was definitely not a liar. He was a player, exactly as advertised. None of these women had been able to change that and Elise couldn't either, whether she took it day by day or not. Her burden was deciding if she could live with no promises and the likelihood he'd be giving that speech to another woman in a few weeks, after he'd moved on from Elise.

Her fragile heart was already closer to the edge of that cliff on Heartbreak Ridge than she'd like.

All the eyes were back on her, burning into her skin. Jenna's were the hottest as she swept Elise with a pointed look that clearly indicated she found her lacking.

"It has everything to do with what kind of company this is. Are you a matchmaker or a gambler? Do women like Candy come in here expecting to meet a compatible man who's also looking for love, only to be disappointed and out a substantial sum of money?"

It was the TV interview all over again, except this time she wasn't naive enough to offer her matchmaking services to Jenna as a way to prove her skills. She had a hunch that woman ate men alive and then let them beg for more. Except for Dax. He'd truly hurt her.

Elise shook her head, hardly sure where to start slashing and burning Jenna's incorrect and provoking statements.

"I'm a matchmaker. Only. I care about helping people find love, even someone like Dax."

"Someone like Dax?" he repeated silkily as he focused his attention on Elise instead of Jenna. "What's that supposed to mean?"

And now everyone had turned against her, even the one person who'd been on her side. Who *should* have been on her side. She and Dax were embarking on something with no label, but which she'd wanted to explore. Or she had before she walked into this confrontation, this *ambush*.

The room started closing in. "It means you don't believe in love, and I naively thought I could show you how wrong you are. But I can't."

Her heart hurt to admit failure. Not only had she failed to accomplish a reversal in Dax's stance with a soul-mate match, she had almost set herself up for a more spectacular disaster by giving in to his day-by-day seduction routine.

She met the gaze of each ex-girlfriend in succession. It wasn't their fault they weren't the one and she held no hostility toward them.

"Dax is no longer a client as of today. So your protest is poorly timed. Candy, I'll refund your money. Expect the credit to appear on your statement within two days. Please see yourselves out."

She fled to her office and shut the door with an unsatisfying click. Slamming it would have been unprofessional and wouldn't have made her feel any less embarrassed. But it might have covered the sob in her throat.

The door immediately opened and Dax ended up on her side of it. He leaned against the closed door. "I'm sorry. I had no idea they were waiting around to pounce on you. It was uncalled for and entirely my fault."

She let her head drop into her hands so she didn't have to look at him. "It's not your fault. And I was talking to you, too, when I said see yourself out."

"I wanted to make sure you were okay."

The evident concern in his voice softened her. And it pissed her off that he could do that.

"I'm not. And you're the last person who can fix it."

"Elise." His hand on her shoulder shouldn't have felt so right, so warm and like the exact thing she needed. "I have to get back to the office, but I'll make it up to you tonight."

Why did he have to be so sweet and sexy and so hard to pin down?

She shrugged it off—the hand, the man, the disappointment. "I can't do this with you."

"Do what? Have dinner with me? We've eaten plenty of meals together and you never had any trouble chewing before."

That was the problem. He wanted it to be dinner with nothing meaningful attached. In a few weeks, she'd end up like Jenna.

"Dinner isn't just dinner and you know it. It's a start and we have different ideas about what we're starting."

"That's completely untrue. Dinner is about spending time together. Making each other feel good. Conversation."

"Sex," she said flatly.

"Of course. I like sex. What's wrong with that?"

"Because I want to get married! I want to be in love. Not right away, but some day, and I need the possibility of that. I need the man I'm with to want those things too," she shouted.

Shouting seemed to be the only way to get through to him. This was not going to work and he kept coming up with reasons why she should feel differently, as though there was something wrong with her because she didn't want to get in line behind the ex-girlfriends.

He swiveled her chair around to face him. "Maybe I will want that. And maybe you want those things but you'll realize you don't want them with me, and you'll think that's okay. Neither of us knows for sure what's going to happen. Nobody does."

No, but she had a pretty good idea what would happen, and it didn't lead to happily ever after. "Did you imagine yourself marrying Jenna while you were dating her?"

He flinched. "Don't let a few disgruntled women spook you."

The flinch answered the question as well as if he'd flat out said *no*.

"I'm not." That might have been the genesis, but the gang of ex-girlfriends had only brought suppressed issues to the surface. "This was a problem yesterday and the day before that. I let a few hot kisses on a park bench turn my brain off."

"So that's it then. You're done here?"

She didn't want to be. God help her, she couldn't let him walk away forever.

"I have more fun with you than with anyone else I've ever spent time with. If we can't be lovers, what's wrong with continuing to be friends?"

He let his hands fall to his sides. "That's what you want?"

"No, Dax. It's not what I want. But it's what I can offer you." She met his slightly wounded gaze without flinching, though her insides hurt to be so harsh. But what choice did she have? "Go back to work and if you still want to hang out *as friends,* you know where to find me."

Friends.

The word stuck in Dax's craw and put him in a foul mood for the remainder of the day. Which dragged on until it surely had lasted at least thirty-nine hours.

What did Elise want, a frigging engagement ring before they could have a simple *dinner* together? He'd never had so much trouble getting a woman to go on a date, let alone getting her between the sheets. He must be slipping.

"Dax?"

"What?" he growled and sighed as his admin scurried backward over the threshold of his office door. "I'm sorry. I'm distracted."

It wasn't just Elise. The Stiletto Brigade of Former Girlfriends had been brutal, digging barbs into him with military precision. He treated women well while dating them, with intricately planned evenings at expensive venues, gifting them with presents. A woman never left his bed unsatisfied. So why all the animosity?

"You don't have to tell me. I needed those purchase orders approved by five o'clock." Patricia pointed at her watch. "Past five o'clock."

"Why can't Roy sign them? He's the CFO," he grumbled and logged in to the purchase order system so he could affix his digital approval to the documents. Why have a chief financial officer if the man couldn't sign a couple of purchase orders?

"Because they're over five hundred thousand dollars and Roy doesn't have that level of purchasing approval. Only the CEO does. As you know, since you put the policy in place," she reminded him with raised eyebrows. "Are you okay?"

"Fine."

He *was* fine. Why wouldn't he be fine? It wasn't as if he'd lost anything with Elise. They hadn't even slept together yet. A couple of really amazing kisses weren't worth getting worked up over.

Actually, to be precise, he and Elise had shared a couple of amazing kisses and a few good conversations. More than a few. Several.

"Why don't you go home?" Patricia asked.

To his lonely, industrial-size loft? Sure, that would fix everything. "Thanks, I will in a few minutes. You're welcome to leave. You don't have to wait on me."

She nodded, backing away from him as if she expected a surprise attack any second, and finally disappeared.

Dax messed around until well after six o'clock, accomplishing exactly zero in the process, and tried not to think about the Vietnamese place where he'd intended to pick up dinner before going to Elise's house. Vietnamese food warmed up well and he'd fully expected to let it get good and cold before eating.

So Elise hadn't been on board with taking their whatever-it-was-with-no-label to the next level after the run-in with the Stiletto Brigade. They'd freaked her out, right when he'd gotten her panic spooled up and put away.

Fine. He was fine with it.

Elise wanted all her check boxes checked before she'd commit to dinner. It was crazy. She'd rather be alone than spend a little time with a man who thought she was funny and amazing and wanted to get her naked.

Actually, that wasn't true. She was perfectly fine with being friends. As long as he kept his hands to himself and didn't complain when she made astute, painful observations about his relationship track record.

He fumed about it as he got into his car and gunned the engine. He fumed about it some more as he drove aimlessly around Dallas, his destination unclear.

Dax shook his off morose mood and focused on his surroundings. The side-street names were vaguely familiar but he couldn't place the neighborhood. He drove to the next stoplight, saw the name of the intersection, and suddenly it hit him.

He was a block from Leo's house.

House, fortress, same thing when it came to his former friend. Leo had excelled at keeping the world out, excelled at keeping his focus where it belonged—on success. Dax slowed as the car rolled toward the winding, gated drive. The huge manor skulked behind a forest of oaks, bits of light beaming between the branches stripped of leaves by the fall wind.

Was Leo at home? Hard to tell; the house was too far from the street. Once upon a time, Dax would have put money on the answer being no. For as long as he'd known Leo, the man worked until he nearly dropped with exhaustion. Occasionally, when Dax found himself between women, he'd coax his friend out from behind his desk and they'd tie one on at a bar in Uptown.

Case in point—Dax had no woman on call. No plans. It would have been a great night to meet up with a friend who didn't ask him pointed questions about why he never stuck it out with a woman longer than a few weeks.

He didn't call Leo. He didn't drive up to the security

camera at the gate, which was equipped with facial recognition software, and would admit him instantly.

Leo wasn't that friend, not any more. Leo had a new playmate locked away inside his fortress, one he'd paid a hefty chunk of change to meet.

Well, not really a playmate since he'd married Daniella. *Married.* That was a whole lot of forever with the same woman. If Elise could be believed, Leo and Daniella were soul mates.

For the first time, Dax wondered if Leo was happy. Because wasn't that the point of a soul mate? You had someone you wanted to be locked away with, someone you could be with all the time and never care if the world spun on without either of you.

If Dax's soul mate existed, she would care very much what was behind his curtain and furthermore, he'd trust her with the backstage mess—the doubts about whether he actually had something to offer a woman in a relationship. The anxiety over whether he'd find out he had more in common with his mother than he'd like. The fear that he actually lacked the capacity to be with one person for the rest of his life. The suspicion that he was broken and that was why he'd never found someone worthy of promising forever to.

Five hundred thousand dollars seemed like a bargain if it bought a woman who stilled his restlessness. Dax had just spent twice that with the click of a mouse, and barely glanced at the description of the goods Wakefield Media had purchased. Whatever it was—likely cameras or other studio equipment—would either wear out or be replaced with better technology in a few years.

A soul mate was forever. How could that be possible for someone like Dax? What if he'd already met her and didn't realize it? That was the very definition of being broken, and it was exactly what Elise had meant when she'd said "someone like Dax."

Before he did something foolish, such as drive up to Leo's house and demand an explanation for how Leo had known Daniella was his soul mate, Dax hit the gas and drove until the low fuel light blinked on in the dash. He filled up the tank and went home, where he did not sleep well and his mood did not improve.

The next day dragged even worse than the day before. Everyone, including Patricia, steered clear, and while he appreciated their wisdom, it only pissed him off. He needed a big-time distraction.

Because he was in that perverse of a mood, he pulled out his phone and texted Elise.

Have a nice evening by yourself?

Well, that was stupid. Either she'd ignore him, tell him what a fabulous evening she had without him or make a joke that gave him zero information about whether she was in as bad of a mood as he was. And he wanted her to be. He wanted her to suffer for...

Beep. No. It sucked. I miss you.

His heart gave a funny lurch and the phone slipped from his nerveless fingers. God, what was he supposed to do with that?

Nothing. She was trying to manipulate him. She knew he didn't like to be alone and wanted him to crack first. That wasn't happening. He wasn't texting her back with some cheesy message about how he was miserable too. She was probably sitting there on that champagne-colored couch in her condo, phone in hand, waiting for his reply.

They weren't dating. Elise wasn't his lover. It shouldn't be this difficult.

He set the phone off to the side of his desk and proceeded to ignore it for the next thirteen minutes while he read the same paragraph of a marketing proposal over and over again.

The phone sat there, silently condemning him.

"Stop looking at me," he growled at the offending device and turned it over.

Elise wanted him to be some fairy-tale guy who swept her off her feet with promises of undying love, and it was so far from who he was, he couldn't even fathom it. So that was it. Nothing more to say or do.

The phone rang.

Elise. Of course she wasn't going to put up with his stupid text embargo. His heart did that funny dance again as he flipped the phone over to hit the answer button.

"Hey, Dax," a female voice purred in his ear. It was not Elise.

Dang it. He should have at least glanced at the caller ID. "Hey…you."

He winced. He had no idea who she was.

"I've been thinking a lot about you since yesterday," she said.

Sherilyn. He recognized her voice now and if he hadn't been moping around like a lovesick teenager with an atrophied brain, he'd never have answered her call. "Yesterday when you and the rest of your wrecking crew stormed into a place of business and started telling the proprietor how to run it?"

Which wasn't too far off from what he'd done to Elise, but he'd staged his showdown over EA International's formula for success on TV. He swallowed and it went down his throat like razor blades. In his defense, at the time he hadn't known how much she hated being in the spotlight. She'd handled herself admirably, then and yesterday. Because she was amazing.

"Oh, I wasn't really a part of that." Sherilyn *tsk*ed. "I went along because I had a vested interest in seeing that you no longer had a shot at getting matched. I'm in the mood for round two with you."

What a mercenary.

"I'm sorry, Sherilyn, but I'm not interested in a relationship with anyone right now. You heard Candy. It would be unfair to you."

He did not want to have this conversation. Not with Sherilyn, not with Candy, not with any woman. He was sick of the merry-go-round.

"Come on. Remember how good it was?" Sherilyn laughed throatily. "I'm not asking for a commitment, Dax. Just one night."

Her words reverberated in his head, but he heard them in his voice, as he said them to Elise. And of course the idea had seemed as repugnant to Elise when it came from him as it did now to Dax coming from Sherilyn.

Why hadn't Elise slapped him? Instead, she'd offered him friendship, which he'd thrown back in her face because he'd wanted things his way, not hers. And he'd lost something valuable in the process.

Dax sighed. "No, actually, I don't remember. Thanks for calling, but please forget about me. We're not going to happen again."

He hung up and stared out the window of his office. He might as well go ahead and admit he missed Elise, too, and had no idea how to fix it.

The Stiletto Brigade hadn't caused his problem with her. The problem had been there from the beginning, as she'd said. He'd discounted Elise's hopes and dreams because they were based on something he considered absurd and improbable—true love. Yeah, he'd done the profile and gone along, but only to win the wager fairly, not because he believed she had some special ability to prove something that was impossible to prove. Yet she'd built an entire business on the concept, and if someone as smart as Leo bought into Daniella being his soul mate, maybe there was more to the idea than Dax had credited.

Maybe he should give Elise's way a chance.

Or…

Love was a myth and now that some time had passed, the new marriage smell had worn off, but Leo was too embarrassed to admit he'd made a mistake. If Dax gave in to Elise without more information, he could be setting himself up for a world of hurt. After all, he didn't trust easily for a reason. Look what had happened to his friendship with Leo.

Besides, Elise wanted to meet her soul mate and Dax was not it. Their vastly different approaches to relationships—and to life as a whole—proved that. So why pretend?

There was nothing wrong with two consenting adults having fun together. They didn't have to swear undying devotion to take their relationship to the next level.

Why was she being so *stubborn* about this?

Leo might be too ashamed to come clean about how disastrous his relationship had become with Daniella, but Elise had lots of other clients. Surely several of EA International's former matches hadn't lasted. An unhappily ever after was a better way to attest that love was a myth than being matched with another Candy, anyway.

All he needed was one couple who hadn't ended up with their soul mate as advertised. Then he could take the evidence to Elise. She needed to understand how the real world worked, and what better way to convince her? He'd have hard proof that even when people started out wanting a lifelong commitment, sometimes it still didn't happen. Sure, she might be a little upset at first to learn she'd held out for something that didn't exist, but then she'd see his point. She wanted him as much as he wanted her, and it was time to let things between them take their natural course.

Guarantees were for products, not people. By this time tomorrow, he could have Elise naked and moaning under his mouth.

Nine

Saturday night, Elise finally stopped carrying her phone around in her hand. Dax hadn't called, hadn't texted, hadn't dropped by. He wasn't going to. The line had been drawn, and instead of doing something uncomfortable like stepping over it, Dax had hightailed it in the other direction. His loss.

And hers, unfortunately. She couldn't shake a slight sense of despondency, as though she hadn't seen the sun in weeks and the forecast called for more rain.

It was a good thing she'd put on the brakes when she had—imagine how hurt she'd be if things had gone any further. Regardless, she was undeniably disappointed he didn't even want to stay friends, which she had to get over.

She needed to focus on Blanca and Carrie, the two new applicants in her makeover program. They were both due to arrive in a couple of weeks and Elise had done almost nothing to prepare.

She tapped out a quick email to Dannie, who helped Elise with makeup and hair lessons when needed. After years at the knee of a supermodel, Elise had enough fashion and cosmetic tips to fill an ocean liner, but Dannie liked the work and by now, the two women were fast friends.

Elise confirmed the dates and attached a copy of a contract for Dannie's temporary employment. Normally, it wouldn't be a question of whether Dannie would say yes, but she and Leo had just returned from an extended vacation to Bora Bora in hopes Dannie would come home pregnant.

Elise would be thrilled if that was the reason Dannie said no.

Then she made a grocery list as two extra mouths required a great deal of planning, especially to ensure the meals were healthy but not too difficult to prepare. Few of the women in her program came to her with great culinary skills. It was one of the many aspects of training she offered, and after a lifelong love-hate relationship with food, Elise brought plenty to the literal and figurative table.

The remainder of the evening stretched ahead of her, long and lonely. She flipped on a movie, but her mind wandered.

The doorbell startled her and she glanced at the clock. Good grief, it was nearly midnight. It could only be Dax. A peek through the window confirmed it. Despite the shadows, she'd recognize the broad set of his shoulders and lean figure anywhere.

Her heart lightened. She'd missed him, fiercely.

She took a half second to fortify herself. He could be here for any number of reasons. Better to find out straight from the horse's mouth than get her hopes up.

"I wasn't expecting you," she said needlessly as she opened the door and cursed the jumpy ripples in her stomach. He was just so masculine and gorgeous. Then she got a good look at his face. The sheer darkness in his gaze tore through her. "What's wrong?"

Tension vibrated through the air as he contemplated her. "I don't know why I'm here."

"Bored? Lonely? Can't find anyone else who wants to play?" She crossed her arms over her middle. Something was up and it was far more chilling than the frigid fall night.

"On the contrary," he said smoothly, his voice like pure honey. "Women seem to be coming out of the woodwork. Except for the one I really want."

Her?

Why was that so affecting in places better left unaffected? It should irritate her to be thought of as an object of lust. The idea shouldn't feel so powerful and raw. But a week's worth of being on edge and missing their verbal swordplay and dreaming about his abs culminated in a heated hum in her core.

"I…" *Want you too.* "…hoped you'd call."

"Did you?" He hooked his thumbs in the front pockets of his jeans, but the lethal glint in his eye belied the casual pose. "What did you hope I'd say? Let's be friends? Let's paint each other's nails and shop for shoes together?"

She should shut the door. She should tell him to go away and forget she'd ever mentioned being friends.

"I hoped you'd unbend enough to admit there's a possibility you might fall in love one day. Barring that, I hoped you'd still want to have lunch occasionally or—"

"Elise. I don't want to be your friend."

"Not worth it to you?" she snapped.

"It's not enough." His hands fisted against his pockets and she realized he was trying to keep himself under control. "I wasn't going to call. I wasn't going to come over. I found myself within a block of your house five times this week all the same."

"But you kept driving."

He nodded once. "I kept driving. Until tonight."

After a long pause, she voiced the question he obviously wanted her to ask. "What was special about tonight?"

"I can't—I don't know how to give you what you want," he bit out. "And I don't know how to stay away."

Her heart stuttered and shoved all her suppressed feelings to the surface. That's why she'd missed him—when he showed her glimpses of his soul, it was more beautiful than the ocean at sunset.

"I never asked you to stay away. You shouldn't have."

"Yes. I should have. I absolutely should not be here on your doorstep." His chest shuddered with his next deep breath. "But I can't sleep. I can't concentrate. All I can think about is you naked, wrapped around me, and that brain of yours firing away on all cylinders as you come up with more inventive ways to challenge me."

The image of her unclothed body twined with his sprang into her consciousness, sparked through her abdomen, raised goose bumps on her skin. She swallowed against the sudden burn in her throat.

"You say that like it's a bad thing," she joked and nearly bit her tongue as fire licked through his expression.

"It's ridiculous. And I'm furious about it, so stop being so smug."

His glare could have melted ice. All at once, his strange mood made sense. Normally when he wanted a woman, he seduced all her reservations away. But he respected Elise too much to do that to her and he was incredibly conflicted about it. The effect of that realization was as powerful as being the object of his desire.

Combined, it nearly took her breath.

"Poor thing," she crooned. "Did that bad Elise tie you up in knots?"

One brow lifted and every trace of his ire disappeared, exactly as she'd intended. "Don't you dare make a suggestion like that unless you plan to follow through."

"Uh-uh." She shook her head. "This conversation is not devolving into foreplay."

"Not yet." Lazily, he swept her with a half-lidded smoky once-over. "But I appreciate the confirmation that talking dirty to you counts as foreplay."

Now she should slam the door in his cocky face. Except she'd shifted the mood on purpose, to give him a reprieve for confessing more than he'd probably intended. And the last thing she wanted was for him to leave.

But did she want him to stay? This wasn't some random drive-by; it was a showdown.

Between his mercurial mood and the hum in her core, this night could end up only one of two ways—either she'd let him into her bed and into her heart, or she'd give him that final push away.

Dax was still on the porch. Waiting for her to make the decision. And Dax would never let her forget she'd made the choice.

Who was tying whom up in knots here?

"Why are you here, Dax?" She took a tiny step behind the door, in case she needed to slam it after all. Of course there was a good chance he'd slam it for her, once he crossed the threshold and backed her up against it in a tango too urgent and wild to make it past the foyer. "And don't feed me another line. You know exactly why you got out of the car this time."

His reckless smile put her back on edge. "Why do I find it so flipping sexy when you call me on my crap?"

He thought her no-filter personality was sexy. He really did. She could see the truth of it in his expression. The wager was over and there was no reason for him to say something like that unless he meant it.

"Because you're neurotic and deranged, obviously." When his smile softened, she couldn't help but return it, along with a shrug. "We both must be. If you want the real answer, you said it yourself. You like that I challenge you. If it's easy, you don't value it as much."

His irises flashed, reflecting the bright porch light. "I would definitely classify this as not easy."

"And you still haven't told me why you're here."

He crossed his arms and leaned on the door frame. "Have you ever followed up with any of the couples you've matched?"

"Of course. I use them as referrals and I throw parties every few months for both former and current clients as a thank-you for being customers. Many become friends."

"They're all happy. All of them. They've all found their soul mates and say you were one hundred percent responsible." He said it as if Elise had single-handedly wiped out a small village in Africa with a virus.

"You talked to my former clients?"

The shock wasn't that he'd done so, but that he'd *just* done so. Why hadn't he had those conversations at the very beginning, when they were still operating under the terms of the wager?

"Not the recent ones, only those matched over five years ago. They should be miserable by now. Happily ever after doesn't exist." His rock-hard expression dared her to argue with his perfunctory statement.

Except he'd learned otherwise, and clearly it was throwing him for a loop.

He hadn't talked to her clients before now because he'd assumed he didn't need to. That he'd only be told what he already believed to be true.

It was hard to be handed back your arrogance on a silver platter.

"I offer a guarantee, Dax," she reminded him gently. "No one's ever asked for their money back."

Instead of bowing and scraping with apology, he stared at her. "Aren't you going to invite me in?"

"Why would I do that?"

His gaze burned through her. "Because you want to know what else I learned when I talked to your clients."

He'd learned *more* than happily ever after happened to people on a regular basis? Oh, yes, he had and he was going to make her work to find out what, running her through his maze until she dropped with exhaustion. Or solved it and won the prize. It was a ludicrous challenge. And it was working.

But she didn't for a moment believe he only wanted to

tell her about his findings. The prize wasn't simply information and they both knew it.

She held the door open wide in silent invitation and
prayed she wasn't going to be sorry.

She shouldn't have answered the bell. But now she had
to know if talking to happy couples had somehow opened
his eyes. Maybe gotten him to a place where he could see
a future with one woman.

What if she *could* be that woman? She didn't want to
send him on his way before finding out.

"Dax?"

He met her gaze as he stepped over the threshold.
"Elise."

Searching his beautiful face for some small scrap of re-
assurance, she put it all on the line.

"Please don't do this unless you mean it."

Dax shut the door behind him and leaned back against
it, both hands flat against the wood.

The click reverberated in the silent foyer.

Elise's eyes were shiny and huge and he didn't mistake
the look for anything other than vulnerability, which just
about did him in where the last week of awfulness hadn't.

Why had he stayed away so long?

It didn't matter now. He was surrounded by Elise and
everything finally made sense again. He breathed her in
before he hauled her into his arms right there in the foyer.

Tonight wasn't about slaking his thirst in the well of
Elise, though he'd be lying if he said he wasn't hopeful
they'd eventually get there. He'd have sworn this was all
about taking pleasure where pleasure was due. But now that
he was here…it wasn't. He still wasn't sure *what* tonight
was about, what he truly wanted—or what she wanted—
but the fragile quality to her demeanor wasn't doing his
own brittle psyche any favors.

Don't do this unless you mean it.

He didn't pretend to misunderstand. Her voice broke as she'd said it and it echoed in his head, demanding an answer—which he didn't have.

They needed to shake off the heaviness.

"Don't do what?" he asked lightly. "Tell you about the nineteen conversations I had with blissfully happy couples? It was nauseating."

Her quick smile set off an explosion of warmth in his midsection.

"Nineteen? That's a lot of conversations about true love. What I don't get is why you'd subject yourself to that."

He shrugged. "Seek-and-destroy mission. I was sure I'd find at least one couple embroiled in a bitter divorce settlement. Needless to say, no one was. On the heels of that estrogen ambush in your office, I needed to figure out some things."

Guilt flickered across Elise's face. "I'm sorry that happened. Some of that must have been really hard to stomach, especially coming from women you were formerly intimate with. I was selfishly caught up in my own reaction and didn't think about how you must have felt."

"Uh…" He'd been about to brush it away. But this was Elise. She'd see through him in a second. How had she known the whole thing had bothered him so much?

So much for lightening the mood.

"I was more worried about you than me," he said gruffly. "But thanks."

Such a small word to encompass the full generosity of Elise's apology. A lot of women—most women—would have said he'd gotten what was coming to him. And maybe he had. He'd treated Jenna pretty shabbily. He sighed. There was a possibility all of the women had genuine grievances. Relationships were not his forte.

But he wanted that to be different.

Elise motioned him out of the foyer and walked into the living room. "So while talking with my clients, what did you figure out?"

He followed, caught up with her in a couple of steps and grasped her hand to swing her around to face him in front of a gas-log fireplace, the flame lowered to a romantic glow.

Don't do this unless you mean it.

But that was exactly it. He *wanted* meaning, wanted something to finally click.

"I figured out *I'm* the one missing something." And only Elise held the answer. "I got out of the car tonight because I want to know what it is. You're the relationship expert. Tell me."

Her skin was luminous in the firelight and he wanted to trace the line of her throat with his lips, then keep going to discover the delights of the trim body waiting for him under her off-white sweater. But he wanted to hear her response just as much.

She looked up, hand still in his. Flesh to flesh, it sparked and the answering awareness leaped into her expression. Something powerful that was part chemistry and part something else passed between them. He let it, embraced it, refused to disrupt the moment simply because he'd been off balance since the moment this woman insisted he call her Ms. Arundel.

He tightened his grip. He wasn't about to let her step away, either.

"Tell me what I'm missing, Elise."

"What if I show you?" Her voice scraped at him, raw and low.

"What if you did?" he murmured. "What does that look like?"

"It looks like two people connecting on a fundamental level." Without breaking eye contact, she slid her free hand up his chest and let it rest over his heart, which sped up under her fingers. "It looks like the start of a long kiss that you can't bear to end. It looks like a friendship that's made more beautiful because you've opened your soul along with your body. Have you ever had that before?"

"No," he said, shocked at the catch in his throat. Shocked at how much he suddenly wanted something he'd had no clue existed.

"Me, either."

The wistful note of her admission settled over him heavily, binding them together in mutual desire for something meaningful and special.

"How do we get it?"

"It's right here," she whispered, tapping the place over his heart once with an index finger, then touching her own heart. "For both of us. All we have to do is reach out at the same time. That's what makes it wonderful."

Everything inside woke up at once, begging to dive into not just the sensations, but the swirl of the intangible. He'd called off the wager strictly because he'd begun to suspect he was about to lose. Spectacularly. And as he looked into her soul, it was done.

He was lost.

"Elise." He palmed her chin and lifted those luscious lips to his and hovered above them in a promise of pleasures to come. "I mean it."

And then he fell into that long kiss he hoped would never end and wrapped Elise in his arms. When his knees buckled, he took her to the carpet with him, twisting to break her fall, sliding into a chasm of pure joy.

She found the hem of his shirt and spread her palms hot against his back. He groaned and angled his head to take the kiss deeper, to explore her with his tongue, to taste the beauty of her.

This wasn't an urgent coupling, a slaking of mutual

thirst. It was more. Much more. Profound and meaning-ful. And he couldn't have stopped if his life depended on it.

He wanted Elise. Wanted it all, everything she'd offered, especially the emotional connection.

She lifted her head a fraction. "Dax?"

"Hmm?" He took the opportunity to run his lips down the column of her neck, exactly as he'd envisioned, and yes, it was sweet. She moaned, letting her head fall back to give him better access.

"Don't you want to go upstairs?" she asked after a good long minute of letting him taste her.

Upstairs was far away and required too much effort to get there.

"Not especially. I don't think I can wait that long." That gorgeous blush rose up in her cheeks. Mystified, he ran the pad of his thumb over the coloring. "What's this all about?"

"We're in the living room," she whispered.

"I know," he whispered back and snaked a hand under her sweater to feel the curve of her waist in an intense ca-ress. "I'm becoming very fond of your living room. The fireplace is a nice touch."

"I just…you know. The living room is for watching TV. The bed is for…lying down. In the dark."

More blushing. Despite the rock-hard bulge in his pants and the near-breathless state of desire she'd thrown him into, he recognized a woman in the midst of uncertainty. But over what?

"I'm not a particular fan of darkness. I want to see you."

"There's uh…not much to see." She wiggled a little until his hand fell from her waist, and then she yanked the hem of her sweater down over her exposed skin with a little too much force.

Sitting back on the carpet a bit to give her space, he reached out and took her hand gently. The last thing he wanted was for her to be uncomfortable. "What happened to opening yourself body and soul? Isn't that what this is about?"

"Easier said than done." She made a face. "Especially when I'm up against such stiff competition."

Competition?

Then it dawned on him. The Stiletto Brigade. They'd not only spooked her, they'd given Elise a complex about her appearance. His heart flipped over painfully but when it faded, a strange sort of tenderness replaced it.

"Look at me." When she complied, the earlier vulnerability was back tenfold. "There's not a way to say this without sounding arrogant, but roll with it for a minute. Don't you think I could be in the bed of any woman I chose?"

Her brows furrowed. "Yeah, but that wasn't really in question."

He gave her a minute but her anxiety didn't fade. A smart woman was still susceptible to being deceived by her own self-consciousness, apparently. "Then wouldn't it be safe to assume I'm with the woman I want? And that I think you're beautiful beyond compare?"

Except he'd done almost nothing to convince her of that because their relationship had evolved in such an out-of-the-norm manner. He'd never sent her flowers, never bought her jewelry, and certainly never spent an evening flattering her over dinner.

But he didn't want to do those things with her. He'd done them with other women. A lot. And it had never amounted to more than a shallow bit of nothingness designed to get a woman in bed.

Elise deserved better.

He slid a hand through her hair and smoothed it away from her face. "Instead of telling you how I feel about you, how about if I show you?"

Ten

The corners of Elise's mouth lifted. "What does that look like?"

Obviously she'd recognized her own words as he repeated them back to her.

"It looks like something so stunning, I can hardly breathe." Watching her intently, he fingered the hem of her sweater and lifted it slowly until her stomach was bared. Then he stopped. "Do you trust me with the rest?"

Surprise flitted through her expression. "I…I never thought about this being about trust."

"Of course it is. We're reaching out at the same time, but doing so requires a measure of faith. On both sides."

She stilled, taking it all in, and in a flash, he got the distinct sense she had a lot less experience with men and sex in general than the majority of women he knew. She talked such a good game he'd missed it, but with all the discussion around competition and being embarrassed about the locale he'd chosen, not to mention how often he found her home alone on the weekends…it all fit.

Then she nodded and lifted her arms, silently offering him access to completely remove her top—and placing utter trust in him at the same time. It just about broke him. Sucking in oxygen, which did not settle his racing pulse, he took his time unveiling her, inch by creamy, gorgeous inch.

She wasn't wearing a bra. And her breasts were perfect,

topped by peaks that went rigid under his heated gaze. He muttered a curse as his hands involuntarily balled up, aching to stroke her from neck to belly button. *Take it slow, Wakefield.*

"You're exquisite," he ground out through a throat gone frozen, and tossed the sweater aside, unable to tear his attention from her half-naked form. Nonsense spilled from his mouth, murmured words of praise and awe. So maybe he'd tell her how much he liked her body in addition to showing her.

"Your turn," she whispered.

Immediately he complied, whipping his shirt off as fast as humanly possible because there was no way he was letting fabric block his ability to drink in the sight of gorgeous, uncovered Elise.

"Look your fill," he advised her. "Here in the light."

Look her fill she did, hesitantly at first but then with a hungry boldness that somehow turned erotic instantly. As her gaze traveled over his bare torso, heat flushed across his skin and coalesced at the base of his spine. All the blood in his head rushed south, leaving him slightly dizzy and enormously turned on.

She was going to kill him.

"Get used to me without clothes," he continued. "I'm about to be a whole lot more naked. I want you to see how much you affect me when I look at you. How much I want you, how gorgeous you are to me."

No time like the present to shed his jeans. He stood and with the heat of the fire at his back and the heat of Elise at his front, he flipped the button. She watched, silently, her head tipped up and her lips parted, hands clasped in her lap tightly.

He should have opened with a striptease because she'd totally forgotten her own nakedness. Win-win.

Then he was fully undressed and she huffed out a strangled gasp. It was potent to render a woman with such a quick wit speechless.

"See this?" he pointed at the obvious erection straining toward her. "This is all you, honey. You're not even touching me and I'm about to bust."

He wasn't kidding. Show and Tell was turning into his favorite foreplay game ever.

"What if I wanted to touch you?" she asked coyly. "Is that allowed?"

He strangled over a gasp of his own. "That's more than allowed. In fact, it's encouraged."

Crawling to him, she wiggled out of the remainder of her clothes unprompted and knelt at his feet.

With incredible care, she ran her hands up his legs, fingering the muscles of his thighs, breezing by his erection. She grazed it and his eyelids fluttered with the answering spike of unadulterated pleasure.

She climbed to her feet to continue her exploration and he fought to stay still. Every nerve vibrated on full alert, poised to pounce at the first opportune moment.

"You still have gorgeous abs," she murmured as her fingertips read the muscles of his torso like braille. "They feel like warm, velvet stone."

"Looked me up on Google, did you?" He grinned, pleased for some ridiculous reason. Millions of people had seen those ads and he'd never given it a moment's thought. But the idea of Elise taking secret pleasure in looking at pictures of him—it was hot. "Put your hands a little south of my abs and you'll find something else that feels like velvet stone."

There came the blush again and he should totally be chagrined that he'd provoked it on purpose. But he wasn't.

Glancing at the real estate in question and back up again quickly, she gave a little sigh of appreciation that sang right through him. "I do that to you? Really?"

He groaned in disbelief and frustration. "You have been for weeks and weeks. Years. For an eternity. And now I'm moving on to the 'show' part of this demonstration."

Catching her up in his arms, he fitted hungry lips to her mouth and let all the pent-up desire guide the kiss. Instantly, she melted against him and he took full advantage, winding his embrace tighter to fit her luscious little body against him.

She felt amazing, warm and soft, and he wanted to touch. So he did, running his hands down her back, along the sweet curve of her rear, and he nearly cried out when she responded in kind. Her hands were bold and a bit clumsy with eagerness and combined, it swirled into a vortex of need more powerful than any he'd ever felt before.

This was so far beyond simply taking pleasure and returning it, he couldn't fathom it.

The urge to make this cataclysmic for her became more important than breathing.

He picked her up easily and laid her out on the couch where he could focus on loving every inch of her. Kneeling between her amazing legs, he inched over her until they were skin to skin, but his full weight rested on his elbows on either side of her.

"Talk to me," he murmured as he nuzzled her neck.

"Talk to you about what?" she asked.

He lifted his head so he could speak to her directly.

"Tell me what you like, Elise."

As passionate as she was about connection and relationships, she'd probably be incredibly responsive to anything he did, but he'd prefer to start out educated.

She bit her lip, contemplating. "Shoes. And this is a horrible thing to admit, but I really, really like chocolate."

He couldn't even laugh. She truly had no clue he'd meant for her to tell him what she liked sexually. Probably no one had ever asked her before or she had less experience than he'd assumed. The seriousness of the trust she'd shown hit him in a place inside he'd never realized was there.

"Why is it horrible to like chocolate?"

"Because it goes straight to my hips. I gain weight easily."

"That's impossible." Because he wanted to and he could, he shifted onto his side and ran the back of his hand down the curve of her waist, over the not-chunky hip and around her thigh, and it was nice indeed. "You're so thin you'd have to run around in the shower to get wet."

She snorted. "Thanks, but I didn't always look like this."

The small slice of pizza, the unfinished lunches, came back to him suddenly. She really didn't eat much. And somehow, this fear of gaining weight was tied to her self-image issues.

"You'd be beautiful to me even if you weighed more." In fact, she could stand to gain a few pounds.

"I thought we were doing the show part," she said pertly and slid her leg along his, opening herself without seeming to realize it. It was so unconsciously sexy, he let her change the subject. Plus, the new subject was one he happened to approve of.

"Yeah?" he growled. "You like it when I show you how much you turn me on? Let's begin with exhibit A."

And then he mouthed his way down her stomach to the juncture of her thighs, parting them easily, and she gasped as he tasted her sweet spot, laving it lightly to give her time to adjust to such an intimate kiss.

Her hips rolled, shoving his lips deeper against her wet center, and he sucked. She moaned on a long note and that was it—she pulsed against his tongue with a little cry that he felt clear to his toes. His own release almost transpired right then and there. It took all he had to keep it together.

He couldn't wait to be inside her any longer.

Slipping on a condom with quick fingers, he rose up over

her and caught her gaze, communicating without words, letting all his desire for her spill from his expression. She stared back, eyes luminous with satisfaction.

Slowly, so slowly, he bent one of her gorgeous legs up and nestled between her thighs to complete their connection. She sighed lustily as he pushed. When he'd entered her fully, a wash of pleasure slammed his eyelids shut and he groaned in harmony with her.

It was a dazzling thing to be joined with Elise, and he couldn't hold back. Her name tumbled from his lips, over and over, as he spiraled them both higher. Nearly mindless, he sought to touch her, to caress her, to make her come again before he did…because there were rules. But she shifted, and the angle was so sweet, he lost complete control. Splintering into oblivion, he cried out as answering ripples of her climax sharpened his. The powerful orgasm sucked him under for a long moment, blinding him to everything but the release.

With the fireplace crackling merrily and the warmth of an amazing afterglow engulfing him, he lay there, unable to move. Elise cradled his spent body, both of their chests heaving as one, and he experienced the most profound sense of bliss.

That's what he'd missed.

Happily ever after just might begin with one day of happiness that you found so amazing and wonderful, you woke up the next day aching to repeat it. And didn't let anything stop you.

Elise finally coaxed Dax into bed and they thoroughly christened it in what was the most monumentally earth-shattering experience of her admittedly short list of sexual encounters. So far, she'd managed to keep her total cluelessness from him, but she couldn't let this particular first slide.

She snuggled up against his absolutely delicious body and waited until he'd pulled the sheet up around them to spill it. "You're the first man I've had in this bed."

"Ever?" His voice was soft with a hint of wonderment. As if she'd given him a special gift he'd always wanted but never received.

Was she *that* far gone over a couple of orgasms? She was assigning all kinds of emotions to Dax that she had no business assigning. Her head needed to be plucked out of the clouds really fast, before she got ideas about what was going on here that would only lead to disappointment.

She'd consented to sleep with him, but not to fall for him.

She nodded against his shoulder and opted for candor. "I bought this set about a year ago and I didn't want to sleep here night after night with memories of a past relationship gone wrong still haunting it."

The hand intimately caressing her waist stilled. "Guess that means you figured out how to exorcise the ghosts of past lovers. Or you think I'll be in your bed for the rest of its life."

The post-orgasm high vanished as the heaviness of his real question weighted the atmosphere.

"Um…" Well, she really hadn't thought through how that particular confession was going to go, had she? "Door number three. I thought you were worth it regardless."

He slid a hand up to her jaw and guided her head up so he could look at her. Something misty and tender sprang from his gaze. "That's the best thing anyone's ever said to me."

How could that be? Surely someone had told him he had value before. But his expression said otherwise.

She couldn't look away as a powerful and intangible current arced between them. It was more than the connection she'd told him was possible. More than the deepening of their friendship that she'd sought.

Then he laid his lips on hers in a sweet kiss that went on and on and sent her into the throes of a whole different kind of high. So what if her head was firmly in the clouds?

She was in bed with Dax and he was beautiful and precious and it was the most amazing night in her memory.

And it didn't appear to be ending anytime soon.

"Lay here with me." He spooned her against his warm torso and held her as if he'd never let go, as if it was the most natural thing in the world.

"So are you…staying?" She bit her lip and left it at that, though the question was so much bigger.

"What, you mean overnight?" he mumbled. "Since it's nearly two a.m., I assumed that was pretty much a given. Do you want me to leave?"

"No!" Horrified, she snuggled deeper into him in apology and his arms tightened. The last thing she wanted was to wake up alone. "Just checking. I'm happy with you where you are."

No man had ever slept in this bed, either, and she wasn't sorry she'd waited for Dax to be the first. He fit into it perfectly and if he wasn't careful, she would invite him to spend a good long while in it.

That was actually what she'd hoped to establish by asking whether he planned to stay. Not just overnight, but when tomorrow came, then what? Was it too soon to talk about it? Was it implied that this was the start of a relationship in every sense?

Or was she supposed to know this was one night only?

"Good. Get some sleep. You're going to need it. And Elise," he whispered in her ear. "I might stay tomorrow night, too."

Apparently he'd read her thoughts.

Whether she'd given herself permission or not, it was too late to pretend she wasn't falling for him. She tucked the feeling away and held it close to her heart.

She fell asleep with a smile on her face and woke up with the same smile. Dax made her happy and she wanted to do the same for him. But he wasn't in the bed. Covers thrown back, his side was already cool. Frowning, she strained to hear the shower. Nothing.

He wasn't downstairs either. She sighed and pulled the sash on her robe tighter, cursing herself for thinking...well, it didn't matter. Dax was free to leave. She'd just hoped he wouldn't. He hadn't made promises—false or otherwise— and she hadn't requested any.

But she'd put a lot of faith in him based on his insistence that he meant it and his pretty speech about trust. Perhaps she should have established a better understanding of his definition of "I mean it."

When the front door swung open and Dax called out cheerily, she nearly dropped her freshly brewed cup of coffee.

Dax sauntered into the kitchen all windblown and smiley. It shouldn't be possible to look that delicious after only a few hours of sleep. She didn't bother to hide her openmouthed gaping.

He dropped a kiss on her temple and handed her a bag. "Hey, gorgeous. Bagels. I hope that's okay. Breakfast is the most important meal of the day, after all." He grinned and eyed her robe. "But now I'm wondering what's underneath there. Breakfast can wait a few minutes, can't it?"

"Maybe. Depends on how good the bagels are." She smiled as he glared at her in mock dismay. Then she noticed the other bag, hanging from his shoulder. "That, um, looks like a suitcase. Taking a trip?"

He shrugged. "Picked up a few things while I was out. I don't live far. Figured I'd like to be dressed in an actual suit Monday morning when I show up for work."

Oh, my. Obviously he'd decided to spend Sunday with her. And the whole of Sunday night too. Dare she hope he'd undergone such a miraculous conversion that he was ready to spend every waking second with her?

Or was this blissful weekend the beginning of the end?

"So what are we doing here?" she blurted out, suddenly panicked and quite unable to pinpoint why. "You're staying all day, tonight and then what? I'm sorry, I can't just go with it. I need some parameters here."

The bag dropped to the floor and he leaned against the kitchen counter, his expression blank. "What kind of parameters do you want? I thought this was a pretty good compromise, bringing some stuff over. It's not day by day, but no one's made any promises they can't keep. Were you expecting me to show up with more stuff?"

She'd been expecting *less* stuff, far less. She had no idea what to do with all the stuff he'd unloaded. Relationships were supposed to be structured, predictable. Weren't they? Why hadn't she practiced a whole lot more before this one? The two relationships she'd been in before were vastly inadequate preparation for Dax Wakefield.

"I wasn't actually expecting you to show up at all," she confessed. "I thought you'd bailed."

"I sent you a text. Isn't that our thing?" He grinned. "I thought you slept with your phone in your hand, pining for a message from me. That takes me down a few notches."

Frowning, she scouted about for her phone and finally found it in the side pocket of her purse. On silent. She thumbed up the message.

Don't eat. I'll be back asap with breakfast. Can't wait to see you.

All righty then. She blew out a breath and it turned into a long sigh. She kept looking for reasons not to trust him and he hadn't disappointed her yet. What was her *problem?*

"Hey." He pulled her into his arms and rested his head on top of hers. "You really thought I wasn't coming back? You don't do one-night stands. I respect that. I wouldn't have come here last night if I didn't."

"Sorry," she mumbled into his shirt in case she'd offended him. In truth, he didn't sound anything other than concerned but she'd somehow lost the ability to read him. That scared her. "I'll shut up now."

"I don't want you to shut up." Pulling back slightly, he peered down at her. "Your mouth is the sexiest thing on you."

With that, the tension mostly blew over. Or rather she chose to ignore the lingering questions so she could enjoy spending the day with a man she liked, who liked her back. It *was* a good compromise—for now. She didn't like not knowing the plan or what to expect. But for today, she knew Dax would be in her bed at the end of it and that was something she readily looked forward to.

They had fun giggling together over a couple of Netflix movies and ate Chinese delivery for lunch.

"Let me take you someplace really great for dinner," he suggested as he collected the cartons to dispose of them. "If you'll actually eat, that is."

He hefted her half-full takeout carton in deliberate emphasis.

"I'm not all that hungry," she said out of habit, and then made the mistake of glancing up into his slightly narrowed gaze, which was evaluating her coolly. Of course he hadn't bought that excuse.

Instead of taking the trash to the kitchen as he should have, Dax set the cartons back on the coffee table and eased onto the cushion next to her. "Elise—"

"I ate most of it. There's no crime in not being hungry." Her defensive tone didn't do much for her case.

"No, there's not." He contemplated her for a few long moments. "Except you're never hungry. I didn't press you on it last night when you told me you gain weight easily because, well, I was a little busy, but I can't ignore it forever. Do you have a problem I should know about?"

"Like anorexia?" The half laugh slipped out before she could catch it. This was not funny *at all* but he'd caught her by surprise. "I like food far too much to starve myself entirely, thanks."

How had the conversation turned heavy so fast? And when precisely had they reached a point in their relationship where it was okay to throw it all out there, no censor, no taboos?

"Maybe not *entirely*," he stressed. "But you don't like yourself enough to have a healthy relationship with food either."

Gently, he took her hand and she let him. His concern was evident. But he could stop with all the psychobabble any time now. She didn't have a problem other than an intense desire to never be fat again. Nothing wrong with that.

"Thanks for checking in, but it's okay. My health *is* my concern." She glanced away. He saw too much but it was the price for opening up to him. "This will be hard for you to sympathize with, I realize, but I was an ugly duckling for a long time. A fat girl. When I finally lost all the weight, I vowed never to gain it back. Portion control is my friend."

"Elise." He stroked her knuckles with his thumb in a comforting caress. "I don't know what it's like to be fat. But it's not fair to frame your struggles as if no one else can comprehend them. To deliberately shut me out solely because I have a few strands of DNA that put my face together like this."

He circled an index finger over his cheekbones, and the darkness underneath the motion, in his expression, startled her.

"I'm not trying to shut you out." Was she?

The alternative meant she'd have to let him glimpse her innermost secrets, her deepest fears. It would mean trusting him with far more than her body. It would mean trusting him with her soul.

But hadn't she already done that when she invited him into her bed?

"You may not be consciously trying to. But you are," he said mildly. "And not only that, you're making an assumption about me based on my appearance. Like I can't possibly know what it feels like to have disappointments or pain because of the way I look."

Speechless, she stared into his snapping, smoky eyes. She'd hurt him with her thoughtless comments.

She *had* made assumptions and drawn her fat-girl self around her like a familiar, impenetrable blanket.

Dax had called it during their discussion on the park bench. She ran screaming in the other direction before a man could get close enough to hurt her.

Had she already screwed this up—whatever *this* was—before it started?

"I'm sorry," she said sincerely and squeezed his hand. He squeezed back and her heart lightened a little. "I'm sensitive about food and about being fat. It's an ugly part of me. I'm not used to sharing it with anyone."

"There's nothing ugly about you," he shot right back. "Why in the world would you think a few pounds makes you ugly?"

She debated. It was so much easier to make a joke. But she'd been patiently explaining the components of happily ever after to Dax for weeks, which had everything to do with honesty, vulnerability and trust. Was she really going to balk when it was her turn to lay it all out?

"You've seen my mother. You've been in that world. Surely the pursuit of thinness is not so mysterious an ideal."

He shrugged. "But you're not a model. Neither are you your mother. So your weight is not a requirement for your job."

Easy for him to say. It was different for boys no matter what they looked like.

"It's not that simple. I grew up surrounded by swans and constantly aware I wasn't one of them. In case I didn't feel bad enough about being overweight, my mother made sure I didn't forget it for a moment."

"She's the one who made you self-conscious about being fat?" Dax scowled. "That's horrible."

His unconditional support squeezed her heart sweetly. "It turned out okay. I buried myself in algorithms and computer code instead of hanging out in the spotlight, which was, and still is, cruel. I built a business born out of the desire to shut myself away from all the negativity. Only EA International could have gotten me in front of those cameras where we met. Even now, I give deserving women makeovers because I know how it feels to be in the middle of all those swans, with no one on your side."

"I'm glad you found the fortitude to venture onto my set." Dax smiled. "And I like that you made something positive out of a bad experience."

"There's more." And it was the really important part. "That's why my profile questions dig into the heart of who you are. So my clients can find someone to love them for what's underneath, not what they look like."

Which was not-so-coincidentally what she wanted too—someone to love her forever, no matter what. She'd never had that before.

The smile slipped from his face and he gazed at her solemnly. "I get that."

Of course he did. She'd made sweeping generalizations about him because of his appearance and she'd bet it wasn't the first time someone had done that. Not only did he understand the point about loving someone's insides; of all the people she'd shared her philosophy with, he had the singular distinction of being the only one who'd seen the pain that had created it.

And she was terrified of what he'd do with all this insight.

Eleven

Dax took Elise to eat at the top of Reunion Tower, a place she'd never been despite having lived in Dallas for years. They dined while overlooking the downtown area as the room revolved 360 degrees inside the ball. It should have been a wildly romantic evening.

It *was*. But Elise couldn't quite relax.

When they returned to her house from dinner, Dax took her keys and opened the front door for her, then swept her up in his arms to carry her over the threshold. Solid and strong, he maneuvered through the door frame without hesitation, and it was undeniably sexy.

"What's this all about?" she asked as soon as she unstuck her tongue from the roof of her mouth.

"I seem to have a lot of trouble getting past your front door. This way, I'm guaranteed entrance." He grinned at her cockeyed stare. "Plus, I've got a very special treat planned and thought I'd start it off with a bang."

"Really?" Her curiosity was piqued as her tension lessened. "What is it?"

He let her slide to the ground braced against his gorgeous body and took her hand. "Follow me, Ms. Arundel, and see for yourself."

That made her grin, dispelling more of her strange mood. She trailed him upstairs and the second she entered the bedroom, he whirled her into a mind-numbing kiss.

Her brain emptied as his lips devoured her and heat tunneled into every last crevice of her body. *Oh, yes.*

Bright, white-hot desire flared in a sunburst at her core, soaking her in need and flooding her with Dax, and she couldn't catch her breath. She wanted him to love her exactly as he had last night, perfectly, completely.

Slowly, he backed her to the bed and when she would have stumbled, he tightened his arms. Then he sat her down and drew off her boots, one zipper at a time, and kissed her uncovered calves, all the way to her heels.

She watched him through heavy eyelids, a little unable to process the sight of such a beautiful man at her feet, all his attention on her. He glanced up, his gaze full of dark, sinful promise, and she shuddered as he centered himself between her legs.

With deft, strong fingers, he gathered the hem of her dress and slowly worked it up over her thighs, caressing her bare skin as he went, following the fabric with his mouth and tongue.

A moan rose in her throat and she strangled on it as he licked at her nub through her damp panties.

"I want to see you, Elise," he murmured and slipped off her dress with skill. Quick-like-fox, he had her bra and panties in the same pile as her dress.

As he raked her with a smoldering, hungry once-over, she fought the urge to crawl under the covers.

"You are so beautiful," he croaked, as though he might be coming down with something. Or she'd affected him enough to clog his throat.

Wasn't that amazing? *She* affected *him.*

He stared down at her as he lowered himself to the bed next to her, still fully clothed. "I want to make you feel beautiful."

"You do," she said automatically. Well, actually, he made her feel good. Beautiful was a little more difficult to come by.

His brows arched. "Maybe. But I can do better. Much better. So tonight is about that."

He reached under a pillow and withdrew a bag of Ghirardelli chocolate chips. She'd recognize the bag a mile away. Her mouth started watering. And then her brain caught up. "Why is that instrument of torture in my bed?"

Dax grinned and winked. "You told me you liked chocolate. *Voilà*. We'll get to the shoes another time."

The wall her insides had thrown up crumbled and everything went liquid. "You were paying attention to what I said?"

"Of course." He scowled in confusion. "Why would I have asked if I didn't want to know the answer?"

Heat flamed through her cheeks and she shut her eyes. "I thought you were being polite."

Laughing, he kissed both of her shut eyelids in succession until she opened them. "One thing I am not is polite. But I am interested in giving you an amazing experience. Starting now."

With a wicked smile, he laid her back and tore open the bag, spilling chocolate chips all over her bare stomach.

The chips rolled everywhere, and she jackknifed automatically to catch them, but he stopped her with a gentle hand to her shoulder. Then he grasped a piece of chocolate between his fingertips and traced it between her breasts, up her throat and to her lips, teasing her with it.

The rich, sweet smell of chocolate drugged her senses. She wanted to eat that bite of heaven in the worst way. But she couldn't. A moment on the lips…and it went straight to her hips. She didn't keep chocolate in the house for a reason.

"Open," he instructed. "None of these calories count because honey, I promise you're about to burn them all."

The temptation was humongous. She wrestled with it. And lost.

How could she do anything else but eat it? Chocolate burst on her tongue and a moment later, his tongue twined with hers, tasting the chocolate along with her in a delicious kiss.

The twin sensations of Dax and chocolate nearly pushed her over the edge. She moaned in appreciation. Desire. Surrender.

Trailing chocolate kisses back down her throat, he paused to line up several chips around her nipple and proceeded to lick each one, smearing more chocolate on her breasts than he got in his mouth. He proceeded to suck off the sweetness, sending her into a taut spiral of need that could only be salved one way.

As if he'd read her mind again, he lowered himself between her thighs, opened them and kissed each one. Muscles tight with anticipation, she choked on a breath, waiting for the sweet fire of his intimate kiss.

He didn't disappoint her. She felt a chip graze her nub and then Dax's tongue followed it, and her eyelids slammed closed as her senses pulsed with pleasure.

"You taste delicious," he rasped and stuck another chip under his tongue, laving so hard, she came instantly in a starburst of sparkles that bowed her back and ripped a cry from her throat.

Immediately, he rose up and treated her to a chocolate, musky kiss, twining all the flavors together into an overwhelming, sensual bouquet.

"See how delicious you taste?" he murmured and cupped her with his hand, sliding fingers through her folds and into her damp center, yanking yet another climax from deep inside.

Still in the throes of a chocolate orgasm, she couldn't sort one sensation from the other and didn't want to. Finally the ripples faded, leaving her gasping and nearly blind as dots crowded her vision.

"Delicious," he repeated. "Beautiful."

Then he put the icing on it.

"By the way," he said casually. "In case it wasn't crystal clear, this was me showing you how gorgeous you are. Remember this every time you put chocolate in your mouth, which better be a lot. Because I don't want you to ever, ever forget that you're beautiful or that the sight of you eating chocolate is so hot, I'm about to lose it."

She blinked and focused on his wolfish smile. He'd been trying to psychoanalyze her with this little stunt?

So now every time she thought about chocolate, she'd make all kinds of associations that it should never have, like unbelievable pleasure, a gorgeous man's mouth tasting of sin and sugar, and the pièce de résistance, that watching her eat chocolate turned him on.

It was…brilliant. The benefits of sleeping with a man who understood both psychology and a woman's body couldn't be overstated.

And she wasn't simply falling for him; it was more like being dropped off a cliff, straight into a mess of emotion she had no idea how to handle.

She would have thought herself capable of understanding love, if indeed that's what was going on. Certainly she would have said she could recognize it. And it did not resemble this crazy, upside-down thing inside that was half thrilling, half terrifying and 100 percent Dax.

What if this *wasn't* love but an orgasm-induced hallucination? Worse, what if she went with it, straight into a broken heart? Her fat-girl blanket usually kept that from happening, but she'd lost it.

Or rather, Dax had stolen it from her with chocolate.

And he'd completely piqued her curiosity as to what he planned to do with shoes.

Dax picked up Elise and took her to the bathroom, where he filled the tub and spent a long time washing the chocolate from her body. He wanted to sink into the steaming

water and sink into Elise, but he was too busy breathing
her in to stop.

She smelled like chocolate and well-loved woman and
home, all rolled into one bundle he could not get enough
of. He'd only meant to worship her gorgeous body and en-
able her to eat something she liked at the same time. He
had *not* intended to forever alter his perception of chocolate, but he'd never taste it again without getting a hard-on.

Which wasn't necessarily a bad thing.

Finally he couldn't stand being separated from her any
longer and stripped to slide into the tub. She watched him
unashamedly, ravenous gaze flickering to his rigid erection as he bared it. Last night she'd had a hard time with
that, as if nakedness were shocking.

Not so tonight. But he didn't dare say he was proud of
her lest he frighten her back into that shell. Besides, the
heat in her eyes sent such a shaft of desire spiking through
him, he couldn't do anything other than slide into the tub,
gather her against his chest and dive in.

He kissed her, openmouthed, sloppy and so very raw.
She melted into him, fitting her lithe body into his. Water
sloshed out of the tub, which she didn't notice and he didn't
point out.

He needed her. Now.

After an eternity of fumbling due to wet fingers and wet
body parts and far too much "help" from Elise that nearly
set off what would be a nuclear explosion of a release, Dax
got the condom in place.

He never had this much trouble. But his fingers were
still shaking as he slid into her with a groan and then he
simply clung, hands gripping Elise's shoulders. Flinging
his head back, he let the sensations bleed through him and
only some of them were physical.

That profound sense of what he could only label as *happiness* saturated the experience, lighting him up inside. It

felt as if it would burst from his skin and pour out in a river. He savored the harmony, the rightness of it.

Elise, clearly impatient with all the savoring, planted her knees on either side of him and took over the rhythm, and he let her because it was amazing. The faster she moved, the higher he soared, and a growl ripped from his mouth unrestrained as she pushed him to the edge.

Nearly incoherent and almost numb with the effort to hold back, he fingered her in an intimate caress, silently begging her to let go. Instantly, she tightened around him in an answering pulse that triggered his release, and he came in a fountain of blessed relief.

She slumped on his chest, cheek to his skin, and he shut his eyes, reveling in the boneless bliss that he'd only ever experienced at the hands of Elise.

Being with her evoked so many things he had no way to describe, things he hoped never went away. But since he didn't know how it had happened in the first place, what guarantee did he have he wouldn't wake up tomorrow and find himself back in the real world where Elise wasn't "the one"?

Because here in this alternate reality he'd somehow fallen into, it felt an awful lot as though she was a…soul mate.

Against all odds, he wanted to believe the concept existed, that it might be possible for him. For them.

After they dried off and got comfortably snugged together in bed he murmured, "Elise, you have to promise me something."

"Anything. After the chocolate, you name it." She sighed, her breath teasing the hair on his torso.

"Don't stop. Keep doing whatever you're doing and don't stop. Even if I tell you to."

She stirred and raised her head to peer at him in the darkened room, lit only by the moonlight pouring in through the opened blinds. "Why would you tell me to?"

"Because…"

I'm broken.

That's why he'd never found a woman worth promising forever to. Why Elise's matchmaking efforts had failed, despite participating in her profile sessions to the best of his ability. Not because there was something wrong with the women he'd dated, or even Candy, but because something was wrong with him. How could he explain that he pushed women away on purpose, before things got complicated?

But then, he didn't have to explain. Elise knew that already. She had spelled it out in painful detail on the park bench. If he was being honest, that had been the tipping point, the moment he knew she'd snared an unrecoverable piece of him he'd never meant to give up.

He tried again. "Because I'm…"

Falling for you.

His eyelids slammed shut in frustration and fear and God knew what else. What was wrong with him that he couldn't voice a simple sentence to tell this amazing woman how she made him feel? Or at least confess that she made him want to be better than he'd ever dreamed possible?

He wanted to be the man she deserved. For the first time in his life, he didn't want to push her away.

But he knew he was going to anyway.

He couldn't say all those things because Elise wasn't *his* soul mate. She was someone else's and he was in the way. For her sake, he would have to end things eventually.

That realization nearly split him in two. Appropriate to be as broken on the outside as he was on the inside.

"Hey." Her soft hand cupped his jaw and her thumb rested near his eyes, brushing the lashes until he opened them. "What's going on? You're never at a loss for words."

He laughed in spite of himself. She'd been tying him up in knots from day one. Why should this be any different?

"Yeah, this is all kinds of abnormal."

"Start with that. What's abnormal, being in bed to-gether?" She cocked her head and smoothed the sheets over them. "Are you about to tell me your reputation with women is vastly inflated? Because I won't believe you. The things you do to me can only be the result of years of careful study."

"I've had a lot of sex, Elise. Make no mistake," he said without apology. "But it wasn't anything like this. What's different is you. I can't explain it. It feels…bigger. Stron-ger. I don't know what to do with it."

She stared at him, wide-eyed. "Really? It's not like this with other women?"

"Not even close. I didn't know it *could* be different."

If he had, he would have hunted down Elise Arundel about a decade ago. Maybe if he had, before he'd become so irrevocably damaged, things might have worked out between them.

He could have actually *been* the man she needed instead of merely wanting to be.

Wanting wasn't good enough. She deserved someone unbroken and he needed to give her space to find that guy.

But it didn't have to be now. He could wait a few days, or maybe longer.

"But I'm just me." Bewilderment crept over her face. "I'm not doing anything special."

"You don't have to do anything special. It just is. You don't feel it, too?"

Slowly, she nodded and a sense of relief burst through his gut. Relief that this wasn't all one-sided. Guilt because it might already be too late to get out without hurting her.

"I feel it. It scares me and I don't know why." She gripped his hand. "It's not supposed to be like this, all mixed up, and like I can't breathe if you're gone. Like I can't breathe when you're here."

Exactly. That's how he'd felt all week as he'd talked to the couples Elise had matched and then drove around aimlessly, out of sorts, with no clue how to absolve the riot of stuff seething under his skin. Elise was his affliction. And his deliverance.

Maybe she was the answer, the only woman in existence who could fix him. If he wasn't broken anymore, maybe he could find a way to be with Elise forever. Maybe he *could* have her, without pushing her away. But only if he could finally let her behind his curtain.

"I have to tell you something," he said before he lost his nerve. "Your mother made you feel bad about your weight. Well, I understand how mothers can shape your entire outlook on life. Because mine left. When I was seven."

Tears pricked at his eyelids. He'd never spoken of his mother's abandonment and somehow, saying it aloud made it An Issue.

"Oh, honey, I'm so sorry." Elise pressed her lips to his temple and just held him without another word. The odd, bright happiness she evoked filled him.

"It's stupid to still let it affect me. I know that," he muttered and let his muscles relax. He wouldn't flee into the night and not talk about this.

Elise, of all people, understood the twisted, sometimes warped pathways of his mind, often when he didn't get it himself. He could trust her.

"Dax." She gave him time to collect himself and that small act meant a lot to him. "If you don't want to let it affect you, then stop."

"Oh, sure. I'll wave my magic wand and everything will be fine. Better yet, why don't you wave yours?" he said magnanimously. She didn't laugh.

Instead, she leaned forward and pierced him with a somber gaze. "That's exactly what I've been trying to do. By matching you with your soul mate, so you could be happy with someone. I want that for you."

"What if I said I want that too?"

Twelve

She froze, confusion flitting through her expression. "You do?"

"Yeah. Maybe."

She blinked and swallowed several times in a row before speaking. "You mean commitment, emotions, forever?"

Hope shone in her eyes.

For a brief moment, he felt an answering tug of hope in his heart. Forever sounded amazing.

And then reality took over and squelched everything good inside. These feelings would change—or fade—and he'd prove he was just like his mother by walking out the door.

He was wrong for Elise. She had all these visions of true love he could never measure up to. Being with her made him want things he couldn't have, and it wasn't her job to fix him.

That was the final nail. Just because he wanted to be unbroken didn't make it so. Why hadn't he kept his mouth shut and his curtain closed? He couldn't continue this charade, as though there was a future for them.

For once, he'd thought about trying. That's why he'd shared the truth with her. That's why he'd gotten out of the car.

He shouldn't have. And he had a hundred reasons why he should walk out right now before it was too late. He wasn't cut out for this, for relationships. He had to get out now, before he hurt her even more later.

Ruthlessly, he shut off everything inside, especially the part that had started to believe.

"Why do you sound so stunned?" he said instead of answering her question as he scrambled for a way to let her down easy. "This is your area of expertise. Didn't you set out to change my mind about love?"

"I'm not that good," she blurted out and bit her lip.

"Of course you are. The couples you matched think you're every bit the magical fairy godmother you claimed. Take credit where credit is due."

A grin spilled onto her face. "Does that mean I won the wager?"

His chest had the weight of a skyscraper on it and all Elise could think about was the wager? "The wager is over."

"Sorry." Her confusion wrapped around him, increasing the tension unbearably. "What about marriage? Are you on board with that, too?"

The longer he dragged this out, the more hope she'd gather. Heart bleeding, he shrugged and looked away. "Maybe someday. With the right woman."

"Wait a minute." Unease flitting over her face, she sat up, clutching the covers to her bare breasts. "I thought you were talking about having a relationship with *me*."

Carefully, he composed his expression as if this was no more than a negotiation gone wrong and both parties just needed to walk away amicably.

It nearly killed him.

"Come on, Elise. You and I both know we won't work. I got out of the car because I knew I was missing something and I needed you to tell me what. So thanks. I'm good."

She wasn't buying it. Elise was far too sharp to be put off by half truths. That's why it never paid to let anyone behind the curtain.

"Dax, we have something good. Don't you want to see if we work before giving up?"

Her warm hand on his arm shouldn't have felt so right, as though his skin had been crafted specifically for her touch.

"It doesn't matter what I want. I can't make long-term promises. To anyone," he stressed. "I'm all about keeping my word because my mother didn't. I can't stand the thought of caring about someone and then figuring out I don't have what it takes to stick around."

Nothing like the whole truth to make the point. She needed to understand that this was for her own good, so she could move on and find her Mr. Forever, and he could go back to his empty loft.

"But you can make promises to me because I'm your soul mate."

The soft whisper penetrated his misery. "What did you say?"

"*I'm* your soul mate. Your perfect woman. The computer matched us."

Something dark whirled through his chest, squeezing it even tighter, pushing air from his lungs. "That's not true. It matched me with Candy."

She shook her head. "My name came up first. But I thought I'd made a mistake due to the unorthodox profile sessions. So I messed around with the responses until Candy's name came up instead."

Blood rushed to his head and the back of his neck heated. "You did *what?*"

"It was the ethical thing to do. I thought I'd compromised the results because of how I felt about you."

Ethical. He'd been told Candy was his soul mate and therefore he'd believed Elise was meant for someone else. But it had never felt right, never fit…because he'd thought *he* was the problem.

Instead, it was all a lie.

Letting him think he couldn't do happily ever after, letting him think he was broken—that was her definition of *ethical?*

"Let me get this straight." He pinched the bridge of his nose and reeled his temper back. "You had such deep feelings for me it compelled you to match me with someone who isn't my soul mate?"

"I hoped you'd hit it off. Because I do want you to be happy. Candy just wasn't right for you."

"And who is, you?"

The question was delivered so scathingly, she flinched and didn't respond. Fortunately. His mood had degenerated to the point where he was genuinely afraid of what he might say.

He rolled from the bed and scouted around until he found his pants, and then jerked them on, but stood staring at the wall, fists clenched until he thought he could speak rationally.

"Why tell me now? Why didn't you tell me from the beginning?"

The wager. She'd been trying to win and altered the results in order to do so. It was the only explanation. That's why she'd asked if she'd won earlier. Rage boiled up again, clouding his vision.

"It wasn't a secret," she said defensively. "I thought you'd laugh and make some smarmy joke about how I couldn't possibly resist you. Plus, I wanted you to have a shot at finding your real soul mate."

"Who isn't you."

She couldn't be. His real soul mate wouldn't have let him believe all this time that he was the problem. That he was the broken one and that's why Elise's algorithm couldn't find his perfect match.

He'd trusted her. In vain, apparently.

If she'd just told him the truth, everything might be different. But she'd stolen that chance and thoroughly destroyed his fledgling belief in the possibility of happily ever after.

"I am," she corrected softly. "My match process just realized it before I did."

"Pardon me for questioning the results when it seems your process is a little, shall we say, subjective. In fact, I'd say this whole wager was slanted from the beginning. So save the sales pitch, babe."

Oh, he'd been so blind. From the very first moment, all she'd cared about was proving to everyone that she could change his mind about relationships. She didn't want true love, or at least not with him. It had all been an act to gain the upper hand. If Dax had one talent, it was recognizing a good show when he saw one.

"Slanted? What are you talking about?"

"Admit it. This was all an attempt to bring me to my knees, wasn't it? You planned for it to happen this way." He shook his head and laughed contemptuously. "You're far, far better at this than I ever dreamed. To think I almost fell for it."

She'd dug into his psyche with no other intent than to uncover his deepest longings and use them against him. It was unforgivable.

The only bright spot in this nightmare was that he no longer had to worry about how to push her away or whether he'd eventually walk out the door. She'd destroyed their relationship all on her own.

Thankfully, he'd found out the truth before it was too late.

His mistake had been starting to trust her, even a little.

"Fell for what? Dax, you're not making any sense."

Pulse hammering, Elise sorted through the conversation to figure out where this had gotten so mixed up. What had she missed? Up until now, she'd always been able to sort his fact from fiction, especially when he tried to throw up smoke screens, but that ability had disappeared long about midnight yesterday.

She was losing him, losing all the ground she'd gained—

or imagined she'd gained. Clearly, he'd done some kind of about-face but apparently not in her direction. That couldn't be right. She couldn't be this close to getting a man like Dax for her own and not figure out how to get her happily ever after.

He shook his head and laughed again without any humor. "All this time I thought *you* were looking for a relationship and I *wasn't*. You sat right there on that park bench and told me exactly what you wanted. I ignored it." He crossed the room and poked a rigid finger in her face. "'I want to beat you at your own game,' you said. And you know what, you almost did."

She flinched automatically. Oh, God. She had said that. But the way he'd twisted it around…unbelievable. As if she'd cold-bloodedly planned this to hurt him, playing dirty, fast and loose.

"Listen, this wasn't the game I was trying to win."

Except she'd been pretty focused on winning. From the beginning. Maybe she'd been more compromised than she'd assumed. She'd developed feelings for him without really understanding how to love him.

Maybe she didn't really understand male/female dynamics unless they were other people's.

"What game *were* you trying to win, then? Why is this a game at all?" A dangerous glint in his eye warned her to let him finish before she leaped on the defensive again. "Tread carefully, Elise. You clearly have no idea what you're playing around with here."

"This isn't a game," she cried. "When my name came up as your match, I wanted it to be true. I wanted you for myself and I thought those feelings compromised my integrity."

"You're lying." The harsh lines of his face convicted her further. "If that was true, you wouldn't have played so hard to get."

She couldn't fault his logic. Except he was drawing the wrong conclusion. "The truth is I didn't believe I was enough to change your mind about happily ever after."

"Enough?" he spat. "Enough what?"

"Pretty enough, good enough, thin enough. Take your pick," she whispered.

He laughed again and the sound skated down her spine. "I get it now. You said you don't trust easily, but in reality, you don't trust at all. You didn't ever intend to give me a real chance, did you? That's the game you wanted to beat me at. Get me to confess my feelings and then take my legs out from under me. Good job."

"I *did* want to give you a chance. You said we wouldn't work."

He threw his hands up. "This is why I don't do relationships. This conversation is like a vicious circle. With teeth."

She cursed as she realized her mistake. Misdirection was his forte and he was such a master, she'd almost missed it. He *had* developed feelings for her and they scared him. That's what all this was. Smoke and mirrors to deflect from what was going on back stage.

This was the part where she needed to tread carefully.

"Last night," she whispered. "Before you kissed me. You said you meant it. What did you mean?"

The raw vulnerability in his expression took her breath. And when her lungs finally filled, they ached with the effort.

"I meant I was falling in love with you." His expression darkened as her heart tripped dangerously. "I—forget it. It's too late to have that conversation now."

Dax was falling in love with her? The revelation pinged through her mind, through her heart—painfully—because he'd finally laid it all out there while also telling her to forget it. As if she could.

She'd done it. She'd reversed his stance on love and happily ever after. Shannon Elise Arundel *was* that good. Her match program was foolproof. The algorithm had matched them because she had a unique ability to understand him, to see the real him, just as he did her.

Why hadn't she realized it sooner?

"It's not too late." She crawled to her knees, begging him without words for something she had no idea how to express. "Let's figure this out."

"I don't want to figure it out!" He huffed out a frustrated breath. "Elise, I thought I was *broken*. That the reason you couldn't find my soul mate was because there was something wrong with me. I felt guilty for wanting you when your soul mate was supposed to be someone else, someone better. Instead, you were lying all along. You never trusted me."

In one shot, he'd blown all the smoke away and told her the absolute unvarnished truth. While she'd been pushing him away, he'd filed the rejection under *it's not her, it's me*.

Speechless, she stared at the pain-carved lines in his beautiful face. "I didn't know that's how you'd take it when I told you I was your match. There's nothing wrong with you. This is all about me and my issues."

"I get that you have a problem believing I think you're beautiful." He snorted. "You want to find true love but you won't let anyone in long enough to trust that they love you. That's why you've never had a connection with anyone."

"I've been holding out for someone to love me. The real me, underneath."

I've been holding out for you.

He swept her with an angry look. "Yet you're completely hung up on whether you're beautiful enough. If someone loves you solely for what you look like, that's not true love. Neither is it love to refuse to trust. You have a lot of nerve preaching to me about something you know nothing about."

"You're right." Head bowed, she admitted the absolute,

unvarnished truth in kind. "I didn't fully trust you. I don't know how."

"I bought into what you were selling." His bleak voice scored her heart. "Hook, line and sinker. I wanted something more than sex. Understanding. Support. A connection."

Everything she'd hoped for. For both of them. But somehow she'd messed up. "I want those things, too."

A tear tracked down her cheek and he watched it. As it fell to the bed, he shook his head. "You're not capable of giving me those things. This is over, if it ever started in the first place. I can't do this."

Then he stormed from the room, snagging his bag on the way out. She let him go, too numb to figure out how to fix it. Some relationship expert she was.

Dax's ex-girlfriends had been wrong. He wasn't cold and heartless and he hadn't screwed Elise over. She'd done it to him, smashing his fragile feelings into unrecoverable pieces because at the end of the day, she hadn't trusted Dax enough to believe he could really love her. She hadn't trusted herself enough to tell him they'd been matched. And now it was too late to do it all over.

Happily ever after might very well be a myth after all. And if that was true, where did that leave her and Dax? Or her company?

The sound of the front door slamming reverberated in her frozen heart.

Dax nearly took out a row of mailboxes in his haste to speed away from the mistake in his rearview mirror. Astounding how he'd assumed he was the broken one in their relationship. Only to discover she was far more broken.

While he'd naively been trying to get out without hurting her, she'd actually been one step ahead of him the entire time, determined to break him. And she'd done a hell of a job. She'd matched him with the perfect woman all right—the only one capable of getting under his skin and destroying everything in her path.

It was late, but Wakefield Media did not sleep. He drove to the office, determined not to think. Or to feel. He closed it all off through sheer will until the only thing left was a strange hardness in his chest that made it impossible to catch a deep breath.

Shutting himself off behind his desk, Dax dove into the business he loved, the only thing he could really depend on. This company he'd built from the ground up was his happily ever after, the only one available to him. If he put his head down, maybe he'd come out the other side with some semblance of normality. Dawn came and went but the hardness in his chest didn't fade.

At noon, he'd had no human contact other than a brief nod to Patricia as she dropped off a cup of coffee several hours ago. Fatigue dragged at him. Well, that and a heavy heart.

His phone beeped and he checked it automatically. Elise. He deleted the text message without reading it, just as he'd done with the other three. There was nothing she could say that he wanted to hear.

Morosely, he swiveled his chair to stare out over the Dallas skyline and almost involuntarily, his eye was drawn to the building directly across from him, where Reynolds Capital Management used to reside. Dax had heard that Leo left the venture capital game and had gone into business with Tommy Garrett, a whiz kid inventor.

It was crazy and so unlike Leo. They'd been friends for a long time—until Daniella had come along and upset the status quo.

Bad, bad subject. The hardness in his chest started to hurt and the urge to punch something grew until he couldn't physically sit at his desk any longer.

He sent Patricia an instant message asking for the address of Garrett-Reynolds Engineering and the second he got it, he strode to his car. It was time to have it out with Leo once and for all.

Except Leo wasn't at the office. Dax eyed Tommy Garrett, whom he'd met at a party an eon ago. The kid still looked as though he belonged on a surfboard instead of in a boardroom.

"Sorry, dude," Tommy said and stuck a Doritos chip in his mouth. "Leo's still on vacation. But I'm pretty sure he's at home now if you want to catch him there."

"Thanks." Dax went back to his car, still shaking his head. Leo—at home in the middle of the day on a Monday. His affliction with Daniella was even worse than Dax had imagined.

By the time he hit Leo's driveway, Dax was good and worked up. This time, he didn't hesitate, but drove right up to the gate and rolled down his window so the security system could grant him entrance.

Leo was waiting for him on the front steps as Dax swung out of the Audi. Of course the state-of-the-art security system had alerted the Reynoldses that they had a visitor, and clearly Leo was as primed for a throw down as Dax was. Dax meant to give it to him.

"Dax." Leo smiled warmly, looking well-rested, tan and not wearing a suit. "It's good to see you. I'm glad you came by."

Dax did a double take.

Who was this guy? Because he didn't resemble the Leo Dax knew.

"Hi," Dax muttered, and tried to orient. Leo wasn't supposed to be happy. And he wasn't supposed to be nice. They weren't friends anymore.

"Please, come in." Leo jerked his head behind him toward the house. "Dannie's pouring us some iced tea."

"This isn't a social call," he fairly snarled and then heard himself. Where were his manners?

Leo didn't flinch. "I didn't assume that it was. But this is my home, and my wife wanted to serve you a drink. It's what civilized people do when someone comes by without an invitation."

My wife. The dividing line couldn't have been clearer. But then, Leo had drawn that line back in his office when he'd told Dax in no uncertain terms that Daniella was more important to him than anything, including money, the deal between Leo and Dax, and even their friendship.

All at once, Dax wanted to know why.

"I'm sorry," Dax said sincerely. "Tea is great. Thanks."

He followed Leo into a dappled sunroom with a view of the windswept back acreage of the property. The branches were bare of leaves this late into the season, save a few evergreens dotting the landscape.

Daniella bustled in with a tray, smiled at Dax and set a glass full of amber liquid in front of each man. "Nice to see you, Dax. Enjoy. I'll make myself scarce."

Gracious as always. Even to a man who made no secret of his intense dislike and mistrust of her.

Dax watched her drop a kiss on Leo's head. He snagged her hand to keep her in place, then returned the kiss on her lips, exchanging a private smile that seemed like a language all its own. They were so obviously in love, it poleaxed Dax right in the heart.

Because he didn't have that. Nor did he hold any hope of having it.

Against everything he'd ever believed about himself, the world and how he fit into it, he wanted what Leo and Daniella had.

The floodgates had been opened and then shut so swiftly, he'd barely had time to acclimate, to figure out what he was going to do with all the emotions he'd never felt before.

Then *bam!* Betrayal at its finest. The two people he'd let himself care about had *both* betrayed him. And one of them would answer for it right now.

After Daniella disappeared, Dax faced Leo squarely. "I suppose you're wondering why I'm here."

"Not really." Leo grinned at Dax's raised eyebrows. "Dannie and Elise are very good friends. I'm guessing you didn't know that."

Elise. Her name pierced that hard place in his chest and nearly finished what the lovey-dovey scene between Leo and Daniella had started. Death by emotion. It seemed fitting somehow.

And no, he hadn't realized Daniella and Elise were friends. Daniella had probably been treated to an earful already this morning. "And your wife tells you everything, right?"

"Yep."

Dax sank down in the wicker chair, but it didn't swallow him as he would have preferred. If he'd known his spectacular flameout at the hands of Elise had been trotted out for everyone's amusement, he might have gone someplace else, like Timbuktu.

"Last night was really messed up," Dax allowed without really meaning to. It just came out.

"I sympathize." Leo cleared his throat. "Which is more than you did for me when I was going through something similar, I might add."

That hurt. "Is this what you were going through? Because I don't see how that's possible."

Leo and Daniella had an effortless relationship, as if they'd been born for each other and never questioned whether they trusted the other.

"No, it's not the same because we're different people in love with very different women."

"I'm not in love with Elise," Dax broke in.

He might have been entertaining the notion, but she'd killed it. Somehow it was worse to finally embrace the idea that love wasn't just a fairy tale only to have your heart smashed.

Leo just looked at him and smirked. "And that's your problem right there. Denial. That, plus an inability to give someone a chance."

"That's not true," he burst out. "She's the one who didn't give me a chance. She lied to me. I can't trust anyone."

And that was the really painful part. There wasn't one single person in existence he could fully trust. If it could have been anyone, he'd have put his money on Elise, the one person who understood the man behind the curtain. He *had* put his money on Elise—five hundred thousand dollars—and she'd never lost sight of the prize. He should take a lesson.

"I can give you relationship advice all day long if that's what you're after. But you didn't really come here to find out that you guard yourself by pushing people away? You already know that."

Yeah, he did. He ended relationships before he got invested. He left women before they could hurt him. No mystery there. The question was why he'd let his guard down with Elise in the first place.

Dax sipped his tea and decided to go for broke with Leo. "I came to find out why Daniella was such a big deal. I know you married her. But why her? What was special about her?"

Leo's face lit up. "I love her. That alone makes her special. But I love her because she makes me whole. She allows me to be me. She *enables* me to be me. And I wake up every day wanting to do the same for her. That's why Elise matched us. Because we're soul mates."

Dax nearly snorted but caught himself. The evidence stood for itself and there was no need to act cynical about it any longer. No one in this room was confused about whether he believed in it. But believing in soul mates and allowing a woman who professed to be yours to take a fillet knife to your heart were two different things.

"And that was worth ending a friendship over?" Dax asked.

Stupid question. Clearly Leo thought so and at that particular moment, Dax almost didn't blame him. Look what Leo had gotten in return.

"Dax." Leo sat forward in his chair. "I didn't end our friendship. You did. You weren't being a friend when you said disparaging things about my wife. You weren't being a friend when you demanded I choose you over her. I was messed up, wondering how I could love my wife and still maintain the workaholic life I thought I wanted. I needed a friend. Where were you?"

There was no censure in Leo's tone. But there should have been. Hearing it spelled out like that sheared a new layer of skin off Dax's already-raw wounds. He'd been a crappy friend yet Leo had welcomed Dax into his home without question.

"I was wallowing in my own selfishness," Dax muttered. "I was a jerk. I'm sorry."

"It's okay. It was okay as soon as you rolled up the driveway. I've been waiting for you to come by." Leo held out his hand for Dax to shake, which he did without hesitation.

The hardness in his chest lifted a bit. "Thanks for not barring the gate."

"No problem. I had a feeling you'd need a friend after what happened with Elise. It sounded rough. I'd like to hear about it from you, though."

Dax watched a bird hop from branch to bare branch outside the sunroom's glass walls. "Her computer program matched us. But she wasn't interested in me or finding the love of her life. Or professional ethics. Just winning."

"I watched the interview," Leo said quietly. "You were ruthless. Can you blame her for bringing her A game?"

The interview. It felt like a lifetime ago, back when he'd been smugly certain he couldn't lose the bet because love didn't exist. He almost preferred it when he'd still believed that.

"She screwed me over. I can't forget that."

"You reap what you sow. You started out going head-to-head and that's where you ended up. Change it if that's not what you want."

Leo sipped his tea as Dax shifted uncomfortably. "You say that like I had some fault in this, too."

"Don't you?" Leo tilted his head in way that told Dax the question was rhetorical. "I went into my marriage with Dannie assuming I wanted a wife who took care of my house and left me alone. And that's what I got until I realized it wasn't what I really wanted. Fortunately, she was waiting for me to wake up and see what I had. You didn't give Elise that chance. You ended it."

Of course he'd ended it. "I don't make promises I can't keep."

It was an automatic response, one he'd always said was the reason he didn't do relationships. But that wasn't why he'd walked out on Elise.

The problem was greater than the fear of learning he was like his mother, faithless and unable to make promises to one person forever.

He also feared being like his father—pathetic. Mooning over a woman who didn't actually care about him, waiting in vain for her to come back.

Elise hadn't told him the truth and he could never trust her to stay. And if he let himself love her, and she didn't stay, he'd be doomed to a lifetime of pain and an eternity of solitude because he'd never get over losing his soul mate.

Thirteen

When the doorbell rang, Elise's pulse sprang into double time as she flew to answer it.

Dax.

He'd come to apologize, talk, yell at her. She didn't care. Anything was fine as long as he was here. Hungry to see him again after three miserable days, she swung open the door.

Her heart plummeted.

It was Dannie, dressed to the nines in a gorgeous winter-white cashmere coat, matching skirt and heels. Next to her stood Juliet, the new princess of Delamer, wearing a T-shirt and jeans, of course.

"What are you doing here?" Elise glowered at Juliet. "You're supposed to be on your honeymoon."

The princess shrugged delicately and waved a hand full of bitten-off nails. "It was a working honeymoon and you need me more than His Royal Highness. I left my husband in New York with a host of boring European diplomats. I miss him already, but I owe you more than I can ever repay for giving me back the love of my life."

"I need you?" Elise glanced at Dannie. "You called Juliet and told her I needed her?"

"Yes, yes I did." Dannie bustled Juliet into the house, followed her and shut the door, then held up two bags. "This is an intervention. We brought wine and chocolate since you never keep them in the house."

The heaviness Elise had carried since Dax left returned tenfold. "No chocolate for me. But wine sounds pretty good."

The silence had been deafening. He'd ignored her text messages, even the funny ones. He hadn't called. At first she'd thought it was merely pride, which was why she kept reaching out. But he really didn't want to talk to her.

"Come on, Elise. Live a little. When a man acts like an ass, chocolate is the only cure," Dannie called from the kitchen where she'd gone to fetch wineglasses and a corkscrew.

Tears welled up and the ugly-cry faucet let loose. Dannie flew into the living room and enfolded Elise in a comforting embrace while Juliet looked on helplessly.

Murmuring, Dannie smoothed Elise's hair and let her cry. Sobs wrenched Elise's chest, seizing her lungs until suffocation seemed more likely than a cease-fire of emotions.

Her life had fallen apart. But her friends were here when she needed them.

"It's okay, cry all you want," Dannie suggested. "The endorphins are good for you. It'll help you feel better."

"I know." Dabbing at her eyes ineffectively with a sleeve, Elise sniffled and gave up. "But they don't seem to be working."

"Maybe because Dax is more of an ass than regular men?" Juliet suggested sweetly.

Dannie bit back a snort and Elise choked on an involuntary laugh, which led to a fit of coughing. By the time she recovered, the tears had mostly dried up.

"It wasn't working because it's my fault. I'm the problem, not Dax," Elise confessed.

They might be soul mates, but obviously there was more

to it than that. Happily ever after didn't magically happen, and being matched was the beginning of the journey, not the end. And she had no clue how to get where she wanted to be. That's why she couldn't hold on to Dax, no matter how much she loved him.

Everything he'd accused her of was true.

"That's ridiculous." Dannie *tsk*ed.

"I'm not buying that," Juliet said at the same time. "It's always the man's fault."

Elise smiled at the staunch support. She'd had a hand in these two women's becoming the best they could be, in finding happiness with the men they'd married, and it had been enough for so long to be on the sidelines of love, looking in from outside, nose pressed to the glass.

At least then she hadn't known what she was missing.

"Dax has a hard time trusting people," she explained. "I knew that. Yet I didn't tell him we were matched and he took it as a betrayal."

More than a betrayal. She hadn't trusted that he could love the real her. He'd been gradually warming up to the idea of soul mates, putting his faith in her, and she'd forgotten to do the same.

"So what? When you love someone, you forgive them when they mess up," Juliet declared. "People mess up a lot. It's what makes us human."

"And sometimes, you have to figure out what's best for them, even when they don't know themselves," Dannie advised. "That's part of love, too. Seeing beneath the surface to what a man really wants, instead of what he tells you he wants."

"And sometimes," Elise said quietly, "love isn't enough. Sometimes, you hurt the person you love too much and you can't undo it. That's the lesson here for me."

She'd had a shot at being deliriously in love and ruined

it. She'd always believed that if her soul mate existed, then love *would* be enough.

Juliet and Dannie glanced at each other and a long look passed between them.

"You get the wine." Dannie shooed Juliet toward the kitchen and then extracted a jewelry box from her purse.

Juliet returned with the wineglasses, passed them out and perched on the edge of the couch. "Open it, Elise."

After handing the box to Elise, Dannie sat next to Juliet and held her glass of wine in her lap without drinking it.

Carefully, Elise cracked the hinged lid to reveal a silver necklace. A heart-within-a-heart charm hung from the chain. Surprised, she eyed the two women. "Thank you. But what's this about?"

Dannie unclasped the necklace and drew it around Elise's neck. The cool metal warmed instantly against her skin.

"You gave us necklaces during our makeovers," Dannie said and nodded at Juliet. "We were about to embark on the greatest adventure of our lives. We had your guidance from the first moment we met our matches and it stayed with us every day, right here in silver."

"Open heart." Juliet pointed at Dannie's necklace and then at her own. "Hearts holding each other. Simple but profound messages about love. We wanted to return the favor."

"I had no idea those necklaces meant so much to you." Tears threatened again and Elise blinked them back. "What does mine mean?"

Juliet shook her head with a small smile. "That's for you to figure out at the right time. That's how it works."

"We can't tell you. Just like you didn't tell us." Dannie put a comforting hand on Elise's arm. "I wish I could make it easier for you because honestly, working through the issues I had with Leo was the hardest thing I ever did."

Nodding, Juliet chimed in. "Finn and I are so much alike,

it was nearly impossible to compromise. But we found a way and it was so worth it."

Elise fingered the larger heart with the smaller one nestled inside. Her match was a disaster, not like Dannie's and Juliet's. She'd known their matches were solid from the beginning. Of course, it was easier to see such things from the outside.

What was it about matters of your own heart that were so difficult?

That was it. A heart within a heart.

The necklace's meaning came to her on a whisper, growing louder as her consciousness worked through it, embraced it. The large heart was the love between a man and a woman, which had the capacity to be huge and wonderful, eclipsing everything else.

But inside the larger heart lay a smaller heart.

I have to love myself too.

The fat girl inside hadn't vanished when Dax poured chocolate chips over her. Or when he admitted he was falling in love with her. Because it wasn't enough.

She had to be enough, all by herself, with or without a man by her side.

Until she believed she was worthy of loving a man like Dax and allowing him to love her in return, she wasn't his soul mate. She wasn't his perfect match.

Not yet. But she could be.

"I get it. The necklace," Elise clarified, and took the other women's hands in hers, forming a circle. "I know how to get my happily ever after, or at least how to shoot for it. Will you help me?"

"Yes," they said simultaneously.

"You have a plan," Dannie guessed.

Elise nodded slowly as it formed. "Wakefield Media has a box suite at AT&T Stadium, but Dax never goes. He hates the Cowboys." She didn't recall when he'd shared that information. During one of their marathon profile sessions, likely. "But I need him there on Sunday. Can you have Leo make up some reason why they both need to go to a game?"

"Of course." Dannie smiled mischievously. "Leo will do anything I ask. I finally got two pink lines this morning."

"You're pregnant?" Elise gasped as Juliet smiled and kissed Dannie's cheek. "No wonder you told Juliet to get the wine."

"We're not announcing it. I'm only telling you two because I had to tell *someone*." The glow only made Dannie more beautiful. "But enough about me. I'll get Leo and Dax there."

"Thanks." Elise squeezed both of their hands. "You are the finest ladies I've ever had the privilege of meeting."

The last thing Dax wanted to do was go to a Cowboys game. But Leo insisted and they'd only recently resurrected their friendship. How could he say no and not offend Leo?

Dax would much rather spend the day asleep, but that wasn't an option. He hadn't slept well since that last night with Elise. Spending the day alone held even less appeal. So he went.

The stadium teemed with blue and silver and stars aplenty. The world's fourth-largest high-definition video screen hung from the roof, from the twenty-yard line to the opposing twenty-yard line, and only someone in the media business could fully appreciate the glory of it.

The retractable roof was closed today in deference to the late season weather, which boosted the crowd noise to a new level of loud. Once he and Leo arrived in the luxurious box suite, blessed silence cloaked them both as they ordered beer from the efficient waitstaff and then slid into the high-backed suede stools overlooking the field.

Leo held out his longneck bottle and waited for Dax to clink his to it. They both took a long pull of beer.

After swallowing, Leo said, "Thanks for doing this. I thought we should hang out, just us."

"Sure." Dax shrugged, a little misty himself at the catch in Leo's voice. "No one was using the suite today and the Cowboys are playing the Redskins. It'll be worth it if the 'Skins trounce the homeboys."

The spectacle of the teams taking the field began, and they settled in to watch the game. They sat companionably until halftime, when Leo cleared his throat.

"We've been friends a long time. But some major changes have happened in my life. I've changed. I hope you can respect who I am now and it won't affect our friendship going forward." Leo stared out over the field. "On that note, I have to tell you something. It's huge."

Dax's gut clenched. Leo was about to announce he had two months to live. Or Daniella did.

Fate couldn't be so unkind to such genuine people. And Dax had wasted so much time, time Leo may not have, being stupid and prideful.

"I've been hard on Daniella and on you about her. I'm over it." Over his pettiness, over his inability to be happy for his friend. But not over the slight jealousy that Leo had figured out how to navigate relationship waters with such stellar success. "It's great that you found her. She's amazing and obviously good for you."

"She is. And that's good to hear, because—" Leo grinned and punched Dax on the arm "—I'm going to be a father."

"That's what this bro-date was about?" Dax grinned back as his nerves relaxed. "Congrats. I'm glad if you're glad."

Leo was going to have a family.

Jealousy flared again, brighter, hotter. Shock of all shocks. Dax had never once thought about having a family. Never thought he'd want one. Never dreamed he'd instantly imagine a tiny, beautiful face with dark hair and a sharp wit. A little girl who took after her mother.

"Of course I'm glad! It's the second-best thing that's happened to me after marrying Dannie." Leo swallowed the last of his beer and set it down with a flourish. "And no. That's not why I insisted we come to the game. That is."

Leo pointed at the jumbo screen in the middle of the stadium. A woman's face filled it. A familiar, dark-haired woman. *Elise.*

Dax's pulse pounded in his throat. "What's going on?"

Audio piped into the suite quite clearly.

"Thanks for giving me thirty seconds, Ed," she said, her voice ringing in Dax's ears, filling the stadium as the crowd murmured and craned their necks to watch. "My name is Elise Arundel and I'm a matchmaker."

What was this all about—advertising? Or much more? He glared at Leo. "You had something to do with this?"

"All her," Leo replied mildly. "I'm just the delivery boy."

Dax's gaze flew back to the screen where Elise was addressing the entire stadium full of Sunday afternoon football fanatics. *Elise* was addressing *80,000 people* voluntarily. If he weren't so raw, he might be proud of her. It must have been difficult for her, given that she didn't like to be the center of attention.

"Some of you saw me on the *Morning Show* a few weeks ago, being interviewed by Dax Wakefield. We struck a deal. If I matched Dax to the love of his life, he'd agree to sing my praises at the Super Bowl. Which is in February and unfortunately, I lost the wager."

Lost? She'd been quite gleeful over the fact that she'd won the last time he'd seen her. His mind kicked into high gear. She was up to something.

"So," she continued. "Congratulations, Dax. You win. You get to put me out of the business of happily ever after. I'm such a good loser, I'm going to let you do it at a football game. All you have to do is join me on camera. Tell these people I didn't change your mind about true love and that you still don't believe soul mates exist."

"How can I do that?" Dax muttered. "I don't know where you are."

"I'm here," Elise said. But in the flesh, not through the stadium's sound system.

He whirled. And there she was, gorgeous and real, and her presence bled through the air, raising heat along his neck. She was within touching distance. He'd missed her, missed her smile, her quirky sense of humor. The way she made him feel.

And then he remembered. She was a liar, a manipulator. She cared only about winning.

Except she'd just announced to 80,000 people that she'd lost. And she'd told him in no uncertain terms that only promoting EA International could get her in front of a camera. Obviously she'd found another motivator, but what?

A cameraman followed her into the suite, lens on Dax. He couldn't even muster a fake grin, let alone his "camera" smile, not when Elise had effectively pinned him to a piece of cork after all. "What is this all about, Elise?"

"I told you. This is your shining moment. It's your chance to ruin me. Go ahead." She nodded to the stadium, where this nightmare was playing out on the screen.

Thousands of eyes were riveted to the drama unfolding and it needed to be over. Now.

He opened his mouth. And closed it. Not only was he pinned to a cork, on display for everyone to examine, she was daring him to lie in public.

He wasn't a liar.

So he didn't lie.

"My soul mate doesn't exist."

Something sharp and wounded glinted in the depths of her eyes.

"Tell them I didn't match you to the love of your life," she suggested clearly, as if the stadium deserved to hear every word regardless of what was going on inside her. "That I'm a fraud and my match software doesn't work."

Obviously, this was not going to end until he gave her what she was asking for.

"True love doesn't exist for me and your match process is flawed," he growled as his pulse spiked and sweat broke out across the back of his heated neck, though both statements were true. "Is that what you wanted me to say?"

It was done. He'd set out to ruin her and now everyone in the stadium, as well as those watching at home, heard him say it. His comments would be broadcast far and wide on social media, he had no doubt.

His stomach churned. The victory was more hollow than his insides.

All at once, he realized why. He'd called off the wager and meant it. But only because he refused to lose and calling it off was the only way to ensure that would never happen.

He and Elise were put together with remarkable similarity. Was he really going to blame her because she didn't like to lose either?

Leo might have had a small point about Elise bringing her A game.

Too bad the wager was the only real thing they'd ever had between them.

Vulnerability in her expression, she stared at him without blinking. "Is that all? There's nothing more you have to say?"

"I'm done."

Wasn't what he'd already said enough? His heart felt as if it were being squeezed from its mooring through a straw. Did she not realize how painful this was?

She crossed the suite, closing the few yards between

them, barging right into his personal space. Finger extended, she pointed right at the area of his torso that hurt the worst.

"You need to tell them the *whole* truth. You not only admitted love does happen to others, you started to believe in it for yourself. In the possibility of soul mates," she said. "Because I matched you with the perfect woman. And you fell in love with her, didn't you?"

He groaned. She'd seen right through his carefully worded statements. Right through him. The curtain didn't exist to her.

He crossed his arms over the ache in his chest. "It would be unfair to say either of us won when in reality, we both lost."

Tenderness and grief welled in her eyes. "Yes. We both lost something precious due to my lack of trust in you. But not because you were untrustworthy. Because I couldn't trust myself, couldn't trust that I was the right person to change your mind about true love. I was convinced you'd end our relationship after a couple of weeks and when I fell in love with you, I—"

"You're in love with me?" Something fluttered in his chest as he searched her face.

All her deepest emotions spilled from her gaze, spreading across her expression, winding through his heart.

It was true.

His pulse spiked and he fought it. What did that really change? Nothing.

"I'm afraid so," she said solemnly. "Nothing but the truth from here on out. I thought love conquered all. But without trust, someone can be perfect for you and still screw it up."

She was talking to him. About him. She knew he'd let his own issues cloud their relationship, just as she had. He'd let his fears about turning out like his parents taint his life, never giving anyone a chance to betray his trust.

He'd let anger blind him to the truth.

This had never been about winning the wager, for either of them.

"How do you know if you can trust someone forever? That's a long time."

"Fear of the unknown is a particular expertise of mine," she allowed with a small smile. "I like to know what's going to happen, that I can depend on someone. Especially when he promises something so big as to love me for the rest of my life. That's scary. What if he changes his mind? What if—"

"I'm not going to change my mind."

The instant it was out of his mouth, he realized what she'd gotten him to concede. And the significance of it.

"And by the way, same goes," he said. "How do I know you're not going to change yours?"

How had he not seen they were alike even in this? Neither of them trusted easily, yet he'd crucified her over her inability, while tucking his own lack of trust away like a favored treasure. She hadn't been trying to bring him to his knees. Just trying to navigate something unexpected and making mistakes in the process.

"Let's take it day by day. As long as you're in this relationship fully today, that's the only guarantee I need. I love you." She nodded to the stadium. "I'm not afraid to stand up in front of all these people and tell you how I feel. Are you?"

It was a challenge. A public challenge. If he said he loved her, it would be the equivalent of admitting she'd won. Of admitting she'd done everything she said she would in the interview.

"What are you trying to accomplish here?" he asked.

"I believe this is more commonly known as me calling you on your crap."

Against his will, the corners of his lips turned up. "Is that so?"

Only Elise knew exactly how to do that. Because she got him in a way no one else ever could.

She nodded. "But I had to wade through my own first. When my algorithm matched me with you, it wasn't wrong. But I was. I'm sorry I didn't tell you I was your match. I wasn't ready to trust you. I am now."

And she'd proved it by declaring her flaws to the world on the big screen, publicly. The one place she said she'd go only for her business. But she'd done it for him because *he* was her motivator. Because she loved him.

Somehow, that made it easier to confess his own sins.

"I…messed up, too. I wasn't about to stick around and find out I couldn't trust you to stay, so I didn't. I'm sorry I didn't give you that chance."

The exact accusation he'd flung at her. His relationship philosophy might as well be Do Unto Others Before They Do Unto You. That ended today. If he loved Elise and knew beyond a doubt he wasn't going to change his mind, he wasn't broken. Just incomplete.

His soul needed a mate to be whole.

Her smile belied the sudden tears falling onto her cheeks. "You didn't meet your soul mate because your soul mate wasn't ready to meet you. But I am ready now." She held out her hand as if they'd just been introduced for the first time. "My name is Shannon Elise Arundel, but you can call me Elise."

He didn't hesitate but immediately grasped her fingers and yanked her into a kiss. As his mouth met hers and fused, his heart opened up and out spilled the purest form of happiness.

He'd found his soul mate, and it turned out he didn't want a woman who didn't care what was behind his curtain. He wanted this woman, who'd invited herself backstage and taken up residence in the exact spot where she belonged.

She'd been one step ahead of him the entire time. She

was the only woman alive who could outthink, outsmart and out-love him.

Lifting his head slightly, he murmured against her lips, "I love you too. And for the record, I'd rather call you mine."

An "aww" went up from the spectators and without taking his attention off the woman in his arms, Dax reached out to cover the lens with his palm. Some things weren't meant to be televised.

Epilogue

Elise's first Super Bowl party was in full swing and surprisingly, she'd loved every minute of it. It had been her idea and Dax let her plan the whole thing. And he didn't mind that she spent more time in the kitchen with Dannie and a host of female guests cooing over baby talk now that Dannie was in her second trimester.

"Hon," Dax called from the living room. "I think you'd better come see this."

Immediately, Elise set down her wine and moved to comply. The other women snickered but that didn't slow her down.

"What?" she called over her shoulder. "If any of you had a gorgeous man like that in your bed every night, you'd jump when he said jump, too."

She sailed out of the kitchen to join Dax on the couch in front of the sixty-five-inch LED TV that now dominated her—their—living room. It was the only thing Dax had requested they keep from his loft when he moved in with her at Christmas.

How could she say no? They hardly ever watched it anyway. Neither football nor science fiction movies held a candle to doing everything together—going to the grocery store, dinner and sometimes even to work with each other. It was heaven on earth and it could not possibly get any better.

"I like what I see so far," she told him as her gaze lit on his beautiful face.

Dax grinned and took her hand, nodding at the TV. "You can look at me anytime. That's what you should be focusing on."

The game had cut to a commercial break. A Coca-Cola polar bear faded away as one commercial ended and another began. A familiar logo materialized on the screen. *Her* logo. EA International's, to be precise.

"What did you do?" she sputtered around a startled laugh.

"I owed you the match fee. Watch," Dax advised her and she did, fingers to her numb lips.

A montage of clips from her confessional at the Cowboys game flashed, interspersed with snippets of former clients espousing her praises in five-second sound bites. The whole commercial was cleverly edited to allow Elise's speech about true love to play out in real time in the form of happy couples. Then the last scene snapped into focus and it was Dax.

"EA International specializes in soul mates," the digital version of Dax said sincerely, his charisma so crisp and dazzling on the sixty-five-inch screen she nearly wept. "That's where I found mine. Elise, I love you. Will you marry me?"

Her pulse stopped, but her brain kept going, echoing with the sound of Dax's smooth voice.

The screen faded to a car commercial and the house full of people went dead silent as Dax dropped to his knees in front of her, his expression earnest. "I'm sorry, but I can't call you Ms. Arundel any longer."

And then he winked, setting her heart in motion again as she laughed through the tears that had sprung up after all. "You can call me Mrs. Wakefield. I insist."

Applause broke out and Elise was gratified to feel absolutely no heat in her cheeks. Dax lived in the spotlight, and she'd deal with it gladly because she wanted to stand next to him for the rest of her life.

The crowd shifted their attention to other things, leaving Dax and Elise blessedly alone. Or at least as alone as they could be with thirty people in the house.

Without a lot of fanfare, Dax pulled a box out of his pocket and produced a beautiful, shiny diamond ring, eclipsed only by the wattage of his smile. "I'm assuming that's a yes."

She nodded, shaking loose a couple of the tears. "Though I'm intrigued to find out what you'd planned as a backup to that commercial if I said no."

How could he come up with anything more effective than *that?* He'd declared his love for her, asked her to marry him and endorsed her business in the most inarguable way possible. He was brilliant and all hers.

It was better than a fairy tale. Better than Cinderella because he saw *her*, the real her, underneath. No makeover, no fancy dresses. If she gained a few pounds, he wouldn't care.

"No backup," he said smugly and slipped the ring on her finger, which fit precisely right, of course. Dax Wakefield never missed a trick. "I knew you'd say yes since I proposed during the Super Bowl. You know, because it's less predictable than Valentine's Day."

Her heart caught on an erratic, crazy beat. He remembered what she'd said on that park bench a season ago. That alone made him her perfect match. The rest was icing on the cake.

"I thought being with you couldn't get any better. How like you to prove me wrong," she teased and then sobered, taking his jaw between both of hands. His ring winked back at her from its place on her third finger, perfect and right. "Don't stop, even if I tell you to, okay?"

"Deal." He leaned forward to kiss her sweetly, and against her lips, mouthed, "I love you."

"I love you, too."

Happily ever after had finally arrived. For both of them.

* * * * *

PREGNANT BY
THE RIVAL CEO

KAREN BOOTH

In memory of Holly Gilliatt, brilliant author and fabulous friend. You taught me the importance of embracing the good and the sheer power of defying the bad.

One

"Strangle me? Isn't that a little harsh?" Anna Langford gaped at her friend and coworker, Holly Louis.

The pair stood in the luxe lobby of The Miami Palm Hotel, just outside the bar. Anna was preparing to see her bold business plan to fruition. If only Holly could find it in her heart to say something encouraging.

"I've only been in a few meetings with your brother, but he's going to hit the roof when he finds out you want to cut a deal with Jacob Lin."

Anna glanced back over her shoulder. The bar was humming with people, all fellow attendees of the two-day Execu-Tech conference. As Senior Director of Technology Acquisitions for LangTel, the telecom her father had started before she was born, Anna had the job of scouting out the next big thing. Her brother Adam, current LangTel CEO, had been crystal clear—he expected to be dazzled.

The company had been floundering in the months since their father's death, and Anna had a bead on a game-changing cellphone technology, only Adam didn't know it. She was fairly sure that LangTel's competitors hadn't figured it out either. Unfortunately, getting to the next big thing meant going through Jacob Lin, and he absolutely hated her brother. Adam, without a doubt, despised him right back.

"That's him, isn't it?" Holly asked in a whisper, nodding in Jacob's direction. "Damn. I've never seen him in person before. He's fifty times hotter than in pictures."

Tell me about it. Anna was well acquainted with Jacob Lin and his hotness. She'd been rebuffed by him and his hotness. Six years later and it still stung.

"Does he always have that aura?" Holly swirled her hand in the air. "The one that says he's genetically superior to every man within a fifty-mile radius?"

Anna didn't even need to look. "Yes, and he comes by it honestly. It's not an act."

"Wow." Holly patted Anna's shoulder. "Well, good luck. I'd say you'll need it."

"What?" Any confidence Anna had mustered was evaporating. "Do you really think it's going to be that bad?"

"You're a Langford. He hates your family. So, yes. I do think it's going to be that bad."

"Technically, I could order you to come with me. You're a member of my team."

Holly shook her head so fast it made her curly hair frizz. "My job description does not include suicide missions."

Another wave of doubt hit Anna, but she did her best to brush it off. She had to do this. If she was ever going to convince her brother that it was okay to step aside and allow her to take over as CEO, just as he'd promised her before their father died, she had to make tough decisions and dangerous moves.

Holly wasn't wrong, though. There was no telling how Jacob would react given his history with the Langford family. "I'm telling you right now, it's going to be great." Anna feigned conviction. "Jacob is a money guy and I can offer him a big pile of money. And once Adam sees how huge this could be for LangTel, he'll get past the personal stuff, too. It's business. Nothing else."

"So what's your plan to approach Mr. Hottie?"

"I'm going to ask the bartender to give him a note."

Holly squinted one eye as if she had a migraine. "Oh, because that won't seem weird?"

"I can't call him," Anna pled. "I don't have his cell number." The only number she had for Jacob was six years old, acquired during the week he spent with her family at Christmas, the year she fell for him, the year she'd kissed him. The year he'd told her "no." That old cell number was no longer his. She'd tried it, and no dice.

"You can't exactly go up to him and start talking either. You won't just get the rumor mill going, you'll set it on fire."

"No. I can't just walk up to him." However ridiculous it sounded, if ever there was an understatement, that was it. Everyone in the tech world was aware of the feud between Adam Langford and Jacob Lin. The backstabbing had been ruthless and very public.

"If anyone can make the impossible happen, it's you," Holly said. "Text me later and let me know what happened. Good luck."

"Thanks," Anna muttered. She straightened her

blouse and strode into the room with her head held high, then sidled up to the only available seat at the bar. She discreetly took a piece of paper and pen from her purse. It was time to conjure her steeliest tendencies. No looking back now.

> *Jacob,*
> *I'm sitting at the far end of the bar. I need to*
> *meet with you to discuss a business proposition.*
> *I thought it best not to approach you in the open*
> *considering the state of things between you and*
> *Adam. Text me if you're interested.*
> *Anna*

She added her cell phone number and signaled to the bartender. She leaned forward, hoping the men sitting on either side of her wouldn't hear. "I need you to give this to the gentleman seated in the corner. The tall one in the gray suit. Black hair." She skipped the part about his ridiculously square jaw and sublime five o'clock shadow. She also left out his superhuman sexiness and his perfect, tawny complexion, the product of his Taiwanese and American background.

The bartender raised an eyebrow, looking down at the note.

Give me a break. Anna slid a ten-dollar bill across the bar.

The bartender swiped the money away. "Sure thing."

"And a dirty martini when you get a chance. Three olives." Liquid courage would be right on time. She scratched her head, striving to remain inconspicuous while studying Jacob. He ran his hand through his hair when he took the note from the bartender. She caught a glimpse of his deep brown eyes. It wasn't hard to remember the way they lit up when he smiled, but she doubted her message would prompt such a response.

His forehead crinkled as he read. What was he thinking? That she was crazy? Now that he had personal wealth north of one billion, was incredibly accomplished in the field of venture capitalism, and at the top of his game, it seemed a little childish to have sent a note. And to think she'd once hoped it would end well when she kissed him.

Jacob shook his head and folded the paper. He tapped away at his phone. How had she forgotten how bewitching his hands were? Like the rest of him, they were big and manly. They seemed so…capable. Sadly, her bodily familiarity with his hands didn't go beyond one of them on the small of her back and the other on her shoulder when he'd delivered the stinger that had stuck with her for years. *I can't, Anna. My friendship with Adam means too much.*

It had taken buckets of self-analysis to get over him, and just being in the same room was bringing it all back—in a deluge, where there was no dodging a drop of water. With all of the serious business-related thoughts rolling in her head, her mind kept drifting to their past—every smile, laugh, and flirtatious look they'd ever shared still haunted her. Dammit. She'd been so sure she was beyond this.

Jacob tucked his phone inside his suit coat pocket and finished his drink.

The screen on Anna's phone lit up. Her pulse throbbed in her throat. What would he say? That he wanted nothing to do with her or her family? That she was lucky he didn't call her out in the crowded bar?

She swallowed hard and read the text.

Penthouse suite. 15 minutes.

Anna forgot how to breathe. The message was so like Jacob. Direct. To the point. Just intimidating enough to make her doubt herself even more. She wasn't put off by powerful men. She worked alongside them every day, could hold her own in any tense business situation. But those men didn't have the pull on her that Jacob had once had. Those men hadn't once held her heart in their hands, and she sure hadn't spent years pining for any of them, writing dozens of heartfelt letters that she would ultimately never send.

Jacob stood and bid a farewell to a man he'd been talking to. With the grace of a cat, he wound his way through the jam-packed bar, towering above nearly everyone at six-foot and several more inches, acknowledging the few who had the guts to greet the most formidable and successful technology venture capitalist quite possibly ever.

A shiver crawled along Anna's spine as he came closer. He brushed past her, not saying a word, leaving behind his heady scent—sandalwood and citrus. Fifteen minutes. She had to pull herself together and prepare to be alone with the one man she would've once done anything for.

Anna Langford. I'll be damned. Jacob pressed the button for the private elevator to his suite. He'd spent the last six years convinced that the entire Langford family despised him, a feeling he'd had no choice but to return.

After the note from Anna, he didn't know what to think, which was unsettling. He always knew what to think.

Did he want to meet with gorgeous Anna Langford, youngest of the three Langford siblings, the woman stuck with an untrustworthy jerk for an older brother? The prospect, although ill-advised, was intriguing. He and Anna had once been friends. On one memorable night they'd been a little more. But did he want to speak to Anna Langford, a member of the LangTel executive board? On that count, it depended on what she wanted to discuss.

His plan to engineer a takeover of LangTel wouldn't simply backfire if Anna discovered it—he'd be sunk. The War Chest, a secret high-roller investment group led by Jacob, had watched the decline of LangTel stock after the death of Anna and Adam's father, Roger. The company was vulnerable with Adam in charge—he didn't have the confidence of the board of directors the way his dad had. LangTel was ripe for the picking.

The War Chest's plan had been born over cards and too much bourbon one night in Madrid, at a retreat for key players. Jacob had put it out there—*What about LangTel? Could a company that large be taken over?* It would be a daunting challenge, requiring a massive money pool and meticulous planning, but this was precisely the kind of project the War Chest loved. Without risk came no reward. There was money to be made, and a lot of it, because a company that well established would eventually rebound. Carving out a slice of revenge against Adam by ousting him as CEO would merely be giving Adam exactly what he deserved.

Jacob rode the elevator upstairs. The game had changed the instant Anna walked into that bar. She was no longer a wide-eyed coed. She was a powerful businesswoman—confident, cool, in control. Other men in the bar had taken notice, too—she was formidable for her business pedigree, coming from one of the most successful entrepreneurial families in US history. Her beauty only upped the intimidation factor, with thick brown hair falling around her shoulders, a dancer's grace and posture, and lips that suggested sweetness and hinted of a storm.

Anna's lips had fallen on his once—a few scorching heartbeats still emblazoned in his memory. The way she pressed against him had resonated to his core. She'd been so eager to surrender her body, so ready to explore his. Turning her down, saying he'd destroy his brotherly friendship with Adam if things went further, had been the upstanding thing to do.

He had no way of knowing that Adam would betray him months later by ending their business partnership, making millions from the sale of the company they'd started together and publicly bashing Jacob's contribution to the project. The words Adam had said could never be erased from Jacob's memory. *It's your fault you never asked for a partnership agreement.* And to think he'd trusted Adam…that had been his first mistake.

He keyed into his suite—quiet, sprawling luxury, echoing his private existence at home in New York. Outside of a maid or a cook or an assistant, there was never anyone waiting when he walked through the door at the end of the day, and that was how he preferred it. Most people were nothing but a disappointment—Exhibit A, Adam Langford.

A business proposition. What was Anna's angle? It'd be brave of her if it involved peacemaking. The feud between himself and Adam only continued to get worse.

It seemed as if the more successful Jacob became, the more Adam said crude things about him at cocktail parties and in business magazines. *Jacob Lin doesn't have an entrepreneurial mind. He's good with money and nothing else.* Jacob had given into it, too. *Adam Langford will coast on his family name for as long as the world lets him.* It was impossible not to engage, but it had also occurred to Jacob after the last barbs were exchanged in the newspapers, that words were no way to go. Actions spoke louder. He'd no longer tell the world what he thought of Adam. He'd show them.

Jacob picked up the direct line to the twenty-four-hour concierge.

"Good evening, Mr. Lin. How may I assist you?"

"Yes. Can you please send up a bottle of wine?" He flipped through the room service menu. "The Montrachet, Domaine Marquis de Laguiche?" He rattled off the French with no problem. Years of shuttling between boarding schools in Europe and Asia had left him fluent in four languages—French, English, Japanese and Mandarin, the language his father had grown up speaking in Taiwan.

"Yes, Mr. Lin. We have the 2012 vintage for fifteen-hundred dollars. I trust that is acceptable?"

"Of course. Send it up right away." *Life is too short for cheap wine.*

Actually, he and Anna had consumed more than their fair share of cheap wine during their marathon late-night talks at the Langford family home in Manhattan. That felt like a lifetime ago.

His friendship with Adam had meant the world then. They told each other everything, commiserated over growing up with powerful, yet emotionally reclusive, fathers. They bonded over career aspirations, came up with ideas effortlessly. Jacob had hit it off with Anna equally well, except that he'd only had a sliver of time with her—ten days during which they drank, played cards and joked, while attraction pinged back and forth between them. He'd thought about acting on it many times, but never did.

He'd been raised as a gentleman and no gentleman made a move on his best friend's sister, however tempting she might be. Anna had been supremely tempting. It physically hurt to say "no" to her when she'd kissed him and it wasn't only because she'd given him a mind-numbing erection. He'd sensed that night that he was turning down more than sex. It was difficult not to harbor regrets.

After room service delivered the wine, Jacob removed his suit coat and tie. He was essentially shedding his armor, but it would make things more informal. If the Langfords were aware that a takeover was in the mix and Adam had sent her to spy on him, this would make him seem less threatening. The War Chest investors had been careful, but some tracks were impossible to cover.

The suite doorbell rang. Jacob had given his personal assistant the night off, so he strode through the marble-floored foyer to answer it. When he opened the door, he couldn't help himself—he had to drink in the vision of Anna. A stolen glimpse of her in the hotel bar had nothing on her up close. Her sweet smell, her chest rising and falling with each breath, sent reverberations through his body for which he was ill prepared.

"May I come in?" she asked. "Or did you answer just so you could slam the door in my face?" The look in her eyes said that she was only half kidding. He had to give her credit. It couldn't have been easy to break the silence between himself and the Langfords.

"Only your brother deserves that treatment. Not you." Jacob stepped aside. He'd forgotten about the sultry nature of her voice, the way it made parts of him rumble and quake.

"I won't take up your time. I'm sure you're busy." She came to a halt in the foyer, folded her hands in front of her, playing the role of steely vixen all too well.

"Anna, it's eight o'clock at night. Even I don't schedule my day nonstop. The evening is yours. Whatever you want." The more time he spent with her, the more sure he could be of her motives.

She straightened her fitted black suit jacket. The long lines of her trousers showed off her lithe frame. "You sure?"

"Please. Come in. Sit."

Anna made her way into the living area and perched on the edge of the sofa. Palm trees fluttered in the wind outside. Miami moonlight filtered through the tall windows. "I came to talk about Sunny Side."

Of the things Jacob thought Anna might come to discuss, he hadn't considered this. "I'm impressed. I thought I'd managed to keep my investment role at Sunny Side quiet. Very quiet. Silent, in fact." Exactly as he hoped he'd kept his LangTel investments. Was he losing his touch? Or was Anna that good?

"I read about them on a tech blog. It took some digging to figure out where their money was coming from, but I eventually decided it had to be you, although that was just a hunch. Thank you for confirming my suspicions." She smiled and cocked an eyebrow, showing the same satisfied smirk her brother sometimes brandished.

The times Jacob had wanted to knock that look off Adam's face was countless, but on Anna? Coming from her, delivered via her smoky brown eyes, it was almost too hot to bear. He was intrigued by this sly side of her, more self-assured than the coltish twenty-year-old he'd first met. "Well done. Would you like a glass of wine? I have a bottle on ice."

Anna hesitated. "It's probably best if we keep our conversation strictly business."

"There's no business between you and me without the personal creeping in. Your family and I are forever enmeshed." She could turn this point on him later if she learned of the War Chest's plans, not that he cared to change a thing about it. The ball was rolling.

Anna nodded in agreement. "How about this? Talk to me about Sunny Side and I'll stay for a glass of wine."

Was it really as innocent as that? His skeptical side wanted to think that it wasn't, but it'd been a long day. At least he could enjoy a glass of good wine and derive deep satisfaction from admiring his nemesis's little sister. "I'll open it right now."

"So, Sunny Side," Anna said. "They could be an amazing acquisition for LangTel."

Jacob opened the bottle at the wet bar, filled two glasses and brought them to the lacquered cocktail table. He sat near Anna and clinked his glass with hers. "Cheers." Taking a long sip, he studied her lovely face, especially her mouth. He'd only had her lips on his for a few moments, but he knew the spark beneath her composed exterior. She could so easily be his undoing. He hadn't anticipated this beguiling creature resurfacing in his life. Or that she might disrupt the riskiest investment venture of his career.

"Well?" she asked. "Sunny Side?"

"Yes. Sorry. It's been a long day." He shook his head, trying to make sense of the situation. "Is there a point in discussing it? Sunny Side might consider an offer from LangTel, but the problem is Adam. I don't see him wanting to acquire a company I'm so deeply entrenched with and frankly, I'm never getting into bed with him either." Getting into bed with Adam's sister might be another matter. Loyalty was no longer standing in the way.

She nodded, intently focused. "I'll take care of Adam. I just want to know if you can put me in the room with Sunny Side."

"Just so you know, it's about more than money. The founder is very leery of big business. It took months for me to earn his trust."

Her eyes flashed. She was undaunted by obstacles. If anything, it brought out her enthusiasm. "Of course. The technology has limitless applications."

"It will revolutionize the entire cell phone industry." One thing dawned on him—the War Chest's interest in LangTel was with the mind of turning the corporation into a bigger moneymaker once Adam was gone. Sunny Side would be a major player in the industry, so why *not* put the two together? It could have an enormous upside.

"So, can we make this happen?"

Jacob admired her persistence. Among other things. "Only if Adam stays out of it."

"Tech acquisitions is my department. Think of it as doing business with me."

"How long do you think you'll stay in that job?" He'd been surprised she'd taken a job with LangTel at all. She always seemed to hate being in her brother's shadow.

"Not forever, hopefully."

"Setting your sights on bigger and better things?"

She smiled politely. "Yes."

He was relieved that she saw herself eventually leaving LangTel. She'd still make a boatload of money from her personal stock if he was successful with a takeover, and her career wouldn't be derailed. Adam was his target, not Anna. "Okay, well, if we're going to talk about Sunny Side, Adam has to stay out of it. A negotiation requires compromise and he is incapable of that. He hates it when you disagree with him."

"I'm familiar with that aspect of his personality." She ran her finger around the edge of the wine glass, her eyes connecting with his and sending a splendid shock right through him. "I could never get Adam to tell me exactly what happened. Between the two of you."

Although Jacob wasn't certain what made Adam react the way he had, he suspected Roger Langford was at the root of it all. It started when Jacob spotted problems with Adam's central idea for Chatterback, the social media website they were starting. They needed to rethink everything. Adam vehemently disagreed. He brooded, they argued for days on end. Jacob suggested Adam consult with his dad—maybe he could talk some sense into him. The next day, Jacob had been cut out entirely. "I find that surprising. I assumed he bad-mouthed me to anyone who would listen."

"He did some of that, but he mostly just never wanted to talk about it." Anna wound her arms around her waist.

Did he care to venture down this road tonight? Absolutely not. The details were too infuriating—money lost, countless hours, passion and hard work unfairly yanked away. Plus, he couldn't tell Anna that he suspected her father had been the problem. She was likely still grieving him. "I don't want to be accused of trying to taint your opinion of Adam. He is your brother, after all."

"Okay, then at least tell me that you'll put me in the room with Sunny Side."

His mind went to work, calculating. There were myriad ways in which this could all go wrong. Of course, if it went right, that could be a real coup. "I'll make it happen, but this is only because of you. I don't want Adam interfering."

"Believe me, I won't let him get in the middle." Anna took a sip of her wine. When she set down the glass, she laughed quietly and shook her head. "It was bad enough when he was the reason you didn't want me to kiss you."

Two

Adam's fiancée, Melanie, pointed to the dog-eared pages of bridal magazines spread out on the dining table in Adam's penthouse apartment. "Anna? What do you think? Black or eggplant?"

Bridesmaid's dresses. Talking about the dress she'd have to wear for Adam and Melanie's January wedding felt like a speed bump. Anna'd been trying to broach the subject of Jacob and Miami for nearly the entire week, but Adam kept putting her off.

"Do you have a preference?" Melanie asked.

Anna shook her head, setting down her dessert spoon. The chocolate mousse Melanie had served with dinner was delicious, and perfect, just like Adam and Melanie's life—a well-matched couple giddily in love, wedding a few months down the road. "I'm sorry. What were you saying?"

"Classic black A-line or strapless dark purple?"

Anna choked back a sigh. She was happy for Adam and Melanie, really she was, but their wedding had taken over Langford family life. It was the only thing their mother, Evelyn, wanted to talk about. Just to make things especially fun for Anna, her mother usually added a comment about how her first project after the wedding was helping Anna find the right guy. January couldn't come—and go—soon enough.

She loved her brother dearly. Melanie had become a close friend. It was just that it was painful to watch them reach a milestone Anna was skeptical she'd ever reach. At twenty-eight, being hopelessly single in a city full of men who didn't have eyes for women with lofty aspirations, there wasn't much else to think. Most men were intimidated by her family and the job she'd already ascended to at LangTel. It wasn't going to get any less daunting for them if and when she took over as CEO.

"The black, I guess," Anna said. "But you should pick what you want. Don't worry about me. It's your big day, not mine."

"No, I want you to be happy. I think we'll go with the black." Melanie smiled warmly.

Anna really did adore her future sister-in-law. These days, Melanie was the only thing that made being around Adam tolerable, which was so sad. Adam had once been her ally. Now it was as if she had a grizzly bear for a brother and a boss—she never knew what would set him off, and most days, it seemed as if everything did.

She'd assumed she and Adam would lean on each other after their father passed away, but instead, Adam had withdrawn. He'd holed up in Dad's big corner office and become distant. The tougher things got, the more

Adam shut her out. She'd been exercising patience. Everyone dealt with death differently. If only he'd trust her with more responsibility, she could lighten his workload and remind him that she was well equipped to take over.

Melanie took Adam's hand across the sleek ebony table, her stunning Harry Winston engagement ring glinting. "I still can't believe we're getting married. I pinch myself every morning."

"Just wait until we have kids," Adam quipped. "Then things will really get surreal."

"You're already talking about children?" Anna tried to squelch the extreme surprise in her voice.

"We are," Melanie answered. "Two of my sisters had trouble getting pregnant. If we're going to have kids, I don't want to risk waiting too long."

Anna nodded. She'd worried about how long she would have to wait. Her friends from college were having kids, some their second or third. On an intellectual level, she knew she had time, but after her dad had died, emotion had taken over reasoning, and she panicked.

Feeling alone while watching Adam move forward with his life, Anna decided she wasn't about to wait for a man to show up in hers. She'd looked into artificial insemination. It was a just-in-case sort of thing—a fact-finding mission. Hopefully, she'd find love and a partner and none of it would be necessary, but at that moment when she'd felt powerless, taking action was the only comfort she could get.

Unfortunately, the visit to the clinic brought a devastating problem to light—a tangle of scar tissue from her appendectomy, literally choking off her chances of conception unless she had surgery. If she didn't fix the problem and she did become pregnant, carrying a baby to term was unlikely. With things crazy at work, Anna hadn't done a thing about it, although she planned to. Some day.

"We aren't going to have to try, Mel." Adam leaned back in his chair, folding his hands behind his head. "If I have my way, you'll be pregnant by the end of the honeymoon."

Melanie laughed quietly. "Did Adam tell you about Fiji?" she asked Anna. "Two weeks in a private villa on the beach with a chef and an on-call masseuse, all while the rest of New York is dealing with gray snow and cold. I can't wait."

Fiji. In January. Anna took a cleansing breath. She hated these feelings of envy. She wanted to squash them like a bug.

"We need to talk about that, because we're going to be away for a full two weeks," Adam said to Anna. "If you think that's too long a stretch for you to be in charge at LangTel, you need to tell me now."

Anna blew out an exasperated breath. "I can't believe you think there's a chance I can't handle it."

Adam fetched a bottle of beer from the fridge and returned to the table. "What about Australia? What if something like that happens when I'm gone? We're still sorting out that mess."

"First off, *we're* not sorting out that mess, I am. And you asked me to make those changes. I was following orders."

"If you're going to be CEO, you have to think for yourself." He took a sip of his beer and pointed at her with the neck of the bottle. "There will be no orders to follow."

How she hated it when he talked down to her like that,

as if she didn't know as much about business, when she absolutely did. "And I will do that once you finally hand over the reins." Anna tightened her hands into balls. She was so tired of her dynamic with Adam, constantly at war.

Melanie buried her nose in a bridal magazine. Surely this wasn't a comfortable conversation to sit in on.

"When you're ready and not a day sooner," Adam barked. "You know we're in a delicate position. The company stock is fluctuating like crazy. I keep hearing rumblings about somebody, somewhere, wanting to take over the company."

She'd heard those same rumors, but had ignored them, hoping they were conjecture and nothing more. "Adam, change brings instability. I think you're making excuses, when the truth is that you suddenly have zero confidence in me."

"You don't make it easy when you make mistakes. Half of the board members are old guard. They do not want to see a woman take over the company, no matter what they might say to your face. We have to find the right time."

Anna felt as though she was listening to her father speak. Was there something about working out of that office that made a person completely unreasonable? "You mean I have to wait until you decide it's the right time."

"You have no idea the amount of pressure I'm under. People expect huge things from me and from LangTel. I can't let what Dad started be anything less than amazing."

Anna kept her thoughts to herself. Adam was struggling with their father's death even more than she was. He might not realize it, but she was sure his iron grip on LangTel had more to do with holding on to the memory of their dad than anything else. Tears stung Anna's eyes just thinking about her father, but she wouldn't cry. Not now.

"I can do this. I thought you believed in me."

"I do, but frankly, you haven't dazzled me like I thought you would."

"Then let me dazzle you. I have an idea for an acquisition after the conference in Miami. That's what I've been trying to talk to you all week about."

"I don't want to spend our entire evening talking shop. Send me the details in an email and we'll talk about it tomorrow."

"No. You keep blowing me off. Plus, I'm starting to think this isn't a discussion for the office."

"Why not?"

You might get mad enough to set off the sprinkler system. "Because it has to do with Jacob Lin. I'm interested in a company called Sunny Side, and he's the majority investor."

Adam's jaw dropped and quickly froze in place. "I don't care if Jacob Lin is selling the Empire State Building for a dollar. We're not doing business with him. End of discussion."

That last bit was so like her dad, and such a guy thing to do, attempting to do away with an uncomfortable subject with male posturing. It insulted every brain cell in her head, which meant it was time to forge ahead. She wasn't about to wait for another time. It might never come. "The company makes micro solar panels for cell phones, phones that will never, ever need an electrical charge."

"Sounds amazing," Melanie chimed in from behind the shield of her magazine.

Adam shook his head, just as stubborn as Anna had imagined he'd be. "No, it doesn't."

"Yes, it does," Anna said. "We're talking about a revolution in our industry. Imagine the possibilities. Every person who ever wandered around an airport looking for an outlet will never see a reason to buy a phone other than ours."

"Think of the safety aspects. Or the possibilities for remote places," Melanie added. "The public relations upside could be huge."

"Not to mention the financial upside," Anna said.

Adam kneaded his forehead. "Are you two in cahoots or something? I don't care if Jacob has invested in a cell phone that will make dinner and do your taxes. He and I tried to work together once and it was impossible. The man doesn't know how to work with other people."

Her conversation with Jacob was fresh in her mind, what he'd said about the end of his friendship with Adam. What if things had been different and they had remained friends? "Funny, but he says the same thing about you."

Adam turned and narrowed his focus, his eyes launching daggers at Anna. "You spoke to him about this?"

"Actually, I met with him. I told him that LangTel is interested in Sunny Side."

"I can't believe you would do that."

"Come on, Adam." Anna leaned forward, hoping to plead with her eyes. "We would be passing up a huge opportunity. Just take a minute and look past your history with Jacob for the good of LangTel. You'll see that I'm right."

Adam stood up from the table. "I can't listen to this anymore. I'm going to answer emails and take a shower." He leaned down and kissed the top of Melanie's head. "Good night."

"That's it?" Anna asked, bolting out of her seat, her chair scraping loudly on the hardwood floors. "The almighty Adam passes down his decree and I'm supposed to live with it, even when my idea could make billions for the company he won't hand over because he's so concerned with its success?"

"Look, I call the shots. I'm CEO."

Anna felt as if she'd been punched in the stomach. "You've reminded me of that every day since you took over."

"Good. Because I don't want to talk about this ever again. And I don't want you to speak to Jacob Lin ever again, either." He started down the hall, but turned and doubled back, raising a finger in the air as if he'd just had the greatest idea. "In fact, I forbid it."

"Excuse me?" She remained frozen, beyond stunned. "You forbid it?"

"Yes, Anna. I forbid it. You are my employee and I am forbidding you to talk to him. He's dangerous and I don't trust him. At all."

Three

Jacob ended his first conversation with Adam Langford in six years with a growl of disgust, dropping his cell phone onto the weight bench in his home gym. Where exactly did Adam get off calling him? And issuing orders? Stay away from his sister? Keep your little cell phone company to yourself? Jacob had a good mind to get in his car, storm through the lobby of LangTel up to Adam's office and finally have it out, once and for all. Lock the door. Two guys. Fists. Go time.

Jacob leaped up onto the treadmill, upping his pre-set speed of six miles per hour to seven. Rain streaked the windows. Morning sunlight fought to break through gray September clouds looming over the Manhattan skyline. His long legs carried him across the conveyor belt, his breaths coming quicker, but it wasn't enough. It wasn't hard. It wasn't painful. He upped his speed again. He craved every bit of release he could get—no sex in two months, a powder keg of a job and an infuriating phone conversation with his biggest adversary made him feel as if he might explode.

It was more than what Adam had said, it was the way he'd said it, so smug and assuming. Adam wasn't all-powerful. He never had been, although he loved to act as though he was. Adam did not control him. The suggestion, even the slightest hint that he did, made his blood boil. He'd show Adam. He'd do whatever the hell he wanted. He would get as close to Anna as humanly possible, in any way she wanted to be close to him. If she wanted to do business, they would. If she wanted a replay of that kiss, they'd do that, too.

Jacob quickly finished five miles, every stride only steeling his conviction that Adam needed to be humbled, big time. He'd felt that way before Anna had come into the picture, and although she had no idea, she'd set off a chain of events that left him fixated on his goal. Adam needed to know what it felt like when someone destroyed everything you'd worked so hard for.

That was merely the business side. There were other unpaid debts. When Adam had betrayed him, he'd thrown away their friendship as if it meant nothing. That left a familiar void—Jacob found himself without a close friend, exactly as he'd lived out much of his childhood and adolescence, shuttled from one private school in Europe to another, never having enough time to fit in.

He'd been a straight-A student, but hardly had to try at all—that annoyed the hell out of the smart kids. He came from unspeakable wealth, but it was new money. He'd had to learn the hard way that there was a difference. He didn't have a notable lineage behind his family name. His father was immensely powerful, but that was in the Asian banking world, not the entrenched circles of old-world high society in England and France. Jacob was left in a no-man's-land, with plenty of money for the highest tuitions, the grades to get into the best schools and nothing to focus on but studies that didn't challenge him in the slightest.

The real shame was that his friendship with Anna became collateral damage when things went south with Adam. Their immediate rapport had shown so much promise. He felt truly at ease with her. He could talk to her about anything, especially his upbringing, something he did not share easily. She always listened. If she hadn't had the same experiences, she still empathized, and she found a bright spot in everything.

The night she'd kissed him, he'd been equal parts shocked and thrilled. He'd been pushing aside thoughts of his lips on hers from the moment he met her. She was off-limits, his friendship with Adam too precious. So he'd had to tell her "no." He'd been sure his bond with Adam would be stronger because of it. But that had been a mistake. Every mistake he'd made because of Adam was an open wound, refusing to heal.

What if he and Anna brought things full circle? For just one night? They could start where they left off with that kiss six years ago, this time without Adam in the way. It would be more than physical gratification. A tryst with Anna would be another instance in which Jacob showed Adam just how little control he had.

Jacob muted the bank of televisions airing global financial news in front of him. He sat back down on the weight bench, picked up his phone and called the founder of Sunny Side. He was open to meeting with Anna, but could they do it upstate? Mark and Jacob had homes thirty minutes from each other. Perfect. Out from under the meddlesome reach of Adam.

He ended the call and scrolled through the contacts until he found Anna. Rational thought and urges warred inside his head. Could he cross that line? He would never hurt her. Business or pleasure—Sunny Side or sex, he'd follow her lead, but they could get nowhere until he set them on the right path.

"Jacob. Hello," she quickly answered, hushing her voice.

Her softly spoken words were much like early-morning pillow talk, bringing a pleasant sensation, a rush of warmth. Perhaps it was the knowledge that his actions would enrage Adam. "Anna. How are you today?"

"Good. You?"

She had to be covering. Adam must've been hard on her when she'd brought up the notion of doing business with Jacob. Too bad for Adam—this call was about Anna and Jacob putting together a deal. No more letting Adam get in the way. "I'm good. I wanted to talk to you about Sunny Side. I spoke to Mark, the founder, and he's amenable to the three of us meeting this weekend."

"Really? That would be fabulous."

Jacob was surprised by Anna's lack of hesitation. She'd spoken to Adam about this—Adam had said as much, and yet she seemed undaunted, unwilling to conform to Adam's wishes. A woman after his own heart. "We'll see how things go. If you two talk and it's not a good match, that's the end of that. But I can't imagine you not hitting it off with Mark. I doubt he'll have a defense for the Anna Langford charm."

That last part was the truth, not necessarily meant as flirtation, although he knew very well it came out that way.

"I could always wave a fat stack of cash in his face," she quipped.

"Coming from you, I'd say that sounds incredibly sexy." Visions of Anna seductively thumbing through a bundle of hundreds materialized. That *would* be sexy. Insanely sexy.

"I'll be sure to run by the bank."

A protracted silence played out over the line. It was partly his fault. He'd really tripped himself up with "sexy." He cleared his throat. "So you're up for the meeting?"

"Absolutely."

How he loved her decisiveness, her fire. It made him want to kick himself for ever saying "no" to her. "We're meeting at my place in Upstate New York if you can make that work. Mark bought a house about a half hour from mine. I don't know about you, but I could really use the getaway."

"Getaway? You and me?"

"Just for a night. It's too far to go for just a few hours. Or at least that's what I say to force myself to take a break from work."

"Oh. I see."

Why was going away with him the one point of hesitation? Was she thinking he was making a pass? He didn't want her to think so. "It'll be like old times. If you're lucky, I might even beat your butt at cards."

"We have to have this meeting and talk hard numbers. That's really important."

He blew out a breath. Maybe it was for the best that

she was determined to focus on business. That would make it more difficult for his mind to stray to other thoughts of Anna. It would be trial enough to be alone in the same house. "Of course. Everything you need."

She hummed on the other line, as if mulling over her decision. "Yes. I'll be there. Should I hire a car or is there a flight I can catch?"

"We can ride up together. Text me your address and I'll pick you up early tomorrow morning."

"Oh, okay. Great. Is there anything special I need to bring?"

"Maybe your bikini?" The instant it came out of his mouth, he realized it sounded like a bad pick-up line.

"Not really my go-to for a meeting."

Find a save. Find a save. "And there's nothing like a soak in the hot tub after a tough negotiation."

A getaway. With Jacob. Anna pressed the button to take the elevator down to the lobby of her building. She sucked in a deep breath. Her skin noticeably prickled when she thought about what she was doing and with whom she would be doing it. This was about as wrong as wrong could be—going away to discuss a business venture that was supposed to be a dead issue. Going away with the man her brother despised, the man she'd been warned to stay away from.

But Anna spent every day doing what everyone expected of her and where had that gotten her? Frustrated and running in circles. There was no reward in playing it safe. Of that, she was absolutely sure.

Could she have devised a more tempting plan to make Adam regret ever selling her short? Not likely. So, she'd be spending it in close proximity to the man she had a

certifiable weakness for, a man who'd been sure to remind her to pack a bikini. She was strong, or so she
hoped.

After she and Jacob had gotten off the phone the day
before, the bathing suit talk had sent her rushing to the
salon to get everything imaginable waxed as well as getting her nails done. Sure, it was girlish and vain, but if
she was going to let Jacob see her climbing into his hot
tub, he was at least going to second-guess the wisdom
of ever turning her down.

Anna stepped off the elevator. As she made her way
to the glass doors, a sleek, black SUV pulled up to the
curb. She wasn't sure exactly what make it was, only that
several guys eyed it as they walked by, as if it was a supermodel bending over in a short skirt. Jacob rounded
the front of the vehicle in a black sweater, jeans and dark
sunglasses. Had he managed to get hotter since she'd
seen him in Miami? He was as tempting as ever, square-
shouldered, as if he was bulletproof. *Damn.*

She ducked into the revolving door with her overnight
bag just as Jacob caught sight of her. He came to a halt on
the sidewalk, grinning. His magnetism was so effortless.
It was in his DNA. He ran his hand through his shiny,
black hair and pushed his sunglasses up on his nose. That
seemingly harmless sequence of motions left her dizzy.
Hopefully she'd get reacclimated to Jacob quickly, de-
sensitized to the ways he could make the most benign
action enticing. She had more than a few recollections
of staring at his hands while he shuffled playing cards.

"Ready?" His impossibly deep voice stood out amidst
the sounds of the city.

"Yes," she answered with a squeak.

He reached for her bag, grasping the handle. Their

fingers brushed and her body read it as an invitation, even though her brain insisted it was nothing. Meaningless. Still, if he touched any more of her than that, she was a goner. He opened the passenger door. Something about him standing there, waiting for her to climb in, gave this the distinct feel of a date, even when she was sure it was only because Jacob was a perfect gentleman.

"I'm a little surprised you're driving. I figured you and your driver would pick me up," she said after he'd tossed her bag into the backseat and gotten in on the driver's side.

Jacob shook his head and started the car. The engine roared, quickly calming to a low and even hum. "I figured this made for more quality time to catch up. No prying eyes."

Anna swallowed hard as Jacob expertly zipped into the confusion of cars whizzing by. "Oh. Sure."

"I trust my driver, but he's only been with me a few months and you never know. I've been burned before by people who talk behind my back. This way, it's one less person who knows what we're doing."

She nodded. *What we're doing.* What in the heck were they doing? Tempting fate? Undoubtedly. If Adam found out about this, especially before she had a chance to be out in front of it, he wouldn't merely go ballistic. He would explode into millions of pieces, only after he was certain she and Jacob were in the bull's-eye of the blast zone. "Thank you. I appreciate that."

"Look, the last thing I want is for you to end up in the doghouse with your brother. We have legitimate reasons to explore this business venture, but we need to put some real numbers together before you can entertain it seriously. If this meeting doesn't go well, no harm, no foul. Adam never needs to know it happened."

"Sounds reasonable to me." The covert nature of their trip was appealing for practical reasons, but misbehaving was its own temptation. She was always the good girl, always did what was expected of her. For once she could deviate from plan, even if her confidence about it wavered. She didn't like deceiving anyone, especially not her family.

That didn't change the fact that she had to get Adam's attention and shake him out of the mindset that she wasn't ready to take over as CEO. Jacob had become her very unlikely ticket to doing that. She had to wonder if money was Jacob's only motivation, or if he thought this deal might show Adam that he'd made a mistake by ending their working relationship. He certainly seemed focused on the business aspect. Telling her to bring her bathing suit was probably a slip or Jacob being a good host. It was hard to imagine it was anything else.

There was a big part of her, however, that wished there was something else. She never did well with the idea of possibilities left unexplored. The night she kissed Jacob, she'd already spent many nights imagining what came next, of what it would be like to have his hands all over her, to share the same bed with him. When he'd cut it short, she couldn't help but feel as though she'd been robbed of something. That was difficult to let go.

She glanced over at Jacob as he fiddled with the satellite radio while navigating the snarl of traffic leaving the city. His profile was endlessly enthralling. She could've sat there and studied his strong, dark brows or his uncannily straight nose for hours. That would only lead to the examination of his perfect lips, the way his angular jaw was accentuated by his well-groomed scruff. It would be so nice to trail her finger along the line from his ear to his chin, kiss him again and see if he wanted to explore their unfinished business.

But what if he'd only used Adam as an excuse, a means of covering up the fact that he hadn't wanted to kiss her at all? If she tried anything a second time, he might be honest with her. That would be brutal.

He turned and narrowed his focus on her for an instant, making her heart leap into her throat. "Everything okay?"

She nodded, swallowing back a sigh. "Oh, sure. I was just wondering how long the drive is."

He looked back over his shoulder and sped up, changing lanes like a man who wasn't about to let anyone get in his way. The scent of his cologne wafted to her nose, making her lose her bearings. "Five hours. Four and a half if I can get out of traffic." He reached across and patted her on the leg, the width of his palm and fingers spanning her thigh. "Sit back and enjoy the ride."

She stared down at her lap, the place where he'd left an invisible scorching-hot handprint. Five hours? Alone in a car with Jacob? She'd be on fire by the time they got there.

Four

In the years since he'd graduated from Harvard Business School, the only time Jacob had mixed business and pleasure was right now—taking Anna away for the weekend. Time alone in the car with her had quickly illustrated that being with her made things muddy, messy. Nothing was clear-cut and that made him nervous. Considering the game he was playing with LangTel stock, getting close to Anna was dangerous. It wasn't just playing with fire. It was tantamount to walking a tightrope over an active volcano.

But the fire was so tempting—her sweet smell, the way she pulled out her ponytail and redid it when she was thinking about something. He'd struggled to keep his eyes on the road. The deep blue turtleneck she wore was maddening. His brain wouldn't stop fixating on trying to remember the exact arrangement of freckles on her chest. And then there were the jeans. Sure, he'd held the car door to be a gentleman, but he'd committed every curve to memory, frame by frame, as she'd climbed inside his car.

Finally at their destination, he turned from the main road and stopped between the pair of towering stone pillars flanking the entrance to his estate. Cool autumn air rushed in when he rolled down the window to punch in the security code. Silently, the wrought iron gate rolled aside, granting entry into his retreat, a world that intentionally bore no resemblance to the one they'd left behind in Manhattan. The fall leaves blazed with a riot of brilliant orange and rust and gold. The trees rustled with a stiff breeze, leaves breaking free from their branches, some landing on the hood and windshield, the rest drifting until they came to rest on the white crushed-stone driveway.

The massive house stood sentry at the head of a circular parking area.

"Wow," she muttered, leaning to the side and peering out her window as he parked the car. "It's so gorgeous, Jacob. And huge."

Surely Anna had been to impressive estates, but she seemed quite taken with what he had to offer her for the weekend—pristine grounds, crisp, white clapboards wrapping the spires at each corner of the house, a wide sweep of stone stairs leading to the front door, flanked by hand-leaded windows. His pride swelled. He couldn't help it. He'd impressed her and he was glad that he had.

"The house was built in the twenties. I had it completely remodeled when I bought it three years ago." As much as he loved his job, it was a pressure cooker, and being in Manhattan only exacerbated it. "I figured it was a good investment and I wanted a getaway that would always be here. Something I could depend on. Something comfortable."

Jacob snatched up the keys in his hand and climbed out of the car. He didn't make it around in time to open Anna's door for her, but he was able to grab her overnight bag before she had the chance to do so. He wanted to at least do some things for her. In fact, he'd purposely called the house's caretaker and asked him to give them a wide berth this weekend. There would already be his cook and housekeeper around.

"Seems like a lot of space for one person," Anna said, as they made their way to the front door. "How often do your parents come to visit?"

Family was such an integral part of Anna's life. It was probably impossible for her to fathom an existence that didn't revolve around it. "You'd be surprised." He opened the door and ushered her inside, placing their bags on a bench in the spacious foyer.

"A lot, then?"

He shook his head. "No. Not much at all. Especially not my dad. My mom will come for a weekend once a year, but she's antsy the whole time she's here. I think she probably learned that from my dad." As hard as Jacob liked to work, he had seen his dad take it too far. He made a point of relaxing when he came up here, but that almost exclusively involved getting his hands dirty. Very dirty. He'd have to show Anna his collection after he'd shown her the house.

Anna turned and frowned. "Don't you get lonely up here?"

Jacob was so accustomed to being alone that it didn't faze him at all, but he was smart enough to know that most people didn't live that way. Especially not a Langford. "I won't be lonely this weekend. That's all that matters right now." He chided himself the instant the words were out of his mouth. Why couldn't he answer, "no"? Why was flirtation and leading answers his inclination? He wasn't the guy who had trouble turning off this aspect of his personality. He was usually far more in control.

Anna flushed with the most gorgeous shade of pink. "That's a great way of thinking."

The urge to cup the side of her face and sweep his thumb across the swell of her cheek bubbled up inside him. Stuffing his hands in his pockets was the only way to stop himself. He wasn't about to cross that line. He needed to get a grip and wrap his head around everything he was fighting in his mind. When he'd been irate with Adam, it was easy to imagine getting back at him by seducing his sister. But then he'd picked her up at her apartment and he was quickly reminded of two things—Adam's sister was a woman he cared about, and a path that led to intimacy was not to be taken lightly. A smart man would insist that the risk was not worth the reward, even if the reward did look stunning in her blue sweater.

As in all business, detachment was the most proven tack. For the moment, it meant focusing on his head and ignoring his body. There was a very clear answer to the question of what his body wanted—Anna. He couldn't even fathom what might happen if he made a move. Would she cast away her brown eyes in shyness or would she have the courage to meet his gaze and tell him what she wanted? If he could have anything right then and there, he would've loved to know what she was thinking. Why was she here? What was driving her? Was it really as simple as wanting to broker a big deal? Or was there something else?

He cleared his throat. "Allow me to give you the tour."

Anna nodded and he led the way.

Anna had grown up amidst wealth and splendor, but Jacob's house was truly remarkable—beautifully refinished wood floors, a refined mix of modern furnishings and antiques, every surface impeccable and of the finest quality. Even her mother would've been a bit envious, and Evelyn Langford devoted an awful lot of time and resources to feathering her nest.

They returned to the front door, and Anna assumed they were going to go upstairs to see the bedrooms. Instead, Jacob handed over her coat. "I have something I want to show you in the garage."

The garage? He was aware she knew what a lawn mower looked like, wasn't he? "Okay. Sure."

They walked along a wide flagstone walkway, past the swimming pool and tennis courts. Beyond was an enormous outbuilding. Practically a warehouse, with a keypad entry and a security system Jacob had to disarm once they were inside. He flipped a succession of switches and the lights flickered on, one by one, across the massive room. Anna gasped.

It was an homage to motorized travel—seven or eight very expensive-looking cars, all black, and at least two dozen motorcycles. The entire room was spotless—polished concrete floors, not a speck of dust or dirt anywhere. Chrome gleamed. The aroma of motor oil and tooled leather swirled around her, a smell she'd never anticipated could be so appealing. She'd had men show off collections before—art, autographed baseballs. One guy owned what she'd thought was a dizzying array of antique chess sets. Talk about dizzying—Jacob's display of testosterone-fueled fascination was enough to make her head swim.

"Jacob, wow. I can't even…" Anna paced ahead slowly, Jacob right behind her. She was mesmerized, but afraid to touch the wrong thing. "They're incredible."

They stood before a bike with a worn but polished brown leather seat. "This is my hobby. Everything is vintage. Nothing built after 1958. Some of them I've bought from other collectors, but quite a few were falling apart when I got them. They were a lot of work, but I love it."

She folded her hands. Jacob loomed behind her, so close. She could feel the measured rhythm of his breaths even when she couldn't see him. "You do the actual repairs?"

"Is that hard to believe?"

She shrugged. "I don't know. I'm just surprised you know how to do it, that's all."

He let out a breathy laugh. "At first, it was the challenge of teaching myself how to do it. I was very motivated to learn. Now it's simply that I don't trust anyone with these. They're prized possessions and that means I keep them all to myself."

"Well, they're just incredible. Truly beautiful. I'm very impressed."

He stepped over to a bike in the center of the front row, swung his long leg over the seat and straddled it. "This one is my favorite. A Vincent Black Shadow. Very collectible." The motorcycle popped back off its kickstand, bounced in place a few times under his weight.

His hands—good God, his hands—gripped the handles in a way that said he didn't merely know how to care for the machinery. He knew how to ride.

"Take me out," she blurted.

He smirked, his eyes crinkling at the corner. "It's cold out there. You'll freeze."

"I'll live."

"Have you even been on a motorcycle?" His voice rumbled, low and gravelly.

She had most certainly *not* been on a motorcycle. She'd lived her entire life in Manhattan. Riding on a motorcycle was the sort of thing her parents never, ever would have allowed her to do. As an adult, she'd never had the chance. Nor had she put much thought into how all-out sexy the idea might be until confronted with it.

"No. I haven't. And that's why I want you to take me out." She shook her head slowly, their eyes connecting. His dark stare was like a tractor beam—he could have drawn her across the room with a single thought, not needing to utter a word or even curl a finger. He made her so damn nervous when he looked at her like that, as if he knew how easily he could mold her every vulnerability into something of his own. She didn't have a lot of weaknesses, but there were a few. Did he know that he was one? That look on his face made her think that he did.

"You know what they say about this particular motorcycle?" he asked.

"No clue."

"That if you ride on it fast, for long enough, you're bound to die."

Anna gnawed on her lower lip. What was it about being with Jacob, the man she wasn't supposed to be

with, that emboldened her? Because there was no denying that it did. He could've been about to push her over
the edge of a cliff and she would've jumped off herself
and figured out what to do on the way down. "I'm not
scared."

"You realize that if any part of you gets hurt, your
brother will have my head."

Anna wasn't much for pain, but she wouldn't mind
Jacob wearing her out a little. Or a lot. "So now you're
going to use Adam as your excuse?"

He sat back, tall and straight, brushing the side of the
bike's body with his hand. He granted her the smallest
fraction of a smile and it made her knees buckle. "When
you put it that way, I don't think I have a choice." He
pushed the kickstand back into place and climbed off
the bike, heading for a tall cabinet in the corner. "Let's
find you a helmet and a jacket."

Her mind was at war with itself. *What are you doing?
You came up here for a meeting. Shut up shut up shut
up. Forget work. Forget the meeting. Who turns down
a motorcycle ride with an insanely hot guy?*

"We just need to be back in time for our meeting,"
she said, as if it would make this sensible if she brought
up work.

"That's two hours from now. Plenty of time."

"Okay." Anna trailed over to him, wishing she'd had
something smart or sexy or at least sane to say. She
felt so overmatched, much as she had when Jacob had
come to stay with her family that Christmas. As if he
was guiding her, pulling her in, making her his. Except
that it had never materialized that time. Was it all in her
head? Would it actually happen now? If not, it would be

fantastic to know now so she could preserve her dignity by dodging another brush-off.

He turned, holding out a black leather jacket. "Allow me."

She made a one-eighty, her back to him, steeling herself to his touch, sliding her arms into the heavy garment, which weighed down her shoulders.

He patted her back gently. "A little big, but it'll work."

The sleeves were stiff, and she had to work at bending her arms to zip up the jacket. Boxy and clumsy for her frame, it made her feel like a child in a winter coat a size too big. She faced him and her brain sputtered, fixated on the image of him as he put on his own jacket. Dammit. It fit like he'd been born in it, adding a dangerous veneer to his admirable physique. Where did he get that thing? The Absurdly Tall and Broad-Shouldered Men's Warehouse?

He grabbed a shiny silver helmet, but instead of handing it to her, he curled his hand around her head and reached for her ponytail, gently tugging on it as he pulled out the hair tie. She was so shocked, it was as if he'd pulled her breath out of her lungs at the same time. Her tresses collapsed around her shoulders. He was close enough to kiss. His mouth was right there—lips as tempting as could be, the moment resembling the one that preceded her ill-fated attempt at seduction. They'd been standing in nearly the same posture and stance. Why couldn't he have taken her hair in his hands that night? Why couldn't he have decided that she was more important than Adam?

"One of my old girlfriends always complained that it hurt to wear a ponytail that high with a helmet."

Talk about ruining the moment. He *would* have to

bring up other women, wouldn't he? Of course he'd gone on with his life, including his romantic one, after they parted ways years ago. He was smart. He hadn't wasted untold amounts of time wishing for someone he couldn't have.

She nodded. "I never would've thought to take down my hair."

He zipped up his motorcycle jacket, which was the sexiest meeting of metal teeth in the history of apparel fasteners. "If you want to know the truth, it's just that I find that moment when a woman shakes out her hair after riding on the back of my bike particularly sexy."

Was that his way of throwing down the gauntlet? Issuing a dare? Because she sure as heck could whip around her hair. She might not be the purely confident seductress, but that much she could handle. The raw anticipation of the ride ahead returned to her veins, pumping blood from head to toe.

"Ready?" he asked, climbing onto the Black Shadow.

He pressed a button on a key fob and one of the wide garage bay doors began to open. The crisp air rolled inside, but she appreciated the cooling effect on her ragged nerves. Jacob put on his helmet, then his sunglasses. Lastly, he pulled on a pair of black leather gloves.

"Yep," she answered, sidling up to the bike. She realized then that it wasn't the idea of the ride making her nervous. It was the idea of touching him. Then again, this gave her the perfect excuse, and if this was as close as they got all weekend, she'd find a way to live with it and later weave it into a super hot fantasy. She pulled on her helmet, adjusted the chin strap, and grasped his shoulders as she straddled the bike behind him.

He started the engine. The bike rumbled beneath them. "Hold on tight," he yelled back to her.

She wrapped her hands around his waist tentatively. She didn't want to be so hopelessly obvious. Better to wait until their speed warranted a stronger grip. The next thing she knew, they were moving, albeit slowly, as he turned to close the garage door. Then he sped up, rounding the outbuildings, chugging down the gravel driveway to the road, opening the gate ahead of them with another click of the fob.

He came to a dead stop at the road, balancing them with his foot on the blacktop as the gate closed behind them.

"You can go a little faster, you know," she yelled.

"That was gravel," he called back. "You want fast?"

Anna gulped. "Yes."

"I'll show you fast."

He revved the gas, still keeping them in place. The power of the engine had her body trembling. The bike lurched and they hurtled ahead like a rocket. They flew down the narrow state road, picking up speed, much faster than they'd gone in his car. Maybe it only seemed that way because she no longer had the protection of a steel cage around her. The momentum of the bike pulled her away from him, and she tightened her grip around his waist, clamped her thighs to his hips. Her shoulders tensed, but at the same time, she felt freed. It was the oddest sensation. Laughter and elation bubbled out of her. The wind whipped at her jeans, but the jacket kept her warm. As did Jacob. Very warm.

The engine popped and roared whenever he changed gears. Masterfully, he handled the bike, leading them through a curve. She grabbed him even tighter as he leaned them into the turn, defying the laws of gravity. The way his shoulders shifted, maneuvering the bike through the treacherous bend, was unspeakably hot. She loved seeing him so in control. One wrong move and they'd both be gone. In that moment, she couldn't imagine wrong. He was infallible. Invincible.

They continued for miles, on narrow, serpentine roads. He took her through a small town with a round-about, the changing leaves fluttering around them, people milling about from a coffee shop to a farmer's market, bundled up in hats and scarves. She felt as cozy as could be, as if she was curled up in front of the fire. The fire of Jacob. Once they got back to the open stretches of rural road, he took off like a bat out of hell again. He got cocky on a long straightaway, weaving back and forth. If only he could have seen the mile-wide smile on her face. He'd earned his macho moment. And good for him for claiming it.

Much too soon, the road returned to where they'd started, only this time, from the opposite direction. He took the gravel drive leading to his house slowly again, expertly guiding them into the safety of the garage.

Anna was catching her breath, adrenaline coursing through her. She unclasped her hands from Jacob's waist, but her arms were heavy under the weight of the jacket and they dropped. Dead center. Between his legs. She yanked back her hands as if she'd touched a hot stove. In some ways, that was exactly what she'd done. She gripped his shoulders to climb off the motorcycle. Embarrassment flooded her. She could only imagine what he must be thinking. Was he wondering if that was her awkward attempt at a pass? Because she was wondering the same thing.

Five

Composure was no longer possible. Jacob gripped the motorcycle handlebars, but only to steady himself. Anna and her slender, feminine hands had just stirred primal urges from the depths of his gut. It had been building in the car. The motorcycle ride brought it closer to the boil—her arms coiled around him, her clasped hands pressing into his stomach when he went faster, her thighs pressing into his hips, squeezing him when he took the turns. And then there had been the noises she made—muffled shrieks and cries of excitement. How was a man supposed to live through that without his body responding?

And then she'd touched him there.

He closed his eyes to take the edge off, but the reality was that he wanted her, and he was fairly certain that she wanted him. Was that brush across his crotch her way of sending a message? It didn't seem at all like Anna's style—she was subtle and demure, rarely so bold, but she'd been testing limits of late, with her brother and her career. Was she testing Jacob? He had to find out. Every drop of blood circling below his waist was making it impossible to let the question go unanswered.

He dared to open his eyes. She'd removed her helmet. He'd missed the moment when she took it off, but the result was worth it. Her hair was mussed—tousled, nearly disheveled, not at all its usual glossy neatness. He liked it. He liked it a lot. He could picture the rich, dark color against the white sheets of his bed. Her cheeks were flushed and rosy; he hoped not from the brisk autumn air, but from the thrill of the ride, the rush of being close to each other.

He cleared his throat as he climbed off the motorcycle. Now to figure out a way to get the ten or so paces to the gear cabinet where she was standing—his jeans were too snug to make walking a casual affair. He used his helmet to shield himself.

"That was so much fun. Thank you," Anna said, breaking the silence.

He wasn't in the mood for skirting things anymore. No purely polite response to her gratitude would come from him. "Isn't that what a guy does?" He eased out of his jacket and hung it up in the cabinet.

"Does what?" Anna furrowed her brow, climbing out from under the pounds of leather she was wearing.

"Try to impress a woman by showing off." He placed his helmet on the shelf, then turned to face her square-on. It took considerable effort to obscure his edginess. His attraction to her hadn't manifested itself this strongly before. His mind was racing to keep up.

She cocked an eyebrow. Her warm brown eyes flashed. "Is that what that was?" Her lips remained parted after the question, the flirtation only provocation to the devil on his shoulder.

"Yes." He scanned her face, waiting for one more sign—something that said it was a good idea to do what he wanted to do.

A warmth washed across her face. "If that's you showing off, you can do that all you want."

And there it was. He sucked in a deep breath of resolve and erased the gap between them. He clasped both hands around her neck, pushing his fingers into the silky hair at her nape and lifting her mouth to his, collecting what he wanted with a tender, but insistent kiss. Her lips were even sweeter than he remembered, the kind of dessert that makes you lick the spoon over and over again, craving one more taste.

"Tell me to stop," he said, not relinquishing the grip he had on the back of her neck. His thumb caressed the smooth skin below her ear.

"What?" Her eyes were half open, breaths heavy enough to hear.

"Tell me you want me to stop." His heart raced, part of him begging her to say that she wanted him, part of him knowing that it would be easier on them both if she stopped this right now. Being with Anna, as badly as he wanted her, would be pouring fuel on the flame that had dogged him for too long. "Tell me that you don't want me to kiss you."

Her mouth went slack, eyes wide as the day was long. "I can't," she muttered.

His heart was fighting to pound its way out of his

chest. Whatever it was that she couldn't do, he wasn't sure he wanted to know what it was. "You can't what?"

"I can't tell you to stop because I don't want you to."

A wave of relief crashed over him. One hand went to her elbow, his fingers tracing the underside of her arm until he reached her palm. "Good. Because I don't think there's any way I can."

He snaked his hands around her waist and she popped up on to tiptoes, planting her arms on his shoulders. He didn't even have to kiss her—she was all over him. As if he'd told her she'd earn a million dollars for every second they didn't come up for air. Their tongues wound together in an endless circle. Their noses bumped as she tilted her head and came in for a different approach. She flattened her stomach against him, and he responded by lowering a hand to her bottom and tugging her hips closer to his.

The metal door of the cabinet clanged against the frame when she pushed him into it. He was still trying to keep up with what was happening, trying like hell not to fixate on where it was going. Would their first time be in the garage? That could be insanely hot. But where? Concrete floor? Tool bench? He tensed for a second. He wanted it to be better than that. If they were only going to have one night, one weekend, he wanted them both to remember it. He quieted his mind. This was not the time for overthinking. His body relaxed. That only made him more susceptible to Anna's fire.

She hitched her leg over his hip as if she knew exactly what she was doing. Either she had far more experience than he'd ever bargained on, or she was going on pure enthusiasm. He hoped for the second, that this was her response to him, not just another time with another man.

"Do you have any idea how long I've dreamed about this happening?" Anna asked. Her voice was all sweet desperation.

His body came to a complete halt. *Dreamed?* Did this mean more to her than he'd banked on? If they were going to have their fling, they couldn't make love in a car or on a tool bench. He needed to make this right, not merely salacious and reckless.

"Believe me, I thought about our kiss a few times over the years."

"Just a few?" she asked, seeking eye contact. Her eyes were clear and intent, searching his face.

He couldn't tell her it had been more than that. It would only make things more complicated. There were enough dangerous feelings between himself and one Langford. "Let's not talk about the past anymore. I'm tired of it."

"I don't want to talk anyway."

Jacob caught sight of the clock on the wall. *Oh, no.* "Anna. Our meeting is in ten minutes."

She blew out a deep breath. "It is?" She lowered her head and shook it. An adorable groan leaked from her mouth. "Okay. I guess it's time to get to work."

So much for Anna's resolve that this trip was going to be about business and absolutely nothing else. She'd had about as much self-restraint as a toddler in a toy store the minute Jacob kissed her. She still couldn't believe she'd pushed him up against the cabinet door. Then again, she'd waited a long time for Jacob.

But there was work to be done. She sat and smiled politely as Jacob and Mark got situated in the living room at Jacob's. A fire crackled in the fireplace, the late afternoon sun cast a warm golden glow through the windows. Jacob had his arm spread out along the back of the chocolate brown leather sofa, his leg crossed, his other hand playing with the stitching at the end of the sofa arm. He laughed quietly at something Mark said, and glanced over at Anna with a look that made any sound in the room turn to a low hum. It was a look born of recognition. He wanted her and he sure as hell knew that she wanted him. There were no more questions of that basic intent. The real question was who would be the first to break down. Was she sitting inside the fireplace? It sure felt that way.

Her entire body warmed, in exactly the way a fire builds—a spark, dead center in her chest, became dancing licks of flame in her shoulders and belly, and the heat rolled right through her, making her face hot and her toes just as naturally off temperature. That kiss—that single, brain-chemistry-altering kiss, was more gratifying than any physical encounter she'd had with a man in years. What if more happened? What if clothes started to come off? Would she pass out? She might.

"So, Mark," Jacob started, again sliding a shy smile to Anna. "I'd love it if you could give Anna an overview of what you envision for the future of Sunny Side. I think that'll be a good start and then we can see if partnering with a corporation like LangTel could be a good option."

Mark shifted in his seat, stroking his hipster beard, not looking entirely sold on the premise of corporate anything. He struck her as a man who'd be a stickler on the finer points of an arrangement between the two companies. This deal, if it happened, would require more than the right amount of money. A day ago, Mark's reticence would have unhinged Anna to no end. Today, it was more of an annoyance. If he didn't want to be here, why didn't he just say so? Then she and Jacob could get back to business of an entirely different nature.

Mark nodded and started on his song and dance about Sunny Side. Anna listened, taking notes on projections and plans for future products, ideas he had for the launch of the technology, product integrations and applications. Adam was a damn fool for letting his rift with Jacob stand in the way of this deal. Of course, the fact that he'd ignored the financial upside was testament to how much he hated the man she'd just kissed with reckless abandon in the garage.

"Anna? Do you have any questions for Mark?"

She was on deck. It was time to make her case. Jacob might be distracting the hell out of her, but she needed to focus. "I don't. I've had a chance to look over these numbers and if your projections hold true, I'd say that Sunny Side can pretty much write their own ticket. So the real question is, how do we make that work within the structure of LangTel?"

Mark leaned forward and set his elbows on his knees. "Look, Ms. Langford…"

"Please. Call me Anna."

"Anna. You have to understand that I run a company of two dozen employees. Our product has come to fruition so seamlessly because we're a tight-knit group. Our company culture is immensely important. My worry is that a giant like LangTel will swallow us whole or dismantle us until there's nothing left."

"Let me assure you. We have no interest in dismantling your company. The dynamic of your team is crucial to your success. We will absolutely keep it intact."

"How can you make promises like that? Isn't your brother CEO? I've heard he can be ruthless."

Jacob shot her a sideways glance, as if to remind her that Adam's reputation was of his own making, not Jacob's, and he wasn't wrong. Adam liked knowing that some people feared him.

"Actually, Adam's business thinking is very much in-line with yours. He's started two immensely successful and innovative companies from the ground up…" She stopped herself. One of those two ventures was the one Jacob and Adam had started together, the very source of the rift that made everything such a mess. Her stomach sank. What must Jacob think of what she'd just said? That she was hopelessly callous? She had to recover from her gaffe. "At the end of the day, whether your company is big or small, everyone wants to retain the dynamic that brought you success. Nobody wants to see someone else come in and dismantle what you've worked so hard for."

Jacob cleared his throat and Anna felt horrible. Bringing up his history with Adam had been a mistake. He'd said it himself in the garage. The last thing he wanted to talk about was the past.

Six

Jacob and Anna bid their goodbyes to Mark as he walked out to his car. The brisk night air filtered into the foyer. With a quiet click, Jacob closed the door. They were alone.

"Well? What did you think of Mark?" he asked, bending over to pick up a stray leaf that had been tracked into the house.

Anna stifled a sigh of appreciation for his backside. The man knew how to work a pair of jeans. "I like him a lot. He seemed open to some of the things I suggested, so that's good." Considering where Anna's mind had been that whole time, it was a wonder she'd been able to glean that much from the meeting.

"Good. Definitely good." He nodded, holding the orange leaf by the stem as if he didn't know what to do with it.

"Yep." The air was charged with anticipation. They

both knew where this was going. But no one was doing anything about it. Should she throw herself at him? That was as close to formulating a plan as she could come. "Pretty color." She pointed to the foliar evidence of the fall weather, resorting to painful small talk.

Jacob opened the door again and tossed the leaf outside. A new rush of cool air caused her to shudder. Perhaps it was nature's way of punctuating the fact that this time, he didn't merely close the door. He locked the deadbolt.

"Are you cold?" He dropped his chin, stepping closer, working his way into her psyche with an intense flash of his eyes. His hand gripped her elbow. Energy zipped along her spine.

Finally—touching. Nothing skin-to-skin yet, but at least someone had given in. Anna was hyperaware of her breaths, her galloping heartbeat, the rotating sway of her body in his presence. This wasn't that different from the moment after the motorcycle ride, except then, they'd had to break the ice. She was glad to be done with breaking. Now on to melting. "I caught a chill. I'm okay."

He smiled. "You're so cute when you're deflecting."

"What do you mean?" Even perplexed, her heart flitted at the mention of cute.

"You'll do anything you can to take any and all focus off of you."

She twisted her lips, trying not to fixate on his—the swell, the color, the memory of the way it felt when they were on hers. Why wasn't he kissing her again? Was he going to wait until she started things? "If I do, I never noticed it. It must just be my personality." She wished she could've come up with a sexy answer to the question, but there were too many urges to manage, like the one that told her she'd be a lot happier if he wasn't wearing that sweater. Or those jeans.

"I just find it interesting. Your brother is the complete opposite."

If Anna knew anything, it was this—if he didn't kiss her in the next two seconds, she would go off like a grenade with the pin pulled. "Let's leave Adam out of this. In fact, let's pretend he doesn't even exist."

"Are you flirting with me by describing my Utopia?" His eyes toyed with her. He was reveling in every second of their game.

Her mouth went dry. That kiss in the garage hadn't quenched a six-year-old thirst. It left her wanting more. "And what if I am?" She popped up on to her toes, gripping his shoulders to steady herself. "What if I did this?"

She closed her eyes and went for it—her lips met his, in a kiss that made it feel as if she was no longer standing. There was a millisecond of hesitation from him before his tongue sought hers. Every atom of her body celebrated in a chorus of delight and relief. She shifted her forearms up on to his shoulders, dug her fingers into the back of his thick hair. His lips—soft and warm and wet, became more eager, seeking her jaw and neck. His arms wound tightly around her, pulling her against him, nearly lifting her off her toes.

His hand snaked under the back of her sweater, conveying what she'd been so eager to know—he wanted clothes to come off as badly as she did. His fingers fumbled with the bra clasp, which was so adorable. He was so smooth. It was nice to know he couldn't make the entire universe conform to his will.

"Here. Let me," she muttered. Now flat-footed, she lifted her sweater over her head then clutched it to her chest. "Everybody's gone for the day, right?" It would be so like her to undress while the gardener was watching.

He laughed, a flicker of appreciation crossing his face as he plucked the sweater from her hands and tossed it onto the foyer bench. "Yes." Leaning closer, he poked his finger under one of her black satin bra straps, popping it off her shoulder. "It's just you and me and this big house."

His words didn't merely prompt a rapid wave of goose bumps—they were about to become a permanent feature of her complexion. She bit down on her lip. If this was going to happen, it would be good. She reached behind and unhooked her bra, but left it for him to take off. "Tell me you want me to stop."

"Tell me you want *me* to stop." He kissed the curve of her neck—the most sensitive spot, the one that made her want to squeal with delight.

"No stopping. Please, no stopping."

He didn't tear his gaze from her as he slid the other strap from her shoulder. He dragged the garment down her arms slowly. His vision sank lower. "You are too beautiful to have anything less than exactly what you want. Tell me what you want." Gripping her rib cage with both hands, his thumbs caressed the tender underside of her breasts, as he lowered his head and gave one nipple a gentle lick.

The gasp that rose from the depths of her throat sounded like a lifetime of frustration being cut loose. She dropped her chin to her chest when he did it again. She loved watching him admire her this way, knowing that she turned him on. "I want you. Right now."

"Upstairs," he muttered.

Before she knew what he was doing, she was off her

feet and in his arms, feeling tiny, like she weighed nothing at all. He marched up the stairs and she clung to his neck, desperate to kiss him again.

The hall to his bedroom seemed to stretch for miles. Neither of them said a thing. Their heavy breaths carried the conversation instead. They reached their destination, a grand room with vaulted ceilings and windows overlooking the grounds. He set her down gently on the enormous four-poster bed, smiling.

He lifted his sweater over his head. The soft, evening light showed off the incredible contours and definition of his chest and abs—perfectly smooth, no hair except for a narrow trail below his belly button. His shoulders were far better than any item of clothing had ever suggested. Not even the motorcycle jacket did them justice—square and broad, begging for her touch.

She sat up and flattened her hands against his firm chest, his skin warming her palms. With her arms raised, he cupped her breasts with his hands. She would've dropped her head back in pure ecstasy if she wasn't so anxious to have his mouth on hers again. As if she'd spoken her wish, he bestowed a long, reckless kiss... hot and wet and magnificent.

She was dying of curiosity to know what the rest of him looked like. She unzipped his pants and pushed them to the floor. She dipped her fingers beneath the waistband of his gray boxer briefs, shimmying them down his trim hips. He kissed her again, and she wrapped her hand around his length, relishing the forceful groan that he made into her mouth.

He urged her to lie back, kissing her bare stomach. She watched as he unbuttoned her jeans and wiggled them south. His eyes were on her body as if he were entranced. Everything between her legs was eager for attention. Her entire body tensed with anticipation. "Touch me, Jacob. Please." The words had wandered out of her mouth, the thoughts in her head trickling out.

He tugged her panties down, casting his dark eyes up toward hers as his fingers met her apex. She couldn't let go of her grip on his head as he rocked his hand back and forth. It felt impossibly good to be at his mercy—wanted, desired. The pain of the past washed away like the tide erases writing in the sand. Their gazes locked, and it was as if she could see more of him, parts that he obscured, the vulnerable things he had hidden from her.

The pressure was building, the peak within her grasp too soon. "Make love to me," she said. How many times had she imagined this? Hundreds, and it hadn't come close to matching the real thing.

He dotted her stomach with soft, open-mouth kisses, firmly gripping her waist. When he rose to his feet, he opened the top drawer of a tall, dark-wood bureau. He ripped open the foil packet and handed her the condom. She wasn't about to ruin the moment with mention of the reasons they might not need one. Plus, she liked the idea of focusing on him, just as he had on her.

He stretched out next to her, the most magnificent creature she'd ever seen—strong and muscled, but graceful and lean. He dropped his head back when she wrapped her fingers around him and rolled on the condom. When he returned his sights to her, he looked as if he wanted to consume her, heart and soul.

She arched her back, welcoming him as he sank into her, slowly, carefully, with a reverence she'd never expected or experienced. Her mind was a swirling vortex of thoughts and sensations, the most powerful of which was that she'd suspected he would feel wonderful, but not like this. She couldn't have prepared herself for it feeling this good.

He rolled his hips when his body met hers. It built the pressure in her belly quickly, her breaths coming faster now. Her hands roved over the muscled contours of his back, trailing down to his glorious backside. His kisses were deep and long, matching the steady and satisfying rock of their bodies. She wrapped her ankles around his waist, wanting him closer. Deeper.

She placed her hands on the side of his face, keeping his lips to hers. She wanted to be connected with him like this when she unraveled. Her mind shuffled images—the motorcycle ride, the first real kiss, the moment when he looked at her in the front hall and she knew, with complete certainty, that he wanted her. Everything inside her began to uncoil. She was ready to let go of it all, even the past, and succumb to the bliss she'd waited so long for.

Anna was so close. Jacob could feel it, sense it in every fitful movement of her body. He was fighting to stem the tide, but it wasn't easy. Concentrating on her face was the only way to do it, a beautiful distraction from the energy doubling in his belly.

Her breaths came in frantic bursts. Every sound she made was sweet and sexy, but she nearly blew his mind when she called his name, clutching his back and digging her fingers into his skin. She tensed around him, her body grabbing on to his as if she might never let go.

Deliberate thought was gone. Tension clenched his legs and stomach, pure instinct took over. A blissful smile spread across her face. Breaths shallow, strokes longer and harder. Now faster. The pressure threatened to burst. Anna bucked against him. She fought for it just as eagerly, until finally his body gave in to the pleasure. It barreled through him like a freight train.

"Oh, no," he blurted, stilling himself on top of Anna as the swells ebbed in his body. He'd never had this happen before, but it wasn't hard to guess what it was. He'd felt it. "The condom broke. Don't move."

Anna wrapped her legs around him even tighter. "No. Keep moving. You feel so good." Her voice was catlike, a purr, a fitting match for her reaction. She didn't seem the slightest bit concerned about what he was now panicked about.

"Anna. The condom. It broke. And I just came. Did you not notice?" He pressed one hand into the mattress and slowly began to lift his hips away from hers. What now?

"Oh." She shook her head as he got up from the bed. "I guess I didn't notice."

"Yeah, this is a problem." He rushed off to the bathroom to clean up. "This is a huge problem," he muttered to himself, discarding it and washing his hands. It was one thing to exact revenge on Adam by taking his sister to bed. It was quite another to go and get her pregnant. Plus, a baby? No way. He was the last guy on the planet who had any business becoming a dad.

He stepped into his boxers and rushed back to the bedroom. He could make out Anna's gorgeous curves even in the dark. She'd climbed under the covers, partially covered, lying on her stomach and patting the spot on the bed next to her.

"I missed you," she murmured.

He blinked several times in complete confusion. "I

was gone for two minutes. And aren't you worried? There's a very good chance you and I just made a baby."

She shook her head as he eased back into bed next to her. "I'm almost entirely certain that we did not make a baby. Don't worry about it."

Even with the way things had just gone wrong, being that close to her completely naked form had everything in his body stirring again. "Care to fill me in? Maybe I missed that day in health class."

"Can't you just take my word for it?"

"What? You're on the pill? Then why did you let me use a condom?"

She took a breath and buried her face in the pillow.

He rolled to his side, placed his hand in the center of her back. Why did she not understand what a big deal this was? "Anna. What is going on? Will you talk to me, please?"

She finally turned to look at him. "I can't get pregnant."

"What?"

"Or at least not until I get some of my plumbing fixed."

"I'm sorry. You've lost me."

She rolled over, pulled the sheet up over her chest and sat up in bed. He hated the fact that something he'd said made her want to cover up, but he did need to know what in the world she was talking about.

"A fertility doctor told me I can't conceive. I'd gone to talk to him about artificial insemination."

"You're twenty-eight years old. Why would you think about doing something like that?" He watched a wave of embarrassment cross her face. It nearly took his breath away. He eased closer to her, craving her touch, her smell.

"Losing my dad really made me think about having a baby. About how much I want that in my life at some point."

"Oh." It was hard to imagine ever feeling that way, but lots of people did. Most people, in fact. Or so it seemed.

"All I could think was what if I never find the right guy? Being a female executive is tough. Most men let their ego get in the way."

He had to wonder what sorts of men she'd dated, but he wasn't about to ask. There was no point worrying about that particular obstacle. He'd never get past the barrier of Adam. "I hadn't considered that."

"I've never been serious enough about anyone to want to have a child. And losing my dad underscored how important my family is to me. My whole life revolves around them. Adam and Melanie are building a future together and…" Her voice wavered and she looked up at the ceiling. "This is the world's worst pillow talk. I'm sorry."

He hated seeing her upset. He tried to imagine a scenario in which he could share something like this, something so deeply personal, the sort of thing that left a human hopelessly vulnerable. He gave her a lot of credit for having the courage to be so open. "It's okay. You should tell me about it, if you want to."

"Really? Why?"

He took her hand in his. It wasn't meant as romance, but his inclination to comfort her was strong. "Because I care."

Anna explained everything her doctor had told her about scar tissue and surgery and how that affected her ability to get pregnant. He listened intently, saddened that she'd had to go through that. She clearly cared a lot about having a child. Why else would she have gone to a specialist about it?

"What did your mom say?" he asked.

"I never told her. I never told anyone." The wobble in her voice was back, the one he hated hearing.

If she'd never told anyone, that meant he was the first. The weight of that wasn't easy to bear. Here she was, in his bed, after giving him the most precious thing she could give to him, and now she was baring her soul. He never harbored guilt over a business decision, but his secret weighed on him. He was trying to engineer the takeover of her family's corporation, and she had no idea. What if that came to light? She would never, ever forgive him. And why should she? "Why didn't you tell anyone about what the doctor had said?"

"I wasn't sure I could talk about it without crying."

He was glad she'd been able to hold back tears. He didn't do well when a woman cried. He never knew what to do or say other than give a hug, which he knew didn't fix a damn thing. "But the doctor said it could be fixed, right? With surgery?"

"Yes, but the point was that I just wanted something to be right, to be easy. Everything over the last year has been a nightmare. This was supposed to be my way of looking to the future. I guess I felt a little defeated."

"So we didn't just make a baby."

"We didn't just make a baby."

Relief washed over him again. No baby. Good. Things were tangled enough. Now he just had to deal with his own internal conflict over the LangTel takeover plan, and that might require action on his part. He was excellent at keeping the business and personal separate, and in this case, he'd clearly allowed the two to commingle far too much.

"Are you feeling better now?" she asked. "You were pretty panicked there for a minute."

He laughed quietly. He had indeed let it get the better of him. "I'm fine. Although I wish you would've told me about this earlier. We could've skipped the condom all together. I'm clean. I get tested every year for my physical. Plus, I've never not used one, so it would be virtually impossible."

"You've never felt what it's like without one?"

He shook his head. "Never worked out that way. It can't really be that different, can it?"

A mischievous smile crossed Anna's face. It was so sexy. She scooted closer, until their thighs were touching. She kissed him, sending vibrations through this entire body, especially the parts they'd just been discussing. She took his hand, twined her fingers with his. "I've heard that it's very different."

"Very?" he asked between kisses. His body was ready to discern this for himself.

She climbed on top of him, straddling his hips. "Why don't we test the theory?"

Seven

Jacob finished off his third cup of coffee. Two was his limit, but he hadn't slept at all. It was difficult with a woman in his bed. It was partly sexual distraction, but there was another side to it. Something wouldn't allow him to relax enough to give in to real sleep.

He placed his mug in the sink and strode down the hall to the foyer, where Anna was waiting. "I'll be ready to go in a minute. I need to take care of something in the garage."

"Okay." Anna nodded, smiling thinly. Things were definitely awkward between them now that it was the morning after. How could they not be strained? They'd crossed a line that might've been better left uncrossed, however much they'd both wanted to do it.

He hurried out the door and around back to the garage. He'd deliberated about waiting and making his phone call after they returned to Manhattan, but he had to do it now. He couldn't sit in the car with her for five hours feeling even worse about his secret. He needed absolute privacy, and he wasn't about to kick Anna out of the house. That meant the garage.

He had to take steps to clear his conscience. Could he go through with a LangTel takeover at this point? Even if he and Anna never ended up taking this any further? The answer was a surprising, but decided "no." The guy with the killer instinct for business rarely changed his mind and he never undid his own work, but he was sure. He couldn't hurt Anna. Not after what they'd shared. Even if this weekend had to be the logical end, it wouldn't erase their most intimate moments, and he didn't want to forget them anyway. He wanted to keep them in his head for as long as possible.

He entered the garage and closed the door behind him. He wasted no time pulling out his cell to call Andre, his closest ally in the War Chest. He had to end the campaign against LangTel, even if it might be a tall order. His fellow investors were astute, shrewd, and skeptical to a fault. They would want to know why he was backing off, and he couldn't tell them the real reason. He couldn't tell them that he'd seduced a woman who'd gone and seduced him right back.

"Jacob. What's up?" Andre answered. "Not like you to call me on a Sunday."

"I know. I wanted to talk to you about the LangTel deal. I'm out." He held his breath, not offering any reasons. With his investment record, he could sometimes get away with only a mention that he was making a move and others would follow suit. The why wasn't always necessary.

"You're what? Are you insane? Why would you do that?"

Crap. So he would have to offer an explanation. The cult of personality would only get him so far today. "I don't think the upside is there like we thought it was. And it's such a huge undertaking. We could be knee-deep in this for a year. Or longer. Do we really want that? Do you want that much money tied up like that?"

"With that kind of payday? Yes. Don't forget, you aren't the only person Adam Langford has pissed off over the years. A few guys are eager to knock him down a peg or two."

Everything that had seemed so perfect a few months ago was now quite the opposite. "Isn't the notion of revenge a little outdated? Don't you have better things to do?"

"You seemed pretty damn motivated by revenge that night in Madrid when we first talked about this."

Jacob was skating very thin ice right now. Andre was absolutely right. Jacob had pushed them all. Hell, he'd not only rallied the troops, he'd riled them up. "I can't spend my life worrying about Langford. I'd rather wash my hands of it. And him." That much was the absolute truth, however much he was unsure of his feelings for Anna.

"I don't know what to tell you," Andre said. "You want out. I'm still in. I can't imagine the other members bailing."

Jacob pursed his lips. How could he have thought for even a second that he might get out of this easily? He'd put a nearly flawless master plan in place. All he could do now was control his own holdings, make a few more phone calls and try to convince some others. Otherwise, what could he do? This train he'd put on the tracks had momentum of its own. "Well, obviously I can't tell you guys what to do. All I can do is tell you that I'm out. I'm moving on to greener pastures. Greener pastures with less of a headache."

"Suit yourself, Lin. I don't see any way any of these guys are going to back down any time soon. Plus, there's talk of a new investor in the mix. A big hitter with very deep pockets."

His mind raced. This was news to him. "A new member? Nobody spoke to me about this. I have say over who joins the group."

"This guy apparently has no interest in joining the group. But he already has extensive holdings in the company and is keenly interested in a takeover. Probably just one more person who hates Adam Langford."

Jacob threaded his hand through his hair, the most colossal headache he'd ever had making his eyes burn. "And no idea who this guy is?"

"None. Right now, it's just talk. I have to ask why you would even care? Even if you pull your money out of the deal, you'll still get the fun of seeing LangTel and Adam Langford taken down. That's gotta be worth something."

Funny how the appeal of seeing Adam destroyed had taken on a pall, all because he'd given in to his desire for Anna. How could he even think about moving forward with Anna when this was all going on? He couldn't. It would be reckless and stupid and worst of all, unconscionable. Forget that her brother despised him—he couldn't begin things with an enormous secret hanging over his head. It would never work. That left him only one option. He had to back off with her. If she wanted to pursue things, she'd have to let him know, and then he'd make a decision. For now, he'd have to play it cool.

"Okay. Thanks. We'll talk soon." Jacob hung up and shoved his phone back into his pocket. So much for being a financial wizard. That wasn't going to keep him warm at night.

Anna couldn't sit in the house anymore. She needed fresh air, so she made her way outside to the driveway and set her overnight bag next to Jacob's car.

The notion of the end of their getaway was all too depressing. Last night had shattered her expectations. Just thinking about the things they had done together, his touch against her skin, every white-hot kiss, made her tingle. They'd flipped on a switch and completed a circuit, but that could be turned off just as easily, couldn't it?

She felt as if he'd answered the question mere moments ago, when he went out to the garage to spend some time with his beloved motorcycles. He'd patted her back on his way out the door, like a pal—as a buddy would do. He'd been distant all morning. It was hard not to take the hint. Last night was in the past. Today, he was moving forward.

She kicked a pebble into a puddle. It had rained at some point in the middle of the night, which left behind a grayish-blue sky with only the wispiest of white clouds. They would have a gloomy ride back to Manhattan, a fitting precursor to what was waiting for her when they got there—family, responsibilities that were more important than a fling. She didn't want to think about it too hard. She wanted to be back in Jacob's bed, curled up in the sheets, pillows cast aside, the rest of the world an afterthought.

So if this was a one-time occurrence, could she be content with that? She caught a glimpse of Jacob as he came out of the garage. The answer was clear as she watched the way he moved. One night would not be enough. In jeans and a gray sweater, clothes that were nothing special on any other man, he was stunning. He lowered his sunglasses, which had been nestled in his thick head of hair. Not being able to see more of him, in every sense of the word, would be such a disappointment. But was that realistic? Considering the circumstances, she feared it was not.

"I need to grab one more thing inside," he called to her from the flagstone walkway in front of the house.

"No problem. Take your time," she answered.

A muffled version of her cell phone ringtone sounded. *Who's calling me on a Sunday morning?* She fished it from the bottom of her bag, her stomach flip-flopping when she saw the name on the caller ID. Talk about an abrupt jerk back to reality. Adam. She walked away from the car with a finger jammed in her ear. "Adam. Hi. Everything okay?"

"Hey there, Anna Banana. How are you?"

Anna was about to ask if he was feeling well. He hadn't called her by that nickname in years. "I'm good. What's up?" Paranoid thoughts whirred through her brain. Did he have some way of knowing where she was? Of what she was up to? Every bold feeling she'd had yesterday about throwing caution to the wind was now haunting her; it enveloped her with a crushing sense of guilt. She wasn't the girl to sneak around, to hide things from her brother.

"I feel badly about our talk the other night. I was going to call you yesterday, but Mel and I were doing all sorts of wedding stuff. I'm really sorry about the way I spoke to you."

"That's nice, Adam, but you seemed pretty certain about what you were saying at the time."

"I know, but I was caught up in the heat of the moment. I don't want you to think that I don't want you in place as CEO. I do. I definitely do. And I believe in you. It's just…it's been hard. I think you know that."

Had he called to apologize or was he searching for validation? "I do know that. This has been hard for me, too."

He blew out a deep breath. "Look, Mel and I had a long talk last night. I swear, she's so good at figuring out what's going on with me. It's uncanny. I realize now that losing Dad has been much more difficult than I imagined. I knew it would be tough, but not this bad. And the pressure at work. Well, I think I just haven't been myself."

She hadn't quite expected he would come to this realization, ever. Adam had a real affinity for being detached when needed. The pain of losing her dad sat squarely in her chest. It was somehow more pronounced now, realizing that it weighed on Adam just as much. "I know it's been hard. I should've been more patient with you. I know you're doing your best."

"And I realized just how hard I'm being on you, which is so stupid on my part. You're my biggest ally. You're the one person I know I can trust with anything and I'm shutting you out. It's not only stupid, it's not fair to you."

The one person I can trust. The words echoed in her head. And here she was, hours away, with the man her brother had told her to stay away from. "Thank you for saying that."

"So, starting tomorrow morning, you and I need to get together our plan for moving you in as CEO."

It felt as if her heart had just stopped. Was he really saying that? Was he really willing to finally move forward? "We do?"

"Yes. You know, the board of directors is never going to be happy. If I sit around waiting for them to fall in line, you'll never get to take the job you want and I'll never get to return to what I want to do."

Jacob emerged from the house. The smile on his face was everything she wanted to see, while everything she wanted to hear was coming at her over the phone from her brother. She should've been happy, but she knew full well that these two things did not peacefully coexist in the real world. There was no having both.

"Does this mean you've changed your mind about Sunny Side?"

He groaned, making Anna regret even bringing it up. "I don't want to dismiss your idea again. Let's keep an eye on it. Maybe Jacob will take himself out of the mix. I refuse to touch it before then."

"Ready?" Jacob asked, walking around to her side of the car and opening her door.

"Did you say something?" Adam asked.

Inside, she was begging Jacob to please not say another word. Her heart pounded in her chest. This was far too messy. She had to get off the phone right away. "I have to go, but thanks for calling. I really appreciate it. A lot."

"I have confidence in you, kiddo. I really do. I just

had to pull my head out of my rear end for a few minutes."

She sighed. How she'd longed for this moment—to hear Adam say that she was right about something, about anything, that he had confidence in her. "Thank you. That means a lot."

"See you at work tomorrow."

"Yep. See you then."

Anna put her phone back in her purse. Was she the worst human being on the planet? It felt that way. At best, she was a rotten sister for taking up with Jacob and pursuing Sunny Side behind Adam's back.

"Everything okay?" Jacob asked.

"Yes. Just fine." She nodded and climbed into the car, her conversation with Adam replaying in her head. *You're the one person I can trust.* Was it time to climb out of her dream? To keep Jacob where he was—a fun, amazing fling that had come to an end? The answer seemed clear. She'd scratched the itch and now she had to remain loyal to her brother and her own dream job. She'd worked so hard, and it was presuming a lot to even wonder if Jacob was interested in more. He'd been withdrawn all morning.

He started the car and turned on a news talk station. "I want to get caught up on the financial news. Back to work tomorrow morning, you know."

Anna leaned her head against the car window. *Back to work.* "Yes. I know."

Five hours later, they were pulling up in front of her building. "Let me get your door," he said, reaching for the handle on his own.

"No. Hold on." She grabbed his forearm. "I feel like we should talk." She probably should've brought this up during the ride, but she'd chickened out every time. Maybe this was better. At least she had an escape.

Jacob shut off the radio and turned to her. "Yes. Of course."

"I had a really wonderful weekend," she started, already feeling remorseful about what she was about to say. It was the smart thing to do, the right thing to do. It was also the last thing she wanted to do.

"Good. I'm glad. I did, too."

"It's just that…" she sighed deeply. "I like you a lot, but we need to be honest with ourselves. It probably wasn't the smartest thing in the world, considering that we have my family to contend with. I don't see Adam changing his mind any time soon, possibly ever, and my family is really important to me. I just think it will cause a rift that won't be good for me. Or you, for that matter."

"I see." He took his sunglasses out of the cup holder and put them on. "Whatever you want, Anna. You won't get an argument from me."

Was he hurt? Disappointed? His voice was so cold, his tone so aloof, it was impossible to know, but she had a pretty good guess. The night before, everything she'd dreamed of all those years ago, had been nothing but a one-night stand to him. "Okay. Great. I guess I'll talk to you at some point? About Sunny Side?"

He nodded, looking straight ahead through the windshield. "I'll call you if I have any information to share."

"Perfect." She climbed out of the car, closed the door and didn't look back.

This was for the best, but it felt absolutely wretched.

Eight

Telling Jacob "thanks, but no thanks" was the hardest thing Anna had done in a very long time. Four days later and it felt downright stupid.

"Still nothing from, you know, him?" Holly asked, setting a salad down on Anna's desk. They'd taken to eating lunches together in Anna's office since the executive dining room was no fun. Rumors of a LangTel takeover were rampant, but if it was happening, the perpetrator hadn't come to light.

"Shhh," Anna admonished, leaping out of her seat and making sure her door was firmly closed.

"It's not like I said his name." Holly dug into her own salad as if they were discussing the five-day forecast.

"Sorry," Anna whispered, heading back to her desk. "It's just, you know. If Adam found out, he would not be happy. You're literally the only person on the planet who knows about it."

"I feel so privileged to have this information that could get me fired."

"I'm sorry. I hope this isn't bothering you to know. I just had to tell somebody or I was going to go insane. And like it or not, you're my best friend."

"Don't worry. I'm very good at keeping my mouth shut."

Anna sighed. "To answer your question, no, I haven't heard from him, and it's been four days. I don't know why, but I can't stop thinking about him." Of course she couldn't stop thinking about him. It'd been an aeon since she'd felt so alive. But she'd made the sensible decision, choosing to put her career and family at center stage. Those were things she could rely on. Those were things that couldn't be yanked out from under her. After the last year, she needed to know that she was standing on solid ground, even if this particular patch of land still left her wanting more of Jacob.

"Sex will do that to a person, you know," Holly quipped. "Especially if you've gone long enough without it."

It was more than sex, though. She couldn't bring herself to utter those words, especially not to Holly, the woman of zero filter, but it was the truth. Anna hadn't had that kind of connection with a man, well, ever. Perhaps it was the shared history between herself and Jacob, everything she'd spent years anticipating and thinking she'd never have, but it felt even more elemental than that. They fit together—shared dreams, similar mind-sets and aspirations. The physical fit was certainly impossible to ignore. In bed, the fit was mind-blowing. "I guess. Not much I can do about it, though.

The drama of my family is too much, and he seemed all too ready to agree."

"Men and their axes to grind. Two women would never allow it to get this bad. They'd smile to each other's faces and do that phony nice speak, then bad-mouth them the minute the other person turned their back. It's much more civilized if you think about it."

Talk about uncivilized—one of Anna's coworkers had uttered Jacob's name in a meeting the day before, and Adam literally kicked the guy out of the meeting. No explanation, just an invitation to get the hell out. He'd softened his approach with her, but he was still being extraordinarily hard on everyone else.

Anna was picking through her salad when her cell phone lit up. Jacob's name popped up on the screen. She dropped her fork into the bowl.

"Who is it?" Holly asked. "You look like you just saw a ghost."

"It's Jacob."

"What are you waiting for?" Her voice was at a near-panic. "Answer it."

Anna wiped her mouth with a napkin and picked up the phone. What in the world could he be calling about? Nothing about their circumstances had changed. She stifled the hope that rose in her chest, that he was calling because he had to see her.

"Jacob, hi." She brandished her hand at Holly to shoo her out of her office, but Holly just sat back in her chair. Anna bugged her eyes. "Please go," she mouthed.

"Fine." Holly feigned sadness by jutting out her lower lip and begrudgingly got up from the chair.

"Is this a good time?" Jacob asked. Even when he was

being entirely too businesslike, his voice was so sexy that it shook her to her core.

"Yes. Of course."

"I didn't want to assume, since you're at work, but it's important and I didn't want you to hear this from anyone else but me."

Her heart began to beat furiously in her chest. "Hear what?"

"Sunny Side is going to have to go on hold. The patent has been delayed and there's a design flaw they have to work through. It's pretty routine with a technology like this, but it could be another few months until a sale is in the mix. They want to put their best foot forward with whomever they partner with, and I've advised them that that's a sound strategy."

Anna took in a deep breath through her nose. She fought her disappointment that he hadn't called about something personal. At least he had what might end up being good news—a delay could be fantastic for her. By the time Sunny Side was ready to sell, she might be in place as CEO and she could make the call. "I see. Well, I appreciate you keeping me up to speed on things."

"I hope you don't feel like our weekend was a waste of time because of this."

A waste of time? Does he feel that way? "Of course I don't. It was an amazing trip." There were hundreds more things she wanted to say to him, but could she make that leap? Could she even hint just how badly she wished they could do it all over again? And should she even cross that line again? "It was great. Both personally and professionally."

"Good. I'm glad to hear that you still feel like that."

Her mind was whirring like a broken blender. Why

did it feel as if he was calling about more? And if he was, why wasn't he just getting to it? It wasn't like him to tiptoe about things. "You didn't really think that I only cared about Sunny Side, did you?"

"No, I didn't. I just wanted to be sure." He cleared his throat. "Anna, I have to tell you something else. I'm actually glad that the delay with Sunny Side happened because it gave me an excuse to call you."

"You don't need an excuse. We're friends, aren't we?"

"Friends with a very complicated set of circumstances."

That much was indeed true. It didn't change the fact that she was hopelessly drawn to him. "So just call me whenever. You don't need an excuse." A long silence played out on the other end of the line. Had she nudged things too far? Was he now trying to find a way out of this phone call?

"Okay, good. Because I'm calling you right now to tell you that I can't stop thinking about you."

She smiled so wide that she witnessed the rise of her own cheeks. Her heart had apparently gotten the memo—it sprang into action by thumping her pulse in her ears. "Really?" Anna dug the heel of her pump into the office carpet, wagging herself back and forth in her chair, ultimately propelling herself into a lazy spin.

"It's especially bothersome when I'm trying to go to sleep."

She dropped her foot, stopping the chair. "Oh. I see."

"I just keep thinking about what it was like to be with you. I keep thinking about touching you, kissing you. I want to be able to do that again."

"You do?" Her mind went there—a gloriously wild confusion of every sexy moment they shared together…

the way his butt looked when he walked away from her, the way his mouth went slack when she did something that pleased him. And then there was the dark, intense stare he gave her when he had her pinned beneath his bodyweight, taking his time, making sure she relished every subtle move he made.

"Yes, I do. I also would appreciate it if you would stop asking questions and give me some indication as to how you feel about this. Right now I feel like I'm having one-sided phone sex."

If she blurted out everything going through her head right now, he wouldn't get a word in edgewise for a week. "I can't stop thinking about you, either." Something about making the admission was so freeing, however vulnerable it made her.

"Go on." His voice rumbled over the line.

"And I'm having the same problem. I can't sleep. I just lie there in the dark and replay everything that happened last weekend."

"Good." His declaration had a confounding finality to it.

Anna furrowed her brow. "Good?"

"No more questions. I'm sending a car to pick you up at five."

"I have a meeting at four-thirty."

"Is it important?"

What was it about the velvety quality of his voice that made her want to not merely throw caution to the wind, but send it through a paper shredder? Taking directives from a man was not on the list of things she enjoyed doing. In fact, she usually went out of her way to avoid it, but this was different. She not only knew what he was implying, but precisely what he was capable of. "I'll reschedule."

"That's my girl."

My girl. The words sent electricity zinging through her body. "Where are we going?"

"We aren't going anywhere. You're coming here."

Oh crap. I'm going to have to run home and change.

"And, Anna. Bring a toothbrush."

Nine

Jacob had never done anything quite so weak, but all bets were apparently off when it came to Anna. He'd managed four whole days without calling her. Why give in now? He knew from experience that the first forty-eight hours were the worst, when you know it's in your own best interest to stay away from someone.

In the case of Anna, it had only gotten harder after those first two days. It was like he was being starved for air, which was disconcerting. He couldn't focus on his work. He needed more of her and he needed her now. Damn the consequences, however complicated. Damn the fallout, too. He needed her insistent hands grabbing his body, her strong and graceful legs wrapped around him. He needed to smell her and kiss her, hear her laugh. He needed his fix.

He had to temper the romance. This was a rabbit hole

for him emotionally. He didn't let many people into his life and when he did, he didn't want them to waltz right out. That wasn't the point of trust. If you believed in someone, if you wanted them in your life, they would stay. There was no telling how long Anna would be able to stay, or even if she would want to.

Tempering romance aside, he knew he couldn't start an ongoing no-strings-attached thing with Anna. Even when strings meant the Langfords on some level. This left him with a very narrow tightrope on which to balance, at least for the foreseeable future. The War Chest had closed ranks, forging ahead with the scheme he'd planted in their heads. He refused to regret doing it, but he sure as hell wished he could turn it around. If he could just find someone willing to back down, the rest of them might follow, and that would mean one less thing hanging over his head.

He glanced at his watch. Anna would be here any minute and that made his nerve endings stand up straight and tall, pinging electricity throughout his body. The anticipation brewed an unholy cocktail of adrenaline and testosterone in him. He could only imagine what it would be like when he finally saw her. When he could finally kiss her again, feel her come alive beneath his touch. That was the response he cherished—when she allowed herself to be vulnerable, when she surrendered to him and he could feel and see the tangible results— quivers, shakes and trembles.

He walked out into his kitchen and removed a bottle of champagne from the fridge. Cliché? Maybe. But Anna did deserve at least one or two trappings of romance. He wasn't about to let that go completely unaddressed.

The knock at his door sent his pulse embarking on

a similar staccato rhythm. He retained his composure, fairly certain that it was the smooth, in-control Jacob that she lusted after. The one she wanted to take to bed.

He opened the door and had to fight the impulses of his jaw. This was not the time to do nothing more than stand there, mouth agape, like an idiot.

"Hi." Her grin was equal parts flirtatious and shy. Her cheeks flushed with that gorgeous pink, a slightly paler shade than her lips, all of it hopelessly inviting.

"Hello yourself." He ushered her in, shutting the door.

He followed her into the living room just off the foyer and helped her with her coat. His eyes zeroed in on the view—her black, sleeveless dress was tailored within a whisper of her figure, hugging every gorgeous inch. Good God. Was he still standing? The thing he admired most about her in that dress was that a woman like Anna could get away with wearing something like that to a meeting. Granted, a meeting where every guy in the room might have an impossible time focusing. Her toned legs looked even more tempting in black sky-high heels. Note to self: bring Anna to an important meeting someday. She'll make the deal.

"You look absolutely gorgeous," he said, craving her touch. He tossed her coat over the back of a chair and gripped her elbow. The electricity between them was obscene, like an out-of-control Tesla experiment. He was surprised he couldn't see the sizzling current arcing between them.

"Thank you." Her head dropped to the side, only a fraction of an inch, but he loved to see her soften to him like that, to give him a subtle indication that he was on the right track. "You don't look half-bad yourself." She stepped closer, still needing to look up at him in killer heels. He might have to beg her to keep them on the whole night.

Her hand pressed against his chest, smoothing the fabric of his suit jacket. He watched her, smiling, their eyes connecting. It looked as if there was a fire blazing behind hers—hot and intense. Which one of them would give in first? He had no idea, only that for once in his life he knew that he'd still be the winner if he was the first to show his hand.

"I missed you, Anna. I know we said that this wasn't a good idea, but I missed you. It's as simple as that. I missed standing close to you and looking at you and thinking about all of the things I want to do with you. The things I want to do to you."

Her lips parted ever so slightly and a gentle rush of air passed them. It was the sound of pressure being released. "I couldn't stop thinking about you, either. Every time I thought of the reasons we should stay away from each other, I just kept coming back to that original thought…"

He was reasonably sure of what she might say next, but he wanted to hear her say it. "Thought of what?"

"Of you and everything I was missing by staying away."

Perfect. "So now what?"

Her hand hadn't left his chest. She bowed into him, placing her other hand opposite it. Her fingers played with the knot of his tie. "We have the whole night ahead of us. Maybe we just need to see what happens."

He smiled again, this time much wider. It was hard not to be incurably happy around her. "Like what happens when I do this?" He snaked his hand around her waist and settled it in the curve of her lower back.

"Mmm." Her lips traveled closer to his. "I think the

next thing that happens is this." She tugged his tie loose, watching his reaction. She flicked open the top button of his shirt, taking liberties again. "Oops. I took two turns in a row."

"Taking advantage, I see," he murmured. This game of undressing, however compelling and sexy, would need to be seen to a quick conclusion. He wanted her naked. Now. He reached up for the zipper, pulling it down the center of her back as she made quick work of his shirt buttons. He longed to see that stretch of her skin, the one he'd kissed a week ago. He turned her around, admiring her porcelain beauty as it contrasted with a black bra and as he lowered the zipper further, lacy panties. He eased the dress from her shoulders, savoring every sensory pleasure—her smell, the heat that radiated from her, her smooth skin as he dragged the back of his hand along the channel of her spine. Her presence didn't merely have him primed, he was already teetering on the brink.

The garment slumped to the floor and she cast a sexy look back at him, her eyes deep, warm, and craving. "You made a big jump ahead there."

Hell yes, he had. And he'd do it again in a heartbeat. He grasped her shoulders and pinned her back to his chest, wrapping his arms around her waist. She craned her neck and he kissed her, hard. He cupped one of her breasts, the silky fabric of her bra teasing his palm as she tightened beneath his touch, her nipple hard. Their tongues tangled and Anna righted herself, turning in his arms. He took off his jacket and tie as she unhooked his belt and unzipped his pants in a flurry. He wrangled himself out of the rest of his clothes with one hand while keeping her as close as possible with the other. He wouldn't let go of the kiss either—she'd cast aside sweet for an edge that he couldn't ignore.

With a pop, he unhooked her bra, and didn't bother with the seduction of teasing it from her body. He cupped her breasts, molding them in his hands, his mouth seeking one of her deep pink, firm nipples. The gasp that came from her when he flicked his tongue against her tight skin was music to his ears.

She kicked off one of her shoes and then the other and stepped out of her panties.

Her beautiful bare curves heightened his awareness of how badly his body was driven to claim hers. There was no way he'd make it to the bedroom. He sat on the couch next to them, half reclining, and reached out his hand. "Come here. I need you."

She smiled and cocked an eyebrow, taking his hand. "Are you that impatient?"

"Yes. And we have all night." The breath caught in his chest as he watched her carefully set her knee next to his hip and straddle him. The sky outside was quickly falling into darkness, but the light was just bright enough to show off the dips and hollows of her delicate collarbone. He traced his finger along the contours. "Calling you this morning was the best thing I've done in a long time."

"I couldn't agree more." She smiled, dropping her head to kiss him. Her silky hair brushed the sides of his face. He was almost sorry he didn't have the visual of the moment she took him in her hand, guided him inside, and began to sink down around him. A deep groan escaped his throat as her body molded around him, warm and inviting. He wanted to be nowhere else.

She settled her weight on his and they moved together in a dance he never wanted to end. It buoyed his senses, made him appreciate her beauty and essential nature even more than before. She rocked her hips into his, over and over again, as they kissed and his hands grasped the velvety skin of her perfect bottom. Her breaths quickened and before he knew what was happening, she was gathering around him in steady pulses. She sat back, their eyes connecting for an instant before she gave in to the sensation, closing her eyes and knocking her head back. He closed his own eyes and the relief shuddered out of him, each passing wave invisibly bringing them closer.

Anna collapsed back on the bed, her chest heaving with fast and heavy breaths. Jacob clutched her hand, struggling just as much for air. She glanced over at the clock. It was after midnight. They hadn't stopped for much more than a snack and a glass of champagne since she'd arrived a little after five. How much stamina could one man have? Was he trying to prove a point? Because he had. And then some.

She was spent. Wonderfully, gloriously spent. It struck her as a summertime kind of exhaustion, the kind she'd experienced as a kid, up at the Langford family beach house. After swimming all day, sun-soaked, stomach sore from laughing too hard, you were absolutely starving. You would take your first bite of food at dinner and be sure that nothing had ever tasted so good.

That was Jacob. Nothing had felt so good before him.

"Can I just take the chance now to apologize for what happened that first time we kissed?" he asked. "It's pretty clear that was the wrong decision."

She rolled to her side, smiling, despite the unpleasant nature of the topic he'd just chosen to introduce. "You don't have to pretend that you wished things had ended differently. It's okay. I'm a big girl. Plus, you made up for it tonight."

"Don't you think I regret it? What exactly did I turn you down for? A friendship that would ultimately turn into the worst thing in my entire life."

Had she gone through years of pain over the wrong decision? She didn't want to believe that. It would be more comforting to go with the theory that everything happens for a reason. "As much as it hurt to have you say no, I have to admire the reason you did it, even if it didn't turn out the way you would've liked."

He stared up at the ceiling, seeming immersed in thought. Was his rift with Adam something deeper than warring over a business decision? She'd always assumed that Jacob's side of things was about the embarrassment of being publicly shut out of his first major business deal, about losing his cut of a big payday. Was there something else?

"I'm a loyal person, Anna. You have to understand that. If I let someone into my life, they're there for a reason. I don't do it lightly."

And there was her answer. "So it's not just about business. It's about losing the friendship, too."

He was quiet again, but she didn't want to interrupt whatever was running through his head. The intensity of his reservation was one of the things that had first drawn her to him. She bristled with curiosity, wondering what exactly his brilliant mind was choosing to ruminate over. She placed her hand on his stomach—he tensed at first touch, but just as quickly she felt his muscles give in to her. He grasped her hand and raised it to his mouth, kissing her fingers tenderly.

Anna felt equal parts exposed and protected. Did he feel the same? Was it the power of the afterglow, or was there more? Even when her brother had insisted that she couldn't trust Jacob, Anna couldn't buy into it. Her gut told her that she could. Plus, she didn't want to believe that the man who'd once turned down sex out of respect for a friendship would do anything less than the right thing. She might be inching closer to the edge of a treacherous place, but she wanted to believe that Jacob would tug her back if she put herself in the path of true danger. He had to. She didn't want to think anything less of him.

"I don't want to burden you with the minutiae of what happened between Adam and me," he said, breaking the silence between them. "We're having such an amazing night. I don't dare mess with that."

She propped herself up on her elbow and gazed down into his face. He was so gorgeous that it boggled the mind sometimes, even more so at this moment, when he'd given her a glimpse of how deep the waters running through him really were. Would she ever fully know those depths? If she were to live in this instant for all eternity, she wanted nothing more than to drown in them, sink to the bottom and never come up for air. There was so much to learn—she hungered for it.

But was it the right thing to do? To dive in, knowing the repercussions? Was it her weakness for him that was making her so eager to do the foolhardy thing? Maybe. Probably. Did she care? Not really. There were no guarantees, regardless of the situation two people found themselves in. It was up to them to find a way. No one could do it for them.

He rolled toward her and placed the softest, sexiest, most intimate kiss on her lips, plunging her into the sea she longed to get lost in. His hand wound to the small of her back, fingers drawing delicate circles against her skin. She could do nothing more than press against him—the inches between them felt so absurd. Pointless. Of course they should be together. Even if it might bring everything crashing down.

Ten

Life quickly became a beautiful blur, weeks of week-end trysts and countless late-night rendezvous. Sneak-ing around wasn't Anna's preference, but she couldn't deny herself the glory of time with Jacob, so as difficult as it was, they took great care to keep things a secret.

It was working for the most part, although there were times when it was touch and go. One day in the office, Adam had asked why she was so tired. Was she coming down with something? She couldn't tell him the truth, that she and Jacob had been up until all hours making love, intermixed with eating ice cream in bed and watch-ing bad reality television. So she'd said that she simply wasn't sleeping well. It wasn't a *real* lie, or at least not a big one, but the tiny untruths were beginning to hang over her like a dark cloud.

"What do you want to do tonight? What if we went

out for a change?" Jacob asked over the phone as Anna sat at her desk.

"You know we can't do that. What if someone sees us together?" It was the awful truth, but tonight it was more of a convenient excuse. She glanced at the clock on her laptop and began packing up her things. If she was going to beat Jacob back to his apartment, she needed to leave now. She'd scrambled to put together a small birthday surprise—nothing too elaborate, but she hoped he would enjoy it.

"Anna. We can't do this forever. We need to get out of the house now and then. Not that I don't want to leave you tied to my bed. I do."

She smiled. It was hard not to—he was so good at working in the comments that reminded her how much he wanted her. Her most girlish tendencies lived for those moments. "You're right. We'll talk about it tonight. Your place?" He *was* right. They couldn't do this forever. Something would have to give, and that something bore a remarkable resemblance to her brother.

"Yes," he answered, seeming a bit exasperated. "I'll be home by seven. You have your key?"

"I do." He'd given it to her a few days ago, as a "just in case." She wasn't entirely sure of what that meant, but it made a surprise dinner possible.

"Anna?" he asked, with a sexy, leading tone.

"Yes?" she replied, knowing full well what he was about to say.

"I miss you."

She smiled, absentmindedly trailing her fingers along her collarbone. *I miss you*—three silly words they'd been saying to each other for a few weeks. It was one of their many secrets, the things they hid from the rest of the world. Were they a placeholder for "I love you"? Those particular three words hadn't come yet, however much she hoped that they would. They'd sat on her lips several times, but would he return them? Just like the ill-fated kiss years ago, the thought of that kind of rejection was too much. Wait, she'd told herself. It would happen. They would find a way. She had to believe.

"Miss you, too. I'll see you tonight."

She told her assistant she had some errands to run and tried to ignore the guilty feelings that came along with ducking out of work early. After retrieving a carrot cake from the bakery around the corner from Jacob's building, she let herself into his apartment.

It was certainly strange to be in his place on her own. What would it feel like to come home here? Even with the spaciousness of her own apartment, it didn't have the sprawling splendor of Jacob's penthouse, nor did it have the magnificent Central Park view. She could be more than comfortable here. She could be happy. That would be a wonderful life, if she could ever get to that point. She sensed Jacob was proceeding with caution and how could he not be? Her brother hated him. That would scare even the most formidable man away.

A half hour later, she was making good progress with dinner. She wasn't the world's greatest cook, but she could hold her own with pasta and a salad, and it wouldn't be the same if she'd ordered takeout. Luckily, Jacob was easily pleased. A big guy who worked out five days a week, he'd eat virtually anything you put in front of him, especially if accompanied by a glass of good wine.

Even though the dining room table could easily accommodate ten, she set it for two, placing them side-by-side at one end. She found some candles in the buffet, dimmed the lights. Then she returned to the kitchen to finish the preparations. He was only a few minutes late when he strolled into the kitchen.

"What's all this?" He smiled, seeming genuinely perplexed.

Anna rushed over to kiss him—a surreal moment, for sure. Was that what it would feel like to be husband and wife? She might not have much time to get dinner on the table if and when she became CEO, but she enjoyed this glimpse of domesticity. It felt especially comfortable with Jacob. "It's a surprise. For your birthday."

His brow furrowed. He now seemed even more confused. "How did you know it was my birthday?"

"You had your passport out on the dresser the other day and I wanted to sneak a peek at the picture."

"So you were snooping." He smirked, suggesting he wasn't entirely disappointed in her.

"A little. But that's beside the point. I wanted to do something nice for you. Honestly, I'm a little surprised you never told me about it in the first place."

"I don't really celebrate my birthday." He loosened his tie. "I never have."

"Really? Why?"

"I spent a lot of time away from my parents as a kid. They were always doing their own thing, I was away at boarding school. It just doesn't mean much when you get money wired into your bank account and a phone call."

It was about the saddest thing she'd heard in a long time, but she didn't want to dwell on the negative. She took his hand and led him into the dining room, where she sat him down and poured him a glass of red. She held out her glass to clink with his. "Happy birthday."

Something about the sentiment fell short, like she was supposed to add something about their future or that she loved him.

As to what tomorrow held, or even a month from then, she didn't know. As to the question of love, she knew in her heart that she did. He understood her in ways that no one else seemed to—he appreciated her aspirations, he encouraged her, he commiserated when she'd had a difficult day at work. He was always so focused on her, everything she wanted and needed. No one had ever done that, and he made it seem so effortless. Even better, he accepted her affection unconditionally. He never had an agenda outside of being with her.

It was perfect. *He* was perfect, or at least he was perfect for her. But that made their situation all the more frustrating, stuck as she was between him and her family.

She served their salads and took the seat next to him. How could he have gone his whole life not celebrating his birthday? Her heart felt unusually heavy—birthdays had always been a big event in the Langford household. Always. She wanted him to have that, to have everything she'd had.

"Maybe today can be the start of a new birthday tradition."

He offered her the faintest of smiles. "That's a nice idea."

The start of a new tradition. Did Anna really mean that? Did she see a future for them? Because as incredible as it was to be with her, it felt as if the universe was conspiring against them. It was only a matter of time before the War Chest takeover surfaced.

He ate his salad, listening to Anna talk about her day, feeling more guilty with every bite. Hours before, the War Chest had staged their coup against him—ousting him from the group for daring to push them so hard, vowing to continue with their hostile takeover of Lang-Tel. They'd done to him what he'd once hoped they could do to Adam. Being on the receiving end of vengeance wasn't fun. These people were dangerous, all deep pockets and determination. Experience told him that it didn't take much else to be successful. Not even luck.

Anna served the pasta, which might've been one of the most delicious things he'd ever tasted—ziti with Italian sausage, white wine, saffron and arugula. She'd found the recipe online after having taken note of how much he loved those particular ingredients—so thoughtful of her, and yet he couldn't truly enjoy a single bite. Watching her, the sweet smile on her face, thinking about the effort she'd gone to. She'd planned this incredible evening for him, and he'd planned to destroy the company her father had built. What kind of a monster was he? Had getting back at Adam really been that damn important? Had his father messed him up so badly that his so-called business brilliance was capable of ruining lives?

He had to find a way to stop it—sell every asset he had, pull together a new group of investors to help him. Something. There had to be a way. Because the truth was that he was absolutely falling in love with Anna. He'd known it for weeks now. Hell, he was fairly sure he'd fallen for her during the motorcycle ride. But he couldn't confess his true feelings for her until the takeover was squashed. That was no way to start a life together, with a secret of epic proportions lurking in the shadows, about to reveal itself at any time.

After they finished Anna's meal, she brought in a cake and serenaded him with "Happy Birthday" in her slightly off-tune voice. It was corny and adorable and not at all the sort of attention he'd ever had before he'd met Anna—sweet, genuine and thoughtful. Then she gave him his gift—a gorgeous pair of perfect-fitting black leather gloves.

"They're handmade," she said, watching with excitement as he tried them on. "I called a motorcycle shop out in Queens and talked to the owner, so I knew what kind to get."

"Thank you. Thank you so much." His heart ached, so overwhelmed with this show of generosity from Anna.

"You forgot the card." She flipped over the gift box and removed a small envelope taped to the lid.

His eyes couldn't be torn from her as he opened it. Where had she come from? Was this all a dream?

For Jacob,
There's no one I'd rather be on a motorcycle with.
I'll be the one holding on tight.
Love, Anna

He nodded, struggling to manage the emotions welling inside him. *Love, Anna.* He loved her. She was so warm and giving, so beautiful, inside and out. He wasn't even sure he deserved to be in the same room with her, let alone ever have a place in her heart or her life. "Thank you so much, for everything." He set the gloves aside and took her hand. "Truly. I am so thankful for this evening. It's been wonderful." The card was sitting right there. He wasn't much for sentimentality, but he would cherish it forever, even if things didn't work out, even if the horrible things he'd done came to light. "The gloves are absolutely perfect and the card is just…" He nodded, swallowing back everything he wanted to tell her. *I love you.* "It's perfect, too. You have such a way with words."

She smiled sheepishly. "I have a fair amount of experience with writing you notes and letters."

"I don't ever remember you writing to me."

She downed the last of the wine in her glass and re-filled it, topping off his as well. "After that Christmas you stayed with my family, I had a hard time. Writing to you was my outlet."

"A hard time?" What in the world was she talking about?

She shrugged. "I just couldn't stop thinking about you. A lot of it was just wondering if you'd said no when I kissed you because you didn't like me. It had definitely occurred to me that you might have used Adam as an excuse."

Could she really think that? After all this time? "He wasn't an excuse. I was completely honest with you, Anna. If it hadn't been for Adam, I would've kissed you all night long. Your Dartmouth sweatshirt would've been off in a heartbeat."

She dropped her chin and grinned. "Really?"

"Yes. Really." Just thinking about it filled him with equal measures of regret and gratitude. At least he'd gotten a second chance, but had he unwittingly thrown it away?

"So anyway, I wrote you letters. A lot of letters."

He narrowed his gaze. "But I never heard from you at all."

"I never mailed them. I kept them in a box. I threw them away right before I graduated from college. At that point, it felt pretty silly to still be pining for you, and I had a boyfriend. Although he didn't last for long."

"Why didn't you send them after my friendship with Adam went south?"

"You can't be serious. Didn't you hate my entire family at that point?"

He had to think hard about that. "I definitely told myself I hated all of you, but I never truly felt that way about you. Or your mom. You were both so kind to me."

"Would you have actually read them?"

He had to be honest. "Probably not. I was insanely angry those first few years. I probably would've just thrown them away." If only he could have thrown away that anger instead, he wouldn't be in this position right now. If only things with Adam hadn't ended the way they had. "Can you tell me what they said?"

Her face flushed with bright red. "You would ask that, wouldn't you?"

"I'm curious."

"Of course you are. They were all about you. Who doesn't want to hear about a bunch of love letters someone wrote about them?"

"Just tell me one thing." His curiosity was getting the better of him. It was difficult not to be fascinated by the idea of someone being that preoccupied with him. The thought of Anna feeling that way was nothing short of awe inspiring.

She laughed quietly and walked her fingers across the table until she took his hand. It covered his arm in goose bumps. What she could do with a single touch—it astounded him every time. "It depended on the day. If I was dealing with it okay, I would just write and tell you how much I missed you, but then I would write about normal things happening with me. If I was sad, then it was *a lot* about how much I missed you." She cast her eyes aside as if she was trying to summon her courage. "And then there were the times when I was feeling lonely in other ways. That's when I wrote to you about what I wished would've happened that night."

Now he was really kicking himself for having turned her down that night. "Dammit. Really? And you threw those away? I'd pay just about anything to read that."

"How about if I just show you instead?"

Her eyes glinted with mischief, warming him from head to toe. Was he the luckiest man on earth? Because it sure felt that way. He not only needed her at that moment, he needed to have her as his forever. He couldn't imagine a moment without what they had together. That meant he needed to double his efforts to stop the Lang-Tel takeover. Then he could tell her he loved her. Then he could find a way to smooth things over with Adam. Then he could go to Tiffany's, buy her a big fat ring, and have what he knew he couldn't live without—Anna.

Eleven

Anna could no longer tiptoe around Adam. Hiding her relationship with Jacob had become ridiculous. His birthday had illustrated that they were moving in a good direction, but they were both clearly holding back. She'd sensed it all night from him, that there was something he was dying to say. Was it that he loved her? If those were the words he wanted to say, the only thing she could imagine stopping him was Adam. There was no other explanation.

Could she persuade Adam to set aside the feud? The more she thought about it, the more convinced she was that it could be fixed. If she could get her two favorite guys to bury the hatchet, everything in her life would be better.

Anna buzzed her assistant, Carrie. "Can you let me know when my brother is out of his meeting? I need to speak to him this morning."

"Sure thing, Ms. Langford. Anything else?"

Anything else. *Maybe get Adam's secretary to slip a shot of bourbon into his coffee cup.* "No, Carrie. Thank you."

Twenty minutes later, Anna got the call. "Mr. Langford can see you now."

She strode down the hall, feigning the confidence that wavered inside her. Her relationship with Adam had improved so much since he'd had his revelation about how hard their father's death had hit him, but she still had no idea how he would react to this news. Would he feel betrayed? Would he be angry? He'd be entitled to either reaction. She only knew that the time had come to finally own up to everything. It was her only chance to have Jacob, for real.

"Hey. What's up?" Adam asked, glancing up from his computer screen.

His upbeat and affable tone convinced her she'd gotten the timing right. This was the morning for progress. "I was hoping to speak to you for a few minutes about something personal." She closed his office door behind her and took a seat opposite his desk.

He closed his laptop. "Of course. Is everything okay?"

"For the most part, everything is great, but it could be a lot better if I could just fix one thing."

"I'm listening."

"You and Jacob. I'd really like to see you two find a way to be civil to each other and stop the fighting. It's gone on for far too long."

He shook his head. "I thought you said this was personal. Sunny Side is not personal. And we agreed to table that."

"I'm not talking about that. I'm talking about me."

Did she have the courage to say what had to come next? She had to do it. Now or never. "Me and Jacob. Together. Personally. Very personally."

His eyebrows drew together. "I don't understand."

"Me and Jacob. You know…"

"Working together?"

"Do I have to draw you a map, Adam? Jacob and I are involved. Romantically. Not business. Personal."

He reared back his head as if she'd just told him that the world was flat. "How in the hell did that happen? You can't be serious."

She took a deep breath to steel herself. She'd worried this might be his reaction. "I don't want you to be angry, but I went away with him. To his house upstate. About six weeks ago. That's where things started."

"Why in the world would you do that? Did he kidnap you?"

"Will you stop? That's just mean."

"Anna, this is making zero sense."

It was time to come clean and she knew it. "I went behind your back and met with the founder of Sunny Side."

"You what?" The fury in his eyes surfaced, just as it had the night they'd first discussed this.

She thrust her finger into the air. "Hold on, Adam. Let me finish. I was certain that I could convince you to come around if I had a better sense of the numbers. We need a strong financial upside these days, don't we?"

"That's not the point…"

"Just answer the question. Yes or no."

"Yes. We do."

"Okay then. That's what I was trying to do. And things just sort of happened between Jacob and me. And then it continued when we got back to the city. I want to see where it can go. We mesh together really well."

He twisted his face. "I don't even want to think about you two, meshing."

"That's not what I'm talking about and you know it." She scooted to the edge of her seat, folding her hands before her and resting her elbows on her knees. It was no coincidence that she looked as if she was praying. "I can't be with Jacob if you two are at odds. Family is too important. I can't be torn between the two. I understand that there's bad blood between you, but I need you and Jacob to sit down and work it out. Once and for all. It's been six years, Adam. You were both new in business. You both made mistakes."

He shook his head so vigorously that his normally perfect hair went astray. "If I made any mistakes, I made them because I was reacting to the things Jacob did. He could've ruined a multi-million-dollar idea."

"But he didn't."

"It doesn't matter. Jacob was willing to put our business venture at risk to prove a point. That told me that he was unreliable as a business partner."

"I just feel like this whole thing has gotten blown completely out of proportion. You used to be friends."

"So what are you hoping for? That I apologize and we start playing golf together? That's not going to happen."

"I'm not asking you to be best friends. I'm just asking for enough of a truce that you two can be in the same room without trying to kill each other. That's it. Although I'd be lying if I said I wouldn't be happy if you rekindled your friendship. That would be nice to see."

"You're deluded." He leaned forward in his chair, his eyes pleading with her. "He's scum, Anna. I don't know what kind of line he fed you to get you into his bed, but I'm sure he was just trying to get back at me. You need to stop acting like a girl and walk away from him now, before you get hurt."

Anna was so offended on multiple levels that she wasn't even sure where to start. "Sometimes I think you just don't want me to be happy, Adam. You know, you and Melanie found a way. I don't see why you can't do one thing for me. For your sister."

"I'm not doing a damn thing to help my sister ruin her life. Believe me, some day you'll thank me." He opened up his laptop and stared at the screen.

She sat back, folded her arms across her chest, crossed her legs. She wagged her foot, brainstorming a new approach.

"Is there something else?" he asked.

"Nope." She shook her head with fierce determination. "I'm not leaving until we talk this out. I don't care if I have to sit here all day." She dug her phone out of her pocket. "I can do a remarkable amount of work sitting right here."

"Mr. Langford?" Adam's assistant's voice broke in over the intercom.

"Yes?"

"I'm so sorry to interrupt, but I have an urgent phone call from Samuel Haskins. He says it can't wait."

Anna grimaced. Sam Haskins had held a seat on the LangTel board of directors longer than anyone, even before Anna had been born. He was big on propriety and manners. He would never ask Adam to interrupt a meeting unless it were a life-or-death situation.

Adam picked up the phone. "Put the call through." He tapped his pen on the desk nervously, his forehead creasing. Right then she could see how much things weighed on him. It was the same sort of look her dad had when things at work were a bear. "Sam. What can I do for you?"

His sights darted to Anna after a few seconds. "So we were right all along."

What in the world could they be talking about? And did it have something to do with her? Why else would he look at her like that?

Adam nodded in agreement, but there was anger in his eyes. "Yes, of course. Whatever you think is the best course of action, but clearly we have to stop these guys. Now. I'll clear my schedule and we'll get on it right away. It's all hands on deck." He glanced at his watch. "Yes. I'll see you in an hour."

"What's going on?" she asked, trying to disguise the worry in her voice.

"Your boyfriend? Jacob? He's heading up a secret investment group. They're the ones buying up Lang-Tel stock."

Her heart felt as if it didn't know whether to leap to action or keel over. "What are you talking about? That can't be right. I just saw him last night." *I've been seeing him every night.* This couldn't be right.

"Jacob Lin and a bunch of guys with a lot of money are preparing for a hostile takeover of LangTel. He's trying to destroy the company our father built, Anna. He's trying to destroy our family's livelihood."

"That can't be right." Her eyes darted all over his office, desperate for some sign that this was all a bad dream. "I'll go talk to him. Right now. This must be a mistake."

"It's not a mistake. Sam has the evidence. And if you were looking for proof that Jacob is scum, here it is."

Anna had never just shown up at Jacob's office. Not once. But here she was, standing in front of his desk after storming in, eyes wild, chest heaving, looking as though she was about to explode. What a relief that he'd put the bag from Tiffany's in his desk drawer. From the look on Anna's face, this was not the time to propose marriage.

"I'm going to have to call you back," he said into the phone, not waiting for a response before he hung up.

"Please tell me it's not true," she blurted, a distinct tone of panic in her voice.

Oh, no. His stomach sank as if he'd just swallowed an anvil. "Tell you what's not true?"

"You and your investment group, Jacob. Please tell me it's not true. Please tell me that Adam got some bad information. Because right now I feel like I'm going to be sick."

He closed his eyes and took a deep breath. His worst nightmare had just come true, but he couldn't lie to her. He'd already endured the guilt of not coming out with it in the first place, or even better, not starting the endeavor at all. "Please let me explain."

All color drained from her face. "Oh, my God. It *is* true." Her voice was fragile and delicate, as if she'd just been broken in half. It killed him to hear her sound like that and he was responsible. "I can't even believe this. Did you sleep with me just so you could get information about LangTel? Because Adam thinks you did. Has this whole thing been a big lie?"

"No. Of course not. How could you think that?" He stepped out from behind his desk, but she shunned him with a quick turn of her shoulder. The physical pain of her rejection resonated deep in his body, but he couldn't deny that he had it coming. "Adam knows about us?"

"Yes, Jacob. I went to him this morning to tell him. Do you know why?"

He shook his head. He couldn't imagine what had finally prompted her to share the thing they'd been hiding all this time.

"Because I hated the sneaking around. I wanted to give us a chance, a real chance. And now I find out that you were trying to destroy my family's company all along." The pain of the betrayal was clear as day on her face. She was shaking like a leaf.

He wanted to pull her into his snug embrace and make everything okay, fix the massive problem he'd created, except he couldn't. It wouldn't help anything. He'd messed up, in tragic fashion. "Will you please sit down so I can explain everything?"

"What could you possibly say that's going to make me feel any better?"

Again, she was right. "Look. I know now that I shouldn't have started this, but the reality is that I never in a million years imagined that you and I would become involved the way we have. That came completely out of left field."

"And it would've been so awkward to roll over in bed and whisper in my ear that you were trying to take over the company my dad built from nothing. That definitely would've put a damper on the sex, huh?"

Every word out of her mouth drove the knife in his heart a little deeper, but he didn't dare flinch. He deserved it all. "I went on the counteroffensive the morning after we first made love. That's what I was doing out in the garage before we left. I called my closest friend in the group to try to convince them to back off."

"So what happened? Why are you guys still trying to do this?"

"*We* aren't trying to do anything. They ousted me. Yesterday. They were tired of me pushing so hard to end the LangTel takeover."

"Does that mean you have no more pull with them? They're really just going to go ahead and do it without you?" She sighed and stared out the window. "This is getting worse by the minute."

"They say they're going to. I don't really have a way of knowing. Believe me, I've been racking my brain, trying to come up with a way to stop them."

Her jaw tensed. She shook her head. "What was the plan, Jacob? Tell me the plan you had before I came along. If you want any chance of redeeming yourself in any way to me, tell me the plan."

"We planned to get enough stock to take over the board of directors and oust Adam as CEO."

"Oust Adam or oust the CEO?"

"Is there a difference?"

"In six months, there will be."

He almost wanted to laugh at his own short-sightedness. Of course. The board of directors was probably already trying to oust Adam. He hadn't thought about that. "Do they already have a successor picked?"

"You're looking at her."

It was as if all air in the room stopped moving. *Anna? CEO?* What had he done? "You?"

"Yes. Me. My dad gave his blessing before he died, but they had to put Adam in place first because that had always been the plan. I'm supposed to be the next

LangTel CEO. It's my dream job. Not that it's going to happen now."

No. Good God, no. He'd set a plan in motion to take away the dream job of the woman he loved. "Please let me try to find a way to fix this."

"You just said you've been trying to fix it for over a month. How are you going to magically make it happen now? And how am I supposed to trust you? We've been involved for weeks now, and the whole time you knew there were plans to dismantle my family's company. The company my dad spent decades building. You were best friends with my brother, Jacob. You stayed at our house. And now you want to destroy us?"

"I never wanted to destroy *you*. Never."

"Yeah, well, whether it was your intention or not, that's exactly what you're doing. You're destroying me and I can't sit around and watch it happen. Which is exactly why I never want to see you again. Ever." Her lip quivered. Was it because she was so angry? Or did it kill her to say those words as much as it killed him to hear them?

"I love you, Anna. I love you more than I ever thought it was possible to love someone. Please don't do this. I need you."

A single tear leaked from the corner of her eye. "You love me? Why do you decide to tell me that now? When you have to save your own hide? Why couldn't you tell me last night when I was making you dinner for your birthday or singing you a song or…" Her eyes clamped shut. "Or when I was telling you that stupid story about the ridiculous letters. Do you have any idea how betrayed I feel right now?"

Again he was overwhelmed by his need to touch her,

but everything in her body language said she would absolutely kill him if he took another step closer. "You have the right to feel all of this. I made a huge mistake and I'm so sorry. I just want the chance to make it better."

"I'm sorry, Jacob. I can't give you another chance at anything. Ever."

"But what about my feelings for you? Does that mean nothing?"

She stood a little straighter and looked him square in the eye. "Actually, it would have meant everything to me if you hadn't betrayed me. Because I love you too and now I have to figure out a way to fall out of love with you."

She loves me. The full repercussions of his one vengeful act came at him with full force. He was about to lose the one thing, the one person, he truly cared about—Anna. "Then don't do it. Give me the chance to make it right."

"I can't. You took my love and threw it away. And that means we're done."

Twelve

Optimism. Anna would've done nearly anything to cultivate a single optimistic thought as she stalked through the LangTel halls to her office. The satisfaction she'd once felt about working here was gone. LangTel was officially embroiled in a battle for survival, against a threat that was impossible to defeat because there was no real way to build a stronghold. No one knew who the mysterious big investor was, and as much digging as Adam and Anna did, they came up with virtually nothing.

The fact that Anna had slept with the enemy only made her life more miserable. Luckily, Adam had remained discreet about that fact, but it had made Thanksgiving especially tense. She prayed he wouldn't say something about it to their mother. It was bad enough that Evelyn Langford had to know about the threat of takeover—LangTel was the bulk of her sizable nest egg, after all.

For the moment, Anna's days were spent jumping through hoops for the board of directors, which had gotten her exactly nowhere, as they were likewise all consumed with the threat of a takeover. It all added up to one thing—her dream job felt more out of reach than ever.

And then there was her personal life, which in many ways felt more like her personal death. Having gone from the high of being with Jacob to the low of discovering what he'd been doing behind her back the entire time they were together had been far worse than jarring. It felt as if she'd been pushed off a cliff with no warning and most certainly nowhere soft to land.

Anna's assistant, Carrie, filed into her office with a cup of coffee. "Is there anything else I can get you this morning, Ms. Langford?"

"No, thank you." Anna settled in at her desk for the ten minutes of her day she actually looked forward to—reading the newspaper. At this point, she clung to the little things that made her happy. There weren't many.

"Oh, before I forget, Ms. Louis was looking for you this morning."

Anna glanced at her watch. "Can you buzz her and let her know that now is a good time?"

"Certainly." Carrie closed the door quietly behind her.

Anna unfolded the business section and was immediately sickened by the headline beneath the fold. Sunny Side had sold. To a rival telecom, no less.

She quickly scanned the article, her heart pounding, half out of shock and the other half out of anger. Somewhere in there was sadness, but she hadn't given in to that yet. It said that the sale was orchestrated by Jacob. So much for the big delay on their patent application. Was that another of his lies? Carefully crafted to lure her in? To what end, she did not know—seek revenge on Adam, get inside information on LangTel. Jacob had everything to gain and she'd had everything to lose. She simply hadn't known it because she'd trusted him— with business, with her heart and her body. *Bastard.* Just when he couldn't have possibly betrayed her in any worse a fashion, he had to go and twist the knife in her back. First he'd tried to destroy her family, then he yanked away her most promising business deal.

So that was it. Jacob really had moved on, in every way imaginable. The thought made tears sting her eyes, but she had to face the truth. There hadn't been so much as a peep from Jacob since they'd broken up. Not a single word. She'd spent nights wide awake, wondering why it had all gone so wrong. Why was the perfect guy also the one who most hated her family? Why was he the man who had so easily betrayed her? It felt like some cruel joke, a tragic twist of fate.

And Jacob? He apparently wasn't quite so torn up by what had happened, moving ahead with the Sunny Side deal. Nope. He'd gone right back to work, making his millions. Perfect.

Her eyes drifted to the picture accompanying the headline. Jacob had that smile on his face, the one he wasn't quick to share, the one you had to coax out of him because he played everything so close to the vest. She missed that smile so much that it made her ache. And it was a longing for more than just him, it was a longing for the way she'd been with him—happy. It was also a longing for the possibilities of "us." Between her dad's illness, death and the company's troubles, the future had seemed bleak and uncertain for over a year.

The notion of "us" had lifted her out of that state, but it hadn't lasted long.

Holly rapped on her office door. "Carrie said you have a minute."

Anna shuffled the newspaper aside and collected herself. "Yes. Of course. What's up?"

"I wanted to ask if you can sit in on my meeting tomorrow morning. Everybody seems to react more favorably to bad news when you're in the room, and there's a lot of bad news." Holly sidled in and plopped a muffin down on Anna's desk. "Here. I brought you some breakfast so you can't say no."

"Is that blueberry?" Anna scrunched her nose. The aroma had overtaken her office with an artificial, off-putting smell.

"Yes. Isn't it your favorite?"

Anna shook her head. "Usually. I guess I'm not very hungry this morning. Thank you, though. I appreciate it."

"Let me get this out of your way then." Holly reached for the offending pastry and marched it out of Anna's office. She returned seconds later. "Are you feeling okay today? You look a bit pale."

Anna hadn't been feeling well at all—tired and blah. Probably a bug of some sort. December was right about time for the first cold of the season. "I'm okay. Just a little run-down."

"Yeah, I hear that. I have the worst PMS right now."

PMS. A thought flashed through Anna's mind—when was the last time she'd had her period? Miami? That was two months ago. "I know how that goes."

"So you're in on this meeting? Please say yes." Holly smiled and batted her lashes.

"Sure thing," Anna agreed, now distracted by the new direction in which her malaise seemed to be pointing.

Holly left and Anna immediately pulled up the period tracker app on her phone. The notification was right in front of her seconds later. Forty-two days late.

"I'm never late," she muttered to herself, her brain slowly catching up. She pinched the bridge of her nose. *No. There's no way.*

She shook her head and dismissed it as silly. She couldn't be that. She couldn't be pregnant. It had to be stress. She hadn't just been under a lot of it, she'd been buried in it. Sucking in a deep breath, she ushered foolish thoughts out of her head and got to work.

A half hour later, her stomach rumbled and growled. The muffin might have been disgusting smelling, but she probably should've eaten it. She rolled her chair over to the office credenza where Carrie had stashed some snacks. A protein bar seemed like a good idea, but the moment she tore open the package and got a whiff of chocolate and peanut butter, her stomach lurched again.

It has to be the stomach flu. I should go home.

She packed up her laptop, put on her coat, and stepped out of her office. "You know, Carrie, I think I'm coming down with something. I'm going to work from home for the rest of the day, but it'd be great if you could run interference for me, at least a little. Just tell people to send me an email if they need me."

"And Mr. Langford? What do you want me to tell him if he asks?" Carrie cringed. Adam had bitten her head off last week. It was hard to blame him at this point.

"You're welcome to tell him I'm sick." No use sugarcoating it.

One of the company drivers took Anna back to her

apartment, but she asked him to stop by the pharmacy on the way there. She dashed in, grabbed some pain reliever and seltzer. The line at the register was long, which only gave her more time to think about the improbable. Was she? The doctor had told her it was a virtual impossibility. Virtual. That didn't mean an absolute zero.

She turned back for a pregnancy test, admonishing herself for giving in to these ridiculous thoughts. As if she could be pregnant by her brother's biggest enemy, the man who'd started the war on her family's corporation. The entire idea was ludicrous.

When she got home, she whipped off her coat. Sitting in the car thinking about it had only made her that much more eager to put the idea to rest so she could curl up on the couch, turn on an old movie and slip into a vegetative state.

The instructions seemed simple enough—pee on the stick and wait. She did exactly that, studying the clock on her phone until the five minutes were up. Time to check.

Two blue lines.

She scrambled for the instructions, taking several moments before it sank in that she was reading the Spanish directions. She ruffled the paper to the other side. "Two blue lines, two blue lines," she mumbled, scanning the page. Two blue lines. Pregnant.

Oh, no no no.

The room felt like it was spinning, while her head traveled in the opposite direction and twice as fast. Pregnant? *I can't be.* She stared at the lines, but they only darkened the longer she looked at them, as if they were defying her to question the results. She consulted the directions again. *A false negative is far more likely than a false positive.*

What do I do? Who do I tell? Definitely not her mother. Her mother would freak out, and Anna was ready to freak out enough for a dozen people. She couldn't call Melanie. She loved Melanie, but she would blab to Adam and that would be bad. Very, very bad. The only answer was Holly. Holly was her biggest ally at LangTel, and if she were being honest, the only female she ever did anything fun with, like going out for drinks.

Holly's phone seemed to ring for an eternity. "Anna? You're calling me from your cell? Why didn't you just walk down to my office?"

"I'm at home. Can you talk without anyone hearing?"

"Two secs. Let me close my office door." There was a rustle on the other end of the line. "Okay, talk. Wait. Did you hear from you-know-who?"

"No." Anna rubbed her head. Good thing she'd bought that pain reliever. "I'm pregnant." No reply came from the other end of the line. "Holly? Are you there?"

"I just saw you two hours ago. What in the heck happened after I threw away the blueberry muffin?"

"It wasn't until you said that thing about PMS that I realized I'd completely skipped my period. So I came home and took a pregnancy test."

"Why didn't you tell me? I could've come with you."

"Because I was sure it was a stupid idea, that's why." It was worse than stupid. If she hadn't done it, she could've been going about her normal miserable day. Now she had to go about her pregnant miserable day.

"Do you know who the father is?"

"You can't be serious."

"You weren't together for much more than six weeks. How many times could you possibly have had sex?"

Anna nearly snorted at the question. *You have no*

idea. She and Jacob had been like rabbits. There was no escaping their physical attraction. It had a life force all its own. It had been made even more carefree by the knowledge that she couldn't get pregnant. Or so she thought. "Let's just say that he has a very short recovery time."

"No wonder you were so bummed out to break up with him."

Anna sighed. She had indeed been sad to break up with him, although sex wasn't the reason. She'd fallen in love with the big jerk. "He's probably going to be the reason LangTel will go down the tubes. I couldn't exactly look beyond that." She could never forgive him for that. He not only knew *exactly* what her family meant to her, he'd known it all along.

"No, I suppose not."

"So what do I do?" Anna hadn't even thought beyond this phone call. Making plans was not in her skill set at the moment.

"You have to tell Jacob."

"What am I supposed to do? Just waltz into his office and announce that I'm sorry that the last time I was there I had to tell him what a bastard he is, and by the way, I'm pregnant with your baby?"

"Think of it this way. It'll be ten times more awkward when you run into him on the street a year from now and have to explain where you got your little Asian baby."

A year from now. She might as well have been talking about the abominable snowman. Nothing seemed real anymore, especially not the future. Perhaps that was because she'd grown immune to all of it. Holly had a point, too. There would eventually be a baby to explain, to everyone. There'd be a baby bump before that. "I have to tell my family, too, don't I?"

"At some point, yes. Nothing makes Christmas morning more uncomfortable than a baby nobody knew about."

Anna laughed quietly. At last she had Holly around to lighten the mood. "You know what's ridiculous about this situation? I should be happy right now. I should be jumping up and down in the streets. I really want to have a baby. You know, I went to a fertility doctor about it after my dad passed away."

"Oh, honey. You did?"

"That's when they told me that I had so much scar tissue from my appendectomy that it was impossible to conceive until I had it fixed. I never had a chance to have the surgery."

"This is a miracle baby, Anna. I'm not exactly the sentimental type, but think about that. That's pretty special. Maybe this was meant to be. For whatever reason, the universe decided that you need this baby."

Tears sprouted in her eyes, just right out of nowhere. A miracle baby. "I don't know what to think anymore, honestly, but maybe there is a reason this happened."

"So when are you going to tell Jacob?"

"Can't I wait until after I go to the doctor? Maybe wait until the end of the first trimester just in case something goes wrong? The doctor had said the scar tissue could make carrying a pregnancy difficult."

"You have to tell Jacob, honey. No two ways about that. He deserves to know and he deserves to know now. Every bad thing he did in the past doesn't change the fact that you and he made a child."

Thirteen

Jacob was drowning in the dead quiet of his apartment, but he didn't have the energy to go into the office. Life without Anna wasn't getting any easier. If anything, it was getting harder.

He sat back in his office chair, rubbing at his stiff neck, feeling sore and achy. He'd been working out too much, not sleeping at all, and eating too little. Self-inflicted discomfort seemed only fitting considering the damage he'd done.

It'd been two weeks now, and each day felt as if it stretched on for eternity, a never-ending dirge of meetings and deals and money. He'd once lived on the adrenaline of it. Now it all felt empty. Every night before he went to bed, he looked at the engagement ring he'd bought for Anna. All of his pain, both physical and emotional, served as a reminder of what he was still holding out hope for—that he would stop the LangTel takeover and win her back.

Jacob's phone vibrated on his desk. Did he even bother to look? Just another person wanting something from him, most likely, but he had to force himself to check. When he did, he stared at his phone in utter astonishment. *Anna.*

His heart did a double take, jerking into high gear. Why was she calling? Was it because of the Sunny Side deal? He didn't want to pin his hopes on anything, but he really hoped she was calling for some other, more personal reason. "Hey," he said, fumbling with the phone. Was that really the best he could come up with? He sounded like a teenaged boy.

"Hey," she replied. Her voice was sweet, but distressed, echoing in his mind throughout the most awkward silence Jacob had ever endured.

"How are you?" he asked, deciding the course of polite conversation was the only one to take at this time. He wasn't about to be defensive with her. Everything bad and ugly had already been said.

"I've been better. I need to talk to you and we probably shouldn't do it over the phone. In fact, I know we shouldn't."

"Okay. Do you want to give me a hint?" Honestly, even if she wanted to come over and yell at him some more, he would've agreed. He would've served refreshments. Anything to see her. Even if it would be painful. He was already hurting more than he could've ever imagined.

"Jacob, I just need to talk to you, okay? I can't bring myself to say it over the phone."

His heart went back to acting as if it didn't know what

sort of speed was advised. Had she decided she could forgive him? Could he really be that lucky? And how long would it last if he was? There was still one indisputable fact—somewhere in the world, a very big shark was circling LangTel, and Jacob had dumped the blood into the water. If she lost her dream job because of him, there would be no coming back from that. "Yes. Of course. I'll come to you. Are you at the office?"

"Home."

He frowned. Anna never missed work. Ever. Had she left her job? Another big blow-up with Adam? Neither of those things made sense. She'd made it clear this was between them. Maybe she really was ready to reconcile. Maybe she felt as he did, that the other things between them, although messy, didn't usurp feelings. "I'm leaving right now."

The entire car ride was a lesson in patience, his curiosity killing him and his hopes refusing to be tempered, however much he wanted them to go away. He couldn't help it. He hoped she'd reconsidered.

Anna had left word with the doorman and Jacob took the elevator up to her floor, walking double-time down the hall to her apartment.

"Hi," she said when she opened the door.

The vision of Anna hit him the way an avalanche throws a mountain of snow down to the foothills. Her cheeks were blanched and her eyes pink and puffy. She'd been crying. Whatever this was, it was bad. He filed in to her kitchen, immediately plunged back into the familiar comfort of being with Anna, the one that made him feel as though he never wanted to be anywhere else, even when she was standing before him with her arms crossed, leaving a barrier between them.

"I don't want to make this any more of a big deal than it already is," she said, sniffling. "I'm pregnant and you're the only person who can be the father."

"Pregnant?" He remained calm on the outside, but his mind raced so fast he didn't know which way was up. His brain was a jumble of contradictory thoughts. A baby?

"Yes, Jacob. Pregnant."

Was this some sort of trick? "But I thought you couldn't get pregnant."

"I thought the same thing. The doctor had said it was virtually impossible for me to conceive."

"Virtually? So not completely impossible? Because you told me it was flat-out impossible."

"Virtually, completely. Does it really make that big of a difference?" She rolled her eyes. "Maybe you have superhero sperm. I don't know. Don't assume this is my fault. And remember, we were both there. It's not like I went and did this on my own."

Superhero sperm. His male ego wasn't about to argue that point. He started to say something else, to continue the argument, but one thing that had made him successful in business was his ability to accept facts and deal with problems, rather than burying his head in the sand. A pregnancy—a baby. That was a fact.

He'd told himself he would never have children. Not after the way his parents raised him—moving him from boarding school to boarding school, depending on his father's opinion of whether or not Jacob was being challenged enough with his studies. His dad pushed and pushed. There was no other speed and there was no nurturing any skills beyond academic, except for maybe the years he'd been forced to play classical piano when what he'd really wanted to learn was how to play guitar.

Was it even in his DNA to be loving and caring the way a dad should be? His father had given him a mind for business and that was about it. Such was the legacy of Henry Lin—mold your child in your image and tell him hundreds of times that you expect him to stay that way. Jacob had done it for the most part. After all, he was exceptional at doing exactly what his father did—making money. He had homes and cars and bank accounts to prove it. He merely didn't want to repeat his father's mistake, which had been becoming a dad in the first place.

"Jacob? Are you even listening to me? Are you going to say something?" Anna asked.

He shook his head and ran his hand through his hair. "I'm sorry. It's just that I'd never thought I would ever become a dad. This is just a lot to deal with at one time."

Anna's jaw dropped. "This is a lot for *you* to deal with? Why don't you ask the person who had to pee on a plastic stick how she's feeling about all of this?" She wrapped her sweater around her tightly. "I should've known better than to think that you would even care about this. You care about money and your pride and your stupid motorcycles and that's about it. Obviously the man who decided it was perfectly fine to destroy my family wouldn't care at all about the fact that he was going to be a dad. Goodbye, Jacob. Have a nice life. Don't make me call the doorman and tell him to come up here." She whipped around and rushed out of the room.

He chased her down the hall, grabbing her arm just outside her bedroom door. "Anna, stop."

She turned, not making eye contact, her chest heaving. "Just let me go, Jacob. Just let me go."

Her words, broken and desperate, gnawed at his heart.

How could he let her go? He didn't want to. He'd spent the last several weeks missing her, desperately. "I'm sorry. Truly." The words about to roll off his tongue next, the ones about wanting to embrace her, wanting closeness with her just wouldn't come out. His feelings about Anna hadn't changed since the breakup, but being near her was a powerful reminder of how badly losing her had hurt in the first place. "Tell me what I can do."

She sucked in a deep breath. "I don't need you to do anything, okay? I'm a grown woman and I can handle this on my own. Obviously this is more than you're equipped to deal with, so don't worry about it. I'll have plenty of support from my family. The baby and I will be fine."

A vision materialized—Anna and a baby. *The* baby. *Their* baby. Could he go on with his everyday life knowing they were out there doing the same without him? And what kind of man would that make him? Not only no better than his father, he would be far worse. "No, Anna. You're not going to handle this on your own. I will help you with whatever you and the baby need."

"I don't want you to do this out of some sense of obligation. That's not what I want."

"Well, of course that's part of it. How can it not be? This is just as much my responsibility as it is yours. Just because you're carrying the child doesn't mean that I don't need to share the burden equally."

"Burden? Is that how you see this? Because if you're going to use words like that, I can't even have you around. I need support. My entire life has fallen apart in the last year. I lost my dad, I've probably lost my dream job, and don't forget that my family's corporation is in serious danger of being dismantled, in large part, thanks to you. How is this even going to work, Jacob? How will we ever find a happy medium when my family hates you and you hate them right back?"

When she had the nerve to be so blatant with their circumstances, it certainly did seem as though they were screwed. The weeks apart of wanting her back hadn't changed any of it. "I don't hate your family, Anna. Your brother and your family are not the same thing. I can see that much. I had very strong feelings for you. Much stronger than I ever anticipated. I told you I was in love with you and I meant it. That didn't go away."

"But it did go away. You lied to me."

"I kept the truth from you. To protect you. I couldn't put you in the middle of the mess I'd made. I don't know why you can't see that."

"I don't want to argue semantics. I'm just telling you how I feel. That hasn't changed."

"Okay. Fine. I get it. Regardless, I'm not going to walk away from you and this baby." Had he really just said that? A baby. It was far too surreal. "I'm all-in."

"You do realize this isn't a card game. We're not placing bets."

"Of course I know that. I'm not an idiot."

"And I need to know that you're sure. This is an all-or-nothing proposition. You don't get to change your mind later."

"I'm not going to change my mind."

"We don't even know what's going to happen. The doctor didn't just tell me that I couldn't conceive, he told me it would be nearly impossible for me to carry a pregnancy to term."

How much more harsh reality could there be between them? Not much. "I understand. It doesn't change the

fact that I'm half of this and that means I will partici-
pate and be there for whatever you need."

She sighed deeply and rewrapped her sweater around
her waist, binding it to her body tightly. It was hard to
believe there was a tiny person growing inside her—one
half her, one half him.

"Just so we're clear, this does not mean we're back
together," she said resolutely. "We'll have to work out
the specifics when the time comes, but this partnership
is about having a baby and that's it."

He fought the exasperated breath that wanted to leak
out of him. He deserved this, the universe's way of re-
minding him that every action brought a reaction. He'd
done the wrong thing, and atoning for that apparently
came in the form of partnering with the woman he loved
while under direct orders that there would be no reconciliation. "Clearly, you're calling the shots here."

She looked down at the floor, and when her eyes returned to his, he could see exactly how scared she was.
It brought back, with a vengeance, the all-too-familiar
ache for her. "Well, if you want to be involved, you can
start by coming with me to my first doctor's appointment. Thursday. Ten a.m."

Jacob had a huge meeting scheduled that morning—
a deal he'd been working on for months. "Of course. I'll
be there."

Fourteen

Hospitals. One step inside and Anna was reminded of her dad—the months he spent fighting, in and out of the cancer ward, receiving treatments that they'd pinned so much hope on, only to ultimately lose. She wasn't sure she could deal with another loss like that, and she was already so attached to the idea of the baby.

"We're going up to the sixth floor." Anna pointed to the bank of elevator doors straight ahead. When the doctors realized who Anna was and the serious straits she was in from the beginning, they'd moved her first prenatal appointment to the specialist's office at the hospital. They wanted her to see a physician well-acquainted with high-risk pregnancies. Having that extra care was a comfort, but she really wished she didn't need it at all.

Jacob held the elevator door for her, being as gentlemanly as could be. She shoved her hands into her coat pockets. How she would've loved to be able to take his hand, squeeze it, have a true partner in all of this. But she didn't. He was the obligated dad. It had taken the pregnancy announcement to bring him back into her life. She hadn't heard a word from him after they broke up. Of the many things she had to get past, that now felt like the most difficult.

They reached their floor and stepped out into a quiet hall. There were several clinics along the corridor, theirs a few doors down. A woman at the reception desk welcomed them and had them take a seat.

A man across from them opened a breakfast sandwich of some sort, even when there was a very clear sign inches from his head saying there was no food or drink allowed. Anna loved eggs and bacon, but this morning the smell made her want to hide her head in a trash basket. Why wasn't the receptionist doing something about it? She was just sitting there, shuffling paper.

Anna turned into Jacob's arm, pressing her cheek and nose to the black wool of his coat, closing her eyes and drawing in one of the few scents she found appealing—woodsy and warm and surprisingly calming.

"You okay?" he asked, lowering his head to hers. When she looked up, their noses were inches apart.

She was caught in the fierce intensity of his dark eyes, which left her lips quivering. She would've done anything to be where they were weeks ago. Why did she have to have such strong feelings for him? Things would be so much easier if she didn't still want him. "It's the smell of his sandwich," she whispered.

Jacob stood and took Anna's hand, urging her to join him. "Come on." He marched over to the receptionist's desk. "Yes, excuse me. My wife is feeling a little queasy.

I think she would feel more comfortable if we could be alone back in the examination room, if that's all right."

"Your wife?" Anna mumbled under her breath.

"The nurse will be out any moment now. It won't be much longer," the woman said.

"It's okay," Anna whispered. "You don't need to make a fuss."

"She's uncomfortable. You need to help me fix that." He cleared his throat.

The receptionist glared at him. "As I said, sir. One more moment."

He grasped Anna's hand. "I understand, but it's literally killing me to watch my pregnant wife suffer. So if you could please find us a place to get settled, that would be wonderful."

"Fine, Mr., uh…" She reached for a folder. "Mr. Langford."

Anna prepared for him to explode, but Jacob took it in stride.

"I'm Mr. Lin. She's Ms. Langford."

"Oh, yes. Of course." She picked up the phone. "Two seconds."

A nurse quickly emerged from the door next to reception and brought them back to a private room. "The doctor will want to speak to you and then do the pelvic exam. You can change into the gown after I take your vital signs." She took Anna's blood pressure and temperature, as well as her weight, then left them alone.

"You really didn't have to make a fuss about it, and I appreciate it, but please don't call me your wife," Anna said. There were enough gray areas. They didn't need more.

"Would you have preferred I identify you as the woman

I impregnated? And don't forget it's my job to take care of you." Jacob unbuttoned his coat and put it on the hook, then took hers from her.

"It's your job to help me with the baby, when and if the time arrives."

"You are the vessel carrying the baby, and I don't like seeing you suffer, anyway. It's physically painful for me."

Remarks like that made her wonder if she'd made a mistake by telling him. The baby was not supposed to be a way back in for him, at least not into her heart. She had to protect herself from him as much as she could, however much they were already tied for a lifetime now. Even if the baby never arrived, it would be impossible to escape the fact that they had once shared this. And it would make it unthinkable to ever forget him.

She caught sight of the examination gown. "I need to change. So you need to step out into the hall."

"Anna. I've seen every inch of you. I could probably tell the doctor a few things. Don't worry. I won't stare." He sat down, pulling his phone out of his pocket, quickly reading something, and turning it facedown on his leg. "Too much."

"Uh, no. Close your eyes right now."

"Why?"

"Because I said so."

"Fine." He twisted his lips and did as he was asked.

She shucked her clothes and put on the gown in record time, then climbed up on to the exam table, covering her bare legs with the paper drape they had provided. "You can open your eyes now."

He crossed his legs and gave her a look that was far too familiar. "Next time, I'm looking."

"Next time you're standing in the hall. And you'd better be on the other side of the room during the exam."

A knock came at the door and a trim woman with long, curly red hair entered the room wearing a white lab coat. "Ms. Langford." She shook Anna's hand. "I'm Dr. Wright. It's nice to meet you." She turned to Jacob. "I take it this is Dad."

Jacob cleared his throat, seeming uncomfortable. "Jacob. Lin."

Dr. Wright wheeled over a rolling stool and scanned Anna's chart, nodding and humming. Lord only knew what she was thinking. She didn't show a reaction of any kind. Was that a good thing? A bad thing? After a few minutes, she closed the folder and stood. "All right, Ms. Langford. Let's have a look at you."

Anna lay back as the doctor took out the stirrups. Luckily, Jacob was following orders and had retreated to the far corner of the room. In all actuality, he'd created as much distance between them as possible. This was likely not a comfortable scenario for him, and she did have to admire him for not complaining or excusing himself.

Dr. Wright completed the exam and helped Anna to sit up. "Well, I'll be honest with you both. This is a tricky situation you've gotten yourselves into. I've seen the ultrasound images from your appointment with the fertility doctor. As to how you two got pregnant, I'm mystified. You must've been trying very hard."

Anna's face flushed with heat. Jacob snickered.

"Now, our hope is that this is a big, strong baby like Dad and that as he or she grows, the scar tissue has no choice but to give way. The worst case is that the baby gets stuck in a bad spot and the umbilical cord is squeezed or the baby simply can't grow."

Anna sat frozen. Dr. Wright dealt with dire situations every day, so it all came out of her mouth as if it wasn't a big deal. For Anna, this was a very big deal, and she was trying so hard to keep it together.

"Either way," Dr. Wright continued, "we'll have to watch you very, very carefully. You're most likely to lose the pregnancy early on. I'm guessing from your chart that you're almost eight weeks along, which is great. I need you to watch for spotting. Call us right away if that happens."

Anna sucked in a deep breath. "Okay."

Jacob stepped closer. "Dr. Wright, I'd like to know how many cases you've handled like Anna's and what the outcomes were. I want to make sure that Anna and the baby have the best of the best."

The doctor looked down her nose at Jacob. "I don't know the exact numbers, Mr. Lin. I assure you that I've handled many cases like yours, and I know what I'm doing. If you'd like to seek a second opinion, my nurse can provide you with some referrals."

Embarrassment flooded Anna. How could he do this? "No. Jacob, Dr. Wright has exceptional credentials."

"And I'd be a bad dad if I didn't ask about them."

"If you have concerns, Mr. Lin, you and I can talk about them some other time." Dr. Wright's voice was calm—almost soothing, but there was no mistaking the firm hand she was using with him. "We don't want Anna upset or experiencing any undue stress. It's not good for her or the baby."

"Oh. Okay." He nodded. "Good to know. No stress."

"That's probably the most important thing you can

do, Anna. Avoid it at any cost. Jacob, you need to buffer her from it as much as possible. Sex can help, since it's such a good stress reliever."

Jacob coughed. "Did you hear that, honey?" he asked, wagging his eyebrows at her.

Anna pursed her lips. First he'd pulled the wife thing in the waiting room. Now this. "Is that really safe for the baby?"

"Actually, yes. The baby's so small right now." The doctor pulled a funny-looking instrument, like a tiny microphone, from a drawer near the exam room sink. "Let's see if we can find the baby's heartbeat."

Anna had read about hearing the heartbeat with the fetal Doppler monitor. The notion both thrilled and terrified her.

"Just lie back," Dr. Wright said, lifting up Anna's exam gown to reveal her bare belly. She squirted some liquid on to her skin. "Just a bit of gel. It'll help pick up the sound."

A crackling sound like an old transistor radio broke out in the room. Jacob inched closer to Anna, bewildered. "We'll actually hear the baby's heartbeat?"

The doctor nodded, moving the instrument over Anna's stomach. "The heart forms and starts beating from a very early stage."

More static came from the small speaker the doctor held in her hand. Pops. Snaps. A rapid, watery sound rang out—likes waves at the beach on fast-forward. *Whoosh whoosh whoosh.* A smile spread across Dr. Wright's face. She nodded, consulting the instrument. "There's your baby."

Jacob held his breath. *Whoosh whoosh whoosh.* He'd never been so overtaken by shock and wonder, both at the same time. The miracle of the moment began to sink in, but it wasn't a weight. Not as he'd worried it might be. The baby was not an idea or an abstract—the life that he and Anna had created, against all odds, was real. A tiny human, with a heart and everything. *Whoosh whoosh whoosh.* He'd never been so affected by a sound. That sound and the life force that created it needed him. Anna needed him. And he would not let either of them down.

Anna looked up at him, her eyes wide with astonishment. "Our baby," she muttered.

"It's absolutely incredible," he said, taking and gently squeezing her hand. Maybe it was the wrong thing to do, but he was acting on pure instinct. She didn't protest, which felt like such a gift. "It's so fast."

"It's a tiny heart, Mr. Lin. It doesn't know any other speed."

"And what does the baby look like right now? When can we see it?" *It?* That didn't sound right at all. "I mean him."

"Or her…" Anna added, smiling. It was the first truly light moment of the appointment or for that matter, since she'd told him she was pregnant. He was so grateful for it. Finally, some good news.

"Or her," Jacob agreed. "When can we see him or her?" He was no longer surprised by the excitement in his voice. It was impossible not to get caught up in the moment.

"We'll schedule an ultrasound for next week. I'd like to do some 3D imaging. For now, the baby looks like a peanut with a big forehead."

"Hmmm," Jacob said. Had his dad been this involved when his mother was pregnant with him? Had he gone to a single doctor's appointment? Jacob doubted it greatly.

It was too bad—he'd missed out on so much. Jacob wouldn't have traded this experience for anything. It was only made better by the fact that he was with Anna. Now if he could only convince her to stop tabling romance and let him back into her heart.

The doctor put away the monitor and wiped off Anna's stomach.

"Where can I buy one of those?" Jacob asked. Being able to listen to the baby's heartbeat any time they wanted would be amazing. His mind drifted to thoughts of him and Anna in bed, listening to their baby's whoosh. Certainly their baby had an exceptional whoosh, far better than other babies' whooshes.

"There are inexpensive ones, but they don't work very well. The quality ones are in the neighborhood of six or seven hundred dollars."

"Oh yeah. We need one of those. Can your nurse order one for me?"

"That's a big expense for something you'll only use for another six months."

"And you think I really care about that," Jacob replied. "Because I don't."

Anna shook her head, grinning at him. "He doesn't care about that. At all."

Dr. Wright left after a reminder to watch for spotting, and a promise that they would all talk after the ultrasound. It was a scary, but exciting proposition, the thought of actually seeing the baby. He could only imagine how he would feel then. Everything that had just become so real would be even more so.

Walking down the hospital hall, riding on the elevator, through the lobby and back outside into the cold, gray December day, Jacob could hear that peculiar whooshing in his head. He and Anna and the baby were in the most precarious of situations, and he was determined to hold on to it with both hands. That wasn't at all the way he'd expected he would feel after today, but the heartbeat had changed everything.

Fifteen

"Are you doing okay over there?" Jacob asked as the limo sped along Lexington Avenue to Anna's apartment.

Anna wasn't okay. She wanted to be okay, but her mind kept dwelling on the medical issues. She looked out the window, entranced by the city passing her by, the people bustling along the sidewalks, in a rush that never ended. Had any of them received life-or-death news today? Probably. She wasn't so foolish to think she was the only person with problems.

"Anna." Jacob placed his hand on her shoulder. "Talk to me. It's okay if you're upset after the appointment. It was a lot to take in. I understand."

She closed her eyes for a moment, trying not to fixate on his touch, which called to her, even through her winter coat. Being with him brought back a lot of wonderful feelings, but something tempered it. Could she count on him? For real? She turned back to him, fighting the tears that welled at the corners of her eyes. "Do you, Jacob? Do you really get it? Because our baby is inside me and you said yourself that you'd never planned on becoming a dad."

He nodded eagerly. "And I feel like a fool for even thinking it. I'm telling you, the second we heard the baby's heartbeat, everything changed. I get it. I do."

She sat back in the seat, picking at a spot on the leg of her pants. It was hard to look him in the eye—he was so upbeat and eager right now, but was that just the rush of the appointment? Would it wear off? She didn't have the luxury of worrying whether he would be there for her and the baby. "It felt different then for me, too. Except in some ways, it just made me more scared. I'm going to be crushed if we lose this baby. Absolutely crushed. And every minute that goes by with this child growing inside of me, I'm going to change. I'm going to become more attached."

"Come here," he said, pulling her into his embrace. He rubbed her back as her head settled on his shoulder. "It's going to be okay. I promise."

Part of her wanted to be able to accept everything he'd said at face value, the way a child does when they're worried about monsters under the bed. He rubbed her back and anger bubbled inside her because she loved being like this with him. She wanted things back to the way they'd been before—before the world came crashing down, before he'd betrayed her, except this time, with the baby. Could she find a way to forgive him?

She wanted to let the bad things go, but one thing wouldn't stop nagging at her. If he had truly wanted her back after the breakup, why didn't he reach out?

Why didn't he fight for her? It had taken the pregnancy announcement to bring him back into her life, but that didn't mean he actually wanted to stay. What would happen if she lost the baby? Would he walk away? Would the issues that came along with being with her be more than he wanted to deal with? "Don't promise that everything will be okay. No amount of money or planning or crossing our fingers is going to make everything fine. We have to wait and see what happens and that's going to kill me. It's going to be so hard."

"You have excellent medical care. You're in the best possible hands."

"Thanks a lot for raking my doctor over the coals. What in the hell were you thinking?" She pushed away from him and shook her head.

"I want the best for you and for the baby. You can't fault me for that. Someone has to ask the hard questions."

"I didn't pick a random doctor off the internet, you know. I swear. Sometimes you and Adam are so alike it's ridiculous. Neither one of you trusts me to do what's right."

"That's not true. I trust you implicitly, and I'm sure your brother trusts you, too. He's just gone through a particularly misguided phase since your father passed away."

"It almost sounds like you're defending him. Are you?" She narrowed her stare. It was the first nonvenomous thing that had come out of his mouth regarding Adam. "Because that would be truly weird."

"I'm only pointing out that Adam is a smart guy. He'd have to be an idiot not to see how amazing you are."

She rolled her eyes. "Lay it on thick, much?"

"Anna, come on. I'm just being honest. Can't we be

honest with each other? After everything we've been through and with everything we're about to go through, I think it's only wise that we're truthful in everything."

Truthful? Was he really going to throw that at her now? "Ironic, coming from you."

He choked back the growl in his throat. "I was protecting you."

Protecting me. Really? "Tell yourself whatever you need to. That's not how it felt." The driver pulled up to the curb in front of Anna's building, then got out of the car to open her door. She couldn't even look back at Jacob to say goodbye. That would be too difficult when she was busy grappling with too many emotions. It would be so easy for him to look at her a certain way and she would be hopelessly drawn in, wanting to curl up into him and let him do exactly what he'd promised, the impossible—protect her. "I'll call you when they schedule the ultrasound."

Jacob was saddled with the most uneasy feeling he'd ever had. Anna and their baby were about to leave him. And she was upset. She shouldn't go upstairs and stew for hours. "Let me come in for a minute. We should talk."

"I'm tired of talking. And don't you need to get into the office?"

He was thankful he'd left his phone on vibrate. It'd been going crazy all through the appointment and during the car ride, but she didn't need to know that his business world might be falling apart while he was out of pocket. "You're more important right now."

She shook her head, seeming even more annoyed. "Fine."

They walked into the building and took the elevator upstairs. He liked feeling like this, almost as if they were a couple again, even if she was mad at him. What would it take for her to want him back? A lot of things, most likely—an absolute guarantee that LangTel was safe from a corporate takeover, a reconciliation with her brother.

"You really want to come in?" she asked once they arrived at her door. She had that icy tone in her voice, as if she were trying to freeze him out.

"I do." As they walked inside, he couldn't escape the feeling that this was only half right. He might be clueless about the notion of becoming a father, but he knew that they should be doing this together. If at all possible, this child should arrive with two loving parents, not a mother and a father fighting to remain civil. He didn't want to upset her, but perhaps it was time to just let her say her piece so they could finally more forward. "Anna, will you please tell me what I can do to make this better? Right now I feel like I'm stepping through a minefield."

She pursed her lips. "I'm supposed to stay calm."

"You're supposed to avoid stress, and walking around with all of this anger welling up inside of you is not good. Just let it out. Let me have it."

"Right here? Right now?"

"No time like the present." He took off his coat and slung it over the back of a chair in the living room. He was ready for her to start yelling and he would sit there and take it until she got it all out. "Like I said, let me have it. Tell me every last thing."

"I don't want to rehash our problems. It's not like you don't already know how I feel. What bothers me more than anything is what happened after I broke up with you."

He furrowed his brow. "The Sunny Side deal? Mark found a buyer he wanted to work with. I never meant for that to hurt you."

"It's not that. It's that I never heard from you. You didn't fight it, you just accepted it and moved on. You didn't fight for me. That hurt more than anything."

Good God, if only she knew how much he had *not* moved on after she ended their relationship. He wasn't sure he could even own up to that. He'd never been so miserable, a shell of a man. He didn't want to think of himself like that, the hopeless sap ruminating over his litany of mistakes, staring at the engagement ring he wasn't sure he'd ever have the chance to give her without her throwing it back in his face. "I did fight for you, it was just behind the scenes. I've been busting my hump to figure out who the secret LangTel investor is."

"See? That would have been good information to have, to at least know that you were trying."

"What kind of man would it make me if I came to you with half-filled promises? Trying and doing are two different things. After everything I did, you deserve better than that."

Anna sat down on the sofa, seeming deep in thought, but not saying a thing. Was he finally getting somewhere? He had to keep going.

"Anna, darling, I want you back. I think you know that. My feelings for you didn't go away when you said you were done with me. I still love you." He drew in a deep breath as he sensed his voice was about to break. Just thinking about today, about the baby, made his heart ache. "Now more than ever."

She raised her head slowly, her forehead creased with worry. "Because of the baby."

He took the seat beside her. "Some of it is, of course. There's no separating the two. But my love for you was there before you got pregnant, and it will be there tomorrow. It's not going anywhere. I'm not going anywhere."

"You're on a high right now from hearing the baby's heartbeat, from the excitement of what's new. How are you going to feel when we're forced to deal with my family? How are you going to feel if we lose the baby?"

Indeed, the road ahead was not getting any easier. He simply needed to know one thing. "Do you have feelings for me?"

She looked at him, scanning his face for what felt like a lifetime. "Part of me does. Part of me wants to punch you for what you did. It's hard for me to trust you. When I look back at our time together, all I can think about is everything you were keeping from me. That's hard to get past."

"Then maybe you need to try harder. I'll tell you I'm sorry until I'm blue in the face, but we had good times, too. Spectacular times. We had moments where I wasn't sure another person existed on the planet. Don't give up on our good memories. We can make more." He took her hand, relieved that she didn't fight the gesture. Body warmth traveled so easily between them—why couldn't everything else between them be so simple? Why couldn't things go back to the way they'd been at the beginning? So elemental. "I can't change the past. All I can do is try to build a future, but you hold the key. I can't do it without you."

She dropped her sights to their hands, joined. A tear fell onto her lap, darkening the fabric of her pants. "I need time to think. Today was a lot to deal with."

He nodded. Not that he had much choice, but he could

accept that. He'd make do with a sliver of a chance. "I'll wait, but let me know if there's anything I can do to speed up the process."

"Right now, more than anything, I just need to know that you're not only in my corner, but that you're going to stay there."

"I am Anna. I am."

"I mean it, Jacob. For real."

He sucked in a deep breath of resolve. "I do, too. And I'll find a way to show you. I won't let you down."

Jacob rode the elevator to the lobby, deep in thought. So much had changed in the past few weeks. From the miserable depths of losing Anna, he had new hope. He couldn't afford to doubt the future—she was the one questioning what tomorrow held. He hated seeing that from her. She was the optimist, the sunniest part of his life.

He had to show her that there was more for them. It was the only way back into her heart. That meant showing her that he wasn't going anywhere.

When the doors slid open to the lobby, he was so immersed in his thoughts that he nearly flattened a man rushing on to the elevator.

"Sorry," the man said, holding up a blue Tiffany shopping bag. "Forgot the wedding anniversary yesterday. I'm in a hurry to get out of the doghouse."

"No problem," Jacob answered, turning and watching the elevator doors slide closed. That flash of Tiffany blue was still there in his head.

If he wanted to show Anna that he wasn't going anywhere, he needed to make his overture. The question was when he would find the right moment.

Sixteen

Disbelief choked Jacob as he read the email the next morning—the missing piece of the puzzle, the information he'd been waiting on, sent by one of his informants. The identity of the high roller joining the War Chest was now known. Aiden Langford. And to think he'd woken up wondering when the right time would come to propose to Anna. That would need to be put off for at least another day.

He slumped back in the chair in his home office, sucking in a deep breath through his nose. His brain needed oxygen and fast. This was a huge problem and it had to be solved before it was too late. He knew that each Langford sibling owned 5 percent of the company. With that amount of stock in the mix, it would absolutely be feasible for Aiden to take down LangTel. And with everything Anna had once told him, Aiden had an axe to grind.

He wandered into his bedroom. Fixing the situation

with Aiden wasn't a one-person job, and he couldn't go to Anna for help. It would expose her to far too much stress. He had to protect her and the baby. That left one person, the person he'd vowed to never trust again, especially when it came to business. He had to go to Adam.

He hopped in the shower and dressed quickly. It was time to find Adam, pronto, and there was no time for second-guessing what the outcome might be. The sooner they devised a plan to get Aiden under wraps, the better. Luckily, Adam was notorious for getting into the office absurdly early. Jacob asked his driver to take him to Lang-Tel headquarters, sending Adam a text along the way.

We need to talk. Important. On my way to your office. Don't ask questions.

Adam's response came quickly. I'll tell security.

Jacob could only hope that Adam meant he was instructing security to let him *into* the building, not escort him out of it. He arrived at LangTel in ten minutes and rushed into the lobby. A guard was indeed waiting for him, but only to issue a security badge and instruct him on which elevator to take for the executive floors.

Jacob's head was grinding, mulling over options, devising plans. Short of amassing a huge amount of money to buy Aiden out, how would they stop this? His heart pounded fiercely in his chest as he made his way down the hall to Adam's office.

Adam's assistant was waiting. "Mr. Lin?" She stepped out from behind her desk. "May I take your coat? Can I get you a coffee?"

Jacob mustered a polite smile and handed over his black wool coat. "No, thank you. I'm just fine."

"Mr. Langford is waiting for you."

"Actually, you can do one thing for me. Adam and I are discussing a surprise for his sister's birthday. If she comes by, make sure you don't let her in. Don't even let her know that I'm here." He raised his finger to his lips to encourage her compliance. He had to keep Anna away from this powder keg at any cost.

"Of course, Mr. Lin. Your secret is safe with me."

Jacob stood straighter and took extra-long strides into Adam's office. He tried to think of a time he'd had to swallow his pride any more than at this moment. He couldn't think of one, not even with his dad. Could he keep it together, stop himself from getting sidetracked by old problems?

Adam turned slowly in his massive leather executive chair like a villain in an action movie. "This is a surprise."

Jacob didn't wait for an invitation to sit, taking a seat opposite Adam's desk. "I'm as surprised as you are."

"Are you going to tell me why you're here or are we going to play twenty questions?" Adam tapped a pen on the desk blotter.

"It's the War Chest."

"The gang of thugs you put together to take down the corporation my father built from the ground up? I know all about that."

It was so like Adam to bring up the most damning details. "The investment group I was kicked out of when I pushed them to stop because I didn't want a takeover to ruin my chances at a relationship with Anna."

Adam cleared his throat. "Don't get me started on Anna."

You have no idea. Adam was going to blow up when

he found out that he and Anna were as involved as a man and woman could possibly be, even if the romantic side of things was fragile. "Please, Adam. I know I've done some things you aren't happy about. You can't say that you haven't done the same to me."

"I have a busy day ahead of me. Can you get to the point?"

"Your brother Aiden has joined the War Chest."

"What?" Fury blazed in Adam's eyes.

"With his percentage of stock in the mix, they can take over LangTel. Without much problem, I have to point out. You need to do something about this now."

"Oh, my God. Aiden." Adam's skin blanched, his eyes grew wide with disbelief. It was the first chink in Adam's armor that Jacob had ever seen. "He's been estranged from the family for years and it got worse when my dad got sick, but I never imagined he would go this far."

"Well, he has."

Adam's elbows dropped to his desk, and he pushed his hair back from his forehead. He twisted his lips. His stare narrowed. "Why didn't you take this to Anna? Was your breakup really that awful? I know she's not fun when she's mad."

Jacob had already covered up an awful lot with Anna, and the guilt from that might remain forever. He couldn't take the lies any further. "No, Adam. Anna is pregnant and I'm the father. I didn't want to tell her because stress could jeopardize the baby."

Anna walked through the quiet reception area on the executive floor, making her way to her office. She didn't normally get in so early, but she hadn't been able to sleep much. Perhaps the distraction of work would help clear her head before she ultimately returned to her worries about the baby and whether or not Jacob was really going to stand by her, no matter what.

"Good morning, Ms. Langford. Will you be joining Mr. Langford and Mr. Lin in their meeting?" her assistant, Carrie, asked as she took Anna's coat.

Anna froze in place. "Mr. Langford and Mr. Lin? Meeting? With each other? Here?"

"They're in Mr. Langford's office right now. I just assumed you knew." Her voice trailed off.

What in the world? Confused, she composed herself. "Oh, uh, yes. Yes, I'm joining them." Anna marched down the hall to her brother's office as if this had been the plan all along. A flurry of thoughts was turning her mind into a snow globe of speculation. Was this Jacob's way of fighting for her? Of showing her that he would take the worst of it? She could only hope that this meeting didn't end up with fists flying.

Adam's assistant bolted from her seat when Anna breezed past her and lunged for the doorknob to Adam's office. "Ms. Langford, I'm sorry. Mr. Langford is in a very important meeting..."

"So I heard." Anna marched into her brother's office. She wasn't about to wait to be invited in. Somebody could be dead.

She first saw Adam's response—surprise and shock. Jacob turned and showed a similar horror.

"Well, you're both still alive. So I guess that's good. Anybody want to tell me what's going on?" She planted her hand on her hip, assessing the situation. *What are these two up to?*

Jacob shifted in his seat. "We, uh, had a few things we needed to discuss."

"Right," Adam said, unconvincingly.

"You two can't stand to be in the same zip code. How about we try again?" She glanced over at Jacob, eager to glean from his facial expressions what was going on.

"Maybe it's time to finally change that," Adam interjected.

Now she had to make eye contact with Jacob. She tapped her foot on the floor. Something about this was off and she could see it on Jacob's face.

Adam blew out an exasperated breath. "This is stupid. Nobody's going to believe that you and I can actually talk to each other. Especially not Anna." He pointed at her. "Look. I know everything. I can't believe you're pregnant and you didn't tell me? Your own brother? And Jacob's the dad? I don't even know where to start with all of this. It's like a bad dream."

Jacob stood and grasped Anna's elbow. "I had to tell him. I'm sorry."

She closed her eyes and shook her head, drawing in a deep breath through her nose. The fact that he'd had the guts to come out with it certainly earned him a few points. "We had to tell him eventually. I just can't believe you came here to do this and that you didn't want me here at the same time."

"Well, that's not the only thing we're talking about," Adam said.

Jacob turned to Adam quickly, and even though Anna couldn't see either of their faces head-on, she could tell they were having a conversation without words.

"Will somebody please just tell me what you're doing?" Anna asked. "I'm not leaving until one of you spills it."

"Well?" Adam asked, staring down Jacob. "Do you want to tell her, or should I?"

"Please. We have to stay calm. For the baby's sake," Jacob said, turning to her. "I found out who the War Chest brought in as their big investor. It's Aiden."

"What?" Anna asked. "Aiden? I don't understand."

Jacob looked at her thoughtfully, showing her his miraculous eyes. They were the only thing that calmed her in this unimaginable situation. He explained everything with Aiden as she struggled to keep up with the details. "It's very important that you don't get worked up about this. My first and only concern is for you and the baby."

Anna narrowed her focus on Adam.

"It's the one thing we didn't account for," Adam said flatly. "We're going to lose controlling interest in the company and I doubt there's much we can do about it. He's had a chip on his shoulder forever about LangTel, and you know how he feels about me in particular. Jacob and I were just strategizing on ways to raise the capital to fight this."

Anna sat down in the chair next to Jacob's. This was not the time for panic. There had to be a solution. "No. Adam, you have to reach out to him. Don't fight this with money. That's going to make things far worse. Send him an email. Tell him we know about it. But do it kindly. We don't want to scare him. Tell him that we want to talk, that we want to find out what would make him do this."

"How is that going to work?"

"You have any other bright ideas? He's our brother. If we do anything less than extend the olive branch, he'll never forgive us. Put yourself in his shoes."

"Maybe you should do it. He actually likes you." Adam's voice had an uncharacteristic wobble. Their father had left an awful lot on Adam's shoulders—the CEO position, now this. The root of the problem with Aiden was undoubtedly their father. He'd pitted the boys against each other from the very beginning.

"I think it will mean more from you, especially if you use a softer touch," she said. "He'll expect you to be all bravado, so don't do that. Be his brother."

"This is business. Do you really think that's advised? It sounds awfully girly."

Anna sat back in her chair and crossed her legs. "Then ask Jacob what he thinks."

Adam cocked both eyebrows at Jacob. Anna was amazed they'd managed this much without taking pot shots at each other.

"Anna's right," Jacob said, taking his seat next to her. "If your brother is feeling like he's on the outs with your family, it's going to take a softer approach. If you try to steamroller him, he'll steamroller you right back. Except he can flatten you with this one, Adam. Completely."

Adam looked as befuddled as Anna had ever seen him. "That's a surprising answer coming from you, Mr. Number Cruncher."

"I know exactly what it feels like to be on the outs with the Langford family. It's not a fun place to be."

Anna swallowed, hard. She couldn't argue that point. The good news was that as of now, Adam and Jacob had to be going on at least twenty minutes of being in the same room and everyone was still living and breathing.

Adam visibly tensed. "Okay. I'll do it. I'll play the nice guy and reach out to him." He went to his laptop and started typing. After a few keystrokes, he looked up at the two of them. "Are we done? I have work to do. I'll let you know when I hear back from Aiden."

Jacob cleared his throat and stood up. "Actually, there's one more thing."

"What?" Adam pushed back from his desk and crossed his arms.

"I need you to know that I love your sister more than anyone or anything on this entire planet. And I'm hoping that she and I can find a way to work things out, but we have some obstacles to get past and I want to get rid of one of them right now. You and I need to drop the fighting. It's stupid, and frankly, I have more important things to worry about."

"Do you really think it's as simple as that?" Adam retorted. "We decide to forget it? I can't believe that you, of all people, would think that you could just come in here and declare a truce and make it all go away. It's far more complicated than that."

"Actually, Adam, it's not. It's really very simple. Do we love Anna more than we hate each other?"

A puff of astonished air left Anna's lips. Six years of feuding and Jacob had boiled it down to one question.

"I know what my answer is," Jacob continued. "I love her far more than I ever hated you, which should tell you just how much I love her. Because I really, really hated you."

Adam sat back in his chair, his jaw slack. He was clearly letting this tumble around in his head, and they had to let him process it. "Wow. I guess you really can make it that simple." He looked at Anna, seeming to get a little choked up. "Anna Banana, I definitely love you more than I hate him. I don't know what I would've done during the last year without you."

"Then let's bury the hatchet, Adam. Please," Jacob added.

"If it will make Anna happy, I will give up the fight."

For the first time in a long time, she felt as if she could

breathe without worry. "It would make me insanely happy. There's enough trouble going around for all of us." She stood and walked over to her brother to give him a hug. Relief washed over her.

"I can't believe I'm going to be an uncle," Adam muttered into her ear, holding her close, not letting go.

It would've been so nice to agree that indeed he would, but they weren't out of the woods. "Fingers crossed that everything goes okay."

"Anything you need at all," Adam said, stepping back, but still holding on to her shoulders. "Just let me know."

"Of course. I will."

"As for you," Adam said, reaching out his hand to shake Jacob's. "I didn't really think this day would come. It'll be good to put it behind us."

Jacob smiled. "It's long overdue."

Anna led the way out of Adam's office. "That's not quite how I expected to start my day," Anna muttered to Jacob in the hall. One enormous problem had been resolved, even if another—Aiden—had cropped up.

"Can we talk?" he asked.

Her staff and coworkers were already milling about. The sight of Jacob Lin in the office was prompting hushed voices and sideways glances. "Of course, but not here. My office." She marched ahead, Jacob in her wake. They passed Holly when they rounded the corner to Anna's office. Holly bugged her eyes, but kept her mouth shut. Anna would have to fill her in later. She closed the door behind them, unsure where to start, only that she knew he deserved an awful lot of credit. "That must've been so hard for you to swallow your pride with Adam. I'm just floored that you would do that for me."

"It was for *us*, Anna. It had to end."

She found herself hopelessly drawn to him—his voice, his presence. When he stripped away her defenses, her reasons for being mad or doubtful, he could have whatever he wanted. She looked up at him, peering into his penetrating eyes, the ones that left her undone. She'd asked him to fight for her, and he'd done exactly that. Big time. "I really admire you for it. I don't know what else to say, other than thank you. I know that couldn't have been easy."

"It wasn't, but I don't care about what's easy anymore. I care about getting you back."

Tingles raced over her skin, her breath caught in her chest. That rumble in his voice was there, the one that made her knees threaten to buckle. "Now what?"

"Have dinner with me tonight. My place."

He'd convinced Adam to let bygones be bygones. Could she do the same? Was she ready for this? Because she was certain that if she wound up in his apartment again, she was going to end up in his bed. Was that the logical next step? If it was, she knew very well that it led to a place where it was nearly impossible to be angry with him. Maybe that was for the best—finally just give in to what she wanted, finally just trust that this was the way things were meant to be. "I'd love to."

His smile was warm and immediate. "Good."

He cupped her shoulder gently and leaned in for a kiss—Anna nearly had a heart attack, her pulse erratic and frantic. She closed her eyes, her lips waiting for the reward, and then it arrived, square on her cheek.

She might've been disappointed if it wasn't so sweet, so warm and comforting, telling her that he was still letting her dictate their speed, even after he'd just put on a commanding performance. "Playing it safe?" She couldn't hide her smile. The ways in which he'd figured her out were uncanny.

"Baby steps. Literally." He placed his hand on her stomach gingerly. She felt his hesitation radiate from his core—he was holding back, employing restraint. "I'll see you tonight."

Seventeen

Jacob hadn't even made it down to the lobby before he had a text from Anna. He did a double take when he saw the message.

Don't leave. I'm spotting.

Was this really happening? Just when everything was finally going well? On my way up. What happened?

He stayed put on the elevator when it dropped people at the lobby, having to wait for what felt like an eternity as a new load of people boarded. It was just before nine, everyone on their way to work, which meant that nearly every button, for every floor, was pressed.

He took a deep breath. *Stay calm.* His heart wasn't cooperating at all, nor was his stomach. Everything in his body was on edge. Why now? Why this?

Anna sent a reply. Went to the bathroom and saw the blood.

Good God. Just when things were getting better. Don't worry. Be there soon.

He sent a text to his driver, instructing him to be ready to get them to the hospital as quickly as possible. Jacob would have to wait until he got somewhere private to call Dr. Wright's office. He couldn't announce in a crowded elevator that Anna Langford was in danger of losing a pregnancy. Nobody but Adam even knew that she was pregnant.

On Anna's floor, he stormed past the receptionist and down the hall, rushing inside her office. "I'm here. Let's go. The car is downstairs." His heart was still pounding—seeing Anna and the panic on her face turned everything into an even harsher reality. They could lose the baby.

Anna nodded, putting on her coat. He put his arm around her shoulders, ushering her out of the office. They didn't stop to say a thing to anyone. There was no time for explanations.

"I called Dr. Wright," she whispered as they waited for the elevator. "They're expecting us. She told us to come up to her office. Not the emergency room."

"Good. Okay. It's going to be okay." He had no business guaranteeing anything, but he had to believe it. They were so close to putting things back together. He rubbed her shoulder—anything to calm her, let her know that he was there for her.

Jacob got Anna down to the car and they were quickly whisked through the city, his driver breaking a few traffic laws while dodging taxis, cyclists and buses. Jacob put his arm around Anna's shoulder, pulling her close. She sank against him, turned into his chest, wrapped her arm around his waist. It was the only comfort he could take in that moment. They had each other. Whatever the future held for the two of them as a couple, or the three of them as a family, they would get through it. They had to.

When they arrived at the hospital, Jacob wasted no time getting Anna through the lobby and up to the sixth floor. The nurse was waiting for them and quickly showed them back to an exam room. Anna changed into a gown. Dr. Wright was in moments later.

"Ms. Langford. Mr. Lin. Before I say anything, I want to tell you both to take a deep breath." She motioned with both hands for them to calm down. "I know you're worried, but this isn't always a bad thing. Let's see what's going on."

Anna leaned back on the exam table and Jacob took her hand. She tilted her head, looking up at him as if he held all of the answers. He'd never felt so helpless in his entire life—the two things he cherished most in the world were right here, Anna and the baby—and there was very little he could do to truly keep them safe. How he longed to tell Anna that everything was going to be okay and to be certain of it.

Dr. Wright wheeled back on her rolling stool. "The good news is that your cervix is closed up tight. Let's listen to the heartbeat and make sure there's no sign of fetal distress."

Fetal distress. Those two words felt like a death sentence. The thought of their child in distress brought the most sickening feeling up from the depths of his gut. He hoped to hear that beautiful whoosh. *Please God, let us hear the whoosh.*

"Before we do this," Dr. Wright started. "I want you

both to understand that this is very early days. If the baby is in trouble, there's not much we can do. I want to remind you that you're both so young. You have your entire lives ahead of you. Today doesn't have to be the end."

Jacob's gaze dropped to meet Anna's. Tears streamed down her cheeks. They welled in his as well. He couldn't even remember another time when he'd cried, but he couldn't have stopped it if he'd wanted to. His dream of a life with Anna could still happen, but it would be different if they lost the baby. Neither of them would ever be the same. He would still want her if the worst happened, but would she still want him? She'd worried that he might not be around for the long haul, but the reality was that the same could be wondered about her. Without this child binding them together, and with every mistake he'd made, would she want to walk away? He couldn't fathom how empty his life would be if that happened.

"We understand. Go ahead," Anna said to Dr. Wright.

Jacob nodded reluctantly. "Yes. Please. Go ahead."

The static and pops had a distinctly different tone to them this time—it was hope at odds with itself, a moment born of desperation while clinging to what you already have, not focused on what might be. He'd never piled so many wishes on a single moment before. Jacob looked right into Anna's eyes. If they were going to receive the worst of news, they would experience the pain of that instant together. She would not be alone. Anna clung to his hand, squeezing tight. Static buzzed. The speaker popped. Frantic crackles echoed.

And then the whoosh. *Whoosh whoosh whoosh.*

Anna's eyes sprang to life, quickly followed by her electric smile, jolting Jacob back to a state where he felt as if he could breathe again. Anna raised her head and looked down at her stomach. "The baby…"

"The heartbeat sounds perfect," Dr. Wright said.

"Thank God." The most profound relief Jacob had ever experienced threatened to knock him flat. He closed his eyes and his shoulders dropped from the solace of that perfect sound. He leaned down and cupped Anna's cheek then pressed a kiss to her forehead. His lips wanted to stay there, keep contact with her warm and wonderful-smelling skin.

Dr. Wright turned off the Doppler and sat back down on her stool. Jacob helped Anna back up to sitting.

"I'd like you on bed rest for the next twenty-four hours. Take it easy. It's very possible that this is just normal first trimester spotting and has nothing to do with any of your other issues."

"Normal?" Jacob asked.

"Yes, Mr. Lin. Normal. Possibly."

He'd never quite imagined his glee at hearing that anything was normal, possibly, but there it was. He was ecstatic.

"You aren't out of the woods. There are never any guarantees. But I'd say that everything, for the moment, looks good. Go home. Relax. Together. Dad, no going into work. Stay with her and call me if anything goes wrong."

"You don't have to worry about that. I'm not going anywhere."

Eighteen

Jacob and Anna arrived at Jacob's apartment around one, after running to Anna's place to get her a few things. He insisted they would be more comfortable at his place. She had to agree, and it was also much closer to the doctor's office if they had to return. Although, as Dr. Wright had said, there wasn't much they could do but wait for the bleeding to stop. At least they would be doing it together.

Anna changed into pajama pants and a tank top, unfortunately finding a similar amount of blood when she used the bathroom.

"Well?" Jacob asked, sounding hopeful when she walked into his bedroom.

"Still spotting. But it's not any worse than before, so that's good." It felt as though she was shouldering the weight of the moment. Intellectually, she knew she had no control over the bleeding, but it was hard not to feel responsible. Perhaps that was the burden of being the messenger. It was okay. She'd take it.

"I don't want you to worry about it." He pulled back the comforter and patted the bed. "Your throne, m'lady."

She grinned and shook her head. He could be so silly if he wanted to be, but she knew for a fact that he wasn't like that with anyone else. He reserved his most unguarded moments for her. "Are those your PJs?"

"Of course. I'm not leaving you in this bed alone." He'd put on a T-shirt and basketball shorts. How she loved those glorious, lanky legs of his. "I figure we'll watch bad movies all afternoon. I haven't played hooky from work in well, forever, I guess."

"You know, I think I just want to talk for now. Maybe take a nap." She climbed into bed and he did the same, on his side. This was indeed an odd setup, not really knowing the state of things between them. She knew how she felt—he'd obliterated her doubts about whether he'd fight for her. And he'd been right there with her at the doctor's office, holding her hand. He'd even cried with her, at that moment when they were waiting to hear if the baby was still okay. She knew then that her love for him had never gone away. There had just been other things in the way and she could see now that she'd put a few of those things there herself, or at least allowed them to remain.

"This wasn't exactly what I had envisioned when I was hoping to get you back into my bed," he said, punching his pillow a few times.

Anna laughed. "Right now, this is all the romance I can take." She watched as his expression became decidedly less jovial. "I didn't mean it like that, Jacob. Really. I didn't."

He nodded. "It's okay. I'm just trying to follow your cues. I'm waiting for the moment when you tell me that it's okay for me to love you again."

She rolled to her side and took his hand. Of course he was waiting for her. She'd been the guardian of every roadblock between them, making sure he knew the reasons they shouldn't be together. It felt as though the time had come for her to focus on the reasons they should. "Do you think you can? Love me again?"

"Anna, I never stopped loving you."

"Never? Not even for a minute? What about the day I barged into your office?"

He shook his head. "I still loved you that day. It simply hurt more then. That's all."

She thought of the awful things that had come out of her mouth that day—yes, he had done the unimaginable, but she shouldn't have been so determined to end things, no matter what. "I should have listened to you that day. I was hurt, but you were right about a few things. What you had done didn't change what was between us." She smiled when she noticed the way he was hanging on her every word. "In some ways, it was better that we fell in love in a vacuum, hiding our relationship from my family and the rest of the world. It was really the only way it could happen and be real. There was no outside influence."

"Just you and me, Anna. That's the way it should be. Just you and me." The smile that rolled across his face was so pure and unguarded, it took her breath away. "I love you more than you'll ever know. Forever." He leaned closer and brushed a strand of hair from her forehead. "I started to fall in love with you from that very first kiss, and my feelings have only gotten stronger."

His words floated around in her head—so beautiful, so lovely. She couldn't help but be swept up in the moment. "I'm sorry that being with me has been such a test."

He shrugged. "We tested each other. All couples do. We just got a lot of testing out of the way during those early days."

"In some ways, it's good. If we can survive all of that, we can definitely handle sleepless nights and diapers, the terrible twos and kindergarten."

"You make it sound so glamorous." He reached out and pressed his finger to the end of her nose.

"You know what I mean."

"But that's the baby, Anna. There's more than that ahead of us. If you want it. Do you want more?"

She suddenly found it difficult to breathe. Even if he was merely asking for them to spend more time together, the answer was yes, although she hoped for more. Much, much more. Even these few moments in bed together were enough to remind her that she didn't want anything other than him, at her side. "I do."

"Good, because I can't lose you again. You know that I'm a pragmatist. I deal with numbers all day long. I deal with absolutes. But the truth is that my love for you is an absolute."

The tears came. There was no stopping them. They rolled right down her cheeks. "That's the sweetest thing anyone has ever said to me."

"It's true. All true." Before she knew what was happening, he climbed out of bed and walked over to the dresser. When he turned, he held a blue Tiffany box in his hand.

Anna gasped. It was the most horrifically girly thing to do, but she couldn't help it. "Jacob. Are you?" She sat up in bed, wiping the tears from her face.

His eyes grew very serious. "Shhh. I only get one chance to get this right."

"I know. But I just want to make sure you're thinking about what's happening here. I might lose the baby. Will you still feel like this is the right thing to do if that happens?"

He perched on the edge of the bed. "Anna Langford, I love you with all of my heart and soul. If we lose the baby, that doesn't change my love for you. We will get through it together and we'll find a way to be stronger on the other side. In the end, all I want is you." He presented the box, which was dwarfed by the size of his hand. "If you'll do me the honor of becoming my wife, I promise to love you and put up with your family until my very last breath."

She smiled, staring down at everything he held in his hand—their future, happiness. This wasn't at all the way she'd ever dreamed this moment would transpire, but she wouldn't have traded it for anything. "I love you so much. I want nothing more than to have you as my husband."

He opened the box and plucked a gorgeous round solitaire in a platinum setting from the box. He slipped it onto her finger. It was a little big—in both band size and heft—but it was perfect.

She clasped her other hand over her mouth as she admired the ring and the way it sparkled. "It's absolutely beautiful. I couldn't ask for anything more. Literally. I'm not sure I could carry around a bigger diamond without some help."

He laughed quietly. "I swear it didn't look that big in the store."

"Of course it didn't. Your hands are huge."

"All I care about is seeing it on your hand. It couldn't make me any happier."

He leaned forward and kissed her, softly. It was the first time their lips had touched since the breakup, and it was as if she was being reborn. That gentle brush of a kiss told her just how much they were made for each other. If they weren't, they wouldn't have found a way. This was where she belonged, with him, on the other side of their troubles. Or at least a few of them.

"This would be the part where we tear off each other's clothes and make love all night. Sorry about that," she said sheepishly.

"Don't worry. I can hold off for a few nights until the spotting stops. Then I'll make you mine." He cozied up next to her, wrapping his arm around her, making her feel as protected as she could've imagined. "In the meantime, we wait for what comes, and we go through it together."

She took a deep breath, fighting the tears that fought to take over again. She wouldn't cry—there had been too many tears in the last year, and now was a time to be happy. She would focus on Jacob, the ring. She would focus on the baby, on her hope that everything would turn out okay for once. "It's raining," she said, looking out the bedroom windows, with the glorious view of the city.

"Just like that night upstate."

"I guess it did rain that night, didn't it? I remember the puddles the next morning."

"It rained like crazy and you slept right through it."

"I take it you didn't?"

"Not a wink. I was too busy wondering how I was going to get past your brother to get to you."

"Well, you did it. Big props for that."

"Now we just need to hope he can take care of your other brother."

She turned to shush him. "Let's not talk about the bad. Let's just think about the good."

He smiled and pulled her closer, kissing the top of her head and raking his hands through her hair. "I have all the good I'll ever need right here in my arms."

With morning came the sun. After the steady deluge of rain all night, Jacob could only hope this was a good sign. He hadn't slept at all—consumed with a mix of gratitude for Anna's answer to his proposal and hope that today would bring good things.

Anna was asleep on her side, his arm draped over her. He loved having her back against his chest where he could feel her breaths—that steady, measured reminder that she was here again and wasn't leaving any time soon. They hadn't slept in the same bed in weeks. He'd remembered it as being wonderful, but it was even better with the promise that they would be together. Forever.

Anna stirred. As happy as he was to be able to talk to her, that feeling faded as he realized that she would soon get up and go to the bathroom and they would have news—good or bad.

"You're up," he said, pushing his hair from his face.

"I am," she answered, sleepily, shifting her weight and swinging her legs out from under the covers.

"Are you?" He nodded toward the bathroom.

"I am. Fingers crossed."

He sat up in bed. "Do you need me to come with you?"

She sighed and managed half of a smile. "I'm okay. I'll let you know what happens."

"Whatever happens, Anna. I'm here. Good or bad."

Anna tiptoed off to the bathroom. Jacob climbed out of bed, wondering when it would be okay to ask how things were going. Luckily, the flush of the toilet gave him his cue. "Well?" he called from the other room, his heart threatening to pound its way out of his body.

"Nothing," she called back with an elated squeak. "No more spotting."

Jacob had never moved so fast, arriving at the bathroom door in a flash. "Really? Nothing?"

She nodded, going to the sink to wash her hands.

Thank God. He came up behind her, wrapped his arms around her waist. She was so stunning in the morning—fresh-faced, simply beautiful. The fact that she was carrying his child and had his ring on her finger made her that much more irresistible. He was the luckiest man in creation. "I am so glad."

"I know. Me, too." She looked down and pressed the palm of her hand to her belly. "Me, too."

"You know, you and I are going to make really cute babies," he said, kissing the top of her head. It was the truth—their children would be absolutely gorgeous.

Turning in his arms, she looked up at him. "Babies? Plural?"

"Of course. I want a whole pack of little Lins running all over the penthouse."

She coughed so loud she practically sputtered. "A pack of Lins?"

"Yes, Anna. I had to swallow my pride with your brother. I have to beat him at something. Surely you'll grant me that much."

"Sorry. I don't get your point. Beat him at what, exactly?"

"How ever many kids he and Melanie have, we'll just have one more."

"So this is about being competitive with my brother. That's going to get expensive, you know. What with college and keeping them all outfitted in tiny baby motorcycle jackets."

He laughed. Never had he imagined he could ever be so happy. "Anna, darling. You just leave that to me."

Epilogue

After everything over the last year, Anna had very much looked forward to dancing with her brother Adam at his wedding. She'd imagined the grand hotel ballroom, the legion of happy guests, stunning centerpieces of purple tulips and white irises picked out by Melanie, and the enormous wedding cake that likely took more than a week to create. She'd just never imagined that she'd be watching her other brother, Aiden, dancing with their mother at the same time.

"Aiden seems so happy to be back in the family fold," she said to Adam as he twirled her around the dance floor. He'd just finished his own dance with their mother, during which Evelyn Langford had cried her eyes out. Between having all three of her children in the same place for the first time in years and having her first grandchild on the way, Evelyn had made a point of telling them all how happy she was. There was much to be thankful for on this chilly January day, even the tears that flowed because of it.

"Aiden does seem happy, doesn't he?" Adam countered. "I still can't believe what a number Dad did on him, but I'm glad he was able to see past it. I know for a fact that it hasn't been easy for him."

Anna didn't even want to think about the things that had come to light about their father and his volatile relationship with Aiden—years of misunderstandings, Aiden being passed over in favor of Adam. She only wanted to focus on the good, especially today. "I think it helped a lot that you two talked everything out. He needed to feel like you weren't just toeing the family line because of your loyalty to Dad."

"I loved Dad as much as anyone, but we both know that he could be stubborn and narrow-minded. It doesn't mean he wasn't a good man. It just means that he made mistakes. We've all made mistakes. I've made a lifetime of them and I'm not even thirty-five."

Anna smiled. She wasn't about to rub it in, even though she very easily could have as pertained to Jacob. Adam and Jacob's friendship had rebounded nicely in the weeks since Jacob had dared to demand a truce. They weren't best friends, but they'd come to enjoy time together, and that was as much as she could've ever hoped for. "We all goof up, Adam. It takes happy days like today to remind us that sometimes we have to let those things go." That lesson had been no more important for her than when it had come to Jacob. The minute she put the past behind them, the future had opened up beautifully.

"Speaking of letting things go, why didn't one of us

come up with the idea of running LangTel together as co-CEOs? It's a brilliant move."

She smiled. This had been Jacob's idea, since they were already doing some restructuring in the company in order to bring Aiden on board as a Senior VP of Marketing. "Jacob made an excellent point. No two people are capable of accomplishing as much as we are when we aren't fighting." It wasn't exactly the arrangement Anna had expected. A few months ago, she would have said absolutely not, that she wanted the sole position for herself. But with her pregnancy progressing well, and with an early June due date, taking over as CEO would not leave her the time to be the kind of mom she wanted to be. Her career was important, but not so much that she wanted their child raised by a nanny. That existence had been so difficult for Jacob. She didn't care to repeat the pattern and understandably, neither did he.

"You don't need to worry about any fighting from me. I promise. The co-CEO thing means I can go back to working on my own projects, as well. It's really perfect for me."

"It's perfect for both of us," Anna added.

The song faded to its end and Jacob came up behind Adam with a wide grin on his face. "Hey, Langford. I don't want to be a jerk about it, but I'd like to dance with my bride-to-be."

Adam kissed Anna on the cheek. "Sounds like somebody is tired of sharing you. I can't say I blame him." He clapped Jacob on the back. If anyone had said six months ago that this particular scene would be indicative of the new status quo, Anna never would've believed it. "I'll leave you two lovebirds to it. I have a date with my own bride." He excused himself and waved at Melanie, who was extricating herself from a dance with her uncle.

Jacob swept Anna into his arms, twirling her several times, making the eggplant purple bridesmaid's dress flutter around her. "Finally. I get you to myself."

Anna giggled, the swarm of wedding guests around them fading into the recesses as she became solely focused on Jacob. He really was her dream man. He really was perfect for her. And she couldn't have been any happier.

"We need to get in our time on the dance floor. Just a little more than a month until we're in this same spotlight." They did, in fact, need to clock a few hours of dancing, although their wedding would not be anywhere near as extravagant—fifty guests, at Jacob's house upstate. Neither one of them cared to deal with anything more elaborate. Jacob had actually said he was hoping for a blizzard so no one would be able to show up and he could keep Anna to himself for an entire week or more. She couldn't blame him. It sounded like the perfect plan.

He pulled her closer, his body heat enveloping her, or perhaps it was just his magnetism, the things about him that wouldn't allow her to stay away. He was especially difficult to resist in a tuxedo. "I can't believe you're going to be my wife. Honestly, I can't believe I'm going to be part of the Langford family. I'm having a hard time imagining what it's going to be like. Especially after spending six years in exile."

She reared her head back, looking deeply into his soulful eyes. "Things happen for a reason. I believe that. Maybe you and Adam will end up having an even stronger friendship one day. I certainly wasn't ready to run away with you and have a baby six years ago. So maybe this was for the best, as difficult as it was for you to go through."

He nodded, a slight smile crossing his face. "I'd go through it all for you. Every last minute of it."

She smirked and shook her head. "You're sweet."

"Really I'm just angling to get you out of that brides-maid's dress."

"You and me both. I can't wait to change. It's too tight on my belly." Anna wasn't showing much yet, but her tummy had pooched out a little. Jacob liked to lie in bed and talk to the tiny baby bump. Then he would get out his Doppler for listening to the heartbeat, which had arrived shortly after the spotting scare. He made quite the doting dad-to-be.

Jacob pulled her in tightly, moving her in time effort-lessly to the music. "Are you happy?" he asked.

"What kind of question is that?" Anna whispered, leaning into him as she watched Adam and Mela-nie sway in the tiniest of circles, husband and wife. It wouldn't be long for Jacob and her. The thought warmed her from head to toe.

"It's a perfectly valid thing to ask, especially consid-ering everything we've been through. I want to know that you're happy, Anna. It's the only thing I care about."

She looked up into his eyes, which shone down on her like sunshine on the first day of spring. She could get lost in those eyes for a lifetime and be deliriously giddy. "I don't think it's possible for me to be happier. Truly. Being with you is all I'll ever want."

"Good." He slowed their dance to the most impercep-tible of movements, lowering his head and planting the sexiest, hottest kiss she could've imagined on her lips. It was slow and seductive, a subtle parting of lips and the most tasteful bit of tongue. It left her ready to pass out.

"Jacob. My family is watching," she said when she came up for air, making a mental note that they absolutely would need to continue this when they got home after the reception.

"I thought we agreed that your family had interfered in enough of our kisses."

"True, but it's still a wedding. We don't want to be *those* people, do we?"

He laughed and spun her around, then stopped and laid another steamy kiss on her, this time dipping her back in his arms. He left her breathless, ready to surrender in a ballroom filled with hundreds of people. "Tell me to stop."

She smiled, caught in his eyes and the echo of the enticing rumble in his voice. "Jacob Lin, I never want you to stop."

* * * * *

LET'S TALK

Romance

For exclusive extracts, competitions
and special offers, find us online:

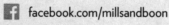 facebook.com/millsandboon

 @MillsandBoon

@MillsandBoonUK

Get in touch on 01413 063232

For all the latest titles coming soon, visit
millsandboon.co.uk/nextmonth

JOIN THE
MILLS & BOON
BOOKCLUB

* **FREE** delivery direct to your door

* **EXCLUSIVE** offers every month

* **EXCITING** rewards programme

50% OFF
YOUR FIRST
PARCEL

Join today at
Millsandboon.co.uk/Bookclub